Praise for EN[VY]

"[Envy] captures the drama of *The Re*... while also bringing this well-developed work of urban... a satisfyingly redemptive conclusion."

—Kristina Giovanni, *Booklist*

Praise for LUST

"Murray has penned hot, steamy scenes in which her protagonist's imagination runs wild, followed by the consequences of her realizing her dangerous dreams. A jarring twist at the end has the reader wondering who the good guys really are."

—*Booklist* (starred review)

"Murray mixes quite a bit of passion, a touch of treachery, and some good old-fashioned revenge."

—*Library Journal*

"Keeps you at the edge of your seat until the last page."

—*Urban Reviews Online*

"A topsy-turvy tale of passion on steroids."

—*Essence*

Praise for STAND YOUR GROUND

"Murray has written a tension-packed novel around the hot-buzz national topic of an unarmed black youth shot by a white male, an act then subjected to the Stand Your Ground rule as a legal defense tactic. . . . Murray's writing admirably shows the often overlooked human emotions following racial violence. . . . The pulled-from-the-headlines story line will captivate readers."

—*Library Journal* (starred review)

"Murray, winner of several African American Literary Awards for fiction, powerfully captures the nuances and tragedies engendered by stand-your-ground laws. A must-read."

—*Booklist* (starred review)

"Using a vivid, realistic premise, she takes a 360-degree view to bring all sides to the forefront for us to enjoy, learn from, judge, and celebrate. *Stand Your Ground* has great literary relevance for our time."

—*USA Today*

Praise for *FOREVER AN EX*

"Murray spices up her story line with plenty of juicy scandals. . . . Readers seeking an inspirational tale with broad themes of trust, betrayal, and forgiveness will do well by choosing Murray's latest effort."

—*Library Journal*

Praise for *FORTUNE & FAME*

"The scandalous characters unite again in *Fortune & Fame*, Murray and Billingsley's third and best collaboration. This time brazen Jasmine and Rachel, who has zero shame, have been cast on *First Ladies*, a reality TV show that builds one's brand and threatens to break another's marriage. Sorry, buttered popcorn is not included."

—*Essence*

"Priceless trash talk marks this story about betrayal, greed, and stepping on anyone in your way. A great choice for folks who spend Sunday mornings in the front pew."

—*Library Journal*

Praise for *THE DEAL, THE DANCE, AND THE DEVIL*

"Murray's story has the kind of momentum that prompts you to elbow disbelief aside and flip the pages in horrified enjoyment."

—*The Washington Post*

Praise for *SINS OF THE MOTHER*

"*Sins of the Mother* shows that when the going gets tough, it's best to make an effort and rely on God's strength. It gives the message that there is hope no matter what, and that people must have faith."

—*Fiction Addict*

"Final word: Christian fiction with a powerful kick."

—*Afro*

Praise for *LADY JASMINE*

"She's back! Jasmine has wreaked havoc in three VCM novels, including last year's *Too Little, Too Late*. In *Lady Jasmine*, the schemer everyone loves to loathe breaks several commandments by the third chapter."

—*Essence*

"Jasmine is the kind of character who doesn't sit comfortably on a page. She's the kind who jumps inside a reader's head, runs around, and stirs up trouble—the kind who stays with the reader long after the last page is turned."

—*The Huntsville Times*

Also by Victoria Christopher Murray

WRATH

A Seven Deadly Sins Novel

VICTORIA
CHRISTOPHER
MURRAY

GALLERY BOOKS

New York   London   Toronto   Sydney   New Delhi

G

Gallery Books
An Imprint of Simon & Schuster, Inc.
1230 Avenue of the Americas
New York, NY 10020

First Gallery Books trade paperback edition January 2021

GALLERY BOOKS and colophon are registered trademarks of Simon & Schuster, Inc.

For information about special discounts for bulk purchases, please contact
Simon & Schuster Special Sales at 1-866-506-1949 or business@simonandschuster.com.

The Simon & Schuster Speakers Bureau can bring authors to your live event.
For more information or to book an event, contact the Simon & Schuster Speakers Bureau
at 1-866-248-3049 or visit our website at www.simonspeakers.com.

Interior design by Lana J. Roff

Manufactured in the United States of America

10 9 8 7 6 5 4 3 2 1

Library of Congress Cataloging-in-Publication Data

Names: Murray, Victoria Christopher, author.
Title: Wrath / Victoria Christopher Murray.
Description: First Gallery Books trade paperback edition. | New York : Gallery Books,
  2021. | Series: A Seven deadly sins novel ; 4
Identifiers: LCCN 2020020001 (print) | LCCN 2020020002 (ebook) |
  ISBN 9781982142926 (paperback) | ISBN 9781982142933 (ebook)
Subjects: LCSH: Domestic fiction. | GSAFD: Christian fiction. | Love stories.
Classification: LCC PS3563.U795 W73 2020 (print) | LCC PS3563.U795 (ebook) |
  DDC 813/.54—dc23
LC record available at https://lccn.loc.gov/2020020001
LC ebook record available at https://lccn.loc.gov/2020020002

ISBN 978-1-9821-4292-6
ISBN 978-1-9821-4293-3 (ebook)

WRATH

Chastity Jeffries

The music was bumpin', the champagne was flowin', and the men were barkin' like they were out to chase the cat. This was the backdrop to the beat that pulsed through the speakers hanging in every corner and crevice of the club.

Bow-wow-wow-yippie-yo-yippie-yeah
Bow-wow-yippie-yo-yippie-yeah.

Men who were *at least* ten years out of college and wearing suits from the most exclusive stores, hopped up and stomped down on the dance floor, their hands raised, flashing their fraternity sign . . . as they barked like dogs.

My eyes scanned Club 40/40, one of the new spots on Fortieth Street, off Fifth Avenue. This place was jammed with the up-and-coming Who's Who of Black Manhattan—a single woman's paradise. But I was unmoved, unbothered, and still very much committed to the sanctity of staying single. Because of songs . . . and men like this.

All I wanted to do was tiptoe past the barking men and thirsty women clad in expensive sheaths with thousand-dollar purses slung over their shoulders. I was more than ready to bounce.

"Can I get you another one?"

I glanced up at the blond bartender, whose sleeveless shirt showed his hours in the gym. Lifting my glass, I downed the last of my pineapple Ciroc. "Close out my tab," I shouted to make sure he heard me over the barking and the beat. "I'm out."

"You're leaving?" The accusatory tone mixed with the music and floated over my shoulder.

First, I nodded to the bartender, my signal for him to continue as I requested. Then I spun toward the voice.

Melanie stood a few feet away, with her right hand perched on her hip, her stance as indicting as her tone. The mighty munchkin. That had been her nickname all through school because for someone who was as vertically challenged as she was, her five-foot-one presence demanded attention always.

"You cannot be thinking about going home already, Chas-ti-ty."

Uh-oh. She'd used my government name, and she only did that when she was annoyed, and Melanie Meadows never spent too much time without her lips spread into a smile.

"Did you know frowning uses one hundred more muscles than smiling and that gives you wrinkles?" Melanie had lectured our Girl Scout troop during one of our overnight trips to Fire Island when we were twelve. "So frown if you want, and then, give me a call; I'll hook you up, 'cause I'm gonna be the baddest plastic surgeon in the city."

She said, "You just got here."

Her words interrupted my memory of her prophecy, and I nodded. "I've been here an hour."

"A whole hour," she said, trading her accusatory tone for a sarcastic one. She rolled her eyes. "All you've done for that whole hour is stand in this whole corner, acting like you're in time-out."

"I've enjoyed myself," I said. "I had a couple of drinks, watched men bark, congratulated you, and now I'm ready to go."

"Chaz, you can't leave."

My shoulders slumped because from her tone, I knew what would come next. A lecture about how she needed her best friend by her side for this twofold celebration: the opening of her private clinic and her being recognized in *Medicine Today* as one of the Forty Best Plastic Surgeons under Forty.

Trying to head her off at the guilt curve, I said, "You know how tired I am."

"Everyone here is exhausted. We work hard; we're making moves." Her hand swept through the air as she gestured to the mass of gyrating bodies, which had slowed with the sounds of Anita Baker.

Melanie had told the DJ to go back to the decade of our birth—only music from the '80s.

As Anita sang: *Sweet love hear me callin' out your name, I feel no shame; I'm in love . . .* Melanie raised her hand above her head and swiveled her hips like she was balancing a Hula-Hoop. "What you've got to do is get out there and bust an old-school move."

"Anita ain't talking to me."

She dropped her hands. "You sure know how to ruin a good party."

"I'm sorry, but it's been a long week. My apartment looks exactly the way it did when the movers dropped that last box on my floor on Saturday, and all I want to do is crawl into my bed, which is the only thing that has been put together in my place."

"Okay, let's make a deal. You stay and I'll help you unpack tomorrow." She paused and tapped her finger on her chin. "Or maybe Sunday or Monday. Or better yet, I'll pay someone to unpack while we sit and sip wine. Just stay. Please."

She pouted like a puppy just as the bartender slid the leather tab closing out my check across the counter.

With a sigh, I signed my bill, then pointed to my glass. To

the bartender, I said, "Bring me two more and put it on her tab. I'm staying, and she's paying."

Melanie nodded at the bartender, then said to me, "Thanks for not bouncing."

"Well, how often will I get to celebrate my girl opening up her own practice?" I paused because I wanted my next words to stand alone. "I'm really proud of you."

"Awww, thanks, Chaz. I guess we did it, huh? A doctor and a lawyer. Just like we said."

"Back in the fifth grade," I added as the bartender slid our drinks onto the counter.

We clicked our glasses together, and then after a sip, Melanie said, "I'm sorry I haven't spent time with you since you've been back."

"You're forgiven, Dr. Meadows. It's not like you haven't been busy being great, and what would I look like, being upset with my new landlord?"

She grinned. "Believe me, you're helping me and Kelvin out. Not to have to worry about collecting that rent, whew! So everything's good at the condo?"

I nodded. "I'm living my best life there."

"And your job?"

"I'm living my rich life there." We laughed. "It's been cool. You know how it is; always exhausting getting up to speed at a new place, but the best thing—I'm back in New York."

"There's no place like home and nothing like landing as a partner at the Divorce Concierge. I fully expect to see you on the front page of some tabloid soon, just like all of their other star attorneys." She shook her head. "Who would have thought this would've been your specialty. Divorce?"

I took a small sip of my Ciroc to stop my words, but Melanie knew when my fascination with divorce had started. After a couple of moments, I shrugged. "People on the other side of love need good lawyers, too."

"And since you don't believe in love, you're on the right side."

Leaning away from her, I said, "Who told you that lie?"

She raised her eyebrows and mimicked my lean. "Maybe I got that impression because your name is not a proper noun, it's a verb."

This woman was about to owe me some free Botox because of how deeply she made me frown. "Do you have to be so crass?"

"*Crass* is my middle name." When I didn't smile, she added, "Come on, I'm telling the truth. You've been so closed off to men for so long that it's unnatural."

"I get my needs met, and I'm happy. That's all that matters."

She shook her head. "You're such a dude."

"Which is it, Dr. Meadows? Am I a chaste female or such a dude?"

"You're my best friend who's home, and I'm hoping this will be a new start with a new man."

"Not going to happen. Work calls."

"That's been your excuse for the last decade."

"I rest my case." I opened my arms as if I were presenting myself to an audience. "The prodigal friend has made a triumphant return as a partner in one of the nation's top law firms. Imagine if I'd spent all of that time dating seriously?" I winked, then laughed as she rolled her eyes again. "Don't act like you didn't get something out of this, too. I can afford your Central Park West condo. You needed me to be chaste—at least emotionally."

"Well, even if you are the love Scrooge"—she grabbed my arm and leaned her head on my shoulder—"I'm glad to have my best friend home."

Since Melanie was the yin to my yang in all ways, but especially our height, I had to lean over to rest my head on top of hers and return her hug. "Thanks."

She stepped back. "Now all we have to do is change your mind about a man . . ." When I plugged my fingers into my ears, she added, "I just want you to have the kind of life Kelvin and I have."

That made me smile. Because Melanie and Kelvin were the poster kids of true love. From undergrad at NYU, through medical school and beyond, they'd stayed strong together, navigating through long residencies, and then they'd doubled down as they studied their specialties: plastic surgery and emergency room surgery. Through all of that, they dated, became engaged and married, and were now making their medical names. Theirs was a great love; they made me believe in what I'd never seen.

In the middle of that nostalgia, Melanie groaned. "Oh, lawd."

My eyes followed my friend's glance. To a man approaching. My brows edged upward. He was impressive. But it was beyond the high thread count of his navy suit and his white shirt, which remained crisp even after the long hours of this day. And it was more than his features—his light brown eyes, his square jaw, and just a shadow of a beard. All of that was imposing, but was not what stood out the most. What was most impressive . . . was his swag. He strutted like he was slow-walking with a crew, and I pegged him as a music executive. Or maybe he was an entertainer I didn't recognize. One thing I knew: he was a New Yorker with all of that sway. He'd been born, bred, and built in this city.

Melanie interrupted my inspection with, "This guy has been following me."

"Hello again, pretty lady," he said in a deep voice that matched his aura.

Then I watched Melanie do something she'd never done before. My overly polite, always respectful friend, turned her back
on the man.

My glance darted between the two.

The guy said, "All I want to do is talk, get to know you
better."

Melanie did a slow spin toward him. "My husband has this
thing about the two of us remaining faithful."

"You really are married?"

Melanie pushed her ring in his face, though with her attitude, she could have been raising another finger. "My husband,
who will be here any minute, will not appreciate you stalking me."

He raised his hands as if he were surrendering to the police.
"My bad. You should've mentioned your husband before."

"You should have respected this ring." A kaleidoscope of
colors bounced off her diamond from the lights above.

"A woman wearing a ring in a club?" He chuckled. "That's
the oldest trick."

The slow smile that spread across Melanie's face was a con-
fession because she (we) had used that trick (though our rings
had come from a corner store) back in the day. "Okay," she said.
"No foul, no worries." Then, after a pause, she grabbed my hand
and spun me in front of her. "But this is my best friend; she
doesn't have a ring. Talk to her."

Before I could blink or breathe, she sashayed away. My
plan was to chase her down and choke her, but before I could
take a step, the dude stopped me from being breaking news on
Channel 2.

"This must be my lucky night," he said.

Now I studied him openly, taking in his height, which was
something I always noticed, since I was five eleven myself. Even
with my three-inch pumps, he had two or three inches on me.

And then he smiled—well, it was a half smile. Only the left side of his lips twitched upward. It was a smile that matched his swag.

But even all of that didn't stop me from saying, "Don't even front. You wanted to talk to my best friend, not me."

"That's not true."

I crossed my arms. "She said you'd been following her."

"I was," he admitted, "just so she could introduce me to you. You're the one I've been looking for, and I'm so glad she helped me find you."

Against every part of my will, the ends of my lips quivered, though I was able to stop a full-fledged laugh from seeping out. "That's a good line." I pointed my finger at him.

He laughed, a robust guffaw that I imagined would have come from Santa Claus. He held out his hand. "I'm Xavier King."

For a moment, I let his hand dangle in the air, feeling, for some reason, that if we pressed flesh in this greeting, my night would change. And I didn't want it to. Now that Melanie was gone, getting the heck out of this club was my number one priority.

But because Pastor and Mrs. Jeffries hadn't raised a savage, I took his hand. "I'm Chastity Jeffries."

His eyebrows raised. "Chastity?" His one-sided grin became wider.

Any cheer I'd felt was gone. I said, "Don't say it," as I held up my hand.

"What?"

If I had a dime for every man who asked me if I was my name . . . Shaking my head, I said, "Nothing. Just call me Chaz. My friends call me Chaz."

He no longer grinned; he gave me a soft smile. "I like that."

"Thank you."

"I wasn't talking about your name, I like that you're already calling me a friend."

This guy had great lines, but still, I glanced at my drink on the bar's counter. I'd only taken one sip, so I had two choices: to finish my drink or just allow this $12 to be the price paid for me to get away.

I chose the latter since it wasn't my credit card being charged. "Well, Xavier, it was nice meeting you."

"Was it something I said? I mean, you don't even want to finish your drink?" Before I could go into my monologue of how tired I was, he said, "Come on, at least finish your drink. You're the only person I know in this place."

"You don't know me," I said.

"And isn't that pitiful? I just happened to walk into this club, looking to have a drink, and there's a whole party going on, and I don't know a soul. So can't you just help a brotha out so I don't look so wretched?"

His words were so sorrowful, spoken with that sly smile. Without saying a word to Xavier, I sauntered back to the bar, grabbed my glass, and took a sip. But when I put the glass down, he took his own sip of my drink.

I leaned back as he smiled and said to the bartender, "I'll have what the lady is having." Then, turning to me, he said, "So, Chastity . . ."

To the bartender, I said, "Bring me a fresh drink, please. And put it on his tab." Then, without letting a beat pass, I said to Xavier, "I told you, Chaz is just fine."

He smirked when he said, "I'm a proper kind of guy. Love proper names. Plus . . . I really like your name." My chuckle made him ask, "You don't believe me?"

"I didn't say that."

"You didn't have to. I read body language."

"Is that what you do for a living? Read bodies?"

He shrugged. "In a way." He paused as if he was trying to decide if he should say more. In those quiet seconds, I wondered about this fine man who'd been so talkative, and now his silence was so sudden. What did he do for a living? Clearly, my earlier guesses had been wrong if he was this reluctant to say. And his hesitancy made me suspicious. Was he hiding from the police?

The bartender placed our glasses side by side, and Xavier took a sip (of his own this time), before he said, "I'm a lawyer," and then returned the glass to his lips as if that would stop him from saying more.

I gave him a moment's stare before I giggled. He frowned as he shifted from one spit-shined Ferragamo shoe to the other.

"I said I was an attorney, not a comedian."

That turned my giggle into a laugh out loud. "I'm sorry," I said as I pressed my hand against my chest, trying to gather myself. "If you knew what I'd been thinking . . ." Stretching my hand out to him, I said, "It's always nice to chat with a fellow counselor."

His eyes narrowed, his body stiffened as if he thought I was making some kind of joke. But when I nodded, his eyes widened with surprise, then amusement, and he laughed, once again filling the air with Santa Claus's joy.

We laughed, even as those around us gave us long glances. It was crazy, we were laughing at nothing, but in the few minutes that we'd stood at the bar, I had a feeling of delight I hadn't felt in years. So I grabbed my glass and let Xavier lead me away to the cushioned seats against the wall.

We were still laughing as we found a space away from all of the barking that was roomy enough for two.

✦   ✦   ✦

FOR THE LAST hour, I'd laughed with Xavier, trading all kinds of self-deprecating jokes about lawyers, something we all did as attorneys.

"How does a lawyer sleep?" Xavier had asked me.

"Well, first she lies on one side and then she lies on the other," I said.

We laughed as if we hadn't heard that joke fifteen million times.

"My turn," I said. "How many lawyer jokes are there?"

He flicked invisible lint from his shoulder as if he were about to win a competition. "Only three; the rest are true stories."

Again, we buckled over, before we tossed more barbs back and forth. Xavier raised his hand, in a pause, as he motioned toward one of the waitstaff. As he asked the young woman to refresh our drinks, my eyes wandered to the dance floor, where bodies still gyrated.

Woke up today, looked at your picture just to get me started . . .

"So, do you have another joke?"

Turning back to him, I shook my head. "Nope, now I have another question."

"Shoot!" Then he held up his hand. "No, wait. I shouldn't say that. I'm a lawyer."

I chuckled. "So, what do you like best about being an attorney?" I asked, though I was careful not to ask where he worked. Not only did I not care but that kind of question led to questions about me.

He paused, thoughtful, then said, "I'm finally settled. I've been at the same firm coming up on seven years now."

"You've moved around a lot?"

That question didn't seem deep to me, but his eyes lost a bit of their shine. "I guess it depends on your definition of *a lot*. I wanted to experience a couple of places before I settled down. What about you? Why'd you become an attorney?"

I'd thought my question had been safe, had never expected him to turn it around. Now I was the one who darkened a bit. "Someone I love went through some pretty deep things. I thought by becoming an attorney, I'd be able to help."

"Ah . . . so, did you help?"

I shook my head. "Not in the way I wanted to, but I ended up with a career I love."

"Well, that's always a great thing." When I tilted my head in question, he leaned a bit closer. "It's always wonderful when you're in love."

His words, and then that sexy smile, made me set my glass on the table. "It's time for me to get up and get out."

"Was it something I said?"

"Nope, just ready to go."

"Well, if I can't talk you into staying, can I get your number?"

Without thinking about how my next words would sound or what they would mean, I asked, "Are you seeing anyone?"

His response came just as fast. "Would I ask for your number if I were?"

I shook my head for a couple of reasons. Truly, I'd enjoyed our hour together, but I needed to dismiss any consideration of giving this man my number. For what purpose?

"So," he interrupted my thoughts, "your number?"

"Why don't you give me yours?" My usual line always worked for men and always worked for me when I ended the night tossing their business cards into my trash can.

"I can respect that." But then Xavier did his own tossing. Threw me a curveball I hadn't expected. "Pull out your phone."

"What?" I asked as if I no longer understood English.

"If I give you my business card, there's a chance it could accidentally fall into the discarded dudes file."

He smiled, but I didn't. Had he just read my mind?

Gesturing toward my purse, he said, "So pull out your phone and lock me in."

It was a new approach, one that showed me he was serious about seeing me again. And the DELETE button would indicate my seriousness—when I was out of his sight, of course.

Taking out my phone, I awakened the screen. There was no chance of me pretending anything with the way Xavier looked over my shoulder.

He watched as I typed in what he told me was his cell, and it wasn't until I pressed SAVE that he smiled and scooted back on the sofa.

"Are you satisfied?" I held up the phone for him to see his number and his name.

"I will be when you call. When will that be?"

"Thirsty, aren't you?"

"Not really," he began with a shrug. "I'm just a successful man who knows what I want, and I want to talk to you some more."

"I'll call you tomorrow," I said and wished I could cross my fingers behind my back, a move that, even at the age of thirty-four, was something I believed in.

"Set a reminder," he said.

"What?" Again, I'd lost my comprehension of my native tongue, because this dude was speaking words in a combination I'd never heard before.

"Set a reminder so you won't forget," he explained as if his request were a natural thing to say to a woman he'd just met.

Right then, he was too bizarre for me, but I set a reminder because I just wanted to go. I'd delete it all when I got home. "Satisfied?"

"Very." He gave me that half smile that brightened his whole face, and just like that, the thoughts I'd had about him softened. "It was nice to meet you, Ms. Chastity." Before I could protest, he said, "I know, Chaz. I love your full name."

My answer: I stood, smiled, and sashayed away just as Marvin Gaye crooned: *Let's make love tonight* . . .

2

Xavier King

The heat of the morning sun burst through my window, making me groan. How had the new day come so soon? I rolled over and, with my eyes still closed, reached across the expanse of my king-size bed. The surprise of the cool sheets made my eyes pop open.

For a moment, I stared at the empty space. It was still a bit shocking, sickening, that this happened to me . . . again.

Pushing myself up, I leaned against the headboard and massaged my temples. This hangover was real, but it wasn't from the drinks I'd had at Club 40/40 last night. This was one of those hangovers I'd learned about from Diana Ross when my grandmother played "Love Hangover" back in the day.

My grandmother . . . I was just about to shake my head to rid it of any memories of that woman or that time, when the three beeps of my front door alarm took my attention away.

The sound made me stiffen, made me move with the stealth of a lion as I rolled across the bed toward the nightstand, where my protection and five bullets lay. A second before my hand touched the drawer's handle, I pulled back. Because I felt her, I smelled her . . . and when I sat up in the bed and faced the door, finally, I saw her.

Roxanne paused at the threshold, pressing her hand over her heart. "I didn't know you were here." She took steps back as if she wanted space between us. "I was sure you'd be gone already. Playing golf or at the gym."

"Had a late night," I said. "Probably won't go out today. Maybe tomorrow." I chattered like she cared, though her caring had stopped a week ago.

"Well"—she glanced down at her feet before she looked back up—"since I'm here . . . and if you don't mind . . . I came for the rest of my things. I don't have much. Just a suitcase, probably." She chuckled, though there was no joy in that sound. "I never planned to leave that much here . . ."

"I've always wanted you to move in, and even now . . ." I paused, waiting for her to raise her eyes, but she wouldn't keep contact for more than a second, as if she didn't want to chance any connection. I tried to conjure up words to change her mind. "Even now"—I picked up where my voice had dropped off—"I want you here; I want you to stay."

Her feet shifted, and her glance did the same, from the window to the closet to the dresser. When she turned back to our bed, she gasped.

It was a soft sound, but I heard it. I'd surprised her by standing and strolling toward her. Now I held her eyes and I had her attention. I stood before her in my birthday glory. This was a trick, but it was all I had in my arsenal.

When I was close enough for her to sniff my morning breath, she finally glanced away from the parts that made me the man she'd loved just last week. But she didn't back away.

That gave me hope, especially when she said, "I came . . . for the . . . rest of . . . my things."

My girl was rattled; she never would've been stuttering if she were not flustered. So I used this time to tell her what she already knew. "I love you."

Her eyes were laser focused on all parts of me from the neck up. "I know that, but I also know that sometimes, love isn't enough."

I stepped back, needing distance between me and her words. But I also hoped her glance would once again wander so she'd see the rest of me and remember.

It worked. For just the shortest moment, her eyes soaked in my nakedness. But she didn't remember, because she turned away. She moved to the right toward the closet we'd shared.

And I pivoted the other way, taking the few steps into the master bathroom. Leaning against the sink, I tucked my chin into my chest as images of my life with Roxanne flashed in my mind: our meeting at a professional singles mixer just about a year ago; our engagement at Masa six months ago; last week, when this all ended.

I had failed because I was unworthy.

Those words made me blink. Took me back to the time when I first realized just how unworthy I was.

February 14, 1991

Gran's laughter thundered from her bedroom, and I made my move, tiptoeing and dodging the wooden plank that creaked at the end of the hallway.

Inside the living room, I hopped onto the sofa and peeked through the curtains. Only Mr. Washington's beat-up Ford sat in front of the cemetery across the street; no sign of Mama.

But she was coming. She'd promised she'd come home today and take me for pizza. For my birthday. The best birthday gifts ever: pizza and Mama coming home.

"Didn't I tell you to stay off my sofa?"

I leaped from the couch, shocked that Gran stood hovering behind me. How had I missed her heavy steps?

"Don't you put your feet up there again, boy." She slapped my head, and although it stung a bit, it wasn't a switch, or the broom, or the electrical cord she'd used a couple of nights ago when she caught me sneaking my broccoli into the trash.

"And if you mess that suit up, you're gonna get it, do you hear me?"

"Yes," I said, reeling from the stinging right above my ear.

She glared as she stepped so close her belly pressed against my nose. "Yes, what?" Her words, her tone, were her warning that I'd better get it right.

I stepped back from the stench of her rage. "Yes, ma'am."

She nodded. I breathed. "Now go over there and sit down." She pointed to the corner chair that looked like a throne. "Wait for your mama there—she probably won't come anyway."

There was no way I could tell my grandmother what I was thinking: that she was a mean liar, because my mama was coming. She'd promised me last Saturday, right before she'd left, and I'd been counting the days.

Gran watched as I climbed up on the chair, careful not to let my shoes touch the fabric. When I sat, she turned and grumbled her way out of the room.

As soon as she was out of sight, my thoughts went back to Mama. Forget about the pizza, I only wanted one birthday gift—for Mama to tell me she'd found another apartment so we could leave Gran's house forever.

I closed my eyes and remembered when it was just me and Mama. When we were together, it wasn't all good, but it was all love. Yeah, there were nights when dinner was nothing but peanut butter and bologna, but even though I went to sleep with my stomach growling, it was okay 'cause my mama hugged me until those hunger pangs went away.

"One day it's going to be better, X," Mama said. "As long as we're together, just the two of us. Because we have love and we're a family."

Being a family with Mama was the best. We did everything together: watched old movies that always made Mama cry or watched cartoons that always made me laugh. When Mama had money, she'd buy chocolate ice cream (my favorite) and we'd eat it right out of the carton as the radio played and we would dance and dance and dance.

It's driving me out of my mind . . .

My eyes popped open. At first, I thought I was imagining that music.

That's why it's hard for me to find . . .

No! It was coming from outside. "Mama!" I shouted. That was her song. She said she'd change her name to Poison if she she could.

I jumped off the chair, then hopped onto the sofa. I tucked back the curtain, my mouth open wide at the sight of that big shiny red car.

"Who's blasting all that noise?" Gran growled behind me.

I froze, waiting for another slap. But her attention was on the music, the car . . . and my mama, who slid out of the front seat after this really tall guy opened the door for her.

"Mama!" I exclaimed, hoping she was taking me to get pizza in that car. All the kids who wouldn't play with me would change their minds after this. I jumped down, ran a half circle around Gran, then made a mad dash to the front door.

When Mama stepped inside, she lifted me off my feet and swung me around like one of those rides at the carnival.

"How's my big boy?"

"I'm six today, Mama."

"I know. Happy, happy birthday."

I grinned and craned my neck around her to see if the car was still there. It was. "Mama, I'm ready to go for pizza. I got dressed up."

Just that fast, her smile turned upside down. "Oh, baby. We're not gonna be able to do that." My shoulders slumped, until she said, "I've gotta pack."

Pack? We were moving away from Gran!

I followed my mother into the living room, where Gran waited with folded arms. "Pack?" she said, without even saying hello. "Where you going?"

"I'm going . . . with Charles," Mama said. "He has a restaurant over in Natchez, and I can work there and make some good money."

While Gran huffed, I stood behind my mama, shivering. I didn't know where Natchez was, but I was excited to be going there.

"Chasing after another man, huh?" Gran growled. "Whose husband is he now?"

"Mama, please." It sounded like my mother was about to cry. "I'm chasing a job, not a man. So I can take care of me and my son."

"Hmph." Gran's eyes moved to me. "You taking him with you?"

Mama looked down at me. "That's what I wanted to talk to you about. Would you mind . . . if he stayed here . . . until I get myself together?"

Before Gran could say anything, I shouted, "No!" Both of them turned to me, though they wore different expressions. Gran glared at me, but there were tears in Mama's eyes.

"No," I whispered when she crouched down.

"Baby," she said. "If there was a way, I would take you right now. But I'm gonna work, and save money for us."

"I wanna go now. I don't care if you don't have money. I won't eat a lot. I promise."

Before my mother could answer, Gran asked, "What's wrong?"

She hovered above us like a thundercloud. "This new man of yours don't like kids?"

"He likes kids plenty," Mama snapped. "His place isn't big enough." Then Mama turned back to me. "But as soon as I get my own place, I'm coming for you."

"Mama, please."

"I'mma need you to be a big boy. Just remember, I'll be back." When I didn't move, she added, "I always come back, right?"

I gave her a little nod.

"Okay"—she stood—"I'm gonna grab a few things. Charles wants to get on the road."

"How long have you known this one?"

"Mama, I just need to know if it's all right for X to stay with you."

"For how long?"

"Does that matter? He's your grandson."

"He is." Gran glanced down at me and mumbled, "At what cost?"

My mother held me tight against her leg. "Not in front of him. Just yes or no," my mama said.

My grandmother glared at me. "You gonna pay me?"

With a sigh, my mama nodded. "You can have my food stamps, and then, whenever I get paid, I'll send you something, too."

Gran didn't say another word. She just stomped from the room, the floor planks shuddering under her weight. By the time my mama crouched down again, tears were tracking down my face.

"Are you going to be a big boy?"

There was so much I wanted to tell her about the belts and the switches. And so much I wanted to show her about the broom and the marks on my back.

"Please, X, I can't get a job here in Sumner, so I'm gonna go someplace where I can make some money, okay?"

There was nothing I could do but nod, then crawl back into the chair as my mother went into the bedroom we shared whenever Mama stayed here and packed. I wanted to go in there to spend these last minutes with her, but I didn't want to cry out loud. So I closed my eyes and did something I saw the ladies at church do whenever Mama took me to service.

"Dear Father God," I whispered, repeating the first words I'd heard. "Can you please tell Mama to take me so I don't have to stay here and get beaten every day?"

I prayed that over and over, until I heard my mama's voice. "Xavier?"

She was by the front door, holding her suitcase. I leaped out of that chair and ran into her arms.

She squeezed me tight. "I love you so much, Xavier."

Those words made me cry out loud as Mama wiped away my tears.

"Come on, I need you to be my big boy."

My answer: my sobs deepened.

She kissed my forehead, then walked through the door and trotted down the steps. The man grabbed her bag, hugged her, and opened the passenger door. He tossed her suitcase into the back seat before he ran around to the driver's side.

I stood sobbing, waiting for Mama to change her mind and come back for me. But neither of them looked back as the car kicked up dirt when it sped away.

"Boy, you better close that door and stop all that noise before I give you something to cry about."

I took my time, not to be defiant, but because once the door was closed, I'd be alone.

"That's why your mama don't want you. Not worth nothin', standin' there cryin' like a baby. Not worth nothin', I tell you, not worth one red cent."

I whimpered, trying to control my tears, but it was hard the way Gran stared at me.

"What are you doing with your hands?"

What was she talking about? I was just trying to push my tears back inside. But I followed her glance to where my fingers curled into tight fists.

"You wanna hit somebody?"

I didn't get that No, *ma'am* out *before Gran whacked me across my head, this time not stopping at once. "You wanna hit somebody?" she repeated. "You wanna hit me?"*

I wanted to tell her I'd never had any thoughts about hitting her . . . until now, the moment when her final blow sent me flying to the floor. I sat there, stunned. But even when the ache began to subside, I couldn't move because there was this heat burning inside of me. It was in my soles, slowly ascending, feeling like fire. Rising, rising, rising to my fists.

"You better get yourself straight, boy."

I stayed there as she grumbled down the hall. My eyes stayed focused on her neck as she moved away. My fingers flexed, then relaxed. Flexed, then relaxed. But my mind didn't stop. The flames didn't stop. And my fingers didn't stop.

Now I knew what I could do with my hands. Now I knew what I wanted to do with my fists . . .

"XAVIER."

Roxanne's voice made me rush from the past, and the first thing I saw was my reflection. That heat from that long-ago day was in my soles now, but when I turned to Roxanne, she was a fire extinguisher. I cooled and calmed from those memories.

"I have everything," she said.

"Roxanne," I whispered. "I want you to know . . . I love you so much."

"I know you do." Then she turned away as if my love didn't matter.

Grabbing my bathrobe from the hook on the door, I slipped into it as I followed her through my condo. At the front door, she paused, turned, and faced me.

"Please know I wish you well," she said.

"What can I do to change your mind?"

There were tears in her eyes when she shook her head. "I always promised myself if any man ever . . ."

"I didn't hit you!" I exclaimed. There was more pleading than volume in my voice, but what Roxanne did next made me want to scream.

She glanced at the wall, and I followed her gaze. To the spot where my fist had made impact. Just one punch, and I'd been surprised at the way the plaster had crumbled beneath the weight of my rage.

"I didn't hit you," I repeated, softer now.

"Only because you missed."

"I missed on purpose."

She rose up, stood taller, full of indignation. "Do you hear yourself? You should never have taken a swing. Last Tuesday, I was the target, and that scared me."

"You're willing to give up everything for one time, when we had so much together? We were going to start a family, build our lives. I don't understand the lack of forgiveness."

"I have forgiven you. If I hadn't, I wouldn't be standing here."

"You're here because you didn't think I was home."

"But I didn't leave once I saw you." She paused. "It wasn't the first time, Xavier. It was the first time your rage was directed at me. But I've seen you out of control—too much."

I pushed down my frustration and said as softly as I could,

"Don't forget the part you played in this. You weren't listening to me."

"And that gives you the right to take a swing, to punch a hole in the wall when I was standing right there?" Again, her ire rose, but I guessed I was the only one in this relationship who couldn't get upset.

"I was just angry." I tried to explain what she already knew.

She shook her head. "No, what's inside of you, Xavier, that's not anger. It's not even rage; it's worse. And I can't sleep with a man who has that kind of wrath." When she glanced down at her hand, I did, too.

I hadn't even noticed she was still wearing her engagement ring. That had to be a good sign, but then she slipped the ring from her finger. With her eyes still lowered, she reached for my hand and pressed the diamond into my palm.

"I'm sorry," she whispered.

"I love you," I repeated, because to me, that should have been enough.

Now she looked up. "We moved too quickly, didn't give ourselves enough time to know each other," she said. "You need time to learn to love yourself first. To find out what's wrong so you can be right for another woman."

I pressed my lips together, trying to keep the words inside. But I felt the heat and lost the battle. "Don't psychoanalyze me. I'm not one of your clients!"

My tone made her glance down. And once again, I found myself following her gaze. Roxanne was fixed on my hands and the way my right hand contracted into a fist. I tried to stop, but my fingers flexed as if that part of my body were separate from my brain. Only after I inhaled, then exhaled slowly, was I able to stop.

Tears flowed from her eyes, and I cried, too, but it was all inside.

She raised her hand, her movement tentative as if she was unsure. Then her palm touched my cheek. And she held it there as if she were trying to commit me to her memory. I closed my eyes and relished her touch. I'd been here before; I knew what the end felt like.

Then she turned around, grabbed her suitcase, and rolled right out of my life.

3

Chastity

And . . . that's a wrap."

The room brightened as Kourtney, the instructor, turned on the lights and everyone in the stretching class applauded the end of this hour. My appreciation came out in a groan. I closed my eyes, feeling as if I could lay there for eternity. This wasn't an aerobics class; this was worse. It was because of the heat. We were only stretching, but it was impossible to breathe in this temperature.

"Really, Chastity."

Her voice made me open my eyes, but that was the only part of me that moved. My mother sat just a couple of feet away from me, yoga-style. With a towel, she dabbed at the perspiration that sprinkled the hairline of her still perfectly styled chignon. There was no sign that Sisley Jeffries just finished an hour of stretching in a room where the thermometer crept toward one hundred. She still looked like the well-groomed Southern belle she'd been raised to be.

"That was so refreshing." My mother sighed.

"Is that what you call it?"

"Oh, come on." Then, using nothing more than the strength of her legs, she rose from the lotus position before she reached down to give me her hand, the same way she'd done a million times in my life.

Even as I took her hand, I groaned, only making it to a sitting position.

"My goodness," my mother drawled, "which one of us is fifty-five?"

"You're not fifty-five, Mom. Grandmom lied to you and Granddad about your true birth date."

My mother laughed just as Kourtney sauntered up to us. "Great class, Ms. Sisley." The instructor, who would have to stand on her toes to be five feet, gave my mom a high five before she turned to me.

I wondered if she'd always been that small or if teaching these heated stretching classes had done this to her.

"I hope we'll see you again, Chaz."

Once again, I was grateful for my mother rescuing me when she said, "Thank you, Kourtney," because all I could do was give a noncommittal grunt.

As Kourtney sauntered away, stepping over mats as she greeted other heat enthusiasts, my mother clapped twice. "Get up, Chastity." She sounded like a schoolteacher trying to get a kindergartener in line. "All we did was stretch."

"So, really?" I groaned. "You do this every week?"

"Hot stretching every Saturday morning," she said as if sweating and stretching with a dozen other women was normal. "The heat is good for you, clears toxins from your body and distractions from your mind. The perfect way to begin the weekend. You need to join me every Saturday." Then with an up-and-down glance, she added, "Because you won't have that body and that metabolism forever."

"Yes, I will. I got my height from Papa, but everything else is all you. I'll be gorgeous till I'm one hundred."

My mother grinned at my compliment. "Let's grab a smoothie from the juice bar." She hooked her arm through mine and led me through the glass door of the studio to the small café. After we ordered our smoothies—a pineapple kale for her and a cranberry banana for me—we sat at one of the circular tables.

My mother reached for my hands, lowered her head, and blessed our smoothies. My parents were *those* Christians— nothing passed through their lips without first a blessing.

After our "Amen," she patted my hands. "You have no idea how happy I am to have you back."

"I'm glad to be home," I said, grateful I'd come to the point where I meant those words.

"Just so you know, we're having a welcome-home dinner for you tomorrow after church."

I rolled my eyes. "Mom, I don't want that. In fact, I was thinking I might not even go to church tomorrow. My apart- ment is a mess, I haven't unpacked, and I want to chill before the grind begins again on Monday."

"Well"—she shook her head—"you'll just have to do all of that after you get home from church and Sunday dinner." When I pressed my lips together, she added, "How in the world did you think you'd get away with not coming to church?" Astonish- ment filled her tone.

Again, I stayed silent.

Her shoulders slumped, and her voice lowered when she said, "You have to see your father at some point."

I fixed my face with a grin. "I wanna see Papa. I cannot wait . . ." My voice trailed off.

"You've gotten away with not seeing him this week because your father just got back last night," she said. "But now you have to face him. And tomorrow in church and then at dinner after-ward is the time and place."

"You're talking like I'm trying to avoid him."

She paused as if she was giving me a chance to take those words back. Then she said, "You've been avoiding him since you graduated from law school." A beat. "You've been avoiding both of us."

"I moved to Atlanta, Mom. It wasn't like I could drop by on my way home from work."

My mother's lips thinned in disapproval before she leaned forward and spoke at a level that only I would hear. "You know exactly what I'm talking about. The holidays when you made excuses or took trips so you wouldn't have to come home."

"You were the one who always encouraged me to . . ."

She held up her hand. "You don't have to defend yourself, but I don't know how many times I have to tell you or what I have to say for you to believe me . . . Our lives are so much better now, Chastity. He's different, and I'm so happy."

I took a sip of my smoothie, holding back the words I was itching to speak. This wasn't the first time she'd said this; over the last six or seven years she'd told me every time we talked. She told me what a wonderful husband my father was . . . now.

My silence gave my mother the space to say, "You left New York because of us."

"I left because of the job prospects in Atlanta."

"The best law firms are in this city, and after you graduated from Columbia, your father could have helped you get hired anywhere you wanted."

"But I didn't want Papa's help." I bounced back in the chair. "I wanted to find a job on my own—which I did. I wanted to build my life, away from the light of you and Papa—which I did."

"That was your excuse to get away from our drama. And I understand. But now you're so blinded by the past, you haven't been able to see the change in your father, the change in us. You would feel different if you accepted that your father is different."

I didn't want to get into a public battle with my mother, but since she didn't want to let this go, I said, "Is he different enough to make me forget all the days I watched you cry?" My question made her take a couple of long sips of her smoothie, and in the space of her silence, I continued, "It was over for me when his last affair hit the tabloids . . ."

Those words hit the REWIND button in my memory, taking me back to that day.

May 5, 2008

It was almost midnight, but even though my roommates and I had been cramming for finals all day, our all-night session was just beginning. The corner bodega on 116th Street was our go-to one-stop for half of our meals, and definitely now for our late-night get-us-throughs.

I was an in-and-out shopper. My hands were filled with a couple of sodas and a giant bag of chips, and less than five minutes after I arrived at the store, I was standing at the counter with my cash, when behind me, Nancy grabbed a tabloid and gasped.

"Oh my God!" Her exclamation resounded through the store, catching the attention of the other dozen or so late-night shoppers.

Nancy was always caught up in some pop-culture moment, but recently my blond-haired, ocean-blue-eyed roommate had been screeching and panting whenever she saw a photo of Senator Barack Obama.

So when she ripped the tabloid from the stand and stuffed the magazine in front of my face, I expected to see some cute pic of the presidential candidate and his wife.

But instead, the bold red-lettered headline of the National Intruder *screamed: Pastor Kareem Jeffries Did Things to Me No Man Has Ever Done.*

The photo of my dad holding hands with the rapper-turned-actress Zena as they strolled up to the doors of the Plaza Hotel took more than my breath away—I had no words.

Nancy shrieked, "That's your dad," as if I needed to be reminded of that in front of everyone in the store.

As my friends hovered around, gasping at the photo and the headline, this should have been the most humiliating moment for me.

"Is that really your dad, Chaz?"

"He knows Zena?"

"Oh my God, what about your mother?"

Their words could have taken me out, but I felt no embarrassment. I was used to the whispers that stopped when my mother and I passed through the church hallways or any event where my mother was known. She'd had to endure the humiliation of my father's infidelity for so long, and although this was bad, I was almost glad. This was so public it would have to be the straw that forced her to finally leave the man I called Papa . . .

"IT WAS HARD for me, Mom," I said, bringing myself back to the present. "I know it was unbearable for you, but for me, when you stayed and supported him, even after he'd disrespected you that way . . . again . . ."

When she glanced up with glassy eyes that held their own memories, I was sorry I'd taken her back through this history. She said, "It wasn't the easiest thing I'd ever done. But I leaned on God because I knew He'd chosen your father to be my husband."

A second before, I'd felt sorry for my mother, but now I fought hard not to roll my eyes. She'd told me this before: How God didn't make mistakes, so she had to believe His choice for her. How the devil had always been after my father because Kareem Jeffries had such an anointing.

"Do you know why I call your father Pastor and not Kareem most times?"

"Yes, you've told me," I said, praying she wasn't going to take me through her explanation again. But my prayer wasn't answered.

"I began calling Kareem Pastor about two weeks after we'd met because I recognized the call on his life. Even as he was in the world, I knew what God wanted for him. When he finally retired from basketball and answered the call, I knew God wanted me to be part of that.

"Even as the world continued to cheer him as the ex-superstar basketball player, I was there to remind him of his true purpose." Then, she added, "It wasn't just for him, though. Through the first twenty-eight years of our marriage, I called him Pastor to remind me."

I sat back a bit; my mother had never told me that last part. But . . . twenty-eight years out of the thirty-five that they'd been married?

She continued, "That was how I stayed through all of those women, Chastity. That was how I stayed to help him get to where he is now." She paused and peered at me as if she wanted to make sure I heard the next words. "Your father has become that man because I stood steadfast, doing what I was supposed to do no matter what the world . . . or you . . . said or thought."

Her last words were sharp, but then she leaned back, her shoulders relaxed now.

"Mom, I never meant to judge you . . ."

She held up her hand. "Yes, you did, but I get it. Every woman I knew and the thousands I didn't were judging me and calling me all kinds of names that led back to the definition of *stupid*. But I was never moved because I will never allow any man or woman's voice to ever be louder than God's."

That rebuke made me lower my head, but my mother reached across the table and lifted my chin. "I'm just telling you this so you can understand where your father and I are in our lives. It took him a while—a long time, really. But God helped him to learn how to truly love and completely cherish me."

When I nodded, she leaned back and blinked hard, fighting the emotion in her words. "I hate what those challenging years did to you, though." Her voice trembled as she rummaged through her backpack and grabbed a package of tissues. Dabbing at her eyes, she added, "That will always be my regret: how much this affected you. You became a divorce attorney, for God's sake!" With the heel of her hand, she hit her forehead and chuckled, and I laughed a little with her. "When you could have been playing in the WNBA." She sighed. "I just hope you'll finally see me and your father for who we are now."

"Mom, I was just . . ."

"Speaking your truth," she finished for me with a shrug. "And sometimes the truth hurts. But at the same time, the truth comes with facts, and the truth today is your father is a changed man who tries every day to live up to greater expectations. Your father suffered, too, after his affair with . . ." She paused, not speaking the rapper/actress's name. "When that story hit the papers, that's what brought him to his knees, completely back to God and to me. And that's where he's been ever since."

It was hard to believe my father had received so much grace. Between the gospel grapevine and the Hollywood rumor mill, the story of my father and his mistress of the moment had been headline news from sea to shining sea. All of those quotes from Zena had set tongues and fingers wagging.

I'd expected my father to step down from the church right before he and my mom were chased from the city. But after a tearful pulpit mea culpa and a thirty-day leave of absence to reconnect with God and my mother, my father had returned to his church, Greater Grace, with resounding praise. The African American Christian community blamed the devil and the wiles of Hollywood (and not my dad) for his downfall.

In the middle of his leave from the church, I'd taken my leave from my parents, moving to Atlanta without even having a job. I'd begged my mother to come with me, but her heart hadn't been open to anything except standing by her man.

"It's time for you, Chastity," she said, breaking into my memories, "to make room for the gift your father has become." Just as she said those words, her cell phone vibrated, and the smile that crossed her face revealed who was on the other end before she even said, "It's your father."

I held up my finger, then slipped from my chair, giving her privacy to talk to the man I hadn't seen or spoken to since I'd flown into New York a month before for my last interview with my law firm.

I sauntered to the refrigerated shelves, checking out everything, looking for nothing, my thoughts still on our conversation. Glancing over my shoulder, I saw joy shining all over my mother as she talked to my father. She wore the expression of a woman who was hearing sweet everythings in her ear.

My mom was happy, and she'd moved on. So why was it so difficult for me? Maybe it was because of the years I'd spent living with my mother's misery, which began when I was just six . . .

February 14, 1991

My tiara was tilted; I couldn't go to my birthday party that way. It had to be right because Papa said I was a princess.

Rushing from my bedroom, I dashed down the long hallway. Mommy would fix it; Mommy fixed everything. But then, as I got close to her door, I slowed down. Someone was crying. Maybe it was the TV—except Mommy and Papa didn't have a television in their bedroom. I tiptoed to the door and then just stood there, too scared to move.

My eyes were stuck on Mommy at her vanity. Her back was to me, but I could see her face in the mirror, though her eyes were covered by her hands.

But the sounds that came from her, the same sounds I'd made last week after I'd tumbled down the church steps . . . Had my mom been hurt, too?

"Sweetheart."

I hadn't noticed that my mom had spotted me.

"Sweetheart." Mommy sniffed the way I did when I was trying hard to stop crying. She held out her arms, and I ran to her.

"Mommy." I leaned back and wiped her tears away with my fingertips the way she always did for me. "Did you fall down?"

"What?" She seemed confused.

"You're crying," I said.

Even though tears stayed in her eyes, a small smile graced her lips. "No, I didn't fall down." She grabbed a tissue from the silver holder on her vanity.

"Then, why are you crying?"

"I'm not crying." She dabbed at her eyes. "At least not the regular kind of crying." After she sniffed a few more times, her lips curled into a full grin. "It's your birthday, and I'm so happy." She hugged me. "You're six years old today. And look at you with your tiara."

"Papa gave it to me."

Her smile dimmed a bit.

"And it's tilted."

"Well, I can fix that," she said.

"CHASTITY."

Blinking back from twenty-eight years ago, I made my way to my mother. With each step, my mind traveled through the years that followed my sixth birthday. All of the tears, all the years of hurt. It had overwhelmed me. Changed my views of men . . . even the papa that I loved.

"Where did you go?" my mother said.

"I stayed right over there."

"I called you a couple of times and you didn't hear me."

"Oh, I was just thinking . . ." I left it there, didn't want to tell my mother that I was still holding on to her pain . . . even if she wasn't. "That was Papa?"

She nodded, but her smile dropped as if my question brought back the memory of where we'd left off. "He said he can't wait to see you tomorrow." With her straw, she stirred the little bit of smoothie that was left, and without raising her eyes, she whispered, "So, don't you think it's time to forgive your father?"

It was a crazy question. He had cheated on her, not me. Yet she knew the scars I wore.

"It's just all here." I pressed my hands against my chest. "The memories of your tears and your humiliation."

She nodded her understanding. "But those were *my* tears, *my* humiliation . . ."

"That I felt."

"I know, and I hate that." Her sadness was palpable. "This is why you're not married today."

"Whoa." I held up my hand like a stop sign. "That's not the reason," I said, even though we both knew I wasn't telling the whole truth. "I'm not married because I haven't met anyone, but primarily because I've focused on my career."

She gave me a come-on-now glance. "As if you're the first woman who's busy with a career. You could have done both if you hadn't been scarred by your parents."

"That's not it." There was such weakness in the tone of my denial.

She said, "Release this, Chastity. Your father has been forgiven by God, by me, by his church members. It's time for you to see what we see—that all we can do is strive to do better today than yesterday." She paused. "Don't let the sins of the father, especially a father who's changed, stop the daughter from striving and becoming the woman she was meant to be."

I looked at my mother in all of her perfection: every hair still where it was supposed to be, her face makeup-free but her sandy-colored complexion still glowing. Even with tears in her eyes, she was filled with a jubilance I'd never seen in her.

My mother stood and hovered over me. "James two-thirteen," she said.

I quoted her favorite scripture: "'Judgment without mercy for anyone who doesn't show mercy,'" I said.

"That's close enough." My mother smiled. "Be merciful as the Lord says mercy triumphs over judgment." She kissed the top of my head. "I'm going to talk to Estelle," she said, referring to her best friend, who owned the studio. "Do you want to wait and we can Uber uptown together?"

"No." I shook my head. "I need to get home so that . . . I can make it to church in the morning."

The wattage in her smile could brighten this city. "Church and dinner." She raised her finger as a reminder before she pivoted in a move that showcased the dancer she used to be. But then, just as quickly, she twirled back. "When you give people room to be human, you have to give them the same space to make human mistakes. That's what grace is all about."

My eyes followed her as she sauntered with the stride of a woman who looked decades younger. I watched her until she disappeared to the opposite side of the studio.

Give them the same space to make human mistakes. That's what grace is all about.

I'd just sat through a whole sermon with my mother. And she'd more than told me, she'd shown me grace.

She was so right: I needed to see my father, have the hard talk, make a new judgment, and not hold on to something old.

The buzzing of my phone snatched my attention away. In the center of the screen was the reminder of a man I'd forgotten all about: *Call Xavier.*

I'd meant to delete this reminder because his request last night was certainly disqualifying . . . if I'd been interested.

But then my glance returned to the door on the other side of the studio, where I was sure my mother sat with her best friend, laughing and filled with all the delight I'd seen in her today. Even when I'd made her cry, she seemed to have such peace.

I turned back to my phone, I held it up, and with the memory of my mother's tears in my mind, I smiled.

4

Xavier

The banging startled me, and I bolted up on the bed . . .
no, wait, I was on my sofa. A quick glance at the sixty-
five-inch television mounted to the wall across the room
helped me to see that, yes, I was in my living room.

So now I knew where I was, but what had happened? What
day was this?

Another flurry of FBI-hard knocks grabbed my attention
again. I stumbled toward the door and swung it open without
checking the peephole. I wasn't too worried about skipping that
precaution. If anyone had made it past the doorman and concierge and was trying to bring trouble to my door, I was six foot
four and a solid 240 pounds. Trouble usually took a look at me
and walked the other way.

"Bruh, you ain't hear your phone ringing?"

One glance at my best friend and I wondered who I needed
to contact in management here at Lenox Luxury Condos to have
the doorman fired.

Turning away from Bryce, I said, "Clearly, I did not. And
you need to demand a refund from NYU, specifically from your
English professors." I hobbled back to the living room.

"I've been calling you," Bryce said, ignoring my attempt to insult him.

"And since I didn't answer, that should've been a clue." I sank into the softness of my oversize leather sofa.

"What's up with that, X-Man?" Bryce said, plopping down in the matching chair across from me, clearly not taking any hint. Before I could respond, he said, "You look terrible."

"Thanks."

"You look like you were run over by a garbage truck up on Lenox or something."

"Thanks."

"So what's up? Why you asleep in the middle of the day, and why do you look so bad?"

"I had a long night."

He grinned, then sat all the way back, relaxed now, as if my answer relieved him. "With Roxanne?"

The mention of her name brought back everything that had ruined my life: the way she'd pressed her palm against my cheek—her forever good-bye. I sighed, pushing that image aside. "Nah, I hung out at Club 40/40 last night."

"Oh, yeah?" He sat forward. "What was happening there?"

"A private party. I went in to grab a drink and stayed awhile. It was better than coming home alone on a Friday night."

He chuckled. "You need to use your Obamacare and get that checked out, bruh. You're a grown man. You can stay home by yourself." He glanced around. "Where's Roxanne? She go out of town to visit her folks?"

Her name triggered another memory: Roxanne slipping the ring from her finger this morning. My glance wandered to the coffee table, where the diamond glittered beneath the sun rays filtering through my window.

As the diamond held my stare, I remembered more: I'd laid

the ring there, then rested on the sofa, staring at the ring until the glitter had lulled me to sleep. Sleep, the instant elixir for heartache.

My stare made Bryce notice. He released a soft whistle, then rose up a bit and picked up the engagement ring that would forever be a symbol that another woman had left me.

The way he held her ring felt like a violation, and I wanted to snatch it away, but I was too exhausted, in all ways, to do more than glare at him.

"Does this mean what I think?"

I shrugged. "I don't know how you think."

He nodded. "Yeah, you know, bruh. More than fifteen years of history, you know."

I hardened my glare; my intent was to make him put that ring down, shut his mouth, and just walk out of my door, leaving me alone.

But that was my hope; that was not Bryce. He dropped the ring back onto the table, and then he stood but only made it as far as my kitchen. I couldn't see him, but I heard the opening of the refrigerator, and I imagined him grabbing two beers.

When he came back, he held only one bottle, though. The cap already off, the top of the bottle was already pressed against his lips. He leaned back in the chair. "I'd offer you one," he said as if he were the host. "But it seems as if a beer is the last thing you need, fam." He swung his legs up and rested his heels on the glass top of my coffee table, which had been shined spotless by my cleaning lady just the day before.

He took another swig. "So"—I could tell by his tone he was settling in for a long talk—"did Roxanne pull a Diane, Mattie, and Trina on you?"

I felt it, starting at my feet with the mention of those names. That fire again, slowly burning, slowly rising. My eyes narrowed,

I clenched my fingers, wanting to punch something. One punch would give me relief. One punch always did.

After another swallow of my imported beer, Bryce placed the bottle on my table. "What happened this time?"

Bryce, his words, his tone, poured fuel on my fury, and I wanted to throw him out. But the truth was, I needed to talk this out. Maybe even help me devise a plan to get Roxanne back.

So I answered, "She got upset."

He shook his head. "I told you before with the others, women don't break off engagements because they get upset."

"I never gave Diane a ring," I said. "She doesn't count."

"But Roxanne counted, and she didn't break off your engagement over something small."

"Yeah, she did," I said. "It was over something small and crazy. I wanted to go out and she didn't seem like she wanted to and then she said she would and asked me what she should wear." The fire within me burned hotter with the memory, and I stood to get relief. "I told her it didn't matter what she wore." I paced away from Bryce. "But she kept pushing. She kept talking until . . ." I slammed my fist into the palm of my hand.

There was nothing but silence as Bryce stared at me. After many moments, he said, "Is that what you did to her?"

I glanced down at where my hand was still in a fist, and I lowered my arms. "No." I shook my head. "Of course not. I didn't hit her. I would never . . ."

Bryce raised an eyebrow, and I sank back down onto the sofa.

"I didn't hit her," I repeated. "I love Roxanne."

"You loved Diane, too."

I paused and remembered that day of rage. I'd just resigned from my second law firm, a resignation that had been strongly suggested by my boss after a client had threatened a lawsuit because I'd gotten a little angry. I'd come home, wanting space and solace, but Diane had drilled me with question after question after question, until I'd tossed her down on the bed. "I didn't hit Diane . . ." Then I repeated, because I needed Bryce to understand what I hadn't been able to get Roxanne to hear, "I love Roxanne."

My best friend nodded. "I know you do." The heat within me began to cool with his acknowledgment, but then he had to add, "Just like I had no doubt you loved Diane and Trina and—"

"Would you stop saying their names?" I shouted, pressing my hands against my temples.

"X-Man, you're gonna have to do something."

"About what?" The words were hardly out of my mouth before I regretted them, knowing what he was going to say. So I preempted him. "Yeah, I get angry sometimes, but who doesn't?"

He shook his head. "No, what you experience isn't anger, bruh. It's beyond that, and I don't know how many women have to leave you or how many jobs you have to lose before you see that. Before you're ready to do something to take care of yourself."

"So what am I supposed to do? Tiptoe around people? When I have something to say, I say it."

"No, when you have something to say, you punch something, and what you need to do is get help before you finally cross the line and that some*thing* turns into some*one*. You need to speak to somebody about this rage."

"I'm speaking to you," I said because I didn't have another response.

"And if I could help, I would. But you need far more help than what a black man with an MBA from Stern can give to you. You need to see a therapist, a psychologist, a psychiatrist, one of those doctors from *Grey's Anatomy*—I don't know, fam. But you need to see someone."

I glared at Bryce, but he didn't flinch under the heat of my stare. So I leaned across the sofa and grabbed my cell phone from the side table, tapped on Instagram, and scrolled through my timeline. Not that I'd ever spent too much time on social media; I never posted anything. But the posts from the people I followed were interesting enough to keep me from having to deal with Bryce. I was tired of folks telling me I needed help. It was like a black man couldn't get upset about anything anymore.

After a few minutes passed, Bryce said, "So this is how you're gonna handle it?"

I just kept scrolling through pictures and posts that I paid no attention to. My mind was still on what Bryce had said and what Roxanne had said and what all the others had said. It was times like these when I felt so alone. Like not even the people who were supposed to have my back tried to hear me.

My condo was silent except for the summer sounds that seeped through my window: children's laughter, the Mister Softee ice cream truck, and the hum of the rubber hitting the road of the traffic that rolled down 132nd Street.

I wasn't going to say a word, and neither was Bryce, I knew that. We'd been here before. But something else I also knew was Bryce wouldn't leave until the last drop of beer had been emptied from his bottle.

That was okay—I had plenty to scroll through. After Instagram, I'd head to Twitter, then finally Facebook. I'd go into social media overload—until Bryce decided to get his happy ass up and out of my apartment.

Finally, that moment came. Bryce stood, but my eyes remained on my phone. "So you got nothin' to say?"

I tapped the phone's screen and switched to Twitter. Even though I didn't look up, I imagined the way Bryce stood, his broad shoulders squared, built like a running back if he'd ever gone out for football. His stature was imposing to many. Just not to me.

When he tired of watching me, he made his way to the door. Still I stayed focused on my phone, but I was aware. I felt him pause, felt his eyes turn once again to me.

For the first time in minutes, I spoke—"Thanks for stopping by, black man"—though I didn't look up.

This time, he was the one who stayed mute as he walked through the door. The moment he stepped outside, I sighed. Bryce didn't get me, and he wasn't the only one. Clearly, Diane, Mattie, Trina . . . and now Roxanne could be added to that list. All I knew was that I was a good man and I'd find that good woman.

Switching to the phone icon, I frowned at all the missed calls from Bryce. But before I could even think about it, the phone rang in my hand—UNKNOWN CALLER flashed across the screen.

I pressed ACCEPT. "Hello."

"Xavier, this is Chastity. I met you last night at . . ."

My smile was instant. "Do you think I need a reminder?" I leaned back, resting my head on the sofa's high cushions. "I've been sitting here all day waiting for your call."

Her laughter was like a cool shower, relaxing me from the heat Bryce had left behind.

She said, "Another good line. Like I told you last night, you're full of them."

"At least you didn't say I was full of it."

She laughed again and now, I swung my legs up and lay down. This time when I closed my eyes, I had no intention of sleeping. All I wanted to do was block out everything except for the sound of music that was Chastity's sweet voice.

As we chatted, every concern I had faded behind the light that Chastity brought. This morning, I never thought I'd smile again. But now, as Chastity and I laughed together, I had a feeling I might never stop smiling.

5

Chastity

reater Grace was rocking; this was the way I remembered the church that had been as much a part of my
life as the Harlem brownstone where I'd been raised.

The praise and worship team sang the last chord of "Every
Praise," and Lauralee, the minister of music, had those singers
hold the last note so long, some of their brown faces turned
crimson as their lungs screamed for relief. When Lauralee
dropped her hands, everyone in the sanctuary breathed and lifted
praises to the Lord.

I stood in the first pew, in the second seat of honor, shoulder to shoulder with my mother. As the atmosphere filled with
worship, I sat, then closed my eyes, pressed my hands together,
and bowed my head. It was a stance of prayer, but that wasn't
what I was doing. I was basking, actually, in the jubilation that I
always felt whenever I came to my home church.

Greater Grace held so many of my first life memories: the
times when I'd crouch under the huge desk in my father's office,
playing hide-and-seek with my dad. Or the first time I stood at
the altar next to my father and recited the 23rd Psalm for Resurrection Sunday. And then there was the first time I'd danced

with the praise dancers under the guidance of my mother, the choreographer.

My mind was filled with good times, good memories.

"Let the church say 'Amen.'"

The richness of my father's baritone reverberated off the walls, and like when I was a child, his voice made me smile even before my eyes fluttered open. I hadn't realized my father had entered the sanctuary.

"Amen!" filled the church, the congregants following my father's directive.

With a smile, my eyes locked on the man I called Papa.

Hovering on the edge of sixty, my father still had the physicality that had made him a basketball star and the mark of too many women. Memories warred inside of me: the man who wrapped me in the best hugs, but then, the same man whom I'd seen embracing women, always leaving me wondering, was this lady the reason why my mom had cried the night before?

I wanted to shake away those memories just as my mother had asked, but they were etched too deeply inside my hippocampus for me to forget.

In the pulpit, my father moved with such grace, his hands gliding like a maestro's as he spoke. But seeing him in the pulpit made me shiver as another memory bombarded me, hitting me hard, hitting me fast:

May 6, 2004

All my life, my parents had done this to me. From my sweet sixteen surprise party they'd sworn I wouldn't have, to the BMW that was my high school graduation gift, they'd always caught me, but today, I was doing the catching!

Swinging my car into Greater Grace's parking lot, I was thrilled about two things: one, Aunt Estelle had been right when she said my parents were still at church after their Thursday-night budget meeting, and two, my dad's Range Rover was the only car left—another good sign, but not a definite. So many took cabs to Greater Grace, so there was still a chance I might have to share my reunion with others besides my parents.

I hopped out of the car, giddy with my excitement that I'd pulled this off, even though I'd told a few tales that had me crossing fingers behind my back. It was Mother's Day weekend, but I wasn't supposed to be home. Both my mom and dad had been sad, though they'd tried to hide it; I hadn't been home since I'd left for London in September.

It was only because my parents were so proud I was spending my junior year at Dartmouth abroad that I was able to get away with the fib that I had to finish an important project. But the whole time, I'd planned this (along with Aunt Estelle); this was going to be the best weekend.

I scurried up to the side entrance of the church, used Aunt Estelle's key, and held my breath as I pushed the door open. I paused, not wanting, after all of this, to spoil the surprise by allowing them to hear me. When all was clear, I tiptoed down the hall, my eyes on the light that shined from my dad's office, and with my fingertips, I pressed back my giggles. I hadn't decided if I was going to jump into the office and shout, "Surprise!" or if I would stroll in as if I were supposed to be there.

After just a few more steps, though, I stopped. I was too far away to see them, but what I heard left me frozen.

"How could you do this to me again?"

The words made me press my back against the wall. Standing just feet away, I took in the sound of my mother's tears. I'd almost forgotten how she sounded, almost forgotten how much she'd cried.

My father's voice was next. "This is not the time, this is not the place."

"And why not?" My mother's volume rose. "This is where she gave me these pictures of the two of you. This is where she had the audacity to . . ."

It was difficult for me to concentrate anymore. Pictures? I moaned. Over the years, I'd had to deal with this too much, since women approached when I was out with my mother or with my father—the tricks, as I'd heard my aunt Estelle refer to them.

But now . . . there were pictures?

"Sisley." My father's plea was inside his tone. "We'll talk about this when we get home."

"No, we're talking now. Look at these," she demanded.

With my back still pressed against the wall, I sidestepped as if I were walking a tightrope, stopping at the door's edge. I'd be able to peek in without my parents noticing, not only because of the way my dad's office was arranged but because there was little that would distract either from what was in front of them.

I peeked inside and watched my mother stand with squared shoulders over my father who still sat at his desk.

"I can't do this anymore, Kareem."

This was one of the few times I'd heard my mother call my father by his name.

She continued, "She's put it in my face. She has to go."

"I can't do that. Cynthia is the best assistant I've ever had."

"You mean the best lay, don't you?"

Her words made me gasp. Sisley Jeffries had taken so much from my father, but she'd always handled it with what I'd come to call Southern grace. It sounded like she'd changed, though. Sounded like she didn't have a bit of grace within her.

"Really, Sisley? You want to disrespect the house of the Lord this way? Is this how you want to speak as you're standing just feet from the altar?"

That was his response? He thought this was the moment to rebuke her for what she'd said after what he'd done?

The one thing I'd never seen in my parents' house was physical violence. The psychological abuse of my father's numerous affairs had been damaging enough. Surely, though, my father's admonishment would make my mother slap him. But the sound of flesh assaulting flesh was not what I heard next.

Instead, it was laughter, and as I once again peeked around the entrance, I watched my mother, her shoulders hunching up then down as she laughed straight in my father's face. He sat, taking her manic outburst, waiting for her to gather herself back into the prima donna she'd always been.

Just moments before, she'd been buckled over in the pain of her tears, and now she was cackling like she'd gone mad . . .

"AND THAT IS having my daughter, Chastity, home."

I heard the words, but I was still so deep in the eighteen-year-old memory that my mother had to nudge me back to 2019. Only then did I hear the applause, and another motherly nudge sent me rising to my feet.

My eyes locked with my father's, and that beam in his eyes, which always melted my heart, almost melted my memories. Almost.

"Can you believe this is the first time I'm seeing my little girl since she returned to New York last week?"

I chuckled with the people and grinned back at my father with the same adoration he gave me.

"I don't think I need to tell anyone in this sanctuary how much I love my wife and our beautiful daughter." He pressed both hands against his chest. "I don't have to tell you my testimony because you've heard it before. But I'm gonna repeat it because God's grace is just that good."

When Lauralee hit a note on the keyboard, the sanctuary filled with "Yes!"

"I was a sinner in need of a savior," my father sang. "And when I tell you the Lord saved me through His mercy, but then, do you know what He did with His grace? Whew!" he shouted, with his hands raised. "The Lord gave me my wife."

"Preach!"

"Oh, yeah, I don't have to tell you 'cause I've told you before. But I was a ho out there in these streets."

"You better tell it!"

"I knew God, but I'd turned my back on the Lord because I loved the limelight that came with the fame of being KJ on this New York basketball team."

"Speak!"

"But that limelight was nothing but darkness. Until"—he paused and looked at my mother—"God gave me a glimpse of His grace through the woman He'd chosen just for me. She loved me through all of my infidelities that came from all of my insecurities."

Again, my father pressed his hands against his chest, and when my mother blew him a kiss, the sanctuary exploded with applause.

"It still took me a long time," my father said, his tone singed with sadness. Then my father's face brightened when he said, "But once I got it . . ."

Lauralee hit another chord on the keyboard.

"Whew!" my father shouted.

Another chord.

"Thank you, Jesus!"

Then the third chord.

"Hallelujah!"

And then, Lauralee kept on playing. My father danced, and the members and visitors of Greater Grace stood and danced with him. When my mother turned to me and offered me her hand, I got up and danced, too. It was a celebration of how good God had been.

L. Frank Baum had been right. In one of my favorite children's books, *The Wonderful World of Oz*, I'd loved his words the first time I'd read them, and I truly loved them now. There was definitely no place like home.

AS SOON AS the benediction had been given, I rushed through the side door before I could be ambushed by well-wishing church members. It wasn't that I didn't want to acknowledge the people, so many of whom claimed to have known me when I'd been in my mother's womb. But how could I greet anyone when I hadn't properly done that with my father? So I bypassed the reception line where my father and mother stood after every service and retreated to the massive space of my father's office.

When I was a child, this office had felt as grand as our home. Stepping inside now, I was still in awe, but for different reasons. I appreciated that every inch of the custom-built walnut bookshelves that stretched from the floor to the ceiling and lined two walls were stocked with hundreds of Bibles, about four dozen of which were in different languages. Then, there were the two stained-glass windows that, to this day, I'd never seen in an office. Black Jesus was sketched into one, and on the other side was His black mother. Both hovered over and glanced down at my father whenever he sat at his desk.

His desk. The centerpiece. It was a replica of the Resolute desk that had been given by Queen Victoria to one of the American presidents and was in the Oval Office even now. My mother had ordered the piece for my father's first office, his gift from her for stepping into his calling. It was going to be a while before my parents finished touching and agreeing with the people, so I did my absolute favorite thing when I came into my father's office: I sank into the red velvet cushion of my father's chair. This chair with the wooden armrests trimmed in gold always looked like a throne to me.

I smiled, remembering the first time my father scooped me into his arms and lifted me up and into his chair. The cushion had been so soft, like a cloud, the way it felt now.

"You look just like a princess," Papa had said. Then he'd spun me around and around until I was giggling and dizzy.

That memory made me close my eyes and spin in the chair the way I'd done that day and on hundreds of days that followed.

"Weeeeee." Just like back then, I lifted my legs as the chair spun.

"You still love that chair, don't you, princess?"

I grabbed the desk to stop, a little embarrassed I'd been caught acting as if I were seven. My father beamed with the love he'd shown me my entire life. Yes, our relationship was complicated, but in this moment, in this way, all I saw, all I remembered, was that this was my daddy.

He'd been holding my mother's hand, but now he opened his arms to me. I jumped up, eager to step into his embrace. He folded me inside his arms, and even though I had on heels that edged me over six feet, I felt dwarfed in my father's hug.

When he stepped back, he held my hands. "How's my princess?"

"I'm good. How are you, Papa?"

His eyes shined, but this time, the light was on my mother.

WRATH   55

"I am so blessed and so favored by God that all I want to do most days is jump and shout." He released me and rushed back to my mother as if he'd been away from her for too many seconds. He pulled my mother into his chest, and she wrapped her arms around his waist. My parents looked like a soap opera couple.

"And it's all because of the man above me"—my father pointed toward the ceiling—"and this woman beside me." When my mother looked up at him, he kissed her nose, then motioned for us to sit down as he rounded his desk. "I just have a few things to wrap up before we head home." He paused. "We have quite a celebration planned." He chuckled when I rolled my eyes. "You know those facial expressions don't mean anything to me. Didn't matter when you were a teenager and don't matter now."

I laughed with my parents.

"Yes, indeed," my dad continued. "We have so much to celebrate when it comes to you, princess."

"You're making me feel like the prodigal daughter," I said, thinking that was how I often referred to myself.

"Far from it," my father boomed. "Though I do feel as if you've been away for about as long as that son in the Bible." That quickly, the ends of his lips dipped, and in the moment of silence that followed, I wondered if I'd heard a bit of an accusation inside his tone. But then, just as fast, his smile returned. He leaned back in his chair, formed a steeple with the tips of his fingers. "My princess is home, and she's now a partner at the Divorce Concierge, no less."

"Well, I have you to thank, Papa. I wanted to do it on my own, but your connections have certainly boosted my career."

He shook his head. "I made a few referrals, but you did the work." He chuckled, though the sound was filled with regret. "It's a shame I know so many people who want to end their marriages. That's not the way it should be."

I wondered if he was thinking about himself and how blessed he'd been not to be in that situation. I said, "That's the way it is, though. And in today's times, with the amount of money at stake in some of these divorces . . ." I didn't have to say any more.

"I understand that in this fallen world, these types of safety nets must be in place," he said. "Divorce is not God's will, but that doesn't take away from how proud I am of you. Your mother and I"—he paused and gave my mother another one of those adoring glances—"are happy to have you home."

He had to make an effort to reach across his desk, which was a mile wide. But he was able to do it because my mother met him halfway. She rose up a bit, and with her hips in the air, she held his hand. As uncomfortable as they looked, as uncomfortable as that stretch had to be, they held each other, and gazed at each other, and smiled at each other—like in a soap opera.

And for the first time, I saw what my mother believed.

6

Chastity

After I slipped out of the Uber, I marveled for what had to be the 1,932,576th time that I was going on a date—Xavier's word, not mine. But it wasn't like I could pretend that once I stepped over the restaurant's threshold, this would be anything else.

But it was time for me to do this, the first step in releasing my father (and myself) from the transgressions of his past. Finally, I could see it: he was not who he used to be. Sisley and Kareem Jeffries were walking examples of grace—the extender and the receiver.

Still, as I pulled open the huge glass doors of Turning Point, my stomach fluttered. I'd hidden behind my father's infidelity for so long, I'd forgotten all the other insecurities that came from meeting up with a guy. What was I going to talk about? Suppose after five minutes I was bored—or worse . . . suppose after two minutes, he was bored?

"It's just a dinner," I whispered as I stepped inside the new restaurant on the northern edge of Central Park. "Nothing more. It will be fine if I never see him again."

Inside, I paused so my eyes could adjust from the six-o'clock brightness of the August evening to the dim lights inside. The space was body-to-body packed, a scene similar to Melanie's party on Friday. Only this time, there was no dance floor. Just drinks and dining for the young elite, black and white—all mixing their mingling as they wound down from a day of high-powered negotiations in law firms, brokerage houses, consulting groups, and every other kind of corporation.

Right before I stepped to the hostess, my cell phone vibrated with a message:

Look to your right, beautiful.

My head snapped up and there was Xavier, his half smile greeting me from afar. His expression, warm and welcoming, made my shoulders relax, made me grin in response, made me realize that since Xavier had asked me to dinner on Saturday, I'd been looking at this the wrong way—this wasn't a date, this was a gathering of two friends, new friends, who hoped to become good friends.

As he stepped from the bar, I appraised him once again: today, he wore a charcoal-gray suit, as exquisitely expensive as the one he'd worn Friday. Still a crisp shirt, still white (that was *so* this group in New York), and by the time he reached me, I was not surprised when I caught a quick glance of his still-spit-shined-after-a-long-day shoes. "Hey, beautiful."

"Hey yourself."

Xavier wrapped his arms around me, and I inhaled his scent—Creed. Enough men who favored this brand had walked into my office. He held me for longer than a greeting moment; I was the one to step back first.

"I'm glad you came out."

I had to take a breath and another step back before I said, "I'd heard about this place and I'd wanted to check it out, since it's not far from where I live." And when I added, "I'm glad you invited me," that was my truth. Because without his invitation, I would have been home, among my dozens of still-unpacked boxes.

Xavier placed his hand on the small of my back as he led me toward the hostess stand. "There's a wait," he said, "but I'm a regular with a reservation, and so Stephanie told me she'd seat us when you got here."

Stephanie?

All he'd done was mention the hostess's name with a good explanation, but still my radar (which I'd developed in child-hood) shot up. Just a moment later, though, I took a calming breath. Xavier and I didn't even know each other like that; why was I concerned about Stephanie?

At the hostess's stand, a twentysomething blond woman—Stephanie—greeted Xavier with an orthodontist-perfected smile, and when he leaned over, whispered to her, she pressed her hand against her chest and giggled. But then she maneuvered around him and spoke to me. "Would you follow me, Ms. Jeffries?"

There was nothing but charm in her tone, and I followed her through the vestibule of the restaurant into the dining area, where Stephanie stopped at a table that was almost exactly in the middle—the place to be seated to see and be seen.

Xavier moved ahead to hold the chair for me. I thanked him and then, when we sat, Stephanie said, "Mr. King, it was good to see you again." Turning to me, she added, "Enjoy your dinner, Ms. Jeffries."

When she stepped away, I said, "You must come here a lot if the hostess knows your name."

He said, "This is my firm's new go-to spot whenever we want to meet clients uptown. Most of us love getting away from Wall Street."

"Well, this is my first stop at what I'm sure are hundreds of new places that have opened in the city since I left."

"That's right; you said you just got back, but you're a native New Yorker, right?"

I raised my hand. "Proud native here. From the Valentine's Day on which I was born."

He leaned back in his seat. "Really?"

I wiggled my fingers at him. "Go on, bring it. What kind of joke do you have about me being a Valentine's baby?"

Xavier said nothing as he reached into his jacket, pulled out his wallet, then slipped out what I, at first, thought was a business card. But it was his driver's license. "Check this out."

In just seconds, my eyes scanned the relevant information, and then I gasped. "You were born on February fourteenth, too?"

He nodded. "We have the same birthday, though I have a feeling I have a few years on you. Since I'm a gentleman, though, I would never ask for your license."

I glanced at his license once again and laughed so loud, I had to cover my mouth with my hand. "We were born on the same day, the same year."

His eyes widened. "Get out."

"Yup." I handed his license back. "And unless you were born in the very early hours of that Valentine's Day, I might even be older." We laughed, and I added, "What a coincidence."

He shook his head. "I would have thought you were much younger." Then he assessed me in that way only an attorney could. Not a direct stare, but his glance moved slowly, appraising all the vital parts he could see. Finally, he responded to my statement: "I don't believe in coincidences."

I chuckled. "That's what my dad always says."

"Your dad—a smart man."

Pressing my lips together, I glanced down at the menu, sorry I'd let that slip out. Beyond Melanie, I never spoke much about my parents. There was no indication Xavier had any idea who I was, and it was always best for me to keep it that way. "So, as a regular, what's your favorite dish?"

The change of subject was natural. Xavier answered, "Now, that's a two-part question. Are you asking me my favorite dish here or overall?"

I put down the menu, crossed my arms, and leaned forward on the table. "Both," I said.

"Okay, well, here, my favorite dish is the shrimp and grits."

"Get out of here." I laughed. "I've survived off of shrimp and grits for the last ten years—that is, when I wasn't eating sushi."

This time, it was his mouth that opened wide. "You're making that up."

"What? No. I love sushi." I paused, holding up my hand. "Don't tell me . . ."

He nodded. "The first time I had sushi was about ten years ago, but I've eaten about twenty years' worth since." He motioned for the waiter, and I took that moment to do my own assessment of the man. He was, as I remembered, smooth, sophisticated, and even suave, which was a word I was probably using for the first time to describe someone.

He placed our order—a double shrimp and grits—and when the waiter stepped away, Xavier said, "So that's two things we have in common," he said. "Let's see if we can make this three for three. What about music?"

"There's nothing like the nineties."

He grinned. "I'm with you. Maybe it's because that's the decade we came of age."

"Or maybe it's because those were the best of music times."

We laughed before he said, "Whitney, Mariah, Mary J, and that's when Janet came into her own."

"And Johnny Gill, Jodeci, Blackstreet, and Bell Biv DeVoe

with one of my all-time favorite songs." Before he could ask, I sang in the lowest of voices, "It's driving me out of my mind . . . that's why it's hard for me to find . . ." I stopped when Xavier stiffened and his smile faded. "Whaaat?" I dragged that word out. "You don't like my singing?" I asked, feeling as if I needed to make light of whatever had just happened.

Then, just as quickly, his lips pulled into that bright half smile, lighting up the space. "Your singing is fine—beautiful, even." He shook his head. "It's just that song . . . has the best of memories for me. I was just surprised to hear you singing it."

"Okay, good," I breathed.

He leaned back in his chair, loose, once again. "You almost know as much about music as I do."

We chuckled together again, and our laughter continued through our dinner. As time passed, we shared our interests:

"If I'm ever on a deserted island, I need my phone," I said. "And not to talk to anyone. I just love to read."

He pulled out his cell and we compared our digital libraries. His was packed with a bunch of what I called political thrillers—and they weren't even fiction. And then mine, historical, definitely fiction.

Then, we talked about sports—tennis and football—and movies—action and rom-coms.

Over a brownie drenched with chocolate ice cream (because that was his favorite flavor, too), we shared the dessert and our obsession about the current political climate, something I'd never been interested in before 2016, though, again, that was different for Xavier.

"From my first year in college, when I ran for class president, I've been enamored with politics. It's something that, eventually, I'd like to get into."

"Really?" I shuddered. "Too much vitriol for me."

"Yeah, but I can't let that stop me from making a difference if that's what I'm called to do."

His words made me smile inside, but I just nodded. He knew his calling, something my mother believed in.

Xavier continued, "I especially want to work at the local level, where change can really happen."

"So what are you thinking about? Being mayor of New York?" I asked, though I was surprised when he nodded.

"Absolutely," he said. "Of course, I'd start on one of the commissions or maybe even as the public advocate. I've always been intrigued by that office. Then, after that"—he shrugged again—"I think the city is ready for a black mayor again."

Perching my elbow on the table, I rested my chin in my palm. "I think it's admirable you want to go into public service after being at such a high-powered firm like Steyer and Smith." I winced a bit and hoped that Xavier hadn't noticed that, one, I'd flinched, and two, I'd mentioned his place of employment when that wasn't something he'd shared.

After Xavier and I talked on Saturday, I'd gone straight to one of the Internet services I'd used at my firm. I hadn't been out in these streets much, but I was smart and not about to be fooled by some dude I'd met in a club.

After a few minutes, I had a few answers: He really was an attorney, a graduate of NYU for both his undergrad in political science, and then his JD/MBA. He was currently an associate at Steyer and Smith, his third law firm, working in their civil rights division (where he'd received huge settlements on two cases), he owned a unit in Lenox Luxury Condos, and there were no (online) pictures of him with a wife. Beyond his professional photos, there was nothing; he had a very light social media footprint, which indicated he was serious about what he was going to do in the future.

Although I could have gone deeper (I'd learned how to find out a lot since dealing with celebrity divorces), I'd stopped there. Xavier King was who he said he was . . . and he wasn't married. So I trusted him to tell me anything else . . . if we got that far.

"It was my desire to go into politics that led me into the law," he said, not having noticed I'd mentioned his firm. "And it was my desire to make a difference that made me focus on civil rights at Steyer and Smith."

I smiled but kept my lips pressed together as he went on to tell me facts I already knew.

"I just finished up a case with . . ."

I could have mouthed the words with him. He'd been the lead counsel on a discrimination case with the Port Authority that had a multimillion-dollar award at the end.

When he stopped, I said, "This really is impressive."

He shrugged as if what he'd just told me wasn't massive and monumental. "It's what I do. I'm taking on civil rights one case at a time until I can address it on a larger scale . . . through a political office."

"That's going to be your platform?"

He nodded. "But for right now, I'm gonna keep doing it at Steyer and Smith, keeping my focus on becoming a partner. I'm on the verge of that now."

"That's terrific," I said. "I feel like I should say congratulations already."

"What about you?" he asked. "What are your plans?"

I shrugged. "Nothing like yours. All I'm thinking about is being back home, getting acclimated to my job, and doing well there."

"So you don't have any plans to turn the Divorce Concierge upside down and inside out?" When my mouth popped open, he said, "Now, that's impressive. You were brought in as a partner."

When I still didn't speak, he added, "What? Of course I checked you out."

I laughed. "I thought only women did that."

He shrugged a little. "Women . . . and men who are serious."

His words, his tone, reminded me of Friday, when he'd talked about how wonderful it was to be in love. Those words, that tone, had been my cue to leave. Tonight, these words, this tone, made me shift in my chair, but this time, I stayed.

He said, "None of us can be too careful. So"—he leaned toward me—"I liked what I saw when I researched you."

I lowered my eyes a bit, wondering how deep he had gone. I'd done a good job of keeping my parents out of my bio.

Xavier said, "What about you? Did you like what you found out about me?"

No mention of my parents. When I glanced back at him, it took everything inside of me not to be intimidated by this moment or this man. "What I found out through research was all right." He raised an eyebrow. "But what I've discovered tonight—this has been the best."

He grinned, and I didn't know how he did it—it was *his* half smile that lit up *my* whole face. He said, "It means a lot that I've passed your test."

"You passed the test before we even had dinner."

"Really?" He grinned. "What was my winning move? 'Cause I want to make sure I do it again and again." He flexed like he was about to pop his collar.

I laughed. "It was my phone call. You answered." When he frowned, I continued, "You answered your phone when I called. You must have good credit if you answer unknown numbers."

He gave me a blank stare as if he couldn't believe I'd said that out loud. Then his head fell back as he filled the restaurant with his joyful laugh.

7

Xavier

Standing in front of the leaning mirror, I smoothed down my lapel. I'd seen this look in pictures from the Golden Globes—black on black. This was not a natural pairing for me: a black suit with a black shirt, and no tie. A bit too casual for the persona I'd created over the last decade. But the men I'd seen in the pictures, Jamie Foxx and Michael B. Jordan, had rocked this outfit, and that was what I was going for tonight—I wanted to rock it with Chastity.

My cell phone vibrated, and I smiled before I even glanced at the screen. When the name flashed across the caller ID, I hesitated, then answered, "What's up, fam?"

"It's about time you called me to apologize," Bryce said.

Just like that, the tension was gone, and I chuckled. "Bruh, you called me."

"Only because I knew you wanted to speak to me," he said as if that were a fact. "It's been almost a week, and the weekend is coming up, so here's your chance," he continued. "You got something you want to say?"

I shook my head. This was why Bryce was my brother. Not

only did he keep it funny but he gave me room to be me. "Okay," I said. "I apologize for not being nice to you when you showed up uninvited even though you should have known better and I never would've done that to you."

He laughed like I was one of the Kings of Comedy. "That's good enough." After a pause, his tone became serious when he asked, "So, you good?"

Inside his question, I heard his real inquiry, and he needed to know Roxanne was so far in my rearview mirror that not only could she not be seen, I hardly remembered what she looked like. "Bruh, I'm better than good."

He sighed as if hearing that answer had been the purpose for his call. "Well, since you're so good, you can take me out for an after-a-long-ass-week drink as your way of apologizing."

"Didn't I apologize already?"

"Bruh, with the way your temperament is set up, there will be another time. So you might as well take me out for a couple of beers at Sluggers—we can catch a few games, and then in the morning, we can hit the links."

I turned away from the mirror. "Golf in the morning sounds good, and then we can grab a couple of beers afterward."

"Nah, Samantha and I are hanging out tomorrow afternoon."

"Well, that's what I'm doing tonight. I've got a big date."

"Oh, yeah?" His tone was filled with surprise. "So Roxanne forgave your big head?"

"Not Roxanne," I said without hesitation. "The woman who has my heart now . . . Her name is Chastity."

In the expanse of the silence that followed, I wanted to swallow back my words. Because I knew Bryce would take what I'd said, twist it, and make it something it was not.

When he began with "X-Man," I heard it in his tone. "You just broke up with Roxanne; how does some female already have your heart?"

"Sometimes, life is just good that way."

He sighed his exasperation. "You think it's a good idea to be out there like that so quickly . . . again?"

"I think it's a great idea."

"You need to give yourself some time and some space."

"What I need is a friend who will be more supportive in my life."

"A supportive friend tells you the truth. You got engaged six months ago and just broke up with your fiancée, who, by the way, you'd hooked up with less than a month after you broke up with your fiancée before her. And now, a week later, you're talking about some woman has your heart. Who?" he asked as if he couldn't imagine a female on the island of Manhattan who'd want to get with me.

"I met her at Club 40/40 last Friday, and we really hit it off. We've talked on the phone every day, been out a couple of times . . ." I paused. That was a half lie that would become the whole truth as soon as Bryce got off my phone. By the end of tonight, I would have been out with Chastity a couple of times. "Anyway," I continued, "tonight, I'm doing something special with her."

"Okay, that's cool. There're a lot of fine women in the city, but just slow it down, X-Man."

"Why? Here's the thing, Bryce," I began, thinking maybe if I broke it down, my friend would stop with all this psychoanalytical BS. "Chastity and I connected."

"I've heard that before."

"We connected right away."

"That's not a new line either, bruh."

"We talked as if we'd known each other for years. It's easy with her."

"Do you realize you've said that about the women you were supposed to marry?"

"Well, I haven't said this." I paused. "She's an attorney."

So many beats went by that I thought Bryce and I had lost our connection. Finally, he said, "And that means . . ."

I filled in the blank for him. "The foundation is there. I can talk to her about anything."

"The foundation of a relationship isn't your career."

"Man, when did you become Oprah?"

"I'm just sayin'."

"And *I'm* just sayin', you have two choices—you can be happy for me or not. And if you're happy, then we can hook up in the morning."

"Look, X, we've had each other's backs for a long time, and that's what I'm doing for you now."

"You know I have no words for how grateful I am to you, right?" I said, repeating what I'd told Bryce over the years. "But right now, having my back means letting me go so I can be on time for Chastity." Before he could share another judgmental word, I added, "Let's hook up in the morning. I'll text you."

That was my good-bye. I hung up, even though I knew Bryce had more to say. But by the time I'd clicked off the phone, my mind was back on Chastity Jeffries.

Everything about this girl fit. A magna cum laude Dartmouth grad with a law degree from Columbia. The only thing—she was already a partner, but that was cool . . . I was right behind her.

And she was a gorgeous woman. Beyond the obviousness of beauty . . . there was her charm and her humor and her height—I loved it. Together, Chastity and I were striking. It was telling in the way people glanced at us the other night. Inside and outside of Turning Point, we were turning heads.

It was easy for me to see her as Chastity King; I couldn't wait until she saw it, too. And it would happen, because what I knew now was that this was all about timing. There had been too much time with Diane and Roxanne, too much time between my proposal and what would've been our wedding day. If I'd been married, to either Diane or Roxanne, neither would've left me. For better or for worse, we would've worked it out. So, with that lesson learned, if Chastity was the one, I was gonna put that ring on it and marry her right away.

I grabbed my cell, opened the Uber app, and ordered my car. The one I'd sent for Chastity was already on the way to her.

"Three minutes," I whispered as the app alerted me of my car.

Tucking my wallet inside my jacket, I wondered if three would be my new lucky number. Chastity would be my third fiancée. Maybe after three dates, I'd propose, and then three days after that, we'd be married.

I chuckled at that idea; that would scare any woman away.

Or maybe not. I needed to see how tonight went and then keep the number three in the back of my mind.

I HAD NAILED it. My victory was in Chastity's eyes from the moment we'd met tonight. First, when I stood outside the Time Warner building as her car rolled to a stop on the curved curb of Columbus Circle. When I opened the door and held out my hand, both of us gasped. I wasn't sure about Chastity's reaction, but I was taken by everything about her. Just like when I'd seen her the last two times, she was a minimalist, which I loved. Minimum makeup, a simple red T-strap dress, a single David Yurman bracelet. Natural nails, natural hair, a natural woman not hiding behind the artificial because she was confident of her reality. That reality was perfection personified to me.

Together we'd walked into Masa, an exclusive Japanese restaurant—since she'd told me she loved sushi.

"How in the world did you get a reservation?" she'd exclaimed as we were seated inside one of the most expensive restaurants in the country. "Steyer and Smith," I'd told her.

She'd nodded—she understood. Chastity had probably guessed that either my boss, Jackson Steyer, knew Masa Takayama, the restaurant's owner, or our firm handled the restaurant's legal affairs. Either guess would have been correct.

Over dishes selected by the chef, we'd chatted as easily as we had on Tuesday, though that was probably because we'd talked on the phone several times a day.

But it was when we walked out of the Time Warner Center and paused at the edge of the curb that I'd hit that hole in one.

"Your carriage awaits, Ms. Jeffries." I bowed at my waist before I extended my hand.

Her mouth opened wide, but she didn't ask any questions; I liked that. I helped her step into the white-framed horse-driven carriage as if she'd already hooked up with her prince.

When I joined her, the driver checked us, then he turned his attention to the business of the forty-five-minute ride.

The moment we entered Central Park, Chastity said, "I've never done this."

"I wanted this to be a night full of firsts for you."

She leaned away from me as if she was trying to get a better look. "I can imagine why you'd think I hadn't been to the restaurant. But a ride in Central Park? I'm a New York City girl, so how would you know I'd never done this?"

"I'm a thinking man." I tapped my temple. "First, you just

returned to the city, so the last time you would've done this would've been in high school or college. I figured even if any of those boys had been able to scrounge up some pennies, they were boys," I said, tossing shade. "You'd never done this with a man."

She laughed, and like the whole time at dinner, the sound of her made my heart swell.

Then I said, "And if you had taken this ride with a boy or another man"—I paused just for a beat—"you'd never taken this ride with me. So this is a first for you."

This time, she gave me a soft smile; I eased my arm around her, and she accepted my invitation, leaning back into me. Then, together, we exhaled.

The city's music played around us: the rhythmic beat of the horse's hooves, the hum of car motors, the roar of the buses' engines. Each, an instrument; together, an orchestra that performed for me and Chastity. I'd taken this ride before, but with Chastity in my arms, the Wollman Rink was more vibrant with the summer sounds of the children, the lake was more alive with the dozens of boaters enjoying the August evening's calm waters, and Strawberry Fields was more tranquil when the horseman paused the carriage for a meditative moment.

That was the best part for me—the silence. Neither of us felt the need to fill the quiet space with anything more than just us. By the time we rounded the park and returned to the south side, I was ready to be with this woman forever.

I jumped from the carriage, tipped the driver, then held out my arms for Chastity. I stood close so all she could do was slide into my arms. Another moment when no words were needed as I held her there, staring into her eyes. Before, my thoughts had been my hope; now, my thoughts were my desire.

I wanted time to stop so that this moment as I eased toward her would stay with me forever. I never wanted to forget how she tilted her head. I always wanted to remember when our lips met.

Our contact sent a surge through me that didn't end at my center the way it always did with a first kiss; this current rushed straight to my heart. When I pressed against her, I wanted Chastity to feel what she'd done to me; I wanted her to know that from this moment, she could have all of me.

The sounds of the city dimmed as our tongues became acquainted, and once again, I asked time to stop so I could remain in the moment when I fell in love.

Finally, we stepped apart, and when she smiled, the deal was sealed. The way she'd kissed me, the way she looked at me . . . Chastity Jeffries was going to be my wife.

8

Chastity

t had only been a week. That was the part I didn't understand. I'd gone from not dating to, after a week, strolling down the southern edge of Central Park with my arm hooked inside a man's whom I'd known for seven days.

Seven . . . God's number of completion. So what did God want completed? Or what had been completed? Maybe that was it; maybe I was completing a part of my life where I'd been stuck inside my father's sins.

So maybe it wasn't the number seven. Maybe God wanted me to keep my eyes on tomorrow, the eighth day. Eight—God's number for new beginnings.

As we continued our saunter west, we were surrounded by pedestrians and traffic, but Xavier and I carved out our own space. The darkness of night had descended, but still, this city pulsed as if it were noon. And through it all, we strolled in our silence. I'd never been with anyone with whom I felt so satiated in the quiet.

"A penny for your thoughts."

I was surprised he'd spoken, but glad that he had. Because

the only thing better than the silence we shared was the sound of Xavier's voice. "Just a penny?"

"Did I say a penny?" He laughed. "I meant a million pennies."

"Hmmm," I hummed. "Ten thousand dollars? We can start with that."

"Okay," he said as if he'd just won a prize. "So, you've been kinda quiet since . . ." He stopped before he said "our kiss," but I knew that was his reference. "You good?"

I pondered for a moment, not because I wasn't sure, but because I was surprised by what I was about to say. "I'm better than good."

He squeezed my arm as if now, he was just as satisfied and complete. "So, is that what you were thinking about? That you were good?"

I nodded. "I was thinking this is good, the night has been good, and my parents would be very happy." I chuckled.

"So they'd like me?"

That mention of my parents had been another slip; Xavier was that easy to talk to. But then, they weren't a secret. And if I continued seeing Xavier, he'd find out. So I continued, "I think so." I glanced up at him. "But honestly, it's more that they'd be happy I was out having a good time. I'm sure they'd think nights like this will keep me from running away again." Another slip, so unlike me. Talking about my parents was one thing; bringing Xavier into that part of my world was another.

"You ran away from home?" He laughed. "I thought you'd gone to Atlanta to work."

"I did," I said. "But you know how parents are."

He said nothing, but this time, his silence sounded different. Felt as if it wasn't coming from the same peaceful place. What had I said to take him away?

Finally, he asked, "Are you close to your mother and father?"

My mind swirled with memories of all the challenges I'd had growing up. "Yeah," I said through my thoughts. "Even though I've lived away for a while, we're close. I'm an only child, so some of our closeness is because of that. What about you?"

"I'm an only child as well," he said, though that hadn't been my question. I wanted to know what he'd asked me—was he close to his parents?

But before I could ask, he said, "What do your parents do?"

This moment . . . of truth. I inhaled and said, "My father's a pastor, and with all that my mother does for the church, First Lady is certainly a career."

"A pastor?" Xavier said, his tone filled with shock, and something else . . . Was it disdain? "I missed that when I was checking you out."

His tone made me pause. Made me forget about telling him my father was Kareem Jeffries. Made me ask instead, "You have something against pastors?"

He shook his head and shrugged at the same time. "Nothing against pastors." His eyes were away from mine when he said, "But God . . . that's a different story."

My pace slowed. "Whoa. You don't believe in God?" If there was one thing I knew, it was we were all at different levels in our spiritual walk. I'd known Christians who couldn't find Genesis in the Bible, and then I knew folks who thought they knew more scripture than the Lord. But no matter where each was, all believed in God. I'd come to think that was the black code, part of our DNA.

It took a moment for Xavier to say, "I believed in Him." After a pause and a breath, he added, "I believed in God so much when I was a child, I called out to Him all the time. But . . ." His shoulders slumped and then, in a voice I could hardly hear over the music that was Manhattan, he told me, "God never answered a single prayer."

His words made us both stop at the Columbus Circle intersection, where, for a moment, we just stared at each other. Xavier didn't ask, so there wasn't a question for me to answer. He just rounded the corner and, still holding on to his arm, I ignored the flutters I felt, and followed him.

Now, we headed north on Central Park West about two miles away from where I lived on the corner of 100th. It would only take us about a half hour, if that long, to make it up to my place.

This hadn't been my plan. I'd expected to say good-bye to Xavier right in the place where I'd said hello. Expected to catch an Uber and head home alone.

But we'd made that turn toward my condo, and even though I was nervous, I was willing. Because what he'd said about his childhood cries to God . . . Xavier needed to talk, and I wanted to listen.

So I moved in rhythm with him, our stroll still slow, and inside, I prayed God would use me to help him. Xavier stayed silent, but I was not concerned. He'd speak soon.

It wasn't until we crossed Sixty-Fourth Street that I spoke words I hoped would let him know I was a safe place. I said, "I'll give you two million pennies for your thoughts. Two million pennies for why you say God didn't answer you." I held my breath and prayed Xavier wouldn't think I was making light of the burden I knew he carried by the words he'd spoken.

His smile was faint, but still, it was there, and I exhaled. "The stakes have gotten higher," he said, his voice light, though still serious.

I nodded. "But only if you want to talk."

He stared straight ahead, his thoughts seemingly deep. Then,

"When I was growing up in Mississippi, I spent so much time praying to God."

He paused for so long (almost two blocks) that I wondered if that was all he was going to say. But I didn't dare ask more. His tone made me not want to press.

Then he picked up as if he hadn't stopped. "My childhood was filled with heartache, heartbreak, and loneliness."

When he paused, I felt—no, I needed to say, "I'm sorry."

He shook his head. "You didn't have anything to do with the misery that was my life." Now he looked at me. "You weren't part of that past; you're here now. And being here with you is a wonderful reminder of how far I've come." When he paused and shook his head, I could tell he was remembering. "Just being in these streets, in this city, with a woman as beautiful and accomplished as you. Just working at one of the most prestigious firms. None of this seemed achievable or believable when I was growing up inside my grandmother's house."

His grandmother. Was that why he hadn't answered my question about his parents? "You were raised by your grandmother?"

He gave me a joyless chuckle. "*Raised* would be a strong word. I lived in her house, that's about all I can say. At first, my mom was there, too, but then . . ."

This time, the silence stayed with us for about four blocks, until Xavier spoke again. "Once my mom left," he continued as if he hadn't paused for minutes, "my life . . . It was filled with all the things you'd imagine for a child who was somewhere he wasn't wanted. But the physical abuse . . . even at six, seven, and eight . . . I could handle that."

I shuddered, and Xavier squeezed my arm as if he was assuring me.

He continued, "I knew the pain, the scars of the beatings, would fade. That wasn't why I prayed to God. I prayed to Him because of the other stuff." His expression was almost like he'd talked himself into a trance. "Not having my mother, not being part of a family, not having that unit of love and protection. It was too much for a little boy. I missed out on a lot . . ." After a pause, he shook his head as if he was releasing himself from his hypnotic state. "Whew, it's a lot to handle, right?"

It wasn't until he glanced down at me that I realized I'd been holding my breath. But I breathed when he smiled, though it came from his lips alone. The rest of him was shrouded in sadness, all the way down to his soul.

Even with the dysfunction of my parents' marriage, I'd never doubted their love for me. I couldn't imagine what life had been like for Xavier. Before, all I'd wanted to do was listen; now all I wanted to do was hold him.

"I'm sorry you had to go through that," I said, giving him the only thing I had.

Again, he squeezed me, giving me reassurance, as if he wanted to make sure I was all right. "That's why I've struggled to let people in. I've always been afraid of connections and consequences. Afraid that I'd be the one to end up with a broken heart."

To this point, all the things we had in common had been fun to uncover. But it was sad to discover that Xavier and I were similar in this way, too. It sounded like he was just like me, in his thirties, yet he hadn't made any real connection to anyone because of his childhood. This time, when he turned to me, his smile went all the way to his eyes. "All that matters is I've achieved what my child's mind's eye could never conceive. Couldn't see a time when something as simple as taking a walk in the best city in the world would make me happy. But I've walked these streets before and have always enjoyed New York; the difference now, though . . . is you."

His words always moved me. Tonight, though, it was his emotions that were touching me.

I didn't think about the fact that we'd only had two dinners and one kiss when I stopped walking and then, with a little tug of his arm, made Xavier turn toward me. This time, I was the one who closed the small distance between us, sealing that space so there was barely room for air. This time, I was the one who cupped my hand behind his head, and, with our eyes locked, I was the one who eased him closer. I closed my eyes just a moment before we connected. Our second kiss, right across the street from the Museum of Natural History.

Just like an hour or so ago, my heart quickened as our kiss went on and on and on. Even as cars crawled by and honked, we kissed. Even as a couple of teenagers giggled and clapped as they passed, we kissed. We kissed until we had to stop because we needed to breathe.

When we stepped back, I understood that inkling I'd had when we'd made that turn onto Central Park West. Because something had shifted. When I reached for his hand, Xavier entwined his fingers with mine. Holding his hand felt far more intimate than how we'd connected before.

We stayed that way as we continued our stroll, and now, Xavier really opened up. Told me more about his younger days. On Ninety-Sixth Street, we sat on a bench and he talked some more. We stayed that way until the traffic thinned and fewer pedestrians passed by. We stayed and talked as windows darkened and the music of the city quieted to a softer beat.

It was after midnight when he escorted me to my door and left me at the threshold with a hug and a kiss. And I left him with a promise of an even better tomorrow.

9

Xavier

I shot up in bed, my sheets soaked with sweat. But after a few deep breaths, I lay back down. Another nightmare, the third in the last week.

Raising my head, I glanced at the clock. Just two hours between now and the ringing of the alarm. This, I couldn't afford, especially since I was now working on what looked to be another huge civil rights case, this time against one of the city's biggest cable companies.

For minutes, I stared at the ceiling, and when my eyes wouldn't close, I pushed myself up. A breeze wafted through my window, and I looked out into the blue-black sky of the night.

I was exhausted, the result of fighting demons inside dreams. In all the years since I'd escaped Mississippi, I hadn't been haunted like this. Yeah, I had dreams, but nothing I couldn't roll out of bed and forget. Nothing that came night after night with images so vivid, I awakened with the scent of Mississippi hay in my nostrils.

At least I knew where this was coming from—Chastity. Not that I blamed her. It was our connection that made her so inquisitive and led to her asking questions that no woman had asked before. And because she already had my heart, I gave her the key to those memories. So when she asked me a question yesterday over lunch, I answered:

"What was it about your grandmother? Why did you have that kind of relationship with her?"

My response was measured when I said, "She didn't want me there. That's the beginning and the end. But she kept me because I came with a check. I guess I have to be grateful to her for two things: one, she was so strict and heavy-handed that she kept me out of the streets. And two, she watched Oprah, *and my hearing Oprah's voice every day after school taught me education was the way out. She'd made it out of Mississippi and so would I."*

I'd told Chastity the truth about Oprah, but I'd left out the whole truth about my family. Because if I told Chastity that, there would be no way she'd stay. No woman would want to be with a man who started life that way.

No matter what I said, though, it wasn't enough. Chastity's questions continued. It wasn't curiosity alone; she wanted to help even after I reminded her nothing could be done about the past. But she did what no other woman had cared enough to do—she continued to press, getting me to talk about all that I'd repressed.

We'd just met thirteen days ago, yet she knew me well because she felt me the same way I felt her. So after our date tonight, when she asked, I wanted to answer. "You didn't enjoy the play?" she asked when we slid into a cab in front of the West Village theater.

"No, I did," I told her quickly. "It's just that there were parts that reminded me of some pretty bad times."

"Oh," she said. Then she took my hand. "I understand if you don't want to talk about her, but it might help if you share a little about your grandmother. Maybe get rid of some of what you've been holding inside."

As the cab made its way uptown, I wondered if I could do

this. It was because of our connection that she knew I hadn't told everything, but could I really talk to her about all I hadn't shared?

Looking down to where she held my hand, I felt all of her care and concern. Chastity was a safe place. So I began . . .

December 3, 1997

I trotted down the steps of the school bus, turned to wave, but like always, there was no one looking out for me. Or maybe it was that the bus windows were too dingy for me to see anything.

That was what I preferred to think, though I didn't have friends. Yeah, Richard talked to me sometimes, but that was it. It was impossible to have friends with the way Gran corralled me.

I walked toward the house, kicking up dirt where grass was supposed to be. At least Gran didn't have an old car, a beat-up sofa, or a toilet sitting in front of her house like just about everyone else's did in this neighborhood.

The four steps creaked and cried as I climbed them to the front door, but when I pushed it, the door didn't budge. I tried again, this time jiggling the knob. I moaned. Gran always left the door open when she was home. That meant if I went around to the back, her car wouldn't be there.

I blew out a long breath and then bounced down onto the steps, which cried out once again. Certainly, I was old enough to have a key. But Gran never made any part of my life easy. So I zipped up the Members Only jacket I'd gotten from the Salvation Army, then cupped my hand over my eyes to glance at the sky. I hoped it wouldn't rain like the last time Gran left me out here. Today, the sun beamed, but like everything else in my life, there was no certainty in what I saw. I trusted no one and nothing. Not even a bright sun in the sky.

My stomach growled, bringing my attention back to my current situation, and I pulled out my textbook from my favorite class—Civics—so I'd have something else to focus on. But before I opened the book, I heard the sound of metal scraping along the asphalt. Once again, I shielded my eyes to see the approaching car, even though I knew who was inside before she came into view. I watched Aunt Virginia screech her fourteen-year-old more-rust-than-paint Impala to a stop. It took her about five minutes to gather herself, then slide out and amble up the path.

Aunt Virginia may have been Gran's sister, but having the same parents was where any similarity ended. The biggest difference—she was kind.

"How you doin', little man?" she asked in a tone I never heard from my grandmother.

"I'm fine, ma'am."

When she reached the top step, she let out a long breath as if she'd just run a mile, then she did something that no one—except for my mama—ever did. Aunt Virginia hugged me.

"You sure are gettin' big, little man." She turned to the door, unlocked it, and I followed her inside. "Now, Gertrude told me to let you in, but to tell you not to touch nothin'."

"I won't."

She paused, glanced into the living room to her right and then to the kitchen on her left. "Well, you gotta eat."

"I'm not hungry," I said, even though any second my stomach would protest again. But I'd gone without food before.

Aunt Virginia sucked her teeth, waved her hand, and turned to the kitchen. "You gonna eat somethin'." She opened the refrigerator and then turned to the cabinets. "Even if I just make you a sandwich."

Since this was her idea, I couldn't get in trouble with Gran, so I slid into one of the chairs around the kitchen table. Aunt Virginia mumbled as she pulled out the bread, then the peanut butter and jelly.

"*Don't make no kinda sense the way she treats you, little man.*"

I stayed quiet, knowing I wasn't expected to speak.

"*I keep tryin' to talk to her. But she won't listen to me. Always tells me she's the oldest and to stay out of grown folks' business. Hmph.*"

She kept on, mumbling about how Gertrude should be ashamed of herself, treating me like all of this was my fault.

"*And then to not let your mama come back here . . .*"

"*My mama can't come back?*" I asked.

She faced me, and it must've been the shock on my face that made her say, "*Don't listen to me, I'm just talkin' 'bout nothin'.*"

Because she'd put the sandwich in front of me, I didn't ask her anything more, even though that question resounded in me. Why wouldn't Gran let my mama come back? All I said, though, was "*Thank you,*" before I took a bite so big almost half of the sandwich was gone.

Aunt Virginia returned with a glass of milk, and then she stood with her hands punched into her hips. I began to chew slower as she stared at me.

"*You certainly are your daddy's twin.*"

Every question I had about my mama was put on pause as I placed the other half of my sandwich down. No one, not even Mama, ever mentioned my father. When it was just Mama and me, I didn't care. Then, after Mama left, I didn't want to ask Gran.

Courage rose inside of me. "*You know my daddy?*"

Aunt Virginia nodded. "*Everybody knows your daddy.*" Then she chuckled before she added, "*Everybody 'cept for you.*" She tilted her head. "*But you know what? It's time you know. How old are you now, little man? Sixteen, seventeen?*"

"*I'm twelve, ma'am.*"

She raised an eyebrow. "*Well, still, you need to know your daddy. I keep telling Gertrude to stop all this foolishness.*"

Whatever she was saying about Gran, I didn't care. All I wanted to know now was, "Who's my daddy?"

She didn't hesitate. "Bobby Washington."

Two words—a lifetime of information. But it was only a name. I needed more: What did he look like? Why didn't he come see me? And now, I wondered . . . would he come and get me since Mama couldn't come here?

I chose one question to ask. "Do you know where he lives?"

She laughed. "He got as far away from here as he could 'cause your grandmother was so mad, she could have chewed up nails and spit out a barbed-wire fence. He could've stayed, though—Gertrude would've got over it. But he decided to move on, headed to New York."

New York. All I knew about New York was what I'd learned in school: the Statue of Liberty, the Empire State Building, the World Trade Center. And I also knew that New York was far away. But the question that came out was "Gran didn't like my daddy?"

"Gran loved your daddy, boy. She'd loved him for a long time. But after you came out of your mama looking all caramel like Bobby, with his thick eyebrows and those lips, he didn't even try to deny it."

My mind was like one of those calculators my math teacher showed us how to use. Only I wasn't adding up numbers. Yeah, I was only twelve, but I knew how babies were made. And that meant my daddy couldn't be my daddy if he was Gran's man.

"Bobby always had a thing for your mama," Aunt Virginia went on to explain. She shook her head. "I tried to warn Gertrude, told her to keep Bobby away from your mama, but she wouldn't listen, and it turned into a big mess. Your mama had one story, and Bobby had another, but all of it added up to you being born and looking just like your daddy." She stared at me for a long while again. "I believed your mama and everyone else in Sumner did, too, because we all knew Bobby Washington and his past. But your grandmother didn't believe her own child." Aunt Virginia sucked her

teeth like whatever had gone down still bothered her. "And she's still punishing your mama." This time, as she shook her head, she grabbed her bag. "Finish up your sandwich, then don't touch nothin' in here. I don't want to hear Gertrude's mouth." She hugged me. "Take care, little man."

She was so casual the way she kissed my head, then waddled out the door as if she hadn't just rocked my world. As if she hadn't just explained why I lived inside a house of hate.

I SHOOK MY head, escaping from that memory. I remembered Chastity's face tonight, filled with care for me but with horror for what I'd been through. When we'd walked to her door, she'd hugged me and said, "I want you to know that even when you don't think He is, God is always there."

My reply was just a kiss good-bye. Because while Chastity had heard me, she didn't understand. God hadn't been there. He hadn't been there for me or my mama. I was about sixteen when I came to really understand Aunt Virginia's words: *Your mama had one story, and Bobby had another.*

Like Aunt Virginia, I believed my mama. I didn't know what my mother's story was, but I knew what Aunt Virginia's words meant: Bobby wasn't just my father, he was a rapist.

Just thinking about that ignited the fire within me, and now I grabbed my cell phone, scrolling to the selfie Chastity and I had taken before the play tonight. Her image was my balm. With my fingertips, I traced the outline of her face, her photo bringing me the peace I needed to lay the burden of my paternity down.

I held on to the cell phone, though, as I folded then tucked the pillow beneath me. I stared at her picture until the phone's screen darkened.

Then I slept, too.

Chastity

For the last month, I'd found it difficult to believe I walked the halls of the Divorce Concierge, this successful firm housed on the twelfth, thirteenth, and fourteenth floors of the Vanderbilt building on Park Avenue. I'd sat in meetings in the oak-paneled conference rooms, and then I'd mingled in the firm's corporate lunchroom, where tuxedoed waitstaff served me as I sat shoulders touching with some of the nation's most notorious attorneys.

Over the weeks, though, I'd settled down, adjusting to the ambience of this place, just in time for my first big case, which would bring quite a bit of publicity to the firm.

"I'm so excited about working with you," Tasha Rose gushed through the phone. "Chastity Jeffries." From the moment we met about a month ago, this was how Tasha addressed me, as if I were the famous one. "Just the sound of your name has Derrick on the run, girl. And what y'all uncovered yesterday? I cannot believe he had all those offshore accounts. And where did he get that money? I better not find out some of that was mine."

"We have great people working with our firm and so, whatever we need to know, we'll find out."

"Thank you, Chastity Jeffries."

Tasha cracked me up; I was the one who should have been fangirling.

Tasha Carter Rose was my favorite TV sitcom actor from the '90s, and I could point to her as one reason why I'd had top grades. My parents' rule: no TV until homework was not only done but done well. So on Thursdays, if no other days, I was on it.

"I just don't think a white attorney would have worked this hard for me," Tasha raved.

"Tasha . . ."

"Of course the Divorce Concierge is a top firm, but black folks understand black folks, and a black woman is gonna take down a dog of a black man." She yelped out a "Hallelujah," and I flinched.

Taking down a black man was not my intention—giving top-shelf legal representation was. Tasha needed the best because Derrick and his attorney were taking prisoners for real, with the goal of sending Tasha to prison as they accused her of everything from child neglect (even though their youngest was sixteen) to laundering drug money, though, according to Tasha, she wasn't the one involved with drugs.

She had her own accusations, with scars she wore as proof. For years, Tasha had been the victim of domestic violence, and I was determined to help her get up and get out.

Whatever came of this case, this was going to be a tragic ending to a fairy-tale beginning. Tasha and Derrick had met when they starred together on *Just the Two of Us*, where they dated, married, and then followed that script in real life. After their marriage, Tasha's star began a meteoric rise, and within seven years, she'd won a Tony, a Grammy, and an Emmy. At the same time, Derrick struggled to find any role once *Just the Two of Us* was canceled.

From the beginning, the tabloids shared gossip about cracks in their marriage, and now after twenty years, the cracks had turned into craters and a new War of the Roses.

"Yes," she repeated, "Chastity Jeffries, you've got to bring these men down."

I told her, "I'm not trying to take Derrick down. I want to leave him standing so he can do right by you."

"See what I'm talking about? I'm so glad you're on my side."

"Okay," I said. "I wanted to make sure you got the papers . . ."

"I did."

"And you have the date on your calendar . . ."

"I do."

"Then just call me if you have any questions."

"I will," she said.

After our good-byes, I leaned back in my chair, exhausted, which was how Tasha always left me. At least today, we hadn't discussed any of the violent incidents she'd suffered at Derrick's hands. Even after ten years in this business, it was hard to get used to the number of women who suffered abuse but continued to live in those situations.

Swiveling my chair toward the window, thoughts of the women I'd worked with faded as I took in the view of Park Avenue and the MetLife Building. This vista was second only to the salary I'd received to join this firm.

I leaned back, mesmerized by the buildings' lights, which shined through the early darkness of the night. And I let my mind wander.

"Xavier."

I did that a few times a day—whispered his name aloud. I'd say his name and smile; it was hard to stress with a grin.

In the four weeks since we'd met, we hadn't been able to spend the new-relationship kind of time with each other we both wanted. Our careers kept us too busy for daily lunches or dinners. Still, it felt as if I was in the middle of a whirlwind because Xavier made every hour we were together better than the last.

The stakes had been high after dinner at Masa, the horse and carriage ride, our first and second and third kiss. How could that night be topped?

But Xavier King was a man who always leveled up and who proved that it wasn't the money (though he had it and was willing to spend it), it was the time that mattered. From the Yankees game to the Saturday brunch at Tavern on the Green to strolling through the Morgan Library & Museum because of our mutual love of books—whether he spent one thousand dollars or one thousand pennies, as long as we were sitting together or holding hands or kissing, we had an amazing time.

I was beginning to care about him. Beyond our time together, I loved that he was a warrior. Every day he told me a bit more about his life. That was why he had me. His intelligence, his looks, his résumé—all of that counted, but all of that paled when compared to what he'd been through and how he'd come through.

While he'd told me much about his grandmother, he hadn't opened up too much about his mother. His history was filled with so much pain that, while I probed, I didn't pry. When he shut down, I let go. He told me what he wanted to now; he'd tell me what he was able to later.

The light knock on my door made me swivel in my chair and then tap on my computer, awakening the screen. "Come in," I said, thinking I'd look up at either Andrea, my assistant, or Stanley Covington, the partner who was responsible for my being at this firm.

But when I glanced up, I jumped up. "What are you doing here?"

"I came to collect the rent." Wearing light blue scrubs, Melanie blew into my office with all of her mighty munchkin energy, but after just two steps, she paused, rested her hands on her hips, and released a long whistle. "My goodness. Look at all of this." She took in the opulence of my executive desk and matching chair, which also matched the burgundy wall paneling. That was what had Melanie's attention. "What kind of paneling is this?" she asked as she fingered the material. If my friend hadn't been a top plastic surgeon, she would have been a top interior designer.

"Purple wood, I'm told," I said, then hugged her. "I'm so glad to see you." Taking her hand, I moved toward the love seat, but my friend twisted away from me, ending up standing in front of the window. Her mouth opened wide.

She turned to me. "They gave you this office?"

I chuckled. "Well, it's not like I'm a junior associate. I'm bringing ten years of experience and plenty of big-name clients, who may start off with a divorce, but who pass their other business to our other divisions, so yeah, they gave me this office."

"I guess." She sauntered over and then plopped onto the other end of the sofa.

"I'm glad you stopped by, but I would've met you somewhere for dinner."

"Oh, you're gonna still treat me to dinner, but I wanted to see you in the middle all of this fabulousness." She twirled her hand in the air.

I laughed, then pushed myself up when my cell phone rang. "Excuse me," I said, rushing to my desk.

"Sure, girl, handle your business."

I was a few feet away, but already smiling because I saw Xavier's photo on the screen. "Hey, you," I said, the moment I answered.

"I've been waiting to hear you say that all day."

Turning toward the window, I lowered my voice. "I know, we haven't connected. I figured you were busy."

"And I figured the same about you. How's your day been?"

"Busy." We laughed.

I said, "How's the cable case?"

"Good. This is the toughest part." He sighed. "Preparing for the depositions. This stage is always . . ."

"Tedious," I said. If we'd been FaceTiming, I would've seen Xavier's smile. He always did that when we finished each other's sentences. He said, "I wish we could get together tonight."

"You know if anyone understands, I do. Work calls."

"It does, but I can handle this work—or anything—because of you. Really, Chastity, over these last few weeks . . ." When he paused, I imagined him shaking his head, filled with the same disbelief I felt. "I've never been able to talk to anyone the way I talk to you."

My smile was my response. It was enough, I was sure, because I knew he felt it.

He added, "We'll definitely get together tomorrow. Something special to celebrate our four-week anniversary."

I laughed. "Really, Xavier? Are we going to do this every Friday?" I asked, though that wasn't a complaint.

"For the rest of our lives."

Like always, his words made me swoon; I could have listened to him for the rest of forever.

"I just wanted to hear your voice," he said. "I'll probably be here until well after midnight, but call me before you go to sleep?"

"Don't I always?"

"You do—that's the only way I can sleep. I can't wait to see you tomorrow and then all the tomorrows after that."

After he said good-bye, I held the phone, staring at the screen, wanting to call back just so he'd say something else so sweet to me. But I just sighed, then pivoted and almost bumped into Melanie. It was a bit jarring because I'd forgotten she was here.

"That didn't sound like a business call to me." There was an accusation in her tone.

Tossing my cell onto my desk, I said, "I never said it was," though I kept my eyes away from her.

"Hmph." Her eyes narrowed. "So do you want to tell me what's going on?"

"What?" I didn't mean to be so secretive. It was just that the best part of our relationship had been that my parents hadn't met him, Melanie hadn't met him (except for that first night), and I hadn't met any of his friends. It was just us.

But the grin on my face told all kinds of secrets, and the way Melanie's nosiness radar was set up . . .

"Don't play with me." She wagged her finger in my face. "So you're seeing Xavier?"

"I told you that."

"No, you didn't. You told me you went out to dinner the week after my party."

I shrugged. "Well, you never asked about him again."

She threw up her hands. "I never asked you because you don't go out with a person a second time!" She crossed her arms. "And if you ever did, I just knew you'd tell your best friend."

I pressed my fingers against my lips because if I opened my mouth, four weeks of wonderfulness would spill out, and hearing those kinds of words from me might traumatize my friend. So all I did was weave around her and drop back onto the sofa.

But even though I hadn't said a word, Melanie acted as if I'd spoken. "You're looking like you're in love or something."

Her eyes widened. "Are you two in a relationship?" There was so much astonishment in her voice.

"Well, I can't say I'm in love," I said, finally speaking up because I really wanted to talk about all of this. "I haven't known him long enough to be anywhere close to that, but yes, we've been seeing each other, and yes, it's been a whirlwind, and yes, I have enjoyed it and him so much."

She stood so stiff. "You?" And then she withered onto the sofa as if she'd fainted. If Melanie hadn't been a top plastic surgeon or a top interior designer, she would have been an Oscar-winning actor—at least, that's what she thought.

I rolled my eyes, but that didn't stop me from laughing.

When Melanie "came to," she pushed herself up. "I never thought I'd see this day. You, the one committed to singleness."

"First, I never said that, and second, I've learned some things since I've been home. I've learned a lot about forgiveness . . ."

"You're a preacher's kid. You should have already known that."

"And," I continued, ignoring her, "I've learned a lot about how people can change if they have the right person in their corner. My father is thriving because my mother stayed. Watching them has opened my heart a little." I shrugged. "Or maybe it was just that I was supposed to be closed so I could be open for a time such as this and a man such as Xavier."

She pressed the back of her hand against my forehead.

"Stop." I shoved her away. "It really isn't that big of a deal, except . . ." I hiked up my skirt and twisted so I could sink deeper into the couch's cushions. "I've never met anyone like him."

"Well, it's not like you've given too many guys a chance."

"Maybe I would have if I'd met someone like Xavier. I've never been with anyone where I felt so connected. Like the two of us were meant to be so that we could make each other better."

She nodded like she understood. "Like soul mates."

"Yeah," I said, never having thought of it that way. "We have fun and we laugh, but then we can be serious, too. I know if I cry, he'll hurt and cry with me."

"Wow. So where do you think this is going?" She paused as if she hesitated even saying the next words. "I mean, how serious are you? Do you think . . . like, he's the one?"

"You're that anxious to get me married?" I didn't give her space to answer. "We're a long way from that. Just four weeks in, we're enjoying getting to know each other."

"So you're not in love?"

I shook my head. "Not love, but I'm in real serious like." I giggled.

Her eyes narrowed. "Hmmmmm. That giggle. It sounds like you're in lust."

"Not that it's any of your business, but we haven't gotten that far, which is something else I like about him. Most guys are ready to jump into bed the first night. But while I know he wants to, he wants us to build something first."

She shook her head as if what I was saying was unbelievable. "Girl, marry this dude." I laughed, and she added, "But first I have to meet him and make sure he passes all of my tests. Maybe I'll cook for the two of you." She paused. "Let me stop lying. Invite him to your parents' place, and Kelvin and I will be there."

"Oh, that will be perfect," I said, filling my tone with sarcasm. "Having my mom, my dad, my best friend, and her husband grilling my man."

She raised her eyebrows. "Your man?" Her grin made her whole face bright. "Be careful, it's a short trip from your man to your husband." She stood, grabbed my hand, and pulled me up. "Come on. You need to buy me a drink after admitting you're in love."

"Your words, not mine," I said as I stuffed two files into my tote.

"You're protesting too much. Yeah, you're in love." But this part of the conversation was over, as far as Melanie was concerned. She'd already sashayed out as if she were a foot taller, on a fashion runway, and dressed in something besides scrubs.

I laughed, but then, as I followed her, my chuckles faded. I wasn't in love, was I? Nah. No one with any sense fell in love in a month.

That was the thought I had as I turned out the lights.

11

Xavier

I felt like a teenager, wobbly knees and all, as the Uber rolled to a stop and I opened the door of the Toyota.

Chastity took my hand and slipped out of the back seat, and when she wrapped her arms around me and said, "Hey, you," my anticipation morphed to expectation.

As it always was when I saw her, it took a couple of seconds for me to breathe, and finally, I was able to eke out, "Hey, beautiful."

She stepped back with a little frown, and as the daylight of the last days of August dimmed toward night, the heat of her stare felt like a spotlight. "You okay?"

My hug, my smile, weren't enough to fool her, our connection already beyond the superficial.

As she tilted her head, her frown deepened, but even with her furrowed brows, she had never looked more beautiful. She still wore her navy knee-length Brooks Brothers suit, with a tailored shirt, a women's style that matched the one I wore. I already knew she hadn't had time to go home.

Her question was still in her eyes. I answered by taking her hand and leading her into the hotel, where we made our way toward the elevator. As we waited, I scrolled through my day in my mind. Unlike Chastity, I'd left the office early, a couple of hours after noon, something I hadn't done in the seven years I'd been at Steyer and Smith. But there were arrangements to be made and plans to set.

We still held hands as we stepped into the hotel's glass elevator, and as we began the slow rise forty-two stories up, the chaos of Times Square sprawled out below us. Chastity gasped, but her eyes stayed on the view. When the elevator doors parted, I gave my name to the maître d', and then we followed him to the window table I'd reserved at New York's only revolving restaurant.

It wasn't until we sat down that Chastity spoke, although all she uttered was "Wow."

Her excitement continued as we ordered our entrees from the three-course dinner menu—the loin of Colorado lamb for her, the surf and turf for me—and every few moments, her glance turned back to the window as the restaurant continued its slow revolution.

"It doesn't feel as if we're moving at all," she said.

I nodded because my thoughts were racing too much for me to speak.

"How long will it take for us to go around once?"

"About an hour."

This time, she was the one who nodded. "This is amazingly beautiful."

Her face shined over the flickering flame of the candle, and once again, I inhaled a few deep breaths to steady myself. I was thrilled when she began chatting about the case she called the new War of the Roses. As she shared only the details she could about Tasha and Derrick Rose, my mind skipped ahead hours, wondering if she would be pleased with my plans.

It wasn't until our food was set on the table that I relaxed into the company of this woman I was so growing to love. We chatted about work, about life, and it wasn't long until we fell into the easy rhythm that had become us.

We laughed over a new bad lawyer joke: "What do you call an attorney gone bad?"

She frowned, shook her head, and when I said, "A senator," she laughed so hard, tears pooled in the corners of her eyes.

Once we gathered ourselves, our conversation shifted to the more serious.

"Jackson Steyer has been stopping by my office on the regular for the last two weeks."

There was as much hope in her eyes as I felt in my heart. "That's a good thing, right?"

"It is. We'll be getting lots of media coverage with this case, and he wants to make sure I'm in lockstep with the firm, which I am. But his visits are about me becoming a partner." Before she asked, I added, "He hasn't said that, but they have to be considering me now."

Her smile turned into a beam, her emotions shining through her eyes. "I'm so proud of you."

Like always, her words, her tone, her expression, filled me with all I hoped we'd be. She hadn't said it, but her love for me was so apparent, I felt it down to my soul. With Chastity, I was finally content, finally complete.

Once again, her attention turned to the view. "An hour must've passed," she said. "We're back at Times Square."

Now the neon lights from billboards that towered high above the street beamed bright through the night's darkness.

When Chastity pulled out her cell phone, I groaned. "Are you really going to do the tourist thing?" She snapped a photo as if she didn't even hear me. "You're a New Yorker, for God's sake."

She snapped another, undeterred by my words and my laughter. She had more than two dozen pictures before she pleaded for me to join her for a selfie. One Times Square and the glittering 2019 ball faded over our shoulders as the restaurant began another 360-degree revolution of Manhattan.

When I returned to my chair, Chastity sighed her satisfaction. "Mr. King, you always outdo yourself."

Reaching across the chocolate mousse cheesecake we shared, I asked, "So what did you like best? The food, the view, or"—I paused for just a beat—"me?"

She released her fork and took my hand. "The company, of course." Chastity leaned across the table, her lips aimed for mine. We both had to stretch to connect, but I would have walked across shattered glass to kiss her.

She eased away with a smile that warmed every part of me. "I love being with you," she said, speaking as if she were reading what was written in my heart.

At this moment, I wanted to pull out my cell phone and snap my own picture, though a photo wouldn't have been sufficient to capture all of the love in Chastity's expression. Still, I'd send the picture to Roxanne, Diane . . . and my grandmother, if she were still alive.

"So . . . what else do you have planned for tonight?"

Her eyes were away from me, on the city's skyscrapers, giving me time to gather myself. By the time she faced me, my expression was innocent enough.

With a shrug, I said, "Let's just see where the night takes us."

After I paid the check, we made our way through the restaurant back to the glass-encased elevator, leaving the top of the world. Outside, though, was just as exciting; Times Square was Friday-night lit, especially since this was the beginning of the end-of-summer holiday weekend. New Yorkers mingled with tourists, strolling through and soaking up the chaos. We moseyed through what felt like a giant celebration, holding each other as we passed Bubba Gump Shrimp Co. and people who were dressed as the Statue of Liberty and Spider-Man, and, of course, the Naked Cowboy. On Forty-Second Street, we passed Madame Tussauds and Ripley's Believe It or Not! before we circled back. As we moved by one of the street vendors, Chastity stopped.

"Let's get one of these," she exclaimed with a child's glee as she pointed to the street artist sketching caricatures.

I whipped out my wallet and pulled out a fifty. "I want one of us together."

The man snatched the money, then nodded. Chastity sat on a cushioned milk carton, and I knelt beside her. When I laid my hand on her leg, she rested her head on my shoulder.

The artist's face stiffened with a scowl of concentration, and as I inhaled the fragrance of the jojoba oil and coconut cream that scented Chastity's hair, I closed my eyes and breathed in this moment. My prayer was this was only the beginning of tonight.

In less than fifteen minutes, we were thanking the man for our rendition before Chastity rolled it into her purse. We continued our slow stroll, holding each other, passing people, hearing nothing. Finally, I paused purposefully, turned to her, and when I pressed my lips against hers, we were there again—in the center of Manhattan's madness, all by ourselves.

We were breathless when we pulled back and I glanced up at where we'd stopped. In front of the hotel, right where we'd started.

Chastity followed my glance, and she also followed my thoughts, because she said nothing, only gave me a hesitant smile. I took her hand and led her back inside.

This time, we stepped into a different elevator, and as Chastity faced the glass, watching the chamber rise over the lobby, she whispered, "You have a room?"

My hands trembled a bit when I turned her toward me. With the tips of my fingers, I lifted her chin and searched her eyes for her message, but there was nothing I could read.

I nodded. "I got a room earlier today because I was hoping." But then I added, "If you're not ready, it's okay," I said. "You're more important to me than this. So it's—"

Before I could say more, her lips were on mine and she kissed me with a passion she never had before. The elevator stopped, but that didn't stop us. When the doors parted, we found a way to step out, still connected. I was so grateful we were in room 2701, right by the elevator.

I pulled away from her, just so I could grab my cell to use the digital key. But once the door was open, my lips returned to hers, and I pulled her into the hotel room.

12

Chastity

L ust, with a bit of lunacy, had taken over. That was the only way to explain why I'd kissed Xavier that way. We'd had plenty of public displays, but what we'd just done in the elevator had gone beyond affection. That was nothing but overwhelming lust.

With lips connected, we stumbled into the hotel room. The door slammed behind us; I wasn't sure how Xavier had done that, but before I could question it, he pushed me away, making me cry out, and spun me around, though he still held me close, pressing his front against my back.

As he held me, the sight of the room made me gasp. "When did you do this?"

The suite was illuminated by hundreds of flickering flames, a dazzling glow in the darkness. Candles were everywhere—on the two end tables that flanked a chintz sofa and on the table in front of the matching floral chairs.

But what captivated me most were the dozens of candles on the floor that lit a path of rainbow rose petals from the front room through the sliding doors where a four-poster bed as wide as the ocean (and covered with roses) awaited.

"My goodness," I whispered, taking in the whole scene. I'd never seen anything so romantic.

Turning around, I faced Xavier, and this time, my kiss was filled with a gentle passion, wanting him to feel all of the care I had for him. Xavier moaned and melded his body into mine.

He returned my affection with the same tenderness, his desire so apparent. Slowly, he backed me toward the bedroom, but then, after just a few steps, he lifted me into his arms, his lips never leaving mine. He carried me as if I were a feather, and inside the bedroom, he laid me down with the same tender care.

The bed became our oasis, our place where we explored terrain we'd never traveled before. The hardness of every part of this man left me panting, left me wanting, and then, when he pulled his tongue away from me, left me gasping. But then he sent me swirling when his tongue tickled my neck. I moaned, leaning into the pleasure. If I could have spoken, I would have begged for his tongue to return—or maybe never return so he could do what he was doing forever. But I couldn't speak because Xavier had taken my breath, my words, my mind away.

My man was on a seek-and-search mission that guided his tongue down, down, down. I raised my chest to greet him, wanting to give him full access to all of me. And he took it—in a single stroke, he ripped my blouse away. Buttons fluttered across the bed, onto the floor, but I had no cares about that.

"Come back," I murmured, but it was as if he didn't hear me, and I settled into the feeling of his tongue, once again exploring me, feasting first on my breasts through the satin of my bra. He stayed there, as if he were trying to caress me into unconsciousness, licking, biting, for several minutes, or maybe it was a few hours.

Then his excursion continued as he cruised lower, tickling

my belly. When he broke away from me, I cried out, missing him already. He lifted my hips and, with the deftness of a magician, he had me naked from the waist down (skirt and panties gone!) before I could breathe or blink.

When he spread my legs, my hope seeped through my lips in a gasp. I so wanted him, I so wanted more. But that *more* would have to wait, because now his lips were back on mine as he slipped my jacket away from my shoulders. My buttonless blouse and bra were next.

The air was cool, I was sure. But unless the thermostat was set to arctic, it wasn't any good to me. Every inch of my skin was afire with the desire I had for this man; there was only one thing that would extinguish this flame.

But once again, he pulled away, leaving me throbbing. As he hoisted himself above me, his eyes were a mirror of my craving. His lips twitched as if he was trying to smile as his gaze drank in all of me. "You are so beautiful."

My response: I pushed him back and rocked onto my knees. Now I kissed him as I slipped his jacket from his shoulders. Next I shredded his shirt, and then I made my way to the treasure hidden inside his pants. I moaned my appreciation; he moaned his gratitude.

I touched him, I held him, and then I begged him to take me, and he granted my wish. I didn't breathe as he filled me, little by little, more and more, until finally, he reached my brim, and I exhaled. Or maybe I screamed as we began to sway to the same beat. With all that made him a man, he sang praises to me as a woman. And I sang with him, a new song, our song. Then he rolled me over and now I led the dance—a new dance, our dance.

We sang and we danced until our serenade reached that crescendo where, even if we'd wanted to, we couldn't hold our notes any longer. There was nothing we could do except waltz through heaven's gates . . . together.

It took me a few moments to roll over and away from Xavier, and when I did, I knew I'd never breathe the same way. It wouldn't be possible. Not with the memory of what we'd just shared forever in my mind.

We lay together, staring up, hypnotized by the shadows of the candle's flames dancing on the ceiling.

When Xavier panted, "How are you feeling?" I wondered if he would ever breathe the same way, too.

It took me a moment to roll onto my side, and I pressed my hand against his chest. I wanted to stay there for a while, touching and agreeing with his heartbeat. "Wonderful," I whispered.

He turned onto his side, too, and our noses almost kissed as we lay there smiling. "I hope you're okay with . . ."

I pressed my fingers against his lips. "I wanted to be with you," I said. But a moment later, a familiar feeling washed over me, making me roll onto my back.

He pushed himself up and looked down at me. "If you were okay with this . . ."

The rest of his question—*what's wrong?*—was in his tone.

Again, I pressed my fingers against his mouth, but this time, it was just because I wanted to touch him. "Nothing's wrong." I answered the question he hadn't asked. "Being with you was wonderful . . ."

"But . . ."

His frown made me sit up. "This may not be the time to talk about this. Especially after . . ." I glanced down at the sheets. "I just want to be honest."

When his fingertips traced the side of my face, his touch made every part of me tingle. "I want you to be honest with me."

I nodded, though it was difficult to think with Xavier so

close, and his fingers going lower, lower, lower. I grabbed his hand so I could focus. "True confessions," I began.

He nodded, with a grin. This man knew what he'd done to me.

Still, I continued, "I haven't been with a lot of guys."

His grin widened.

"Because at times like this, I feel a bit guilty."

Just like that, his grin flipped.

I continued with a shrug, "I'm a preacher's kid. I can't get away from that." I held up my hand. "Not that I want to. Because I truly believe that making love should be in the context of marriage."

"Oh." He nodded as if he were considering my words. Then, "Are you asking me to marry you?"

"No!" I exclaimed. "Of course not," I added, wanting to make sure he understood me. "I mean, I'm not saying I wouldn't marry you. I would. I mean, someday." The more I spoke, the wider his grin, and finally I shook my head. "Oh, God. Why can't I shut up?" I flopped back onto the bed and pressed the pillow over my face, trying to smother myself for real.

He laughed as he wrestled the pillow away, and now I used my hands to cover my embarrassment that made me forget any guilt I'd felt. But Xavier pried my hands away, then warmed my eyelids with his lips, kissing one, then the other. He kissed me over and over until I opened my eyes.

"I understand what you meant, and trust me, I understand baggage. We all have some."

"But you must think I'm some kind of prude, and I'm not, it's just that being Kar . . ." I paused, not believing I'd almost uttered my father's name. But then here I was naked in bed with this man—we were beyond my having any doubts that Kareem Jeffries being my father would make any difference.

He tilted his head. "What were you going to say?"

Sitting up, I combed my fingers through my hair, which had to look a whole mess right now. "I don't know what this is about," I began, tugging the sheet over me. "I've never felt the need to confess everything . . ." I glanced downward, and Xavier reached for my hand.

"You can tell me anything."

His voice was soft, sweet, and his eyes were filled with such—*love?*—I blinked and shook that thought away. I was just stalling, seeing things that weren't there. So I inhaled, then exhaled, "You've told me a lot about your family, but I haven't shared much about mine."

"Well, let's see." He leaned back, mirroring my posture. "I know your father's a pastor."

"Yeah." I twisted so I could see his face. "Whose name just happens to be . . . Kareem Jeffries." I pressed my lips together.

His eyes narrowed a bit as if my words were going through the computer of his mind. Then I saw the moment when he understood, and his eyes widened.

"Wait a minute," he said. "*The* Kareem Jeffries?"

I nodded.

"And you're Chastity Jeffries, his daughter." It wasn't a question, so I just sat there as he hit his forehead with the heel of his hand. But then he turned to me with a frown. "Why . . . why?"

I gave him a one-shoulder shrug, knowing what his question meant. "So many people have tried to get close to me because of my dad. It got so bad at one point, I thought about changing my last name."

"Wow."

"But at the same time, I've received a lot of privileges because of my parents. And they've done a great job keeping me out of their limelight."

He stared at me. "I knew he had a daughter."

"Yeah, but especially in the last ten years or so, I've been out of sight." I added, "On purpose."

He cupped my cheek with his palm. "I never thought about it, but I guess it's tough to be a celebrity's child."

I nodded, though I was sure we were talking about different reasons. He thought it was hard because of my dad's fame, when it was because of my dad's women.

"Well, this is what I have to say about Kareem Jeffries being your dad." He pressed his lips against mine and eased me down onto the bed. I moaned as he caressed my chest, my desire rising, making me want to sing a new song.

But then he pulled away and his lips were only a few inches from mine when he whispered, "I don't want you to feel bad about the guilt you sometimes have or who your parents are."

My fingers stroked the top of his head.

He continued, "We all have baggage, things we never plan to tell anyone."

I nodded, but before I could thank him for his understanding, he said, "And since we're sharing, there's something you should know about me."

I tilted my head, thinking he'd already told me so much.

"I introduced myself to you as Xavier King. But that's not who I am."

13

Chastity

This was my favorite part of the hot stretching class—the end, when we lay on the floor in the dark for three minutes, allowing for muscle recovery. But the Lord knew this was restoration for my soul. I'd made it through another hot-as-Hades session.

"Close your eyes and free your mind," Kourtney sang as she dimmed the lights.

Like instructed, I closed my eyes, but I didn't free my mind. Instead, I did what I'd done for the last week whenever there was space for an idle thought. My mind had stayed stuck on Xavier since our night that had turned into a weekend a week ago.

When I pressed my back into my mat, I remembered the feel of him. I inhaled and recalled the scent of him, and then I had to do everything in my power not to lick my lips, because if I did, I'd moan aloud at the memory of the taste of him.

But even with the wonder of making love for the first, second, tenth, and fiftieth time, what stayed with me most were the words he'd uttered:

"I introduced myself to you as Xavier King. But that's not who I am."

I opened my eyes, remembering the way those words had shook me, and in the passing seconds, my mind had overloaded with murderous conspiracies . . . and then thoughts that he was in the witness protection program . . . and then imaginings that he was a spy from the Maldives. Before I could reach for the phone and call the FBI, he saved me from that embarrassment.

Eight days before:

"My name is Xavier, but my last name, the name that was on my birth certificate, is Owens," he said. "But I changed it." He paused as if I was supposed to let him end the story there, but I had so many questions. Before I could go through the list, Xavier rolled away from me. As his eyes stayed on the ceiling, he continued, "Like everything else, this goes back to my grandmother. The older I got, the less she and I communicated. It was fine by me. I had a plan to get out of Mississippi and never look back."

"Is that when you came to New York?"

He nodded. "I spent a lot of time in the library reading up on New York after Aunt Virginia told me about my father. So I saved the money I received from odd jobs around the neighborhood and . . ." He paused, and I could tell he was deciding how much he wanted to say. "Gifts I'd received. The night before my high school graduation, I decided to ask Gran if she wanted to attend the ceremony. To be honest, I didn't know if she knew I was graduating or not." He stopped, as if he had to soak in the memory before he continued. "Maybe I wanted to give her a final chance to make amends. But when I asked her, she stared through me as if I weren't even standing there."

This time, when he stopped, I leaned into him, wanting to be close as he remembered that awful time. He wrapped his arms around me, and I rested my head on his chest, feeling the strong beat of his heart.

"*My grandmother never said a word, so I went back to my bedroom and stuffed a duffel bag with every single piece of clothing I owned. I left out my suit, my good shoes, and a box where I'd kept my money. All I had was that money and my dreams, and the next day, I left before my grandmother woke up. When I marched across the auditorium's stage, there was not a single person there to celebrate me.*

"*Two hours later, I was on a bus to New York, leaving more than the dust of Sumner behind. No matter where I ended up, I didn't want to be Xavier Owens, that worthless kid from Mississippi. My mom had given me the name Xavier, so I kept that. But Owens . . .*" He shook his head. "*Owens was my grandmother's last name. So I became what she thought I'd never be. I changed my last name to King.*"

"AND . . . THAT'S A wrap," Kourtney sang.

When the lights came up, I popped up and, for the first time since I'd been coming to this class, I beat my mom standing up.

"You're getting the hang of this." My mother laughed.

I'd been home for well over a month, and the sheer joy that emanated from my mother still surprised me.

"It's taken a while, but I'm finally enjoying this."

"Hmmmm," my mother hummed. "I'm still salty you missed class last Saturday . . . and then Sunday, too?" she said, as if I were still a child under her roof and the rule of *No matter what you did on Saturday, you have to go to church on Sunday* still applied.

"I told you, Mom, I had plans last weekend." That had been my story. But right now, my thoughts weren't on last week; all I could think about was what was going to unfold in the next few minutes.

I glanced at my watch.

My mother tilted her head. "You have an appointment?"

"No," I said without looking at her. "I just, you know, wanted to know the time."

She frowned like my words sounded as odd to her as they did to me, but then Kourtney strolled by and took my mother's attention away. I strolled to the cubes, where I'd left a bigger bag than I normally brought with me.

I inhaled, trying to calm the flutters within. As the minutes ticked closer, I wondered why I had done it this way—This. Was. A. Setup. And now that I'd had time to think, I wanted to call it off, because setups never went well.

But it was too late, and all I could do was pray, *Please, God*, over and over.

At about my tenth *Please, God*, the studio door opened and Xavier peeked inside. His eyes passed over my fellow stretching enthusiasts, clad in boy shorts and capri leggings, sports bras and the skimpiest of tees. But my man's eyes didn't pause—not until his glance rested on me.

Then his grin was the bolt that lit the room, and my stomach somersaulted. It had been just a couple of hours since I'd rolled from his bed, but I had missed him.

"Hey, you," he said, sounding like he'd missed me, too. He didn't give me a chance to respond before he pulled me into his arms and our lips locked in a kiss. When he leaned away, he asked, "You ready?"

"Chastity?"

That quickly—truly, it had happened that fast—I'd forgotten. That's what Xavier did to me—he made me forget: forget where I was, forget that I had home training, forget about the plan . . . the setup.

But now all of my sensibilities rushed back. I whipped

around and faced her with what had to be the silliest grin. "Oh, Mom, I forgot."

"Forgot what?" she drawled. Then, "Never mind, I can see." Her words were meant for me, but her eyes were on my man. "And who is this gentleman?" Every bit of her Southern roots came out in her tone and her manner.

"Oh," I said, as if this meeting had been completely coincidental. "This is my friend, Xavier King, and Xavier"—I turned to him—"this is my mom, Sisley Jeffries."

Both of their eyebrows rose in surprise, though Xavier didn't match the smile on my mother's face.

"Xavier. What a stately name," my mother said. She held out her hand. "It's very nice to meet you, though I have to say I'm a bit surprised." Then my mother turned to me and shoved me, as if we were just girls. "You've been keeping secrets."

This was the first time I'd ever seen Xavier stand so still, so stiffly. "Uh, Mrs. Jeffries, you're not the only one surprised."

"My mom met me here at my stretch class," I said to him, hoping my mother wouldn't out me and tell Xavier she met me here every Saturday. Then, to her, I said, "And Xavier and I are driving up to Bear Mountain."

"Really?"

"Uh, yeah. We're going to take a day trip, and he came to pick me up."

"No wonder you've been looking at your watch." She turned back to Xavier. "So I hope this is just a day trip, because I have a feeling you're the reason Chastity missed church last Sunday."

"Uh . . . uh," he stuttered.

"Mom!" I exclaimed. "I told you what happened."

She shrugged. "I was just making a simple statement." Then, with the broadest of smiles, she said to Xavier, "She certainly can't miss two Sundays."

"Uh . . . no . . . ma'am," he said. "She . . . can't."

"Great. And I hope this means you won't miss church tomorrow either, Mr. King. I hope you'll be joining us."

I held my breath as Xavier said, "Ma'am?"

"Any friend of my daughter's is certainly a gentleman her father and I would like to get to know. So let this be a proper invitation for you to join me, Pastor, and Chastity for church tomorrow and then dinner at our home afterward."

How had a casual meeting turned into church and dinner? My plan had been that my mother would meet Xavier, then she'd run home, tell my father, and after a few weeks of the two of them probing and prodding, I would talk Xavier into a formal meeting. But that was supposed to be weeks, even a month or three, from now.

"Uh . . . Mom," I said, now stuttering myself. "Uh, I think Xavier has plans."

"Well, certainly, you're free tomorrow morning," she said to him. "Even if you can't make it to dinner, church will be just fine," she pressed.

Why was she doing this? Why had I done this?

"So, we'll see you, then?"

"I, uh . . . I'll let you know."

"I'll take that as a yes." My mother did one of those claps where her hands barely touched. I wanted to slap her hands to her sides, right after I slapped myself.

"We have to get going," I said, afraid of what else my mother might say.

"You two have a great time, and it was so nice meeting you, Xavier King." She hugged him, even as he still stood stiff as a stone. When she stepped back from the embrace, she added, "We'll see you tomorrow." She dismissed me with an air-kiss and a whisper, "Yes, you've been keeping secrets. I hope you haven't been telling lies."

I didn't respond, just took Xavier's hand and dragged him from that place. In silence, he led me to the car he'd rented for the day, and after he opened the door of the BMW and I slipped inside, I held my breath as I watched him round the car.

When he slid into the driver's seat, I said, "I'm so sorry," before he even started the ignition.

He didn't respond as he backed the car from the spot and eased into the lane.

"My mother was so overbearing, and that's not what I meant to happen," I said, swiveling in the seat so I faced him. "I didn't expect her to ask you to come to church." I chuckled. "Of course, you don't have to go."

When we edged out of the parking lot and onto Riverside Drive, he pulled the car to the curb.

I kept on, "Because it was too much. I can't believe . . ."

He slammed his hand on the steering wheel, startling me, making my head rear back. "Why would you do that?" he shouted—no, he screamed, a sound that made the windows rattle. "Why would you put me in that situation? Didn't you think I'd want to be prepared to meet your mother?"

"Yes, but . . ."

"You set me up!"

I sat still because I was so shocked. It took moments for my brain to send a message to my lips. Slowly, I said, "I just wanted you to meet her." I paused to steady my voice. "I wanted you to have a casual meeting with no pressure. I didn't want to set up something formal because I didn't want you to think I was pushing this relationship. I'm not; I just wanted you to meet her. That's it."

"And now she invited me to church!" he said, as if that were the sin. At least his voice had dropped a decibel, though the way his fingers curled around the steering wheel, I was sure it would break in half.

It took a few silent moments before I said, "I'm really sorry, Xavier." I was more stunned than apologetic.

His fingers flexed, then relaxed, flexed, then relaxed, almost in sync with the throbbing in his temple. After too many moments of that, I said, "I'm sorry," again, before I reached for the car door's handle. But by the time I slid out, he had jumped out and ran around to my side.

As Xavier came toward me, my heart raced, and I wondered if there was any way to outrun him. But then I saw his eyes and the apology that shined from him. I recoiled when he reached for me, but when he pulled me into his arms, I released a long breath into his shoulder. Still, it took me a moment before I wrapped my arms around him.

"I'm sorry," we said together.

He said, "I was just shocked." He stood back. "First your mother, then an invitation to church? That's a lot."

"I know, and it wasn't supposed to go down that way. I just wanted you to meet her in a situation that didn't feel like a big deal. But it turned out to be one anyway. I'm sorry," I said, looking into his eyes. "This was all my fault."

He nodded as if he agreed, and that surprised me. I thought he'd say something like the fault belonged to us both. Yes, I was the action, but he was the opposite and inappropriate reaction.

I said, "And forget about what my mother said about church. That was just my mom being my mom."

He stared over my head, and I knew he was having another memory. Then he said, "It's been a long time since I've been to church. Maybe it's time."

My mouth opened as wide as my eyes. "Really?"

Another moment, then, "Yeah, especially if I'm going with you." A pause as if he was giving himself time to think. "Yes, it's time."

"Okay," I said. "If you really want to, I'd love to have you with me."

"Good. Because I want to go, even if you did set me up."

"I'm sorry," I said, hoping he wasn't going to make me apologize all day.

Again, he nodded, without any acknowledgment of his part. Instead, he pressed his lips against mine, and I fell right into that good feeling. Until my memory flashed back to: Xavier and that steering wheel.

I tensed, and Xavier leaned away. "You okay?"

This time, I was the one who nodded.

He asked, "We're okay?"

A beat passed. "Yeah." Another beat. "Definitely."

"Great. Let's get on the road." He opened the car door, and I hesitated for a second before I slipped inside.

Once I clicked on my seat belt, Xavier leaned in, and I tensed as he kissed my forehead. He leaned back with a bit of a frown, but then he smiled when I did.

He slammed the door shut, and by the time he trotted around and jumped back into the driver's seat, I was convinced I was overreacting. Of course Xavier had been angry. I'd set him up in what had to be one of the most uncomfortable positions for a man. And now I was making too much of his reaction.

Then, in my mind, I saw his fingers and the steering wheel. But I pushed that image aside. He'd been upset, and it was my fault.

Nothing like this would happen again.

14

Xavier

I grinned as I glanced at Chastity, her fingers speed-texting.

"Okay," she exhaled. "I told my mother we'll be there in less than five minutes." She peered out the car's window. "Oh, God." Like she'd done the last dozen times after she'd exclaimed those words, she lifted her compact, smoothed her hair, checked her makeup, then glossed her lips. As she snapped the compact shut, she asked, "Do you think my father will know?"

Because asking me this question was another thing she'd done a dozen times, I knew what she was talking about. Still, I answered, "Know what? That you're a freak in bed?"

I wasn't sure what horrified her more—my words or the way the driver glanced at us with a sly grin.

I laughed, but when she moaned, I pulled her back into my arms. "Would you just stop?" I whispered.

"I can't," she hissed. "We're about to step into my father's church, and he can see things. You don't know, but he's going to take one look at us and"—she lowered her voice even more—"he's going to know we slept together last night."

I shifted to inside-voice mode when I murmured, "We didn't exactly sleep much, so if that's what he sees, we're good."

She shoved me away and then twisted so that her back was against the car's door. "Xavier, I'm serious." She folded her arms.

"I know you are—that's what makes this so funny."

"My father is going to take one look at us and then . . ." She moaned the end of her sentence.

"Would you relax? First, your father isn't going to be able to look at you and see that three hours ago we were sweating between the sheets, and even if he did, you're a grown woman."

"A grown woman who was raised in the church."

I waved my hand as if that wasn't a factor. "I've known lots of church girls, and . . ." The heat of her stare stopped my revelation.

"Oh, really?" Her left eyebrow rose. "How many church girls have you known?"

"All I'm saying," I began, "is you don't have to worry. I'm going to be on my best behavior, your father will love me, and we will enter then leave that church with your virtue intact. And do you know why?"

Her eyes, her tone, were still doubtful. "Why?"

"Because I love you."

Inch by inch, she melted until her arms were by her sides.

Her dumbfounded stare made me cup her chin with my fingertips. "I love you," I repeated, "and you don't have to say it back. I said it because I want you to know what love means to me. It means I've got you; I've got you with your parents, I've got you with your job, I've got you with your friends, I've got you wherever and whenever you need me. I've got you because I love you."

My words had shocked her, and really, I was a bit surprised myself. This hadn't been the way I planned to say that; I'd wanted to create more of a memory. But those words were what this moment needed, and since I was ready, I was fine with it.

After more moments of silence, Chastity leaned forward, her lips aimed toward mine, but before we touched, the car edged to the curb and she pulled back. "We're here," she whispered, and I could have sworn her voice trembled.

As she slapped on her sunglasses, I thanked the driver, then pushed the car door open because Chastity hadn't made a move; I still had to give her a little nudge before she slid out. But then she went into high gear.

"We're going in through my dad's entrance," she said, lowering her eyes as if she was avoiding contact with everyone. We weaved through the parishioners who packed the outside of the church and rounded the corner.

"Hiding me from the people," I teased as I trotted to keep up with her sprint.

"No." She slowed her steps, then leaned into me as she cracked her first smile of the morning. "I want to introduce you to the world, but the first person you need to meet is my father."

"Ah, but he won't be the first. Remember . . . your mother . . ."

The cheer she had a moment ago faded, and I regretted my words. I'd taken her back to yesterday.

But after we climbed the three steps that led to the side of the church, Chastity leaned in and kissed me, telling me she forgave me. I was swept away by what she stirred inside me, falling deeper and deeper into the feeling until . . . the door of the church opened, and we were both startled. Clearly, we'd forgotten where we were.

"Mom!" Chastity exclaimed. "How did you know we were out here?" And then she glanced up, and I did, too, both of us taking in the sight of the surveillance camera.

"Have you been standing here the whole time?" Chastity asked her mother.

"No, I was in your father's office when he saw you walk up.

You remember we had that camera installed a few years ago, right? When he saw you, I came out to greet you. I wanted to escort you back to see Pastor." After she hugged Chastity, Mrs. Jeffries turned to me. "How are you, Mr. King?"

"I'm great. But please, call me Xavier."

Her approval was in her smile. "We don't have much time; I expected you to be here a bit earlier, so we could have all shared a cup of tea before service."

"Xavier and I had to . . . meet up . . . so we could ride together," Chastity said, and it took every part of me to keep my face straight with her smooth lie, even as she stood in her father's church. "I didn't want Xavier to come here by himself."

"Well, you're here," Mrs. Jeffries spoke to me. "Pastor is anxious to meet you."

As we moved behind her mother, I reached for Chastity's hand, hoping that was a reminder of what I'd told her in the car. At the end of the hall, we paused at a door that opened into an expansive office.

From where we stood, I saw Chastity's father, the infamous Kareem Jeffries. His head was lowered, his eyes on the pages of an opened Bible. It didn't look like he was reading, though. He was just staring, as if he was soaking up the words.

Was that his superpower? Did he just absorb the Bible? Maybe Chastity had been right—maybe after one glance, her father knew all things.

After two taps on the door, Mrs. Jeffries said, "Pastor?"

It was interesting that's what she called her husband, and I wondered if she just did that at church.

As the pastor raised his head, Chastity dropped my hand. She rushed toward her father as he whispered her name, and when they embraced, he half lifted his daughter from her feet. A bittersweet memory consumed me—my sixth birthday and my mother lifting me in greeting. She was the only person who'd ever been that happy to see me.

"How are you, princess?"

I watched as he stepped back, still holding her hands but taking in every inch of her. He looked at her completely, the way my mother had looked at me. Whatever he saw in Chastity this morning pleased him, because his smile had enough wattage to power New York.

"I'm really good, Papa."

"You don't know what these Sunday mornings do for me when I have a chance to worship the Lord, and see you and your mother sitting in the front pew. Now that I know I'll see you *at least* once a week." Then after a pause, he added, "Sometimes."

"Is that some low-key shade?" Chastity asked, and we all laughed. She continued, "You know how busy I've been, and then last week . . ."

I wondered what lie would she tell now, but she didn't add anything.

Her father said, "I understand. You're just living your blessed and big life in the city."

Those words must have made him remember that his daughter had arrived with a guest. He pivoted toward me, but his only greeting was the extension of his hand; there was no smile on his face.

Mrs. Jeffries said, "Pastor, I'd like to present Mr. Xavier King," as if this formal introduction was her job.

His hand swallowed mine, which was a feat, because I wasn't a small dude. But standing in his shadow showed me why Kareem Jeffries had held it down on the basketball court back in the day.

"It's nice to meet you, Pastor Jeffries."

"The pleasure is mine." He held my hand with a grip that was one degree removed from arm wrestling, and he held on to me for so long, I wondered if he was waiting for a bell to ring so he'd be declared the victor. When he released me, he gestured toward the chairs in front of his desk.

I resisted the urge to massage the ache from my knuckles. No, he was not going to see that he'd caused me a little pain, though I knew that was his intent.

As I sat, I peeped the more informal setting on the other side of the office: the two overstuffed sofas facing each other with a coffee table in between. A place to entertain, if not friends, people a pastor would want to know better. I was not one of those—yet.

I sat up straight but not stiffly—respectful, not intimidated.

"I'm very happy to meet the first man my daughter thought worthy enough to enter this church."

Worthy. I nodded. "It's certainly an honor to be here with you."

Pastor Jeffries sat in his chair, his fingers tapping together, forming a steeple, while Mrs. Jeffries stood at his right side, her hand on top of his chair. The two of them were connected, an emotional bond that was easy to see. I didn't know much about the Bible, but the way Mrs. Jeffries stood, she was the embodiment of his helpmate. At the same time, he was her protection; from the way he held my hand I knew he'd drag a man (and maybe even a woman) if anyone stepped incorrectly to his wife . . . or his daughter.

I received the message, accepted it, internalized it, and couldn't wait for the day when Chastity and I stood the same way.

Pastor Jeffries said, "So, where did you two meet?"

Before I could respond, Chastity interjected, "At Melanie's party, when she opened her clinic," as if she wanted to make sure the correct answer was given.

Her father nodded. "Ah, Melanie. Another daughter I see on occasional Sundays."

When he laughed, he reached over his shoulder for his wife's hand as if she were not close enough.

"Well, Chastity"—I turned to her—"is the one who stood out in the crowd. In an offhanded way, Melanie introduced us. And we ended up talking all night, and—"

"All night at the club," Chastity spoke up quickly, as if she wanted it to be clear. "We talked for the rest of the night at the party. Before I left to go home."

With the way her parents nodded, I now understood the concern she'd had in the car. Truly, they thought their daughter was her name.

I had to hold my laugh inside before I continued, "It was a great night. We found it easy to talk to each other, both of us being attorneys, having the same birthday, the same interests."

"Really," her parents spoke together.

We mimicked her parents when we nodded together and said, "Yes."

Chastity picked up the story. "It's been a good time, and we're great friends."

"Friends," her father responded to her, but peered at me.

As an attorney, I'd learned many lessons beyond the books. This was one of those moments for one of those lessons. So even though the heat of KJ's stare was enough to warm the sun a few degrees, I didn't shift. Even though my eyelids itched, I didn't blink. I didn't give away the truth when I said, "Yes, we're friends," and then added, "but if this is up to me, I hope one day Chastity and I will be more than that. I'm quite taken with your daughter."

The moment I spoke, I wanted to hit reverse. Not because my words weren't true, but because I saw the heat rising beneath the sienna tone of Chastity's skin. It wasn't because she was embarrassed; it was because she remembered how we'd spent last night.

Her mother beamed, but my words had not moved her father.

"Well," her mother spoke for the first time since she'd made the introduction, "it looks like the praise and worship team is about to begin."

I followed her glance to the fifty-inch television screen that seemed to show the church's sanctuary. Right next to it was a screen of the same size that showed the door where we'd just entered.

Mrs. Jeffries continued, "Let's give Pastor his time before he has to go before the people." She kissed her husband, but when she made the move toward us, he grasped her wrist.

"Sweetheart, would you mind staying?"

"I thought I should go out there with them," she said to her husband. "You know, block all the church people who will want to get into our daughter's business."

"Let Jesus be their fence," my dad said. "Chastity and Xavier can handle it, and I need to speak with you."

"We certainly can." I stood and helped Chastity do the same. When I stretched toward Pastor Jeffries and took his hand again, I hoped for a warmer parting. But it was the same as the greeting—the same grip, the same expression, the same message that Chastity was his daughter. He studied me, his assessment incomplete in the five minutes we'd spent together. But I was fine; it would get better. All Pastor Jeffries needed to know was that I was going to treat his daughter right.

He said, "Enjoy the service, Xavier. And we're looking forward to you joining us in our home afterward."

I smiled, nodded, then followed Chastity from her father's

office. There would come a day when Pastor Jeffries would shake my hand as if we were on the same side. He'd shake my hand as his son.

My thoughts paused. I'd only thought about Chastity as my family, but I'd have an extended one. A mother and a real father. KJ Jeffries at that.

That made me smile all the way into the sanctuary.

15

Xavier

T he sanctuary surged with electricity as the congregants
sang and danced, praised and worshipped. It was un-
abashed adulation unto the Lord, and I stood a bit be-
wildered. The joy was palpable; this was something I had never
experienced. But while I didn't have the connection to God these
people had, I shared their gratitude. Because while our reasons
were different, I was as glad to be in this place as they were.

I glanced at the reason for my joy. Chastity's eyes were
closed, her head back and her arms raised in adoration. While
she adored God, I adored her and this moment we were sharing.
This was what I'd wanted since I'd met her—a chance to create
our own memories. That had been difficult because while the
city offered much, there were few things that met my standards.
So the carriage ride through Central Park—I had done the
same with Diane. Dinner at Masa—where I'd asked Roxanne to
marry me. And riding up the elevator to the top of the hotel for
dinner—that was Valentine's Day for Diane *and* Roxanne.

But this? I had never stood, shoulders touching, with either
of my ex-fiancées in the front pew of one of the most promi-
nent churches in the city. That alone made me rock with the

band, made me give my own praise. I hadn't realized I'd closed my eyes until Chastity reached for me. She entwined her fingers with mine, she squeezed my hand, her message that now, she had me.

Yes, this was a new memory, but as I looked down at her hand in mine, my consciousness took me back to another time, the last time I'd sat in church . . .

September 2, 1990

We stopped at the storefront, but my mama didn't open the door. "Let me adjust your tie before we go in." She knelt and sighed. "Whew, it's hot enough to roast a lizard."

I giggled. "Mama, nobody roasts lizards."

"Well, they could if they wanted to in this heat. Now stand still so I can straighten your tie."

"I don't like wearing a tie," I whined, trying to back away from her prying fingers. "It makes me hot and makes me itch."

"Really?" Her voice was filled with disappointment when she pulled her hand away. "But it makes you look like so handsome."

Then she smiled, and just like that, I cooled off and stopped itching.

"Okay." After one more tug, my mother stood, then grabbed my hand. "We're ready." But still she didn't push open the door. She took a deep breath as if she needed some kind of special energy to step inside the little church that used to be a liquor store.

"Lord, I need to hear a good word, today, I really do," my mother whispered. "I need you, Lord, to answer these prayers. I need a real blessing, 'cause after next week," she paused, "I don't know what my little man and I are gonna do." She took a deep breath, but she didn't move, as if she wanted to first make sure the Lord heard her. She added, "A blessing, Lord," she reminded Him, then she

squeezed my hand. When she said, "Come on, little man," there was more than a smile on her face—I heard the hope in her voice.

We stepped up the single stair, and when Mama pushed open the door, the first thing that hit me was the heat that wrapped around and hugged me. It was almost one hundred degrees outside; that's what Mama said as we walked the two blocks from where the bus let us off. But outside felt like the air-conditioning in the community center compared to this church.

When we stepped all the way in, I couldn't breathe. "Mama," I whispered. "It's too hot."

"Can you be my little man just for a little while?" she whispered back. "We won't stay long. I promise."

There were only five long benches in the whole church, and on the end of the second-to-last one, there was enough space for about one and a half people. Mama pushed me into the row first, and I wiggled down next to the lady who wore a red hat that was bigger than me. When my mama sat down, I half sat on her lap, making it feel like the temperature had soared another two hundred degrees.

How was I supposed to be still when all I could think about was how hot it was and how I wanted to take off this tie? That was all—until the preacher stood up. He was a big man, like a football player. He was huffing and puffing before he even said anything.

Then he began, but he didn't talk; he kinda sang. And then he danced, too, putting on a whole show.

"God's gonna take care of you."

The preacher hopped like a bunny across the stage, and someone shouted out, "Amen."

"No matter what you're going through, God always takes care of you."

Now he skipped the other way, and someone else yelled, "Hallelujah."

"So if He's done it before, He's surely gonna take care of you now. Fear not!" he screamed and then danced in place, moving his feet fast, like the blades on the fan that Mama kept in our window.

"*Preach it!*" *the whole church stood and shouted at the same time.*

As everyone stood, shouting and singing, Mama sat, rocking back and forth.

"*God's got you!*"

When the preacher said that, my mama began to cry.

"*Mama, are you okay?*" *I asked, making sure I used my inside voice so she wouldn't get more upset.*

She reached into her purse for a tissue, then blew her nose as she nodded. But still she cried.

"*The Lord has a blessing with your name on it,*" *the minister sang.* "*All you have to do is stand!*"

I hopped up, then pulled my mother's hand. "*Come on, Mama, you have to stand. You have to stand for the blessing!*"

But no matter how much I tugged, my mother wouldn't get up.

"*Come on, Mama. Stand!*" *I pleaded, knowing how much she needed a blessing. She'd just asked God for that.*

She would not be moved, though, and I wondered if her tears stopped her from hearing. So I repeated everything I'd heard him say: "*Don't worry, Mama, God's gonna take care of us,*" *I sang, the way the preacher had.* "*God always takes care of us. He's surely gonna take care of us. All we have to do is stand for our blessing! Amen, Hallelujah, preach it!*"

Mama's head shot up, and though her eyes were still so glassy, she busted out laughing. "*Now you're my little preacher man,*" *she said and reached for my hand . . .*

THAT MEMORY BROUGHT a smile to my lips, but also the ache that always came with thoughts of my mama. Especially this reflection, because just weeks after that, Mama and I had moved in with Gran and life had never been the same. I'd always wondered what would have happened if my Mama had just stood up that day in church . . .

I felt the tug of my hand and glanced up as Chastity was trying to get me to stand with her. I'd been so lost in my thoughts—I had no idea what was going on.

"So before we welcome all of our guests," Pastor Jeffries said from the altar, "I wanted to give a special welcome to my princess and her friend, though she is certainly not a guest at Greater Grace."

"Amen!" It seemed as if all two thousand of the people in the sanctuary sang together.

"Welcome, Mr. King," her father said, and I nodded, hoping that was all I was supposed to do. "I pray this will be a day of spiritual enlightenment and joy for you."

"Thank you," I said.

Pastor Jeffries turned to the entire congregation. "Now I'd like to ask any other visitors to please stand so we can welcome you to Greater Grace."

As Pastor Jeffries spoke to the other visitors, I understood why this had never happened with anyone else. After my mother, the only woman I was supposed to sit next to at church had to be the woman who was meant to be my wife.

When Pastor Jeffries asked the members and guests to greet one another, I turned to Chastity. And the look in her eyes let me know it wouldn't be long. Because I had a feeling she knew she was going to be my wife, too.

16

Chastity

S unday-afternoon dinners at our home were always filled with the merriment of Christmas. A festive gathering of family and friends, every seven days, celebrating the passage of another week over a soul food spread that rivaled any restaurant's menu.

But this Sunday was different. Of course, I'd had friends come home with me for these weekly celebrations, and growing up, Melanie had been here just about every week. Never, though, had there been a male to walk through the front doors of this brownstone who made me smile the way I smiled at Xavier right now.

As he stepped away from the buffet table, Xavier said, "Pastor and Mrs. Jeffries, you really have a beautiful home."

"Thank you," my mother said. "We'll give a tour of the other floors after dinner." She led us to the formal dining table, which was always set for twelve.

"I'd love that," Xavier said as he moved to the chair where my mother directed him. "These brownstones have always amazed me."

"We were blessed to find this one and then renovate it. We

were a little concerned about Pastor"—she paused—"well, he
wasn't a pastor then. But while he was playing basketball, we were
concerned about living someplace where people could just walk
up to our front door." She said that as if living that way still
amazed her.

"Now, Sisley, tell the man the truth, that was your concern,
not mine." Turning to Xavier, my dad said, "I didn't want to live
anywhere else, except here in Sugar Hill. I loved the history of
this neighborhood, and just rolling through these streets, recog-
nizing the African Americans who were here before me, makes
me proud. This area has always been the best of Harlem."

"Well, we were fine," my mother acquiesced. To Xavier, she
said, "Between Pastor, the security guards, and even the few
times Pastor took me to the shooting range"—she chuckled—
"we were safe, and it turned out to be a wonderful place to raise
Chastity."

Because it felt like my mother was about to take my man
down my childhood memory lane, I asked, "So, Mom, how did
this happen?" She squinted, not understanding. "Just the four of
us," I added. "Has there ever been a time when I sat at this table
and not every seat was taken?" My parents laughed as I recalled a
lifetime of dinners, sitting across from those whose hearts were
closest to my parents and who broke bread with us through the
best of times and the worst of days. But today, my parents had
closed the doors to their home, it seemed. This was a private
dinner, which I appreciated.

"This was all your father." Then my mother turned to
him. "Pastor, do you want to tell Chastity what you told the
people?"

He chuckled. "I told them I was conducting a job interview."

"A job interview?" I repeated and then laughed because I was
nervous, not humored. This wasn't supposed to be anything like

that; I just wanted to have a nice dinner, a great chat, and then Xavier and I would leave, happy we'd had this time together.

When my father added, "I had to say something to keep the people away," I relaxed—especially after he chuckled.

My man wasn't fazed by the interview comment, though. Because he just piped right in, "I enjoyed your sermon this morning, Pastor Jeffries."

"Thank you," my dad said. "We just started this seven deadly sins series last week."

"Well, I enjoyed your sermon on greed. What did you preach on last week?"

"The basics. I had to begin with everyone understanding the seven sins aren't listed in the Bible."

Xavier raised an eyebrow. "I didn't know that."

My father nodded. "Of course, they originated from Christian tradition," he began, "but they went through many variations and changes . . ."

As my dad continued, I loosened up. I should've known my father wouldn't stray far from spiritual topics.

And just when I had that thought, my father asked, "So you're from Mississippi?"

My shoulders hunched all the way up to my ears. This *was* a job interview.

"Yes, sir," my man said, though through his tone, I felt his tension.

"What part?"

Xavier paused, using the time to wipe the edges of his lips with his napkin, and I wondered how much of his story he was willing to tell. "From right outside a town called Sumner." Then he added quickly, "It's so small—just about five hundred people—I'm sure you never heard of it," as if he wanted to run past this and move on.

My father raised an eyebrow. "Isn't that where the trial for the murderers of Emmett Till was held?"

It was Xavier's turn to show surprise. "Yeah. The court-house has been turned into a museum."

"Wow, Papa. How did you know that?" A natural question I hoped would steer the conversation away from anything that would cause Xavier pain.

"I've read a lot."

My mother laughed. "I always tell Pastor he needs to get a spot on *Jeopardy!* Who knows? He just might make something of himself." She waved her hand and giggled, tickled by her own words.

But all the laughter didn't stop my father. "So are your people still in Sumner?"

"No, sir," Xavier said. "I come from a small family, and there's no one left there."

"That's something else that Xavier and I have in common," I jumped in again. "We're both only children."

My effort did nothing; my father returned Xavier to the witness stand. "So where are your parents now?"

I moaned inside. My father had entered the red zone. There hadn't been a time when Xavier shared his past that I hadn't heard his struggle. "I never knew my father," he said, and I was glad he left that story there. "And my mother . . ." He paused and swallowed. "She died."

I held my gasp inside. I didn't want my parents to know Xavier had never shared this with me. His mother was dead?

"She passed away some time ago."

Inside those words, I heard the stored-up pain of the years—however many—that had passed. I didn't want Xavier to have to go through this anymore. I was ready to object and end this line of questioning.

"I'm sorry to hear that," my father said.

I was sure my father would stop now. But then it was Xavier who kept it going. "It's been many years, about twenty. So I've had time to process it and leave that grief and everything else behind. I came to New York and built quite a life, and now"—he paused and glanced at me—"I'm looking forward to my future."

"You left that grief," my father said. When he added, "I see," his eyes narrowed.

With that, I knew Xavier was in for a long dinner.

My father said, "Twenty years ago, you were very young. Were you able to talk to someone about losing your mother then?"

Xavier shrugged. "No, but I handled it. I had to."

My father leaned back, and when he pressed his fingers together forming a steeple, I knew Kareem Jeffries, my father, had left the table. He was in full pastoring mode now. "You know, grief is a deep emotion that leaves its remnants for years, sometimes decades. There are few who've gone through something as tragic as what you've experienced, especially being so young, who have walked away unscathed by that kind of trauma."

It was a statement, but there was a question—actually, a challenge—inside his words. I heard it, and so did Xavier.

"Of course, for a while, I was really upset," Xavier told him. "But I persevered and got to the other side." Then, as an afterthought, he added, "I'm fine," as if those were the words my father was waiting to hear.

My father's eyes never left Xavier, as if he was studying him. His expression was familiar to me, and I wondered, what did my father see?

Whatever he saw, it wasn't on the outside. Xavier didn't crack under the pressure of my father's questions, didn't flounder

under the intensity of his stare. He just sat there, a man on the witness stand, waiting for this cross-examination to end.

My father persisted, "There are levels to this, son. There are stages of grief. Things you have to face so that later in life, you won't have issues and . . ."

Xavier's cell phone vibrated; even though it was inside his jacket, we all shifted, our eyes moving toward the sound. He pulled out the phone and glanced at the screen. "Excuse me." Pushing back his chair, he said, "I wouldn't ordinarily do this, but . . ."

Before he finished his explanation, my mother drawled, "Go ahead, Xavier. If you need privacy, Pastor's office is one level up."

Xavier shook his head and accepted the call at the same time. "I'll just step in here." He moved toward the kitchen.

I followed him with my eyes. "What's up?" we all heard Xavier say.

When I turned my attention back to the dining room, my father's eyes were on me, his brows raised.

I mimicked him and tilted my head in a *What?* expression. Was he annoyed Xavier had taken the call? With the case he was working on, it could have been important.

Except the way Xavier had answered his phone belied that thought.

"Yeah, with Chastity and her parents." Xavier's voice floated from the kitchen.

His side of the conversation didn't give me many clues: "Uh-huh," then, "Are you serious?" then, "Okay, I'll be right there."

I wanted to keep my eyes away from my father's, but I felt his pull. And when I looked at him, I was taken aback by the deep creases lining his forehead.

Xavier rushed back into the dining room. "I really hate to do this . . ."

I pushed my chair back.

"My best friend, Bryce, is at Harlem Hospital."

"Oh my goodness," my mother and I said at the same time.

"Is he all right?" I asked.

Xavier held up his hand. "He's good. Twisted his ankle so bad this morning that he thought it was broken. It was severe, but no broken bones. They've wrapped him up and shot him up with something for the pain, and he can't be released until someone is there to take him home."

"Well, of course you need to go," my mother said as she stood, too.

It took my father a couple more moments to do the same.

"I am so sorry," Xavier said to both of my parents. Then, to my mother, he added, "Mrs. Jeffries, this dinner was magnificent."

"Thank you, darling. I'm just sorry you won't get to enjoy all of it."

"Me too. It's been a long time since I've had a home-cooked meal like this."

"Well, two things: first, you'll just have to come back next Sunday, and second, all of this comes from a good friend, Melba, who caters all of our Sunday meals." She leaned forward. "But no one has to know."

He chuckled and said, "I look forward to coming back," although he made no commitment about next Sunday. When Xavier turned to my father, he didn't receive the same reception; still, he held out his hand. "Pastor Jeffries, thank you for having me."

"You're welcome. And I'll say a prayer for your friend." That was the extent of it. No looking forward to seeing you again. Not even a prayer for Xavier.

I said to Xavier, "I'll walk you out."

He gave my parents a final nod, then followed me into the living room and through the stained-glass double doors of the parlor before we entered the main hallway.

As I reached for the door, Xavier pressed his hand against it, then swung me around and pressed his body against mine. "I'm sorry."

"Xavier," I whispered and glanced over his shoulder. "My parents." And those two words made me remember what he'd just revealed. I wanted to hold him and give him my regrets about his mother. But how could I do that here and now?

He said, "I wish I didn't have to go because I want to be with you again all night long."

"Your friend needs you."

"Well"—he kissed my forehead—"I'm looking forward to"—he kissed my nose—"the day when *you* say you need me." When our lips met, we lingered in the softness, neither of us wanting to break away.

I was the one who pulled away, though I pressed my forehead against his. "I love you, Xavier."

He leaned back, his question so clear in his eyes.

"I love you," I repeated, just so he would know I'd meant it.

Shaking his head, he said, "You don't have to say that." Those were his words, but his eyes told me he hoped I was speaking the truth.

Pressing into him even more, I kissed him again, speaking in *my* language. Our kiss filled with more passion, the kind that demanded more privacy than the vestibule of the brownstone I'd once called home. We were breathless when we pulled away. And again, his eyes searched mine as if he was still questioning me.

I palmed his cheek. "All I want is for you to stay, but right now you have to leave."

"Chastity, you don't know . . ."

"I know."

He shook his head as if I didn't know anything, as if there were hundreds of sentences in his mind, a million words in his thoughts. But he summed it up with, "I love you so much. More than I could ever imagine."

I wanted to kiss him again, but I nudged him instead, because another kiss . . . and I would've walked right out this door with him. And his friend Bryce . . . well, he would have just been at that hospital waiting.

"Go," I whispered. As he backed out, I said, "Call me when you get home."

"What would be even better is if you're waiting there for me when I get home."

I set my hand on my hip. "I don't have a key."

"Oh, we're gonna fix that, baby." He grinned, blew me a kiss, then trotted down the stairs.

Once he was out of my sight, I closed then leaned against the door, my mind filled with all that had gone down today. From Xavier meeting my father, to standing side by side in church, this dinner with my parents, and even his finally sharing about his mother—it was all special. But nothing meant as much as these last three minutes.

I did love Xavier—at least, this felt like love. It was crazy; I was thirty-four and had never really known this kind of love. I'd known sex, I'd known lust, but I'd never known anything that had touched my heart.

Xavier had changed that, and I floated back through the living room to the dining room with thoughts of love on my mind.

17

Chastity

nside the dining room, my parents sat, saying nothing.

I glided back to my seat. "So, what did you think of Xavier?"

"Sweetheart," my mother jumped in, though her eyes stayed on my father, "it doesn't matter what we think. It's what you think of the young man."

My father held up his hand. "No, Sisley, she's right to ask. My thoughts do matter." To me, he asked, "So was that call real?"

I'd been smelling roses, hearing harps, walking on clouds. And just like that, my feet landed with a thud back on the ground. "What do you mean?"

"Did someone just call him so he could get out of here?"

"Why would he do that?" I asked, hoping my father heard my attitude and would back up.

If he heard it, he didn't care. My father hunched his shoulders and gave me the reason he'd asked that ridiculous question. "Maybe the kitchen was getting too hot and Xavier couldn't stand it."

I pushed back from the table. "You think your questions

were too much for him?" I asked, not caring that he heard how offended I was by his question.

This time his response was only a shrug.

I crossed my arms. "Why don't you like him?"

He shook his head. "I didn't say that."

"Well, you're saying something, and it doesn't sound good."

"All right." He bowed his head, and right then I knew this wasn't going to go well. Because whenever my dad made that move, one of two things were happening: either he was talking to God, or God was talking to him.

I sat, waiting for the verdict, my heart pounding. His voice was low when he finally said, "There's something in that young man's spirit, something that has to be resolved."

That made me frown. "What are you talking about? What's in his spirit?"

"I don't know."

His words had gone off in my head like an explosive, and now he was just going to leave that bomb sitting there? I wanted to tell him to bow his head, to go back and ask God for clarification.

"It's something he's aware of," my father continued, "but something he has to do for himself, something that could bring him down . . . and everyone in his world could go down with him."

This was the first time I'd introduced a man to my father, and this was how he was reacting? Even though I understood his gift, I didn't appreciate his discernment right now.

"What am I supposed to do with this? You haven't given me any specifics; you haven't even given me anything in general. So what do you want me to do, Papa?"

I wasn't looking for an answer. My question was more of a challenge, to get my father to back up and stand down.

My father said, "You should do with it what you've been

taught to do. You know how to pray; you know how to hear God's voice. Ask Him for guidance and discernment."

"How do you know I haven't done that already?" The moment I asked, I was sorry. Because just like he was proving right now, my father knew things.

But instead of calling me out, he said, "You know how this works. You can never go to the Lord enough. Seek His guidance in all that you do. And you need to seek the Lord about this young man."

"Chastity." My mother's tone was her attempt to toss ice onto the heat in the room. "Your father isn't saying anything bad about Xavier. He's giving you the advice he would give to anyone about anything."

I whipped my head toward my mother. "So, what should I ask God, Mom? Should I pray the same prayers you prayed for Papa? Should I ask the Lord if Xavier will cheat on me the way Papa cheated on you?"

"Chastity!"

My head snapped back to my father because while we'd had heated discussions, there had been few times when anyone ever raised their voice in our household.

His hands were flat on the table. "You will not speak to your mother that way."

"Why not?" My pushback made my father's head rear back. "You said I should pray, so I just want to be clear. What kind of clarity do I need about Xavier? Not that I have to ask or answer to you. Because in case you've forgotten, I'm grown," I said, sounding even to myself like a teenager right now.

It was probably because the last time I'd told my father that, I was sixteen. And now, like then, he glared at me, his lips pressed together as if he were trying to stop himself from saying or doing something I might regret.

But when he opened his mouth, his volume was lower, though his tone was more stern than I'd ever heard him. "There is only one thing on my mind in this situation, and that is telling you the truth. No matter how old you are or how . . . grown . . . you get, you are still my daughter, and I will always take that responsibility seriously. But what I will not take is you disrespecting me . . . or your mother . . . in *our* home."

While I sat still with my arms folded, I was careful not to return the same glare to my father that he was giving to me. He had never hit me in my life, but the fire in his eyes let me know he might be willing to break that streak today.

"I don't care where you work, I don't care about your title, I don't care how much money you make," he continued as if he wanted to be sure I didn't miss his message, "you need to understand I care about you. We"—he paused long enough to point to the other end of the table—"are your parents. And for your sake, no one in this room better ever forget that."

I tightened my arms, the only defiance I had within me.

And then, as if I was a brat, he asked, "Is that understood?"

I let a couple of beats go by, but I knew I'd been defeated. With a sigh, I said, "Yes, and I'm sorry." I turned to my mother. "I'm really sorry, Mom."

Though she nodded, my mother sat still, as if my words had shocked her into a state where she might never speak to me again.

I tried to explain, "But do you both understand my frustration? Papa, you don't like Xavier—"

"I never said that."

"But you've made some kind of judgment about him after talking to him for thirty minutes."

"I didn't do that."

"You haven't given him a chance." I continued to plead my case. "If you have more questions, ask him; he'll be glad to answer just like he was forthcoming today. He really opened up to you, Papa, and do you know how I know?" I didn't give him a moment to answer. "Because he told you his mother had died, and he'd never even told me."

My father's eyes narrowed. "You never talked about his mother?"

"No," I said, wondering if I'd just revealed the wrong thing. "But I didn't talk about you or Mom either. He didn't find out who you were until about a week ago. We were just trying to get to know each other."

My father nodded. "Well, getting to know each other means getting to know everything. Family structure, how one was raised—those are important factors."

"That's one of the things I like about him. Xavier's had a hard life, he's survived things I never would have, and yet, here he is today. A good man. A successful man. A man I really"— I looked between the two of them—"*like*. And you know I've never said that before. I'm glad to be back in New York, and it has a lot to do with Xavier.

"Papa, the only thing God is telling you is that Xavier has been through some things," I said, as if I were God's spokesperson in this moment. "But the operative word is he's been *through* them. He's created a wonderful life, and all he wants to do is live it." I shrugged. "Just give him a chance."

"Your father and I will certainly do that," my mother said, speaking her first words. Even after what I'd said, she was supporting me, and I jumped from my chair.

"Thank you," I said, wrapping her inside my arms.

"I'm looking forward to getting to know the man you've

just described." Her voice was muffled inside my embrace, but her words made me hug her tighter. When I stepped away, she added, "And I'm sure your father wants to get to know him, too."

When I glanced back at him, he nodded, but before I could rush to him, he said, "I never said I didn't like him, princess. I'm telling you what I feel in my spirit. Now, maybe that young man has been through a lot, but no matter where you start, you better find a way to pull in Jesus. And that's what I'm sensing Xavier needs . . . a whole lot of Jesus." I was just about to fold my arms again, but then my father added, "And you know what? This may be the very reason why God brought you into his life. Maybe He's chosen you to help bring him to Christ."

Relief surged all through me. "So you're okay with me seeing him?"

He leaned back in his chair, crossed his legs, and gave me an up-and-down glance before he said, "I can't stop you. You grown."

We all laughed as I rushed to my father and pulled him into a hug.

My mother pushed her chair back. "Let me get your plate heated up so we can get back to the business of eating this wonderful food."

"No, that's okay. I really have to get going. There's a big case I'm working on, and I want to get a head start on it for the week."

"Well, I'm going to wrap this up for you," my mother said as she picked up my plate and rushed into the kitchen.

I still had my arms around my father when he shook his head. "I'm sorry," I whispered, really meaning it this time.

After a moment, he reached for my hand over his shoulder. "And I'm sorry, too." He swung me around so that now, I faced him. His eyes were filled with sorrow. "I'm sorry because for so many years I . . ." He paused, made a sound with his teeth that sounded like disgust, then continued, "I damaged you, princess."

In the silence that followed, I wondered if he was giving me space to tell him that he hadn't done any harm to me. But there was no need to tell that lie. He knew he'd spoken the truth.

When he didn't get a reprieve from me, he said, "If I had been a better husband, I would have been a better father."

This was where I could give him something. "You were— you are—a great father."

He nodded, but I could tell he hadn't released himself from that regret. "This is something I tell men all the time. How you treat your children's mother will affect them." He sighed. "The greatest gift I could have given you was honoring your mother."

I sat back in my chair, but then scooted it to the edge of the table and took my father's hand. "You're honoring her now. And that's why I've been able to open my heart. I'm dating a great guy because I see the man Mom always believed you to be. So whatever damage might have been there, I'm good now."

He wore his sadness like a mask he couldn't take off.

I said, "Maybe this all worked out in God's timing. Mom is such a great example, and maybe I had to see her help you work it out, so that I can help Xavier work through some things."

"Help him work through, but not fix him, Chastity," my father said.

I tilted my head. "What do you mean?"

He opened his mouth, then pressed his lips together so tightly, it almost looked like he was holding his breath. Then he said, "Just help him find Jesus, and He will do the rest."

I nodded, then hugged my father again. "That's the best advice you could have given me."

"I hope so, princess," he said, still filled with so much sadness. "I truly hope so."

Wanting to ease a bit of his anguish, I said, "I promise you'll love Xavier one day, Papa."

I waited, but my father was silent, and I leaned away from him. Couldn't he find something to say? At least give me an *I hope so*? But his lips remained pressed in a thin line, almost like he planned never to speak again.

But while his lips didn't move, he couldn't hide his thoughts from coming through the windows to his soul. In his eyes, I saw his belief—no, it was more than that—I saw his *knowing* that he would never come to love Xavier.

That made me more than sad; that made me afraid.

18

Xavier

I hopped out of the taxi, then rushed into the hospital in search of the information desk. Bryce sounded fine on the phone, and it was only a sprained ankle. Still, I didn't want to see my fam in any kind of distress.

After being told that Bryce was in the ER, I weaved my way down a couple of long corridors until I found him. One of the nurses shifted the blue curtain to the side, and there was Bryce, resting on a gurney, half covered with a sheet. He was leaning back, eyes closed, one hand behind his head, just chillin'.

My chuckle made him open his eyes. He grinned, though his eyes were glassy as if he had just been given a whole bottle of some good medicine.

"Bruh, really?" I said. "I ain't seen or talked to you in a week, and this is what you're doing? All stretched out here like this is the Four Seasons." I stepped closer to the bed and gave him dap. "How did you get here, man?"

"I told you," he said, his words coming slow. "A pickup game over in Morningside Park."

I laughed. "And I keep telling you, we're past that. You

can't hang with those cats over there. They're eighteen, nineteen, twenty years old."

He swatted my words away. "I don't know what you're talking about, bruh. I still got time to be picked up by some team in the NBA." My laughter didn't stop Bryce. "Just because you've given up your dream of going pro, doesn't mean I have."

"They really got you drugged up."

He shook his head. "I know what I'm saying. Every black man dreams of getting that NBA contract, and until I hit forty, I have time."

This time he laughed with me, knowing for sure he was talking foolishness.

"Okay," I said. "So what do I have to do to break you out of this place?"

"Just a few more minutes." He strained to push himself up. "They got my ankle wrapped," he said, kicking the blanket away with his other foot. "The doctor's going to give me a prescription, then I've got some papers to sign and we can bounce. It's ridiculous they wouldn't let me leave without an escort."

"Do you hear yourself? They got you drugged up, man."

"They could've just put me in a cab."

"Well, your cab is here." I punched my chest, then sat back in the blue plastic chair against the edge of his curtained section. "Though you're gonna owe me a dinner. I was grubbin' with Chastity and her parents."

"Yeah, that's what you said. What's up with that? I mean, I knew you were all into her, since you haven't had time to hit the links with me. But dinner with the folks?"

"Yeah. It was deep." Then I paused, realizing I hadn't talked to Bryce. "Wait, you don't even know. Guess who's Chastity's father."

Bryce frowned as if that was a dumb question. "How the hell would I know? I don't even know her."

"Kareem. Jeffries."

He started out with a tilt of his head, then his eyes narrowed before they widened. "KJ? The basketball player–turned-preacher?"

"The only one."

Bryce released a long whistle. "Man"—he shook his head—"that's what's up."

I held up my hands. "I didn't know who she was, or rather, who her father was, until last week. My being into her has nothing to do with him."

"So you went to church with them?"

"Church, dinner, the whole nine."

"X-Man, she's got your nose wide open if you went to church . . . with her and her parents."

There had never been a time when a guy said those words—nose wide open—when I hadn't pushed back. But this time, I said, "Yeah, I'm telling you, Bryce, she's the one." When he shook his head, I said, "What?"

"Do you know how many times I've heard you say that? You've been in love with more women than all the ladies in the Divine Nine."

"Well, this time is different."

"You've said that before."

"I really mean it this time."

"You keep giving me the same lines."

I shook my head. "I don't know what else to tell you; it's the truth."

He gave me a long look, then switched lanes. "So how was it hanging with her folks?"

I shrugged. "It was cool. Her moms is real sweet. But KJ . . . dude was all in my grill, interrogating me like he wanted to make sure I was good enough for his daughter, even though he's the one with all of those scandals. Remember that big blowup about him and that rapper, actress, or whatever she was?"

"Yeah, bruh. And Chastity's mom stayed with him after that?"

"Yeah, I don't know their story, but the Jeffrieses today are solid. So whatever went down, that man and woman worked it out."

"Good for them." He shook his head as if he couldn't believe what I'd told him. "So you were hanging with KJ. Man, that's something."

"Yeah, he wasn't feeling me."

"Just because he was asking you questions?"

I paused and wondered where KJ would have gone if Bryce hadn't called. "He wanted to know a lot about my past."

He paused, then gave me a nod. "What did you tell him?"

"I told him I didn't know my father and my mother died, but that was it. Didn't mention Gran, didn't tell him what happened to me when I came to New York, didn't say none of that, 'cause I'm good now." I paused. "And I have you and your dad to thank for that."

Bryce shrugged. "That was a dozen years ago. We're fam now. And I don't think you should be worried about KJ. That's just what dads do. You got time to grow on him." I nodded, but my frown made Bryce ask, "What? Is there more?"

I wanted to talk to Bryce about this, but I knew this conversation could go left quick. Maybe, though, since Chastity was KJ's daughter, Bryce might see this differently. So I said, "I really want Chastity's parents to like me 'cause I'm thinking I'm ready to make this move. I'm ready to ask Chastity to marry me."

His incredulity was all over him: in his expression, in his body language, and then in his tone when he said, "How long have you known her?"

His question made that moment flash in my mind. From yesterday. Chastity's face filled with fear. When she'd slipped out of the car before I had a chance to calm down. When she was about to walk away from me forever . . . just like Roxanne . . . and Diane . . . and Mattie . . . and . . .

"Time has nothing to do with it when it's right" was what I said to Bryce, because I couldn't tell him the truth. I didn't want him to know that while I loved Chastity and I thought she loved me, I was afraid she'd see that side of me I tried to keep hidden and her love wouldn't be enough.

But with a ring on her finger—*From this day forward, for better or worse*—those vows would make her stay. I finished telling Bryce, "I just know when it's right, and she's right."

My words must've moved him, because he said, "Okay, I'll give you that."

I breathed with relief. Finally, Bryce got it, and I was grateful. I wanted him by my side when Chastity became my wife.

But then he had to add, "But if she really is the one, why make the move now? What difference will it make if you give it six months or a year?"

Another flash: when I'd held her in my arms outside of the car . . . and she'd trembled, so afraid.

I squeezed the bridge of my nose. "There's no time to wait."

"No time?" He sounded as if he were confused. "What are you talking about? What's the rush?"

I couldn't believe I'd slipped like that. "I mean, there's no need. Not when I'm ready and I think she is, too."

Bryce shook his head. "You're making a big mistake," he said, sounding as if he was now clear of all drugs.

Sitting up straight, I said, "So that's your response when I tell you I'm about to make the biggest decision of my life?"

"You've made this decision before."

"So what?" I said, feeling the beginning of that heat. "Can't you just be happy for me because I finally got it right? Can't you just say congratulations and then roll with me?"

"Yeah, I could do that," he said, his tone so nonchalant. "And if we hadn't been down this road before and if . . ." He stopped there.

"Why you going silent now? Just say what you have to say."

He shrugged. "Okay. If Roxanne hadn't called me."

I stiffened.

"She told me why you broke up, or rather, why she left you." He didn't have to add that final part; he only did it to make a point.

Looking straight into his eyes, I said, "Whatever she told you, that's her story, not mine."

"Are you saying you didn't threaten her?"

My glance didn't stray. "Is that what she told you?" When he only raised his eyebrows, I finished, "I told you we had an argument."

"You left out the part about being so angry that you punched a hole in the wall." His cheeks filled with air, and then he released a long breath. "X-Man, you know I got you, fam, but you've got some things you have to work out; you've got some issues."

Issues—the same word Chastity's father used. A microwave had turned on inside me. "Out of respect for our friendship, we should end this conversation now."

He shook his head. "See, this is what true fam does," he said, flicking his finger between the two of us. "True fam forces you to tell the truth even when you're a liar."

My fingers curled into fists, and Bryce glanced down at my hands, the glaze now completely gone from his eyes.

"You calling me a liar?" I asked, through clenched teeth, battling to keep the fire inside at bay. I didn't give him any time to answer. "You don't know me. You don't know anything about me."

"Keep telling yourself *that* lie. You know I know you. I've had to check you too many times. And that's what I'm doing now, checking you so you don't make this mistake. I'm not saying don't marry Chastity. I'm saying slow your roll. Give the two of you a chance, and if she's the one, she'll be there."

A flash again. Of yesterday. Chastity sliding out of the car. But this time, I imagined how I would feel if when I got to her side, she was gone, leaving a trail of dust in her wake.

"And if for some reason, she's not there in six months," Bryce continued, bringing me back from what I feared most, "then you'll both be better off. You hear me?"

I glared at him. "Well, you need to hear this." His eyebrows rose in question. I said, "Find your own way home."

"What?"

"You heard me. I'm out."

Spinning around, I stomped out of the space, almost knocking down a nurse as I sped by. "Excuse me," I mumbled, though I didn't stop to make sure I'd caused her no harm.

By the time I hit the front of the hospital, the heat had permeated through every cell of my body. I searched for a release. A place where I could free all that burned inside of me. But the building was brick, and the parked cars had exteriors that were just as tough.

I wasn't trying to hurt myself, but I had to hurt something, somebody.

I trotted across Lenox Avenue, and once I got to the other side, I picked up my pace, jogging then sprinting before it turned into an all-out bolt. I ran so fast that people jumped off the sidewalk to get out of the way of the madman in a brown suit, pounding the pavement in a pair of five-hundred-dollar shoes.

A few people began to run behind me, in front of me—as if they sensed danger and wanted to get out of the way.

I ran down 135th Street, crossing Frederick Douglass Boulevard, even though the light was red. I dodged cars, causing a couple to screech to a stop, but I didn't look back, not even as I heard the drivers' shouts. I ran and ran until my chest screamed, and even then, I didn't slow down. I didn't stop until I reached St. Nicholas Avenue.

At the corner, I rested my hands on my knees. My heart hammered so hard that it was no longer a muscle meant to give me life. If it didn't stop pounding so hard, death was sure to come.

But then, maybe that was what should happen. Because without Chastity, it would be like when I lost my mother . . . There would be nothing left for me.

19

Xavier

The phone rang once, then: "Hello, this is Bryce Hamilton. Sorry I'm not available . . ."

Even though I wanted to slam my cell down because I could tell he was sending my calls to voice mail, I needed to give Bryce this pass. So I took a couple of breaths, did what I could to settle my blood pressure, and listened to the rest of Bryce's message, which I'd heard so often since I'd been calling Bryce to apologize.

"Yo, Bryce, it's X again. Listen, I'm sorry. I don't know how many times you want me to say that, but I'm sorry, bruh. I shouldn't have left you at the hospital, but it was the way you came at me . . ." I paused. "Wait, no excuses. What I did was foul, and again, I apologize . . ." That word hung in the air for a moment. "So hit me up. Let me buy you a beer. Because no matter what, we're fam." My voice was softer when I said, "And you're the only fam I got."

A few silent seconds went by before I hung up, though I didn't move from behind my desk. It was true. Bryce was my family, the only person who'd been a constant in my life since I'd arrived in New York. But while I was thankful for him and his dad, he had to understand that Chastity was the one I was supposed to build my life with.

Reaching into my jacket, I eased out the velvet box I'd been carrying around for weeks. When I flipped open the cover, a pinpoint of light burst through the center of the double halo of diamonds and flashed like lightning through my office's dim light.

The Tiffany attendant had answered all of my questions about this diamond ring—the color, the clarity, and the cut—convincing me this was worth my forty-thousand-dollar investment. Roxanne had been worth that investment, too.

With a sigh, I swung around my chair and faced the window. Bryce needed to answer his phone so I could tell him I'd listened to him. That was quite a feat since there were few whose opinions ever mattered.

But Bryce . . . he was my man, and so there were times when he got to me. Like that day at the hospital. I hadn't wanted to hear it, but a few hours after I'd run down 135th Street, a suited madman on the verge of having a heart attack right on the streets of Harlem, I'd calmed and cooled the heat and been able to give thought to Bryce's words.

Bryce had spoken the truth. Chastity did love me in the way that I needed. I wasn't going to lose her; this I knew for sure now . . .

Eleven days before:

This felt like home. We were hanging out in my condo, but with Chastity resting her head in my lap, reading documents on her iPad, while I did the same, this felt like what home was meant to be.

As if my thoughts had reached her, she glanced up and smiled. "What are you thinking?"

I shrugged. "Nothing much." And then I set aside my iPad. "We haven't talked about yesterday. About your parents . . . and me."

She paused, but I was not concerned. As an attorney, I'd learned to only ask questions where I already knew the answers. But still, I wanted to hear Chastity's thoughts.

Her hesitation was part of her answer. "Well, my mother really liked you."

I nodded and checked that off in my mind. "I really liked her, too." Then, "But your dad?"

Now, she set her iPad aside. "It wasn't that he didn't like you, it's that he doesn't know you—but he will," she added with so much hope in her voice. "I promise he will come to feel about you the way I do." She pressed her lips against mine before she laid her head on my shoulder. "His first concern is your salvation. He's concerned about everyone's."

I wondered what her father had said about that. "My mother was the same way. She had a close relationship with God and tried to pass that to me. The only time I went to church was with her."

She twisted so she could face me. "You'd never told me your mom had died, Xavier. I'm so . . ."

Before she could apologize again for situations that had nothing to do with her, I touched her lips. "Yes, her death was bad . . . but her life . . ." I smiled. "I wish you could have known her."

Chastity tucked her legs under her butt. "Tell me about your mother."

My heart always ached, always smiled with her memory. "I don't remember a lot, but what I do, it was all about love. She was the only person who ever loved me. Once she left, that love was gone, and I've never felt it again."

Chastity kissed my forehead.

"She had big dreams, told me how she was going to work hard

so she could give me everything. That's why she moved from Sumner to Natchez, so that she could work."

"And she left you with your grandmother?"

I nodded. "And then . . ." I closed my eyes before I said, "she died." I paused, wondering if I had enough in me to tell Chastity the whole story. When she rested her head on my shoulder, I found some of the words. "I missed her, I missed her promises, and after she died, I missed the hope that my life would get better. Most of all, I missed her love."

Chastity snuggled closer.

"You have no idea how . . ." The words caught in my throat, lodged behind the lump that had suddenly grown there.

Chastity sat up, and with both hands, she palmed my cheeks. Staring into my eyes, she said, "I. Love. You. I love you. Never doubt that. I'm not going anywhere."

A tear trickled down her cheek, and then with gentle lips, she kissed away my tears that I didn't even know were there. That was why Chastity cried; she was crying with me. She kissed me until I felt it—all the love I'd been missing.

I SIGHED. CHASTITY'S love let me breathe; she wasn't going anywhere. So I could have patience. But still, I couldn't wait to get this ring on her finger. Roxanne had loved it, and . . . I blinked, stopping that thought.

It was hard not to think of Roxanne when I looked at this diamond since she'd been the one to pick it out. Not for the first time I wondered if I should sell it and purchase a new one—something that would belong to Chastity only, just like the memories and the life we were creating.

But like I'd done every time that thought came to mind, I shook it away. I'd purchased the best for Roxanne, and Chastity deserved the same, even better. It didn't make sense to change out this ring. It wasn't like she'd ever find out this had belonged to another woman.

The tap on my door made me slip the ring back into place, tuck it inside my jacket, and then say, "Come in." In the split second between my greeting and the door opening, I wondered why my assistant, Felecia, was still here; I'd thought everyone, except for a couple of the partners, had been gone more than three hours before, when the clock struck five.

My eyes widened with surprise when Chastity peeked around the door. Her face glowed, it seemed. Or maybe it was just the halo that I saw whenever I looked at her.

I jumped from the chair. "What're you doing here?"

She sauntered in, wearing an olive-green pantsuit—the color, the style, a nod to autumn, I supposed.

"I wanted to make sure my man was okay," she began, "and to finally check out where you work. I figured both of those were good excuses because I haven't seen you since last Friday."

"Believe me, I know." I pulled her into my arms. "An entire week." Our lips met, but we didn't linger. "I've missed you. But alas, your work has kept you away."

"Oh, no." She pointed at me. "I've been busy, but which one of us worked even this past Sunday and couldn't make it to church, much to my mother's chagrin, I might add?"

I gave her a sheepish smile, and once again thanked the heavens my career was a good excuse. It wasn't a defense I'd be able to use forever, but it would get me out of a few Sundays.

"And tonight," Chastity continued, "which one of us is sitting in our office after eight on a Friday? And which one of us brought the other dinner?" She raised a small green shopping bag.

"Nah! Don't tell me." I grinned as I took the bag from her hand. "Is this . . ."

"Grilled cheese, your favorite. But no fries, just fruit."

"That's good enough for me," I said, leading her to the chairs in front of my desk.

But just as Chastity began to lower herself, she moved toward the window with an unobstructed view of One World Trade Center. "I haven't been downtown since this was totally rebuilt."

I eased behind her and nuzzled against her neck, finding such sweet solace in the warmth of her. She tilted her head, giving me more access, before she swiveled and circled her arms around me. We held each other, both of our eyes on the view of lower Manhattan.

After a few moments, she said, "From one end to the other. Living uptown and working downtown. Your life—the best of Manhattan." She sighed. "It doesn't get better than this."

"Well, it might," I said. "If I was sharing both ends of Manhattan with you."

My declaration made her turn, made her press in, and we kissed as if time were all we had. For a moment, I wondered if there was anything that would ever make us part. Then the knock on my door made us hop back and away from each other.

This time, it was a shock of white hair that peered around the door.

"Mr. Steyer!" I said, moving closer to my boss. "Come in."

Jackson Steyer entered, dragging his feet a bit, the way he always did. But then he stopped. "Oh, I'm sorry." He peered over his gold wire-framed glasses as if he wanted to be sure of what he was seeing. "I didn't realize you were with a client."

"Oh, no, Mr. Steyer," I said. Long ago, he'd asked me to call him Jackson, but I couldn't do that. At least my grandmother had passed something positive to me.

Taking her hand, I said, "This is my girlfriend, Chastity." Turning to her, I said, "This is Jackson Steyer."

"Oh, Mr. Steyer," Chastity exclaimed. "It's so nice to meet you."

His thick snow-colored eyebrows rose high. "Girlfriend." He paused as if he needed a moment to digest that word in relation to me. "Well, Chastity, the pleasure is mine." As he reached to take her hand, Mr. Steyer turned to me. "Where have you been hiding this beauty?"

I chuckled and shook my head. "I haven't been hiding her at all."

The eighty-one-year-old Jackson Steyer always spoke the first words that came to his mind, understanding little about today's work environment and the interactions between men and women, which had changed since he'd opened this firm in 1965. He didn't handle cases anymore, though he still roamed the halls, and he remained active on the board of the now-250+-attorney firm. His key role was he continued to be an active player in the selection of partners with Steyer and Smith.

"Well, I'm glad he hasn't been hiding you," Mr. Steyer said to Chastity. "Because you're beautiful, young lady."

"Thank you."

"Are you a model?"

Inside, I groaned. Really? He saw a tall, beautiful black woman and that was the first thought he had?

"Uh, no," she said. Then, glancing at me, she added, "I'm . . . an attorney as well."

Mr. Steyer reared back a bit. "Really? I thought I knew all of my attorneys. How could I have missed you?"

"Oh, no," she said quickly. "Not here. I work at the Divorce Concierge."

He frowned. "Why?"

She looked at me with wide eyes, though her lips were pressed together as if she was trying hard to hold back a laugh.

Rescuing her, I said, "They offered her a fantastic position over there, Mr. Steyer."

He frowned. "Well, she should be here." Then he turned to Chastity and repeated the same to her.

That gave her room to laugh, and her cheer filled the office, making Mr. Steyer laugh, too.

Chastity said, "I'm going to get out of here and let you gentlemen handle your business. It was nice to meet you, Mr. Steyer."

"You'll be hearing from me," he said. "The reason we are one of the top firms in the country is because we have the best attorneys, and I can tell you're one of the best."

"You can tell all of that just by looking at me?" Her tone was filled with amusement.

"Yes, I can, young lady. I didn't get here by not using this." He tapped his temple. "You're a good one."

She nodded then, turned her bright smile to me. "Maybe we'll be able to get together this weekend?" There was hope in her question. "Maybe a couple of hours for church?"

I nodded, even though, while I did have a couple of hours to spend with her, I didn't plan to waste those hours in church. "Yeah," I said. "I'll make sure of it." I gave her a quick peck because I knew she'd never make that move in front of Mr. Steyer. Then both of us watched her saunter from the office.

I had to clear my throat a bit when I turned back to my boss.

"She is quite a woman," he said as if his three-minute assessment had been enough.

"Thank you."

"So, she's your girlfriend?"

"Yes, sir."

"Is she a good attorney?"

"I think she's the best." I chuckled.

He nodded. "Where did she go to school?"

"Dartmouth undergrad, Columbia Law."

He rocked back, impressed, and then he asked more questions about how long she'd been at the Divorce Concierge, and with her educational credentials, why was she at that tabloid firm?

"She's really happy there."

He pointed his finger at me. "She'd make a good partner." He paused. "You know when we choose partners for this firm, we look at the complete picture. Not only where someone went to school but who are they now. And I know in today's times it may not be considered right by all the politically correct folks out there, but don't let anyone fool you—we look at spouses and family structure, too." He nodded. "Good choice, young man," he said, walking away from me. When he got to the door, he paused. "How's the case coming along?"

"Fine, Mr. Steyer," I said, though my mind was still on the words he'd just spoken. "We'll be going to arbitration in a few weeks. We're in great shape."

"I know we are—because of you." He nodded, then left me alone.

For a couple of minutes after he left, I didn't move. It wasn't a secret; everyone in this firm knew I was here to become a partner at Steyer and Smith. Had Mr. Steyer just given me a clue?

Crossing my office, I rushed to my desk and pulled out the updated firm's profile, which was produced for new recruits but given to all of us. Scanning through the four-color brochure, I skimmed over the bios of the dozens of partners. The pictures were almost all the same: white men, dark hair, blond hair. One black man, five women, though not a black woman in sight. But my focus was on the text, and after a few minutes, I saw it. Yeah, there was a pattern. Not all, but most—more than half—of the partners were married. Was that what I'd been missing? Was a wife the final credential that I needed?

I slipped the ring from my jacket once again. Jackson Steyer had given me the sign that I'd been right all along.

20

Chastity

My eyes fluttered open, and after a moment, I realized I hadn't moved all night. At least, that was how it seemed, because I was in the same position, with my head resting on Xavier's chest, exactly the way I'd been when I'd closed my eyes. And he was still on his back, his arms wrapped around me, as if he had never let me go.

The thought of that made me snuggle deeper into his embrace, and his arms tightened. I smiled; even in his sleep, he held me as if he would always protect me.

It amazed me that I was thinking about Xavier in terms of *always*. But it was hard not to see into the future, hard to think there would be a time when all of this between us would come to an end. Being with him was always so wonderful. Just like last night . . .

Eight hours before:

My first shoe was off the moment I crossed the threshold of the apartment. Once I closed the door, I dropped my tote bag right there, kicked off my other shoe, and began a striptease that left a trail of clothes through the hall, into the living room, and straight to the master bed-room. By the time I stood in front of the jacuzzi tub, I was naked and ready for a relaxing soak.

This would be the first Friday since Xavier and I had met when we wouldn't be together. But that cliché about all good things ending was cool in this case—I needed this time, because the next few weeks were going to be epic with the face-to-face negotiations working out Tasha Rose's divorce.

Within ten minutes of coming home, every part of me from my lips down was soaking in a bath filled with ylang-ylang oil and lavender salts. My own Quiet Storm playlist filled the air, and I closed my eyes, falling into the music.

At your best, you are love . . .

You're a positive motivating force within my life . . .

The song made me push deeper into the warmth of the water. Maybe I'd fallen so hard and so fast for Xavier because he was my motivating force. Or maybe I was his. I settled inside those thoughts as I sang along with new lyrics, dozens of songs, until the water became too chill. Now my plan was to do nothing more than to set up a plate of cheese and crackers, along with a couple of glasses of wine.

Just as I had the food and wine arranged, my landline rang. There was only one reason I had that line—that was my connection to the building's concierge.

"Ms. Jeffries," the gentleman said when I answered. "You have a delivery."

"That's fine," I said, wondering why he was calling when all packages were held for us. "I'll pick it up in the morning."

"It's not a package," he said. "A gentleman has a delivery for you from a Mr. Xavier King."

What had Xavier done? Flowers? A box of chocolate? "Okay," *I said, hoping I didn't sound as giddy as I felt. "Send him up." I wrapped my bathrobe tighter as I made my way to the front door. When I opened the door before the delivery person even rang the bell, I was surprised to find a young black man in a black suit, holding an envelope instead of flowers.*

"Ms. Jeffries." He handed me the envelope.

My smile was mixed with a bit of a frown as I slid out the handwritten note:

I know you're winding down, but after seeing you earlier, I didn't want this Friday to end without being with you. Fridays are our days. So if you get here in the next thirty minutes, you'll beat the midnight hour . . . Love, X.

There wasn't a Cheshire cat in the world who had anything on me when I glanced up at the young man. "I'll meet you downstairs in ten minutes."

The man hadn't even finished nodding before I closed the door in his face. I'd apologize once I got downstairs, but right now, I had to get ready for my midnight rendezvous. In less than ten minutes, I was in the back of a town car, dressed in a pair of jeans, a tank top, and a navy blazer. And by the time the clock ticked to midnight, my lips—and really, every part of my anatomy—were pressed against Xavier King.

THE MEMORY OF the hours that followed made me sigh. But then I rolled away, although I didn't get far. Xavier grabbed my waist and pulled me into a hug.

"Where are you going?" His voice was filled with sleep and lust.

"Nowhere," I said. "I was just . . ."

He rested his chin on my shoulder. "You're feeling guilty?"

My answer: I rolled over, faced him, and kissed his nose.

His response: "You are."

"I'm sorry," I said. "I don't want you to ever think I don't love being with you. And I'll get over it. I always do."

"But guilt is not what I want you to feel when you're with me."

"And it's not guilt, not really. I can't explain it."

"I can," he said, pushing himself up. He rubbed his eyes before he leaned against the headboard. "You were raised a certain way; you believe a certain thing." With his fingertips, he traced the side of my face. "I get it."

My shoulders relaxed. "Thank you for never making me feel ridiculous," I said, grateful I had a man who held no judgment.

"But what are we going to do about this?"

It didn't sound as if he was serious, so I said, "Well, we can be celibate forever," and then I chuckled, expecting Xavier to join me in the joke.

But even though he said, "That's an option," he didn't crack a smile. He added, "Or . . ." He rolled to his left and reached into the nightstand drawer. Even when he pulled out a velvet box, I didn't get it. Even when he turned and faced me, I didn't get it. But when he flipped that box open, my mouth did the same.

"Chastity, there haven't been a lot of good things to come into my life," he began.

I wanted to look at him, but my eyes were stuck on the box, or rather, on the diamond that glittered inside.

He continued, "But I must've done something amazing for you to happen to me. I never dreamed I could be with a woman who would laugh with me, cry with me, a woman who lets me be me."

I pressed my hand against my chest, trying to figure out what was happening, but it was hard to think with this jewel glimmering in my face.

Xavier said, "I loved you from the moment I saw you. And

what I know now is I want to spend the rest of my life trying to make you as happy as you've made me."

"Xavier" was all I could get out.

He kept on, "You've given me peace, you've given me hope, but most of all you've given me love. So can we continue this journey? Together? Can you take this walk with me as my wife?"

His words were so beautiful, even more so than the diamond that tried to blind me. But his words, this ring—what was he doing?

My hesitation made him ask, "What's wrong?"

"Nothing. It's just . . . this seems so fast." Moving my eyes from the ring, I said, "Xavier, we've only known each other two months."

"But I've had so much bad in my life I know when I've found my good thing. So yeah, this may be fast for someone who is looking in, but from where we stand, this is right."

My first response was: *No, this feels wrong*, but I didn't say that. I said nothing, and the silence continued for seconds and seconds and seconds.

It continued for so long that Xavier pressed his lips together, slammed the box shut, and said, "Forget it. I don't know what I was thinking." He stood and shook his head. "I don't know why I thought this could happen for me."

My eyes widened as he paced the length of his king-size bed and the volume of his voice rose. "This is how it's always been, how it will always be," he said, sounding more hurt than angry.

Then he stopped, and, with a grunt, he pitched the velvet box across the room, sending it crashing against the window, making the glass (and me) shake.

"Oh my God. Xavier, what are you doing?" I screamed.

He glared at me before he slumped onto the bed as if exhaustion had taken over. He held his head in his hands. "I don't

know why I thought this was going to be different when everything is always the same."

It took me a moment to catch my breath, and then I scooted
to his side. Pushing myself off the bed, I knelt in front of him.
The cool air made goose bumps rise on my skin, but I ignored
my nakedness. My focus was on this broken man.

"Xavier," I whispered. I tried to take his hand, but his fingers
were like glue against his head. Still, I pried one finger at a time
until he lowered both hands. Again, I whispered his name, but it
wasn't until I used my fingertips to raise his chin that he looked
at me. "Why did you . . ."

"I just give up," he moaned.

"Give up what?" I whispered.

"Trying to be happy."

"What are you talking about?" I asked. "We were discussing
this, and then you went off."

He shifted his glance away, so I sat next to him, though I
didn't let his hand go. We stayed side by side, and it occurred to
me that without anything covering us, we were most vulnerable.
Maybe in this moment, this was how we needed to be.

I held on to him, though I stared at the box, which rested at
the window's base.

He finally said, "I'm sorry." When he tried to pull away, I
held on tighter. He sighed. "I shouldn't have . . ."

"No, you shouldn't have." I paused. "But I understand," I
added, giving him the compassion he'd given me.

He tried to smile, but his lips wouldn't curve upward. It
wouldn't have mattered even if he were able to force it . . . his
eyes were glazed with sadness.

"Can we talk about this, please?"

His eyes narrowed as if he was unsure, as if he couldn't trust
what I would say. But then he gave me a half nod.

When I faced him, his eyes lowered. He'd just noticed my nakedness, but again, I used my fingers to lift his chin and guide his eyes to mine. "I love you, Xavier. I love you," I repeated because I now knew this man couldn't hear those words enough. "But I was shocked. You never mentioned wanting to marry me."

"I have. Maybe not in those exact words, but almost right away I saw my future with you."

How could I fault him? Hadn't I awakened with thoughts of 'always' on my mind?

"Okay, maybe I'm dense," I said, hoping that bit of self-deprecation would ease the tension. It worked; he smiled. I continued, "This is a big deal and I want to talk about it."

"What else can I say besides I love you and I want to spend the rest of my life with you?"

"And you know what? I want that, too," I admitted to Xavier and myself. "I'm just afraid . . ."

His smile was hopeful, though his tone was not. "Of what?"

"We haven't given ourselves enough time."

He took both of my hands into his. "But what does time have to do with anything? Our hearts aren't on a timer; love doesn't come with a clock." He paused. "All you have to do is ask yourself if you love me, and if the answer is yes, then . . ."

His words sounded so right, so why was I concerned? This was only an engagement. We could take a year, maybe two, to get to know each other. This would just show our commitment of wanting to take our relationship to the next level.

"So . . ." He stood.

As he moved toward the window, my mind churned with each of his steps. Inside, I screamed as he lifted, then opened the box, the diamond still shining.

This time, he knelt on one knee. "Chastity Jeffries, will you make me the happiest man on this earth and become my wife?"

Happiest. This man had experienced so little happiness. I stared at the ring, then shifted my eyes and my smile to him. When I nodded, he grinned and slipped the ring onto my finger, so slowly, so focused, as if he was committing this moment to memory. Xavier King was a man who was only going to do this once.

His eyes were glassy when he whispered, "I love you, Chastity." He pulled me into his arms, and I felt his words. But more than that, I felt his relief. As if now he had a place where he belonged.

That made me smile, and I drew him closer. This had to be how my mother felt, her reward for being faithful to the man God had chosen for her.

And then—my eyes widened. My mother. My father!

Oh my God. Xavier should have talked to them first, especially my father. As I held my fiancé, I remembered my father's words. Not the ones he'd spoken; the unspoken ones were more powerful—how he'd never come to love Xavier.

Since he'd said that a few weeks ago, I'd been hoping I'd misread my father. But even if I had then, what we'd just done was going to make everything worse.

21

Chastity

Pushing the heavy burgundy drapes aside, I peeked outside. The October sun made a valiant effort, but the fall night was descending. Glancing down, there was no way I'd be able to see Melanie from the twentieth floor. But looking out the window gave me something to do—besides staring at my ring.

I raised my hand and once again, I was hypnotized by the diamond's rainbow hues that danced in the fading light of dusk. I did what I'd been doing in the forty or so hours since Xavier had placed this ring on my finger—I smiled. And then I did what always followed—I sighed.

Moving back to the kitchen, I checked the two bottles of wine, then returned to the living room and fluffed the pillows on the sofa. When that was done, I tucked my hands inside my jeans, stood in the middle of the living room and slowly spun in a 360, in search of something new to do. Finally, I clicked on the television, then turned it right off before I sank into the sofa.

This was what I was trying to avoid—being still. Because every time I stopped working, stopped moving, I started thinking and remembering and filling myself with anxiety all over again . . .

Two days before:

We fell back onto the bed as if we were performing a synchronized dance, both of us panting from our passion.

"Wow," Xavier breathed after several moments. "If this is what being engaged does, I cannot wait for us to get married."

When he pushed up and smiled down at me, I did the same, but my smile wasn't from that deep place inside. Inside, I felt nothing but uncertainty.

Then Xavier said, "I love you, Chastity," and my angst faded away. He pulled me to him so that I rested on his chest. "You have made me happier than I ever thought I'd be. I am truly the happiest man on earth. You are what I've been searching for my entire life."

My stomach fluttered a bit at his words—what he'd been searching for and not whom. His words felt odd to me—he'd been searching for a thing and not me? Was I just helping him to fill in a blank in his life?

As quickly as those questions came, I pushed them aside. Ridiculous! Not only did I know what he meant, I knew he loved me. I felt it.

He said, "We need to celebrate."

"Okay." I began scrolling through this week's calendar in my head. "I think Tuesday evening works, and then maybe Thursday, but first, I'd want to check and—"

"No," he interrupted me. "I want a real celebration. Something spectacular. A story we'll be able to tell our kids and our grandkids."

What was he thinking? An engagement party? He was going to have to slow his roll. An engagement party would be something only

Sisley Jeffries could plan. The thought of my mother, the thought of my father, made all of my anxiety rush back.

Then Xavier said, "Let's go away," and just like that, my attention was back on him.

"On a trip?" Before he could answer, I shook my head. "We won't be able to do that for a while. I just got to the firm and . . ."

He waved his hand. "I'm not talking about a long trip; we're too busy for that. But I can get away for a long weekend, next weekend. Columbus Day."

"Are you thinking about driving back to Bear Mountain?"

"No, that's not sexy enough." He paused. "What about Las Vegas . . . no, what about New Orleans? Have you ever been there?"

"I took a couple of quick trips with friends when I was in Atlanta. I can't say it's my favorite place."

"Well, you've never been there with me. So let's go to New Orleans next weekend."

After a moment, I said, "Okay," thinking being together for three days could be the first step for us to really get to know each other without the hustle of our lives going on around us.

He hopped out of bed and began pacing again, his energy much different than it'd been an hour before. This time, the air was electric with his excitement, and I tucked a pillow beneath my chin, grinning as I watched him. He said, "I'll make the arrangements; you won't have to do anything."

"Really?" I said, falling into his joy. "I won't even have to pack?"

He jumped back onto the bed, making the mattress rock, and I squealed when he pulled me into his arms. "I will pack for you," he said. "No, forget about packing, I'll just buy you everything when we get there. Just come as you are."

I pushed away from him a little and took in our nakedness. "Just as I am?"

He grinned. "Baby, I love you especially the way you are now."
He held my face in his hands. "I want to give you everything, Chas-
tity. But even if I gave you this whole world, it wouldn't be enough."
This time when we kissed, I felt a little better, a little more
secure about the ring on my finger . . .

THE DOORBELL MADE my eyes pop open. I scooted to the edge of the sofa, but before I stood, I slipped the diamond from my finger and tucked it inside my jeans pocket. Then I exhaled. It was showtime.

"I REALLY LOVE what you've done with my place," Melanie said as she emerged from the second bedroom, which I'd set up as a library.

"Well," I began, "technically it's not your place if I'm paying rent."

"Good point." She chuckled before she flopped down onto the sofa. From the counter that separated the living room from the kitchen area in the open floor plan, I watched her, wondering if I should make my announcement now or wait until she was walking out the door.

"I'm really happy you called me for a girls' night, but you know Kelvin was feeling some kind of way. Except for the party, he hasn't seen you since you got back."

I filled both glasses with wine, but still I didn't make a move.

She continued, "And he wants to meet your new man."

"This is definitely not like when we were in school," I said, ignoring the *new man* part. "We just don't have the time."

"Yeah, making money and making moves can be all-encompassing."

"Exactly."

"Which is why I was surprised you wanted to get together on a Monday night. It only worked because my schedule was light today." Melanie's eyes were on the television she'd turned on.

As she flipped through the channels, I slid the ring onto my finger. Then I picked up our glasses and sauntered toward her as if I were not about to share the biggest announcement of my life.

Melanie's glass was in my left hand, and when I handed it to her, I held on to the stem a bit longer so she had no choice but to look down. It worked; Melanie's eyes got stuck right on that diamond.

At first she frowned, then she tilted her head as if she were trying to get a better look at what she was seeing. When her eyes widened, I pulled my hand away.

First she squealed, then she slammed the glass down on the table, making some of her wine spill over. She snatched my hand so fast and hard, I let out a yelp.

"Please tell me this gorgeous specimen of a diamond is nothing more than costume jewelry you're testing for some amazing Halloween costume or something as absurd."

Tugging my hand away, I took a sip of my wine and walked around the table. Her eyes followed me the entire time, and when I sat, she just stared.

"Chaz?" Before I said anything, she asked, "Are you . . . engaged?" as if that was a word she'd never associate with me.

"Yes; this is why I wanted to talk."

She covered half of her face with her hands. "Oh my God."

"You're the first person I'm telling." The warning that she wasn't to say anything to anyone was in my tone. "I haven't even told my parents."

"Oh my God."

"I didn't go to church yesterday . . . and don't you dare say 'oh my God' again."

"Oh my . . . gospel!"

I rolled my eyes. "If I'd known this would be your response . . ."

"Forgive me if I'm a little shocked." She grabbed my hand, studied the ring, and then said, "Oh my . . ." but instead of finishing, she gulped down her glass of wine.

"Really?" I said when she held her empty glass in front of my face. Still, I took her glass and took my time going into the kitchen. I hoped to give her a minute to process what I'd told her so we could get beyond her calls to the Lord.

When I returned to the living room, she drank about half the glass before she sighed, then leaned back on the couch. "Okay, tell me everything. Tell me how a guy you've known for two weeks—"

"It's been longer than that."

"Okay, take my two and multiply by four. How can you be engaged to someone you've known for five minutes?" She held up her finger, stopping my oncoming protest. "And not only that but a couple of days ago, you told me you didn't love this guy."

"That was more than a couple of days ago, and I meant what I said then. But right after that, our relationship kind of went to the next level."

Her eyes narrowed. "Uh-huh." She pointed at me. "This is why God doesn't want you sleeping with a man outside of marriage, because you get caught up and end up engaged in five days."

"Uh . . . you slept with Kelvin the first night you met him."

"Why you gotta bring up old stuff? I was stressed from

school, and this isn't about me." She took a deep breath. "I really do want to know how this happened. Is this what you want?"

"It is," I said without any hesitation. "Xavier and I kept getting closer and closer, and when he told me he loved me, I hadn't even been thinking that."

"Okay, that's a good sign," Melanie said. "Men are supposed to say it first," she stated as if that were a fact. My best friend had always been into the rules and regulations of relationships— things she'd learned from unmarried experts on television.

"Then, once he said it to me, I realized I loved him, too. I probably loved him when you asked me, but I was caught up in the amount of time we'd known each other. I didn't think it was possible."

"It's just so fast, Chaz."

"But what is the right amount of time to fall in love? A day, a week, a year? The heart doesn't have a clock," I said, repeating Xavier's words.

She held up her finger. "That's a good line."

"It's not meant to be a line. There are people who meet and are married after a week, even less."

"But those people aren't you, and that's what concerns me. You haven't been out there much. You haven't given yourself enough time."

"You weren't out there. Kelvin is your only serious relationship, and maybe something inside of me knew I was never supposed to waste emotions on anyone else. Maybe all of this was saved up for the man I'm supposed to be with." I twisted on the sofa so that I faced Melanie. "He's an amazing guy." And then I went into my Xavier pitch. When I told her his mother died and the horrid stories of his grandmother, Melanie sat with her mouth wide open.

"Why was that woman so evil?"

I shook my head, not wanting to lie but not wanting to reveal what Xavier had told me about his father, something that he shared with so few. "But this is what I know—Xavier King deserves happiness. After all he's been through, this is the first time he's allowed himself to fall in love."

She gave me a side-eye. "Really? At thirtysomething he's never been in love?"

"Why does that seem odd to you? I've never been in love, and just like me, Xavier has been afraid to open up. From the bottom of my heart, I think we met because we were meant to be."

This time Melanie sipped her pinot grigio. "Maybe this is just a love story." She shrugged. "So, has he at least met your parents?"

My voice was lower when I said, "Yeah, but it didn't go well. We went to church, and then the usual dinner afterward. Papa tried to interrogate him, but Xavier had to leave for an emergency." I shook my head, remembering my dad's unspoken words again. "My mom loves him, though."

"Of course. From what I remember, your man is quite easy on the eyes. That's a good beginning for your mom. But what about your dad? What did he see?" She paused. "Wait, am I going to need more wine?"

Melanie knew about my father's gift. We'd experienced his ability when we were kids. Like when he told us to stay away from places we'd only talked about going or he questioned us about places we'd been but had told no one. My father knew things beyond ordinary parental discernment.

I said, "He didn't say much. Just told me to pray for guidance."

"Well, at least they've met him. Now when are you going to tell them?"

I sighed. "That part." I shook my head. "I wanted to test this out on you, and you didn't build my confidence. My parents are going to freak because we haven't known each other long."

"Just tell them that hearts can't tell time," she said, the sarcasm thick in her tone. When I gave her a blank stare, she laughed, then apologized. "Look, you know Kareem Jeffries is not going for that line. So you better be ready, but then, once you tell them, just stand your ground. You're grown."

Those two words made me swallow the rest of my wine and then refill my own glass. "I think I'll wait until Xavier and I get back," I said when I returned to the living room. "We're going to New Orleans for Columbus Day to celebrate, and this way, we can spend a little time together."

"That's cool. So you have between today and when you leave to tell your parents."

"Did you not hear what I said about waiting till I get back?"

She leaned away from me. "Why are you afraid to tell them?" Before I could answer, she said, "Maybe that's a sign. Because if you don't want your parents to know . . ."

"It's not that I don't want them to know. I just know how they're going to react."

"Well, the amount of time you've known each other is not going to change, unless you don't plan on telling them for the next year. But you know your father. If you don't tell him, God will."

Her words made me take another swig.

"Come on, Chaz. You can marry who you want to marry and when you want to do it. Stop making it a big deal."

I nodded, knowing every word she spoke was true.

"So you're going to tell them?"

I nodded again, knowing that gesture was probably a lie. Not a total lie. I would tell my parents. I'd have to . . . eventually.

22

Xavier

etween completing the last deposition and then standing for the first media conference about the civil rights case, this had been the longest day. But at least the depositions were over, I'd patiently answered questions for the press and now the base of the work was done. This case was the final professional check mark I needed to become a partner. I was excited but not as thrilled as I was for what was ahead of me this weekend.

Only two more days to New Orleans, and I had a long to-do list. I'd made the connection with Will Allen, an old college friend who I'd contacted the last time I was going to do this, but he reminded me that not only was I trying to make this happen on a weekend, it was a holiday weekend at that.

The weekend timing wasn't something I'd considered, and it changed so much. Still, it looked like I'd be able to make this happen, even though it was going to cost me a lot.

My plan had been to leave the office as early as I could tonight, head home, and finalize these plans, but because of the message left on my cell phone last night, I was now sitting on

Forty-Seventh Street near Park Avenue, stuck in traffic that made a snail's pace look like a sprint.

"You know what?" I said to the driver. "I'm gonna get out."

"We just have another block to go."

"I'm cool." I thanked him before I hopped out, secured my bag onto my shoulder, then jogged across the wide avenue, even though the light was against me. Traffic wasn't moving uptown, downtown, or across town, so pedestrians had free rein.

Across Park Avenue, I swung open one of the heavy doors of Sweat Box, then scanned my membership card at the front desk. It had been more than a couple of weeks since I'd walked the carpeted floors of this gym.

Inside, I trotted down the stairs to the locker room, changed into sweat shorts and a tank, and then headed toward the space where about a dozen boxing rings were set up. Through the glass doors, I scanned the area filled with men (and a couple of women) and spotted him. As I stepped inside, the sound of boxing gloves making contact filled the air. Grunts and shouts and cheers followed. I passed three rings before I made my way to where Bryce stood, gloves on his hands, his arms crossed as he watched the match in the ring above him. His eyes were narrowed as if he was studying every move.

I eased up, stood next to him, mirrored his pose, and watched the battle in the ring for a few moments before I said, "What's up?"

It still took a couple of beats before my best friend faced me. His expression was solemn, his eyes dark. But then he grinned. And even with his hands hidden by boxing gloves, we embraced in one of those brother-brother greetings, hugging each other tightly, the way fam does.

"Good to see you," I said, meaning every word. Then I made

a great show of looking around the gym. "Strange place to get together."

"Nah, bruh, not strange at all." He unlaced his gloves. "I figured if anything went down like the last time, we could work it out here."

I chuckled, and he did the same as he hung up the gloves. He gestured with a nod, and I followed him to the corner of the massive space where folks waited for their turn.

When we sat on one of the benches, Bryce said, "I'm glad to see you, bruh. I wasn't even sure you were going to show up."

"You call, I come running."

His quick sideways glance made me remember that the last time he'd called, I'd left him behind.

He said, "You stopped calling."

"I called you for weeks."

"So?" he said as if my explanation was insulting. "Calling me every day was your penance. But then you stopped."

"Yeah" was all I said, leaving out the part that I hadn't called since Chastity agreed to marry me. But I added, "I figured you never wanted to speak to me again."

"That was a good figure." He let those words register. "But I missed talking to your big head."

He cracked up, and though I chuckled, I went on to say, "I'm really sorry, Bryce. I shouldn't have left you stranded in the hospital like that."

He leaned forward, resting his arms on his legs. His eyes were back on the boxing rings. "Apology accepted, but your leaving me wasn't the biggest challenge. I caught a ride home, but you getting as angry as you did over us just talking . . ." He shook his head. "That's a problem that can't be solved easily."

My whole body stiffened, except for my leg, which began to shake—my effort to cool down the rising heat.

If Bryce noticed any change in me, it was of no concern to him. Because he continued, "I know you don't want to hear this, but having these tough talks is what fam is supposed to do."

"I'm cool," I said, though I wasn't sure if I said that so Bryce would feel fine to continue or if I was saying that to douse my fire.

"That's why I wanted to see you: to have this tough talk," Bryce said. "You have some deep issues anyone walking this earth would understand. But now, bruh, we have to do something about all of this rage inside of you. Especially because it seems to be escalating."

I wanted to remind him that I'd only walked out because he'd been badgering me. But I was trying to hold it down and quiet my fury.

"I'm concerned; we have to do something before it's too late." He paused as if he wanted me to say something, but I pressed my lips together. Didn't want any words to explode out. So he kept on: "I made some calls, checked out the references, and found someone, a therapist, for you to talk to."

Now I studied the boxers in the ring closest to us, and when one landed a punch, I felt relief as if I'd delivered the blow myself. As I watched the guy drop to the rubber mat, I nodded.

"So you agree?" Bryce asked. "You'll talk to someone?"

"I agree that having someone to talk to may have been the missing link. But that was before Chastity," I said. "I've been talking to her a lot."

There was silence as both of us stared ahead, watching men punch one another out. Bryce said, "I thought Chastity was an attorney."

"She is, but she's helped me open up in ways I never have. Not with you, not even with Roxanne, and she *was* a therapist." Then I added, "But I've really opened up to Chastity, especially after what you said last time," hoping acknowledging his part would make him back off.

For a couple of seconds, all Bryce did was nod slowly. "Talking to her can be a good thing." There was so much caution in his tone. "But I'm talking about a professional."

"Well, she's helped." I paused, then began my lie: "But even if she's not trained, her father is."

Bryce moved in slow motion, raising up and sitting straight. His eyebrows were up high when he turned to me. "You've been talking to KJ?"

"He's not KJ anymore," I reminded my friend. "He's a pastor with counseling skills."

"And you guys talked?" Bryce said, sounding hopeful.

"Yeah, from the first time I met him," I said, leaving out that I'd only met him once. "Remember I told you he asked a lot of questions? Well, I think that was to set the foundation. We've talked about how what I'd been through as a child would affect me as an adult." I shrugged. "It's been good to open up to him."

"I bet." Bryce nodded. "That's cool. So is that gonna continue?"

"Definitely," I said, trying to keep my tone casual. "He and I will be around each other for a long time." I paused, uncertain about what to say next. "I know you think it's too much, too fast, but Chastity is the one."

"I'm not saying she's not, but that 'fast' part—that's where I don't want you to repeat the past. You're moving like you're on some kind of speedway, and I haven't even met her. How you know I'm gonna approve?"

I released a slow breath. He was backing up, thank God. But the part about meeting Chastity . . . I wasn't going to make the mistake of letting Bryce and Chastity get close. Been there with Roxanne, where she felt comfortable enough to reach out to him and tell Bryce about our little incident. Wasn't gonna repeat that. "Well, half of the time Chastity and I've been together, you haven't answered my calls." Keeping my tone light, I said, "But you were right. I don't have to rush because Chastity loves me; she's not going anywhere."

He leaned back. "You're sure about that, now?"

"Yeah. We're committed, and we'll have a future . . . just not tomorrow."

He nodded. "Well, I'm glad you're talking to KJ—I mean, Pastor Jeffries. I guess you won't need the therapist I was going to recommend, but that's good. As long as you're getting real help, that's my only concern. 'Cause all I want for you is the best, fam." He pounded his chest. "We always look out for each other." Then he said, "So, you wanna get out of here?"

I glanced down at my workout clothes. "I thought we were gonna go a few rounds."

"When was the last time you worked out, X-Man?" Before I answered, he said, "I don't want to hurt you."

I held up my hands. "You gotta give me a break—I've been busy."

He grinned. "Yeah, I caught you today at the presser talking about your case. You're doing it over there at that law firm, aren't you?"

"I'm just doing what I do. Putting everything in place to take it to the next level."

"Sounds like a reason to celebrate." He tapped my shoulder. "Let's head over to Sluggers and grab a beer."

Again, I thought about all that was on my plate for New Orleans. But I wasn't ready to break our connection.

"Okay, I have time for one," I said as we made our way back to the locker room. "But it can't be a late night. I have to prepare for a deposition tomorrow," I lied.

"Don't tell me you're working over this holiday weekend," Bryce said.

"Nah." I stopped. As much as I wanted to, there was no way I could share my plans with Bryce. He'd talked me out of this before—when I was setting it up for Roxanne.

"Well, maybe the four of us can get together. You haven't hung out with me and Samantha in a while."

For a moment, I imagined what it would be like if Bryce could see what I saw. If he would listen to me, maybe he and his girl would even join us in New Orleans. But until I could trust his support, I wouldn't bring him into that part of my world.

We were still brothers, though, and we chatted as we changed into our suits, then, with our bags slung over our arms, we walked out of the gym shoulder to shoulder.

23

Chastity

For the last three days, I'd been trying to make Melanie's words come true. I'd tried to figure out how to speak to my parents, but there was no scenario I could work out in my mind where this would work out for me. Maybe if my parents had been more receptive to Xavier the first time, maybe if they'd met him more than one time, maybe if my dad had the opportunity to talk to him for more time—then I'd be able to run to my parents with this news.

But there wasn't anything I could say that would bring my parents around, not even my mother. Yeah, she liked Xavier, but she'd need more than an hour with him before she'd embrace the idea of me marrying him.

Which is why I was sitting here with panic squeezing my gut but a smile on my face as my mother stepped inside this Starbucks. She'd told me last night that an early cup of coffee was the only time she had today. So I'd invited her to Midtown, just blocks from my office.

She slipped off her oversize designer sunglasses, scanned the on-the-way-to-work crowd, then weaved her way past the line and through the dozen tables to where I sat in the back.

As she approached, I stood and once again wondered if I had enough courage to tell her about the ring tucked inside my purse.

"Sweetheart." She air-kissed my cheeks, then slid into the chair across from me. "Do you know how happy I was to get that call from you last night? Even if it's just for a few minutes." She beamed, and I relaxed.

"I ordered your coffee, and here's an unbuttered croissant." I pushed the two toward her.

"Thank you, sweetheart," she purred. But then, in the same sweet tone and signature drawl, she said, "Did you invite me to coffee because you're feeling guilty?"

My heart became a weapon that was about to hammer me to death. "Guilty?" I croaked, licking lips that had suddenly dried.

Her eyes bored into mine. "Is there something you want to tell me?"

She knew! My mother knew. But how? Had God started speaking to her, too?

"Chastity?"

"Mom . . . I . . ." I stopped and looked around at the young men and women, mostly in suits, all on their phones, each oblivious to me dying in the back of this coffee shop.

"Sweetheart, why are you stuttering?"

"Because . . . I . . ."

She reached across the table and covered my hand with hers. "Truly, it's not that serious," she whispered. "You only missed one weekend."

I blinked, bringing her and her words into focus.

"Of course, I love having you join me on Saturdays," she continued, "and you know how your father feels about Sundays, but as you're so fond of telling us, you're grown."

She was talking about missing the stretching class . . . and church? I exhaled a thousand breaths, and she released my hand.

"We know that you have a beau," she started, sounding like fifty years needed to be added to the fifty-five she'd already lived, "and we're going to see you less, though your father and I want the chance to get to know Xavier." She held up her hand. "And before you say it's not serious, we know that, but still, we want to be a part of what's going on in your life."

And just like that, all the relief I had for those ten seconds dissipated.

She finished taking my breath away with "Let's make sure we get together this weekend. With it being a holiday, we can do our regular thing on Sunday and then maybe something special on Monday."

Shaking my head, I spoke my first words. "Not this weekend. We're going away."

"Who's going away?"

I didn't have the guts to tell my mother I was engaged to a man I'd only known for a little longer than fifty days, but I was grown enough to tell her about my trip.

"Xavier and I," I continued, even though her elevated eyebrow almost stopped me. "We've been so busy, and we don't know when we'll have the time to do this again, so we're going to New Orleans for a little fun and to get to know each other."

"Wow." Her surprise made her drawl more pronounced. "You've known him for such a short time. Do you think going away with him is a good idea?"

"I think it's a great idea." I inhaled, then exhaled the truth: "I really like him, Mom. A lot."

"Oh," she said. Her stare bored deeper into me. "Oooh," she said again, this time, making the word sound as if it had seven syllables.

I knew what that meant; she was asking if Xavier and I had been intimate. My mom wasn't a prude; we'd had deep conversations about intimacy, especially about things she'd had to explain to a child about her father's infidelity.

Now, though, was a good time to help her understand what was going on with me and Xavier. Since I was going to have to show her this ring in a week or so, I needed to set the foundation. "I really, really like him" was all the preparation for that talk that I had in me now.

Her stare made me shift from one side of the seat to the other until the edges of her lips twitched into a bright smile. "I'm really happy, Chastity," my mother said. "I'm glad you're finally letting someone in."

I nodded.

"He seems like a nice guy who's been through a lot."

"That's one of the things I love about him." My mom raised her eyebrow again at my slip, but I just continued, "He never gave up, even though he had so many reasons to just give in. He's a warrior."

"And he's quite impressive. Your father and I caught his press conference yesterday."

That made me smile because I'd watched it, too. Except for seeing him on TV and a couple of FaceTime calls, I hadn't seen Xavier all week as both of us worked to clean off our desks before Friday.

"He's on his way to being one of the most well-known attorneys in the city," I said, feeling so proud. "Maybe even the state. He has such big goals. Politics one day."

"Oh, that's something. Maybe both of us will be First Ladies." She chuckled but then waved her hand. "Just kidding. I know you're a long way from talking marriage." Her pause gave me just enough time to groan inside. "But seriously, Chastity, one day, you will meet a man you'll want to marry. And our prayer is that he'll love the Lord first. Because if he truly loves and honors God, he will love and honor you." She held up her hand before I could even think of all the reasons why that didn't sound right coming from her. "I know you're thinking of your father, but here's something you may not understand. Even in his sin, your father knew and loved God. Even in his sin, your father and I were equally yoked because of purpose, and even in his sin, your father knew that, too. That's why he and I are here today.

"So, sweetheart, all I'm saying is that I want the same for you. Not the trials, of course. I want you to live a drama-free life," she said with a shake of her head. "But on those days when that's not possible, I want you to be able to stand on God's word and know that He will get you through because you are with a man who is your purpose. And you will be his purpose, too."

I nodded, then gave my mother a test. "Well, suppose that man is Xavier?" Before she could answer, I continued, "I know his relationship with God isn't strong right now, but his foundation is there. Circumstances pulled him away, but God is in his heart." I paused. "He can come back to the Lord, just like Papa."

She nodded. "Maybe Xavier is the one. The good thing is you have time to discover whether that's true. And if he is, then you'll find your purpose together."

"I believe we will."

Again, her raised eyebrow revealed her surprise. "Well, if you do, I will be there to support you . . . and your father will, too." When I smirked, my mother said, "Pastor wants you to be happy . . . with the right man."

Once again, I thought about all that my father hadn't said, all that I'd surmised. I asked, "Do you think Papa could ever accept it—if Xavier is that man?"

Without a moment's hesitation, she said, "Of course. Truly,

your father has nothing against Xavier. But here's the thing . . . even if he did, even if your father didn't like him . . . if Xavier is the man God has chosen, then your father would be the first one to step up and not only accept him but love him. We both would have no choice. Because God has the final say." She laid her hand on top of mine. "Don't be concerned. Whether it's Xavier or another man, your father and I are looking forward to the day when you tell us this is the man God has chosen for you." When she paused and swallowed, I could tell emotions were rising inside of her. "Chastity, I have prayed for this. You lived through so much of the bad, I want only the best for you now. Xavier has to be special if God chose him to usher you into this time of your life."

Even from across the table, I felt my mom's emotions, felt her love. The foundation had been set; she would accept our engagement. Now I was ready, but I wanted to tell my parents together, with Xavier by my side. We would do that as soon as we returned.

Standing, I took my mother's hand, then hunched down so I could hug her tight. "Thank you for this talk. Thank you for always being there for me."

"And I always will be, sweetheart. You can always count on that."

24

Xavier

Once again, I'd nailed it. Just a little over twelve hours in New Orleans and everything had gone the way I wanted. I'd made this entire trip first-class: seats 1A and 1B on our flight, then, last night, a little before seven, we'd checked into our Ritz-Carlton suite. But I didn't give Chastity time to swoon over the accommodations. We'd dropped our bags then hit the streets, because this was New Orleans on a holiday weekend.

First up were the reservations I'd made for dinner at August, where Chastity feasted on red shrimp salad and blackened tuna, while I opted for the crispy oysters (which I made sure I shared with my lady) and the duckling with grits. Then we strolled through the ebullience of Bourbon Street. Even in October, this place was lit, as people partied like it was New Year's Eve.

Finally, we'd burned off our calories making slow, wonderful love beneath the moonlight that shone through the hotel's windows. All I wanted was for this weekend to be the best for Chastity, one she'd always remember.

That was my thought as I stood at the bathroom's threshold, clad only in the towel tucked at my waist. I leaned against the doorjamb, watching Chastity as she scooped forkfuls of the grillades and grits I'd ordered before I'd hopped into the shower.

"So you couldn't wait for me?"

She glanced up and grinned like a kid caught in the act. "I'm sorry. But you have to taste this." She filled a fork with the beef and grits and offered it to me.

As I strolled toward her, my towel slid away, but even as it dropped, I kept moving. Her glance froze.

"So," I said, my voice suddenly sounding thick, "you like it?"

Her eyes hadn't left what she'd said was the best part of me second to my brain. "I love it," she whispered.

With a chuckle, I stepped back, grabbed the towel, and wrapped myself inside. "We can't do this right now," I told her, even as she pouted. "We need sustenance so that we can do it again"—I leaned over and kissed her—"and again"—another kiss—"and again."

She sighed when I pulled away, then I slipped into the bed next to her. "Well, if we're not going to do that," she said, "then taste this."

As she aimed the fork toward me, I licked my lips and once again froze her stare. For a woman who always felt guilty afterward, sex stayed on her mind.

I grabbed one of the croissants.

She asked, "So, what do you have planned for today?"

I stiffened, mostly from anxiety, but then, as quickly, I relaxed. All of this was going to work just fine. Picking up the remote, I clicked onto the hotel's channel. "Let's see what's going on in the city."

She frowned before she rested her head on my shoulder. "You want me to believe you're looking at television for your ideas?" She chuckled. "Okay, I'll go with it, but I know you,

Xavier King. Not only do you have everything planned, you have big plans."

As she snuggled closer, I was amazed, because she had no idea how true her words were. I pretended I was engrossed in the show's anchor's discussion about all that could be done in New Orleans, but my thoughts wandered to the checklist in my mind and everything I'd set up from thirteen hundred miles away.

I was paying good money for all of it and hadn't received confirmation for the most important part until three days ago, when I'd left Bryce at Sluggers and answered the call on my way home.

"Everything's set, but like I said, the weekend made it tough," Will told me. "My brother will do it, but it's gonna cost."

"I don't care what it costs," I said.

"Roxanne must be a special lady." He chuckled. "I remember when you were going to do this last year. I thought you two had broken up, but I'm glad you're cool. So here's the deal: my brother will do it for five thousand."

I was shocked that he'd mentioned Roxanne's name, surprised that he'd even remembered it. So the first thing I needed to do was correct him, tell him this was Chastity. But the five thousand changed my focus. "I'd said I didn't care, but I hadn't expected it to be that much."

"My brother's taking a lot of chances. Chances cost."

With a sigh and a nod, I said, "Just let me know how he wants to be paid."

"Cash is king, my man."

"Done."

"That's what I'm talking 'bout. Oh, there's just one thing. Like I told you, we need a photo ID: driver's license or passport. But the

202 VICTORIA CHRISTOPHER MURRAY

bad news: He won't do it without your birth certificates. You have to bring those."

"What?" I froze, then said, "Okay, just up the price. How much to get it done without our birth certificates?"

"There is no price. I already asked, but my brother is not willing to go that far risking his license. So if you come without a birth certificate, there's no way it can be done."

I hung up without even saying good-bye, feeling like my plan had just crashed, burned, and now was nothing but ashes. What could I tell Chastity to get her to bring her birth certificate?

I was committed to making this happen, and by the time I got home, I had a new idea. When I called Will back, he told me he would see what he could do. It wasn't until a couple of hours before Chastity and I boarded the plane yesterday that I received the call—it was a go.

"He just wants to make sure you understand this won't be valid."

I'D TOLD HIM I understood, and though this wasn't the way I wanted it, this was the best it could be. I just hoped that not only would this work but if Chastity ever found out, she'd love me enough to understand. Once we left New Orleans, I'd make it right.

Chastity pulled away and looked up at me. "Did you hear what I said?"

I blinked a couple of times to bring her into focus. "What?"

"Where did you go? I've been asking which of these things we are going to do."

"I'm sorry. I didn't hear you."

She twisted to face me. "Okay, what's up? Because if I'm lying next to you and you can't hear me, then something's wrong. Please don't tell me you're getting husband ears."

"What?"

She laughed, having no idea how her words made my heart pound. "Husband ears. That's what my mother calls it. It would be boyfriend ears for you, but you're acting like my father. My mother can be sitting right next to him and he won't hear a thing she says. So is this what I have to look forward to?"

Her question cracked her up, but all I did was stare. She was talking about me being her husband. This had to be a sign.

I held her face in my hands. "I love you, Chastity Jeffries."

"That I know for sure," she said with an assurance I hoped she'd feel forever. "And I love you, too."

"I'm so grateful you came into my life."

My shaky voice removed all of the laughter from hers, and she kissed me, pushing me back and down onto the bed.

I gave Chastity all of my pain, and I released my pleasure. As I lay there trying to hold on to this feeling for every second, I knew there would never be a woman I loved more than Chastity Jeffries.

I PANTED. MY relief was in my release. Chastity sighed as she curled beneath me and I wrapped my arms around her. This was how I wanted eternity to be.

But then she rolled away, and although she said nothing, I knew her thoughts. And her thoughts made this the moment.

Looking down at her, I said, "I have a solution." She tilted her head in question. But my next words were the most important I'd ever speak. "Let's get married."

She laughed as she raised her finger. "Let me introduce you to this beautiful ring that my fiancé gave me." She twisted her hand so that the diamond faced me. "Dude, you already asked me, and I said yes." She raised up, gave me a quick kiss, then added, "And I'd say yes and yes and yes again."

My heart was pounding, my adrenaline pumping. "No, I mean let's get married now. While we're here in New Orleans."

She laughed again, but then her chuckles faded as she kept her eyes on me. I didn't falter.

"Xavier."

"I'm not kidding," I said. Standing, I moved to the closet, grabbed the other bathrobe, then turned back to her.

Sitting on the side of the bed, I took her hands into mine. "Let's just get married. Why wait?"

"I can think of more than a couple of reasons, but two of them live in New York. We haven't even told my parents we're engaged."

"So instead of telling them we're getting married, we'll tell them we already are."

She shook her head so hard, I hoped I wouldn't have to take her to the ER for whiplash. "I can't do that."

"Why not?"

"Because . . ." She paused, searching for reasons. "My parents would want to be part of this. They'd want to plan the wedding and the reception, not to mention my father would certainly want to perform the ceremony."

I needed to leave this city with Chastity believing we were married. If not, I'd lose her, of that I was sure. Maybe not this week, maybe not this month, but definitely sometime this year. Women always left sometime around a year.

They left because we weren't married.

I squeezed her hand. "If we had a wedding, there would be no one there for me except Bryce. I don't have anyone, Chastity, so why would I want to wait for an event that has nothing to do with me? I want to be someplace where it's just the two of us," I said, and in those words I heard an echo. Almost like my mother's voice on top of mine. *Just the two of us.*

"But, Xavier—"

"I don't want to lose you, Chastity."

She snatched her hands away from mine, startling me. But before I could assign negativity to her action, she wrapped her arms around me. "You are not going to lose me. I promise," she whispered over and over. Her breath was hot on my skin, sending sensations I had to fight to ignore. When she pulled back, she cupped my face in her hands. "Why don't you believe me?"

I broke away from her hold and turned away. Staring straight ahead, I said, "You don't understand."

She swung her legs over the side of the bed and then pulled me to her. "Tell me," she whispered. "Tell me what I'm missing."

As my head rested on her chest, I closed my eyes, and in my mind I held her hand, taking Chastity back with me. To the year when it all changed. To the year that was the reason why I had to do this now . . .

February 14, 1999

I didn't have to stand on the chair anymore to reach the top of my closet. Just rising up on my toes, I felt around the shelf and found the brown box I'd made five years before in wood shop. It was a special project, a gift for Mother's Day. I'd carved two hearts in the top of my box, and the words JUST THE TWO OF US. *Even after all of this time, I still hoped for the day when I'd be able to give this to my mother.*

Once I had the box steadied, I cracked open my bedroom door.

"Yeah, Virginia. That pastor was creepin' and . . ."

Easing the door shut, I returned to my bed. There were no

*surprises inside the box, but I did this every year on my birthday.
I sifted through the box's contents—eight years of cards filled with
notes and money. This was my annual ritual: counting, even though
I knew exactly how much I had. To this point: five hundred and
fifty dollars. It felt like a million dollars to me, and I wondered how
much my mother would send me this year. She'd sent me seventy-five
dollars every year, except last year, for my thirteenth birthday, she'd
sent me a one-hundred-dollar bill. I'd never seen one of those. That
made me even more excited about this year. Was there such a thing as
a two-hundred-dollar bill?*

*But the excitement I felt couldn't make up for the sadness
I held. I would return all this money to my mama if she'd just
come back and get me. In the beginning, that's how she'd signed
every card:* I love you so much, X-baby. I promise, I'm
coming back for you. We're gonna be a family. Just the
two of us.

Then last year, she only signed: Love you so much,
X-baby. *I'd stared at those words, refusing to believe that the
absence of her promise meant she wasn't coming back. That thought
hadn't been new; I'd been wondering if I'd see my mom again ever
since Aunt Virginia told me about her and Bobby Washington. Ever
since she'd said Gran wouldn't let my mama return.*

*My hope was that this year, Mama's promise would be back in
my birthday card. When I heard my grandmother's slippers dragging
on the hallway floor, I slid the box under my bed. Her footsteps faded
toward the front, and I grabbed my book, a Richard Wright novel,
from the table, lay back, and opened to the place where I'd left off. But
it was hard to concentrate because I expected Gran to call out at any
moment, letting me know I had mail.*

*After about ten minutes, though, her footsteps returned to her
bedroom. That was weird. Getting the mail was the last thing she did
every night. She didn't let me touch it; she told me I had no business*

in her business. So I left the mail alone, since nothing ever came for me—except on this day every year.

Pushing myself up, I made my way to the door, hearing only the faint hum of her TV. Why was Gran keeping my birthday card from me?

It had been about a year since she'd hit me, maybe because I was a lot taller than her now. Even without a switch in her hand, though, she ruled with a fist that was heavier than iron and a heart of steel.

But there was no way I was going to bed without my birthday card. I made my way to her bedroom and tapped on the open door.

With a scowl, she glanced up from where she was sprawled across the purple-flowered bedcover. Then she growled words that sounded a bit like "What you want?"

"Did my mama . . . send me . . . something today?"

Her glare stayed on me, and even though for almost two years I'd known why she treated me the way she did, it didn't make it easier to accept her hatred.

She waved her hand. "Oh, you're talking about your birthday card?"

That was surprising. In all these years, she'd never said happy birthday. Before, I thought it was because she couldn't remember what day I'd been born. After Aunt Virginia, I realized it was that she wanted to forget. She wanted to forget the day, and she wanted to forget me—except I came with money.

I answered, "Yeah, from my mama."

"How your mama gonna send you a card, boy? She's dead."

I stood there, frowning, not understanding. "Ma'am?"

"Your mama died."

My heart stomped all across my chest. "No." She stared at me without giving me other words to help me understand. "My mama died?"

"Didn't I just tell you that?"

I squeezed my eyes shut, wondering if, hoping that I was dreaming. "How . . . What happened to my mama?" My voice trembled.

Gran's eyes narrowed. "Boy, if you don't get out of here with all that foolishness . . . I don't know why you cared about her; she didn't care about you. Nobody cares about you."

It didn't matter to me if her plan was to insult me all night long. She'd spat out a litany of slurs over the years, but she could repeat all of that and make up new words to wound me—I didn't care. I was going to stand here until she explained what had happened to my mama.

"Did you hear what I said, boy?"

"Why didn't you tell me that she'd died? Where is she now? What about her funeral?"

"All you need to know is that your mama died. She left you, never came back for you, and now she's gone. So you just need to get on out of here."

"OH MY GOD, Xavier," Chasity said, and she held me tighter, pressing me against her breast. The way her body trembled, I could tell she was weeping. My eyes blurred like they had that day, but I had no tears. Instead, as Chasity held me, I silently remembered the rest of that night, the part that I could never share with Chasity . . .

Another time, another situation, I would have done what Gran told me to do. I would have walked away. But I stood in her doorway because I couldn't move. It was the fire that stopped me. The flames that seared through my veins. My eyes bulged; my fingers clutched—I felt like I was swelling into the Incredible Hulk.

Gran's eyes widened as she stared, as if she could see it, too, then her glance slid to my hands, my fingers flexing at my sides.

"You got a problem, boy."

I wanted to know. I had to know. *"What happened to my mama?"* I asked, losing all the deference I'd ever had toward this woman.

My tone shook her, because she backed up, though she didn't back down. *"I don't know,"* she said, her disdain now gone. *"I don't know,"* she repeated, her voice more even than it had ever been.

I pressed my lips together, not to hold back all the curses that were within me, but to hold the fire. Because if I opened my mouth, flames would burst out and I'd beat this old woman. I'd beat her until she told me about my mama, and then I'd keep going until she came to the same end.

Her eyes were still on my fingers, but she stayed in her place. She knew. Tonight our world had shifted.

When I finally cooled enough to pivot, I rushed to my bedroom, then slammed the door. But Gran wasn't coming for me; she'd never come for me again. Because I felt it and she could see it. There was a volcano simmering inside of me, and she was smart enough not to be near when I erupted.

I stomped from one end of my bedroom to the other, with those words pacing my steps: My mama is dead. My mama is dead. My mama is dead.

I paced until I exploded and rammed my fist through the wall. As my knuckles broke through the plaster, the wall screamed, but I didn't. Not even when blood spurted from my hand.

For a moment, I expected Gran to come running. But then I remembered . . . tonight, our world shifted. She'd never come for me again.

I grabbed a T-shirt from my drawer, wrapped it around my hand, and sat there thinking . . . My mama is dead . . . My mama is dead . . . My mama is dead.

CHASTITY SQUEEZED ME tighter, and her embrace brought me back. She held me as if she was trying to shield me from all of my past pain. I sat up and wiped dry eyes. "I didn't mean to dump all of that on you."

"Xavier." Her voice was as soft as her touch as her fingertips glided against my cheek. "I'm so sorry. You didn't even know."

It was hard to look at her. I didn't want to see the pity in her eyes that I heard in her voice. "I never had the chance to say good-bye to the only person who ever loved me. That night, I thought I'd never smile again." I turned to Chastity. "But then I found you. That's why I don't want to wait, baby. I can't. I have the chance to bring balance to my life. You're the good that can help me negate all of that bad. With you by my side, I'll be able to do everything. I'll be able to live up to whatever reason I'm here, whatever purpose I have."

She inhaled a sharp breath, and I wondered what I had said. After too many silent seconds, though, I realized my words, my pain, hadn't moved her, and my heart sank to the arches of my soles.

I stood, stumbling a bit, but before I could take too many steps, Chastity jumped up and pulled me back into her arms.

She whispered, "Let's get married."

Those three words were the life raft I needed. I rested my head in the crook of her neck, and right there, I cried, laying all of my burdens down.

25

Chastity

U sing my hands, I wiped the mirror that had been clouded by the shower's steam. The mist was thick; I'd remained under the heat of the water for at least twenty minutes, as if I was trying to cleanse more than my body. I stopped once the circle on the glass was large enough to see my reflection and I stood, staring at myself.

More than an hour had passed, and I still couldn't get it to make sense. "I'm getting married," I whispered, hoping that speaking those words aloud would aid in my comprehension.

I closed my eyes and took one of those cleansing breaths I'd learned from Kourtney's class, clearing my brain so only those words would settle in. Was this what God wanted me to do?

You are with a man who is your purpose. And you will be his purpose, too.

My mother's words echoed in my head.

I'll be able to live up to whatever reason I'm here, whatever purpose I have.

Xavier's words swelled my heart.

When I opened my eyes, my reflection smiled back at me. This was what God wanted for me. So there was no need to hedge. Together, Xavier and I would work it out, even my parents.

Thinking of them made me pause, it would be tough, I'd get them to understand: *Xavier has to be special if God chose him to usher you into this time of your life.*

My mother's words were true. He'd helped me, and I'd helped him. We were each other's purpose.

Taking a deep breath, I tightened my towel before I stepped into the bedroom. I paused as I took in Xavier, already dressed, casual in jeans partnered with a white golf shirt. His cell was pressed to his ear as he paced.

"Okay," Xavier said, not noticing me. "Okay," he repeated as he continued his jaunt.

I sat on the edge of the bed, watching the man who was about to become my husband.

"I got it. The paperwork and the ceremony."

The ceremony.

"You'll text me with a time?" A pause. "Great. Thanks for everything, Will," Xavier said, then when he stopped, he turned and noticed me. "Thank you for making this the best moment of my life."

The words were to whomever was on the phone, but the sentiment was all for me.

"I'll talk to you soon," Xavier said, his eyes still on me.

When he clicked off, a beat of silence passed before I asked, "So we can do this?"

He nodded but then shook his head. "When I asked you to marry me, I was only thinking about wanting you to be my wife. I didn't consider how we could make this happen, on a weekend and on a holiday. But"—he rubbed his head—"whew. We can do this."

"We can?" I hoped Xavier only heard my question and not the doubt that had, once again, began to rise within me.

"Yeah. I have a couple of connections down here. It's actually a friend from undergrad. His brother is a magistrate, so he'll be able to do the paperwork and the ceremony."

"Wow! One-stop shopping, huh?" I said, trying to lighten the burden of the tension that hung heavy between us.

"It'll cost a bit of money, and we'll have to do it today . . ."

"Today?" I asked. The word kinda stuck in my throat. I knew we were doing this, but . . . today . . . was so . . . immediate.

He nodded. "He only does this during the week, but I told him I'd pay him anything if he could do it today."

I nodded. "So"—I inhaled a load of air—"what do we have to do?"

"Well, we have to get a marriage license; we just need photo IDs . . . oh, and . . ." He held up his finger. "If either of us has been divorced, we have to present our divorce decrees, too." He gave me that half smile that moved every part of me.

I laughed, finally feeling free. "Okay, I'll only need my photo ID," I said, moving my neck with each syllable. "So . . . what about you? Have you been married before?"

He grinned, now seeming as relaxed as me. "I've never even gotten close to marriage because there's never been a woman I wanted to spend my life with as much as you." Those words hung in the air as seconds ticked by. Finally, he asked, "So . . . do you want to get dressed and do it?"

"Are you . . . are we sure about this?"

He knelt and took my hands into his. "Baby, I've never been more sure of anything. I love you; I want to marry you. Today."

Then he kissed me, and I knew not only was he telling the truth, I knew this was right.

✦   ✦   ✦

GROWING UP, I didn't believe in fairy tales and princesses and frogs that turned into princes. By the time I was ten, I pretty much believed in happily-never-after.

With that as my backdrop, I had no dreams of bridesmaids and dresses and flowers and wedding cakes. When I imagined my future, all of my joy was in becoming an enormously successful divorce attorney who helped women walk away.

That's why it felt some kind of crazy that I was here in Saks buying this dress alone. I turned to the mirror and studied my image at every angle in the three screens. After I tried on about a half-dozen options, I chose this ivory crepe fitted dress. It was lovely, stunning really, especially with the plunging V neckline, which Xavier would love. I'd honored his request for a long dress with this floor-sweeping skirt. That had been his attempt to bring some tradition to what we were about to do.

"I want you to look the way I've imagined since I began to dream of you as my wife."

My effort at holding on to some semblance of tradition was that we arrive at the magistrate's office separately.

"While I'm out shopping for a dress, you can change, and then when you leave, I'll come back, get dressed, and meet you there. We'll see each other for the first time just a few minutes before we do this."

I thought that plan would bring a whole smile to Xavier's face. But he looked at me sideways. "You're not trying to get out of this, are you?" Before I could answer, he kept on, "I'm not going to be waiting in the magistrate's office and then you never show up and I come back to this hotel, find that you've packed up, left town, and changed your cell phone number, am I?"

The chuckle was rising inside of me, but then stuck in my throat when I realized there wasn't an inkling of humor in his tone. Right away, I knew . . . he still wondered if I'd leave him.

I pulled him into a hug. "I cannot wait to be your wife." The tension drained from him as he held me. When I stepped back, I pressed my hand against his cheek. "All I want to do is look beautiful for you." He nodded. "And you know what?" I added, "I want you to look your best for me, too. Think about these pictures, think about our kids," I told him.

That brought his grin back, and he moved across the room to the desk. He picked up his wallet and turned to me with his platinum card in hand.

"No." I waved his offer away. "I'm good; I have money."

"I know you do. But you're going to be my wife, and so"——he shrugged——"my money is your money."

"You know what?" I snatched the card from him. "You're right. My dress is on you, with our money."

His smile stretched across his face, and I knew my taking that credit card meant as much as my saying yes to all of this.

I was filled with contentment, knowing I was bringing genuine happiness to this man who'd never had enough of it in his life.

"THIS IS ALL going to be perfect," I told myself through the mirror. Gathering the gown, I rushed from the dressing room, to the cashier, then hopped into a cab, even though I was only a half mile away from the hotel. I checked my watch; truly, the next time I wanted to see Xavier was when we were standing before the magistrate. So I texted him because I didn't even want to bump into him in the lobby:

Have you left?

Not even five seconds passed before he responded:

Just jumped into a cab. Where are you?

On my way to become beautiful for you.

You don't have to do anything for that. You are
already amazing and I love you so much.

I read his words again, then pressed the cell phone to my
chest. Now I knew this moment was right; this man had just
texted his truth: he loved me so much.

I sent him: ❤ ❤ ❤ then leaned back. Canal Street was
jammed with the holiday tourists that crammed the city, but I
didn't mind. The extra time gave me a few moments to reflect.

As the minutes passed, I felt more secure in our decision.
Xavier had to be the man God had chosen for me. There were
too many signs. We'd come to New Orleans, and he knew a
magistrate here. Things like this didn't just come together. Not
unless they were meant to be.

When the cab finally slowed to a stop, I smiled as I used
Xavier's credit card to pay the fare, then with one last deep
breath, I slid out. It was time for me to get ready for the rest of
my life.

26

Xavier

The magistrate's office was only five short blocks from our hotel, but even in October, it was still in the low eighties, too much New Orleans heat for this suit and these shoes. Five blocks would've felt like five miles, so I slid into one of the waiting cabs, then sat back.

Was this really going to happen? I shook my head. For the last couple of hours, that question had played in my mind because I'd never come this close. But I needed to stop questioning what was divine. Glancing at my watch, I nodded. It *would* happen, in a little over an hour.

When the driver rolled to a stop at the address on Poydras, I tossed twenty dollars into his hand, more than doubling the fare on the meter. The driver thanked me, but the moment I'd paid him, my mind had already fast-forwarded to my future.

Like Will had told me, the lobby doors were unlocked, and I took the elevators to the fifth floor. When I stepped into the all-white, leather-and-chrome waiting area, I realized this was a suite of offices, all darkened, all empty, it seemed. Before I could call out, Will stepped from the center office.

"Bruh-man." Will strutted toward me, wearing a shiny bronze

suit with a red plaid bow tie. He reached for my hand, then we embraced in one of those brother hugs. "It's been a while."

"Yeah, the last time was at our fifth reunion, right?"

"That was the last time we saw each other, but I'm glad we've stayed in touch." He led me into the office that was opposite the style of the reception area. This was more traditional, with a cherrywood desk and bookshelves to match. Will gestured for me to sit in one of the oversize wingback leather chairs." So, what's going on with you and this marriage thing? Doing this was a surprise to her, but you want her to think it's legit, even though it won't be?"

It did sound convoluted, but I was not going to explain it to Will. He and I had been friends our first year at NYU, but rather quickly, I discovered Will was a twenty-four-seven hustler. Since I was going into law, I took a step back from him, not wanting to get caught up in some present mess that would drag down my future. By the second year, we were more acquaintances than friends.

But over the years, I'd hit him up occasionally on social media, just having a feeling that one day, I might need some of his connections and skills. My hunch was proven right when last year, after doing a little research and finding out that New Orleans was a no-waiting-period city for marriage, I'd reached out to him.

Finally, I said, "I wanted our marriage to be legit, but with this holiday and all . . ." I paused, hating to go into any of this. "We'll get it fixed. Her father is a pastor." This part of the plan hadn't been thought through yet, but I could make it happen. I'd get her father to issue us a new license, maybe convince him and Chastity we should have a license with his name signed to it. I finished telling Will, "I just want us to do something where it's the two of us. We'll go back and have a ceremony and celebration in New York."

"Cool. My brother will be here in a little while; you got the money?"

I nodded. All one-hundred-dollar bills, as Will had requested. He opened the envelope, flipped through the money, and I wondered how much would get into his brother's hands. But that wasn't my problem. I'd paid; now, somebody was going to stand up and marry me and Chastity.

I reached into my jacket. "Here are the rings. I haven't quite figured out what to say about these since this was supposed to be spontaneous and . . ."

"No worries, I got you," he said. "I got a story ready if she asks. So she'll be here at three?"

I nodded. "What about the paperwork?"

"Milton will take care of that. I got you with this hookup, and he's got you with the paperwork. It'll all look official. No worries, just remember when we mail it to you, it won't be signed."

"That's fine; I'll give you my office address, and you can mail it there."

"No worries," he said. I hated when people said that over and over because it meant just the opposite. "Chill here," Will continued. "I got a call to make, but we'll get started right at three. My brother is always on time."

I nodded. Chastity was a stickler for punctuality, too. So at three, my life would begin.

Will stood, but before he stepped out of the office, he paused. "For reasons I'm sure you'll understand, my brother is gonna come in here and do this. He wants no conversation about this, nothing on the record."

I got that. His brother and I operated in the same legal space. His risk was professional—mine was personal.

Once I was left alone, I exhaled, not realizing I'd been half holding my breath. This was happening; Chastity and I were going to be united. Just the two of us.

Those words were like a shot in a time capsule taking me back to a place I hadn't revisited for so many years . . .

February 6, 1995

"Mama, when are you coming home?" It was the same question I'd asked her for four years, though there was more urgency in my tone now. Couldn't she hear that?

"Now, X, didn't I ask you to be my little man for me?"

"I know all that," I said, thinking she still thought of me as a six-year-old kid. "But, Mama, when are you coming to get me?"

"I'm trying so hard, baby." Sadness spilled from her words. "Please believe me when I tell you I love you and I can't wait to see you."

That didn't answer my question. "If you can't wait, then come home." Right then, I had a thought. "Can you at least come for my birthday?" My birthday was in a few days, and if Mama showed up, this time, she wasn't leaving without me, even if I had to stuff myself in the trunk of her car.

"X," she began, now sounding like she was crying, "if I could come there, I would. But I can't."

Why did she keep saying that she couldn't come?

"I'm going to do what I can, X." There was such conviction in her promise. "Because all I want is for it to be just the two of us. A family. Like I've always promised."

THAT WAS MY final memory of my mother's voice.

Just the two of us, I heard her saying over and over.

If there was any truth to heaven and angels, then I was sure my mother was up there finally fulfilling her promise. She was guiding me to having what she'd promised but never been able to deliver.

I glanced at my watch and tried not to fidget. But it was difficult because in less than thirty minutes, my mother's wish for me and the greater desire of my heart would finally come true.

JUST LIKE WILL had cautioned me, his brother Milton walked into the office and shook my hand as if this were an ordinary meeting.

"So, you guys met at NYU?" Milton asked.

I glanced at my watch. It was just about three, and though she wasn't late, I'd expected Chastity to be here by now, as excited as I was. I let Will answer his brother, since I wasn't interested in chatting. I wanted to stand by that door, a lookout for my fiancée. As I took another quick glance at my watch, I wondered why had I agreed to meet Chastity here. We should have walked through these doors together.

As we sat, Will chuckled as he shared a couple of our freshman exploits. I listened, hardly laughing, completely remembering why I'd been so right to distance myself from this dude. But every minute or so, I took another discreet glance at my wrist and watched the minutes tick solidly past three.

A microwave-type heat burned my soles. Chastity wasn't coming, and my mind fast-forwarded to what I'd find back in our suite . . . the hotel's stationery with her writing: *Dear Xavier* . . .

I was ready to burst. And then . . .

A soft knock on the door, followed by an almost whisper: "Hello?"

The door inched open, and I popped out of the chair. But before I could take more than a few steps, I stopped. Chastity entered, and, like she'd done from the first moment we met, she snatched away my ability to perform even the most elemental tasks. It took seconds for my legs to find their life, and then, finally, I rushed to her.

Her smile embraced me, and then her arms followed. "I'm sorry I'm late," she breathed into my ear. "The first Uber canceled, and I was almost ready to walk, but . . ."

I pressed my finger against her lips, careful not to smudge the burgundy gloss she wore. "You're here now." I wanted to kiss her again and again, but wouldn't a kiss before we stood before the magistrate mess up the little pieces of tradition we were trying to hold on to? Still, I pulled her back into my arms, and I held her until:

"What's up?"

I'd forgotten we were not alone.

Will strutted closer to us and held out his hand. "You must be Roxanne. Nice to meet you."

Chastity frowned, and I stiffened, feeling like I'd been struck by lightning.

She spoke first. "No, I'm Chastity." She looked between me and Will.

"Oh!" He held his fist to his mouth like he was about to swallow it. "My bad. Roxanne . . . is . . . the lady . . . we married yesterday."

"Okay," Chastity said, as if she wasn't sure she believed him. "I just hope you have our names right on the marriage license."

"Yeah, yeah, I never make mistakes . . . on that." Then, trying to be smooth with it, he kept on talking, introducing himself as a very good friend of mine from NYU, and she presented herself as *Chastity*, the woman who was about to become my wife.

"And I'm Milton," his brother called from across the room. "So, are we ready to get started?"

For the first time since Will had called my present fiancée by my last fiancée's name, I breathed. How the hell did Will even remember Roxanne's name from last year, and hadn't I, at some point, said Chastity's name?

"Babe?" Chastity whispered. "Shall we do this?"

It was only because she took my hand that I was able to move. We crossed the room and followed Milton to the windowed corner of his office.

As Milton positioned us and then grabbed a book from his desk, Chastity frowned. "Don't we have to do the license?" She looked among the three of us as if she was confused, then added, "I have my ID," as she tapped the small bag hanging on a chain from her shoulder. She smiled. "To prove that I'm Chastity."

Milton glanced at his brother and Will said, "Yeah, uh, we'll take care of that after the ceremony. It doesn't matter if we do this before or after—that license will have the same legal value." He laughed as the three of us stared at him, and I wanted to swing on him. My glare must've burned some sense into him, so he added, "Uh . . . we can take care of all of that afterward."

"Oh, okay," Chastity said, all concern, all questions, gone from her voice.

It was true, I guessed: when you weren't looking, you didn't see. When you trusted, you believed. Only Milton and I understood Will's joke. And Chastity trusted me.

"Let's get this started," Milton said.

With the sun to our backs, we stood, shoulders touching, and when I reached for Chastity's hand, she grasped mine as if I were her lifeline; she certainly was mine.

Milton stood in front of us, and Will was off to one side— our witness, I supposed. The worn brown leather book that

Milton held was not quite as thick as a Bible, but had enough pages to look official. With a nod, he began:

"We are gathered here today, in the sight of God and this witness . . ." He gave a nod to Will.

I inhaled the deepest of breaths, almost wanting to drop to my knees and give gratitude to the heavens for these words I'd been waiting so long to hear.

". . . to unite Xavier and Chastity in the bonds of holy matrimony."

Was it possible to freeze these moments?

"Chastity and Xavier, is it your desire to take these vows which will unite you at this time?"

As if we were already united, in unison we said, "Yes."

Milton said, "Please face each other."

I did as I was told and now held both of Chastity's hands. Warring desires battled within me. I wanted to slow down time so I could savor this. But time had never shown me any compassion, and the more it passed, the greater the chance this would be taken away. So I willed the seconds to move at sonic speed, getting us to the good part, the finale.

When Chastity squeezed my hands, as if she knew I needed reassurance, I settled into this moment for what it was—not too fast, not too slow, the perfect speed, the perfect time for our wedding.

"Do you, Xavier, take Chastity to be your lawfully wedded wife? Fr—"

It felt as if he'd paused, so I said, "I do!"

Milton looked up from the book. He said, "Wait a minute, let me finish," before he chuckled.

Chastity and Will joined in the laugh; there was nothing funny to me.

Milton continued, "From this day forward, to have and to

hold, for better, for worse, for richer and for poorer, in sickness and in health, to love and to cherish, till death do you part?"

This time, I let a beat pass as I repeated the words inside: *Till death do you part.* Then I said, "I do. I do. I do!"

There were more chuckles, but again, no laughter from me.

As Milton read through the same declaration of intent for Chastity, I held my breath, waiting. When she said, "I do," to me, that was the finale. I wanted to lift her in my arms, swing her around, and get started on all that I had planned for us.

But right after she'd agreed to be my wife, Chastity yanked her hands from mine. There was horror etched on her face as she exclaimed, "Stop!" sending my heart into a downward spiral. Once again, lightning had struck. She said, "We don't have rings."

"Oh, yeah, you do," Will said, stepping forward and opening up the matching velvet boxes I'd given to him.

Chastity frowned. "This ceremony comes with rings?" she asked in a tone that questioned what kind of service was this.

"Oh, no," Will said. "I took X to buy these . . . earlier."

Now she turned to me. "You had time to buy rings?"

"Yeah, well, we do this all the time," Will jumped in since this was his story. "It was one stop, and my man saw what he liked. It didn't take us ten minutes to get in and get out," he said.

I didn't want Chastity thinking I'd spent such little time on our rings, when it had taken me two lunch hours last week, combing through every store in the Diamond District, to find the bands we'd wear for the rest of our lives.

But when Chastity said, "Oh, okay," my heart continued to beat.

"Is it all right for us to get back to this?" Milton asked.

"Of course," Chastity said, and once again, I realized this was all about trust. She said, "I'm sorry. That just came to my mind." In a lower voice, she added, "I wish I could've picked out your ring."

"That's okay, baby. I got us matching bands."

Once she nodded, Milton continued. I floated as we exchanged the rings, and I stayed that way until the moment of the pronouncement:

"Xavier and Chastity, you have come here today of your own free will and have declared your love and commitment to each other. You have given and received rings as a symbol of your promises. By the power of your love and commitment to each other and by the power vested in me, I now pronounce you . . ."

I was in a state of suspension until Milton said:

". . . man and wife. You may now seal your vows with a kiss."

I'd been off my feet, and now, as I kissed my wife, I lifted Chastity from hers.

We kissed and kissed until Milton cleared his throat and Will said, "Dang, dawg, get a room."

This time, I joined in the laughter, and as I held Chastity while we thanked Milton and Will, I paused for a moment to glance up to heaven and my body warmed. But this heat was different from what usually filled me. This time, I felt the warmth that came with serenity, the warmth that came with joy, the warmth that came with love.

27

Chastity

As I signed my name to our marriage license, gone were all the concerns that ebbed and flowed inside until the moment I held Xavier's hand in front of the magistrate. It was because of the love—the love I had for Xavier, but what seemed to be boundless was the love he had for me.

It was in his eyes when we faced each other. Love that he'd never offered to anyone before and love that he'd never received. As I held his hands, I knew for sure we were brought together for a time such as this.

"So, do we have to file this someplace, or do you take care of all of that?" I asked Milton.

Will jumped in front of his brother. "We take care of that. And once it's filed we'll get this in the mail to you."

"How long will it be?" I asked.

It was weird the way Will hesitated and glanced at Xavier. But then, when he said, "We have to file this on Tuesday because Monday is a holiday," I understood. Neither Xavier nor I knew how this worked. I could tell anyone everything about *ending* a marriage, but because I'd never expected to be in this place, I'd never been curious enough to check out how a marriage started.

Not that I needed to know now. I was married, and I would only have one husband: this man.

As I turned to my husband, his expression was my mirror—his face was bright with his grin. Holding my hand, he said, "Well, if that's everything . . ." Xavier didn't complete his sentence, but I could tell he was ready to leave this place.

"I wish you two the best," the magistrate said.

"Yeah, you kids get out of here and get to whatever it is folks do on their wedding night."

Will cracked up at his joke, and we accepted that as his good-bye. With a final nod to the two of them, Xavier and I ran to the elevator banks . . . and we giggled.

"We really did this?" Xavier asked, as if he couldn't believe it.

"Yup!" I nodded.

"So you're really Chastity King."

In the midst of this whirlwind, I'd had little time to think about some very basic components to my new life. In this moment, I preferred to be known as Chastity Jeffries King, a homage to my father as his only child. But this wasn't the time to mention that. This was the time to just savor our wedding day.

When the elevator doors parted and we stepped inside, Xavier pulled me to him and held me. That was all he did once the elevator doors closed—just held me like he wanted me, needed me.

As we stepped off the elevator, I asked, "So what are we going to do now?"

Xavier pushed the lobby door open and then pointed.

When I followed his gaze, I pressed my hands against my face as Xavier trotted toward the pearl phantom sedan that waited with opened doors at the curb. A man dressed in a tuxedo stood there, and Xavier shook his hand.

Then the man nodded at me and gestured toward the back

seat. I slipped inside the Bentley, sliding across the softest leather seat my behind had ever touched.

When Xavier joined me, all I could do was shake my head. "I don't even want to know what else you have planned, and I don't want to know how you did all of this in just a few hours."

"It's what I do." He grinned.

He was right about that, and rest of the evening was like a whirlwind, much like our relationship. First Jason, our driver who introduced himself as we pulled away, told me he was there to take me and Xavier anywhere we wanted to go. Our first stop: Restaurant R'evolution. I'd never heard of this restaurant, but the moment I stepped inside and took in the polished mahogany paneled walls with gilded mirrors and crystal chandeliers (the only lighting throughout), I knew this restaurant was one of the best in the city.

After we were seated inside a corner velvet booth and I studied the menu, I saw that my assumption was correct—at least as far as the prices were concerned. Then the dinner we shared: a dish called Death by Gumbo (which *was* to die for) before we ordered caviar, then ricotta gnocchi with lobster as an entree for me, and the rack of lamb for Xavier, proved that I'd been right about this restaurant being five-star.

Xavier and I moaned (and kissed) our way through the deliciousness of the dinner.

"This is our first meal together as husband and wife," Xavier reminded me.

"I can't believe it," I said, though I didn't feel different. Xavier and I chatted easily and kissed passionately through dinner like we always did.

From the restaurant, Jason drove just a few blocks to Toulouse Street, where, right before we boarded a steamship, I clapped. "I've always wanted to do this," I said as I held my dress above my ankles, stepping carefully over the ramp. Once inside the steamboat, I frowned.

"Are we early?" I scanned the empty ship.

"We're right on time," Xavier said. "We have this to ourselves."

My mouth stayed open wide as Xavier led me to the second level, where a spread of desserts—banana foster, bread pudding, and, of course, an assortment of beignets—was laid out for us. We settled in, and as the boat began its jaunt down the Mississippi River, Xavier explained we had this private cruise for only an hour.

Only? A private steamship where we were being serenaded by a New Orleans jazz quartet that kept me bouncing my head and tapping my foot . . . It couldn't get any better.

The hour moved too quickly, and though I didn't want to leave, I exited so satisfied. I couldn't wait to see where Xavier was taking us next. But when, just about ten minutes later, the Bentley stopped in front of our hotel, I smiled. I was ready for us to go home, too.

We thanked Jason and then held hands as we entered the lobby of the Ritz. When we were in our suite, I stepped into Xavier's embrace, and from there our souls connected. It was so natural when we kissed, slowly, gently. It was more than familiar as we undressed each other, eager yet patient because . . . we had forever.

And then, when I lay with my husband for the first time, it felt sacred because we'd been united before God. And for the first time, after I sang to the heavens and rolled away from Xavier, I was more than satisfied. For the first time in my life, I was not in sin.

28

Xavier

Chastity's limbs were the branches, and I was the tree. At least that's what it felt like, with the way her arms and legs were wrapped around me. I inched away, holding my breath. When I got to the edge of the bed, I paused, making sure my wife still slept.

As I traipsed to the chair by the window, goose bumps rose over my skin, even though I wasn't cold. The temperature felt just right. Or maybe it wasn't the temperature. Maybe it was my life that was finally right.

I settled into the chair and then glanced out into the blue black of the night. There wasn't much of the view from our window. Canal Street was certainly no Caribbean island, but still this view would be one I'd remember. Because this was where I found my happiness.

How had I pulled this off? I was just a poor boy from Sumner, Mississippi, the son of a rapist and a mother who loved me but left me. Even though I'd wanted to believe, I'd never been convinced that happiness would find me.

But now I understood. All of the others who'd left had cleared the way for Chastity.

My eyes focused on the sky. I was a little boy the last time I'd prayed, but now I bowed my head, closed my eyes, and said the only words that came to my mind: "Thank you, Lord."

"Xavier?" Chasity called out to me.

"I'm right here, baby."

Chastity pushed herself up, and I swallowed at the sight of the silhouette of her breasts. "Are you okay?"

I cleared my throat. "Yeah, baby." Making my way back to her, I slipped beneath the duvet and pulled her into my arms. "I just had to get up and give praise to God." She pulled away to look at me, and I continued, "I was praying because I know God exists, even as I've been so angry at Him." I pulled her hand to my lips and kissed her fingers. "But what I've come to realize is that God was saving up every good thing for me for right now."

"Xavier," she said, palming my cheek.

I tugged her hand away and held her, only because I didn't want her to think my words were just another line. "I want you to hear me, Chastity." I had to take a few seconds because I was full—there was so much I wanted her to know. "You are my gift from God. And for the rest of my life I will thank Him by honoring you." I had to pause so I could push out the rest past the lump in my throat. "I didn't get to say any of this to you today, never thinking about the fact that we wouldn't really get to say vows. I didn't get to say what was in my heart."

Chastity blinked more than a few times. "There is so much I want to say to you, too. So let's do this: let's recite our vows here, right now." She scooted in front of me and held both of my hands.

As she balanced herself on her knees, in all of her naked glory, I chuckled. This would certainly be one of the most memorable parts of our day.

I rose up and faced her before I took her hands into mine.

She began, "I've let few people into my life and never anyone near my heart." She shook her head. "I was always afraid that life wasn't perfect. I was afraid I'd follow in my mother's footsteps."

I nodded, wanting now to pull her close to me, but I stayed in the moment. Chastity and I had never talked about her parents, though she knew I knew . . . the world knew. KJ lived his sins in public.

"But the thing is," she continued, "I do want to follow in my mother's footsteps." I raised an eyebrow, and she continued, "My mother gave my father grace, and he grew into the man that God wanted him to be. Of course, I don't want their drama"—her chuckle was void of humor—"but I want to be the woman who loves you, who stands by you, who gives you the grace you need to grow into the man God wants you to be. I am so honored you and God chose me to help you step into all that you are meant to be.

"I love you, Xavier King. I loved you yesterday, and, oh my God, I love you today, and the love I will have for you tomorrow and the day after that is growing within me now. I am so happy to be your wife."

The only reason I didn't move was because she held me in place. But I wanted to do something: kiss her, hold her, make love to her . . . again.

When she said, "Your turn," I took a breath and began:

"You are my blessing. Every morning, every night and the moments when I can in between, I will thank God for you. Not a day will pass when you won't know how much I love you. Let's do this, Chastity King. Let's make this one hell of a marriage, one hell of a life."

When she laughed, I joined her, but then we sealed our vows with a kiss . . . and so much more . . . until the sun began to rise.

Then we slept.

29

Chastity

The moment the tires hit the tarmac, I swiped over to my phone's settings, clicked off airplane mode, and right away my cell vibrated. At first I thought it was text messages, but it was an incoming call, and a thumbnail photo of my mother's official First Lady portrait flashed on my screen.

The sight of her made me frown, pause, wonder.

"What's wrong?" Xavier leaned over my shoulder.

"It's my mother." I stared at my cell as if I couldn't decide what to do. "I wonder what she wants."

"I have a bright idea—why don't you answer and see." His tone was filled with levity, as if he hadn't heard what I said. This was my mother. My plan had been that except for a few calls to say hello, I would stay away from my parents for a few weeks. Work was going to be my excuse, as Xavier and I agreed we'd give ourselves time to get settled before we faced the world's judgment.

Well, I guessed this would be my first call. I'd make it short, quick, and over before my mother asked anything. I tapped ACCEPT. "Hey, Mom, is everything okay?"

"Sweetheart, I was calling to check on you. Are you back?"

"Yes," I said, thinking I could have easily added, *My husband and I just landed*. Instead, I said, "Xavier and I are getting off the plane."

"Great. I hope your holiday weekend was better than ours."

"What happened?"

"Nothing happened, but your father . . . Since you've been gone he's been so concerned."

Right away, my heart skipped. What had God told my father? I asked, "Concerned about what?"

I heard my mother's shrug in her sigh. "I don't know. But I'm telling you, this has gone on all weekend. He kept asking if I'd spoken to you, kept wanting to call you. I had to tell him what you always tell us—you're grown. You would be fine. But he's been on edge since you left on Friday, and on Saturday, it was at its peak."

If I were not a colored girl, everyone on this plane would have seen the blood drain from my face. "Well, I'm okay," I told her, as I wondered how much God had revealed. "Can I call you when I get home?"

"Of course," my mother said. "In fact, don't worry about calling tonight. Get settled, and then your father and I will stop by your place tomorrow evening."

Yeah, God had definitely been talking. Papa and my mother hadn't been by my place . . . ever. The way my family was set up, my parents expected me to come to them—either to their home, church, or even a restaurant of their choice. Now, suddenly, they wanted to come to me?

I groaned before I asked, "Can we do it maybe in a couple days?"

"We won't stay very long." That meant my request had been denied. "Your father needs to see you, Chastity. That's the only thing that will settle him. It took everything to stop him from meeting you at your door tonight. So we'll come by, check on you, and then be on our way."

I couldn't protest too much, or else my father *would* be at my door tonight. "Okay, I'll have a better idea of the time tomorrow when I get into the office. I'll call after I see what's waiting for me on my desk."

"Great." Then she added, "Just one last thing, sweetheart. I'm sure he won't be there, but your father would like to see just you . . . and not Xavier, this time."

Oh my God! "Why?" I asked, hardly breathing.

"Just this once," she said as if that was an explanation. "He wants to talk to just you."

About what? I screamed, but only inside. My outside voice said, "All right," and then we exchanged "I love you" before I hung up.

As the jet rolled to a stop at the gate, my eyes didn't leave my phone.

"What's up with your mom?" Xavier said, resting his chin on my shoulder.

I shook my head. How was I supposed to answer that when I didn't know? I glanced up at Xavier and said nothing. I had just spent the best days of my life with my new husband, but for sure, my forty-eight-hour honeymoon was over.

I WAITED UNTIL we were at baggage claim before I said to Xavier, "My mom and dad want to see me tomorrow."

He tilted his head. "About what?"

My eyes stayed lowered. "All my mother said was that my father has been upset and he needs to see me."

When I glanced up, I could almost see Xavier's brain

analyzing, calculating, then finally making a decision. "Well, that means we'll tell them tomorrow." As our bags dumped onto the carousel, he added, "Honestly, I'm ready. I don't want to keep this a secret. This will be perfect."

Xavier hadn't been listening to me, because not once had I mentioned that my parents wanted to see *us*. And he clearly didn't know Sisley and Kareem Jeffries, because talking to them tomorrow wasn't perfect in any universe. With my father stirred up, *I'm married* were not words that would settle him down.

But I said nothing as we grabbed our bags, and before we made it to the glass doors that led outside, Xavier said, "Let me call an Uber."

"Okay. You call yours and I'll call mine."

It wasn't until he glanced at me sideways that I realized what I'd said. "Oh my God."

"Yeah," he said, "we're married."

"I hadn't thought about that." I paused. "So where . . ."

Before I could finish, he said, "We're going to my place." He spoke with such certitude that I took instant offense.

"How did you decide that without speaking to me?"

He said, "We've always stayed at my place," as if I'd asked a question with such an obvious answer.

"That's right," I said, feeling my ire rise. "Do you realize you've never even been inside my place? Except for escorting me to my door, you've never seen where or how I live." Those words were a fact that hadn't bothered me till now. My God. We knew so little about each other.

He leaned his head back as if he was trying to decide if I'd spoken the truth. And then he only shrugged.

"Xavier!" Slowly, he turned his whole body to face me, his expression letting me know that he had questions. It was another moment of clarity—he didn't even know how my voice sounded when I was upset.

"Baby, what's wrong?" His countenance was the opposite of mine.

"I have a place, too," I said, not backing down. "A condo where I've been living. That's where everything I own is right now. And you're saying I should move in with you without us even talking about it."

"No." His voice remained slow and low. "I'm saying that it's almost ten o'clock, and both of us are tired and have to be up for work in just hours. So instead of trying to figure this out in this moment, I'm saying let's go to my place and we'll handle this tomorrow."

"That's what I mean." I folded my arms. "You're saying . . . we'll go to your place. Without asking me."

"Baby." He posted up in front of me and placed his hands on my shoulders. "I'm sorry; you're right. Let's stay at your place."

I still fumed as he canceled his Uber and ordered another. Once he did that, he hugged me. "Are you good?"

His calm made me feel silly. It wasn't like me to get upset over something so trivial. But my attitude wasn't about Xavier and where we would sleep. This angst was all about my parents.

We were quiet as we climbed into the Uber, then, about thirty minutes later, carried our bags up to my condo. But the moment we stepped over the threshold, I admitted that Xavier had been right. Until we found a space that belonged to both of us, his condo made more sense. His three-bedroom plus den made this space feel like a closet, not to mention that his had been decorated by Aziz, one of the city's premiere designers, while all I could claim was that I'd unpacked.

Xavier followed me inside, then took a twenty-second tour

on his own. "Your place is beautiful, baby," he said when he met me back in the living room.

I laid my head on his chest when he hugged me. But on this, our third night of marriage, all we did was unpack enough clothes to dress for bed, then we fell onto my queen-size mattress, which had little room at the bottom for Xavier's six-four frame.

For the first night since we'd been husband and wife, we didn't make love. While I was sure it was exhaustion for Xavier, I was too wound up for sex or sleep. All I could think about was what tomorrow would bring.

30

Chastity

E ven though I was home, I was doing what I'd done in the office—just staring out the window. I'd been distracted all day, thinking about my parents.

The day hadn't started this way. Over a breakfast of K-cup coffee, a bagel for Xavier, and a PowerBar for me, we'd sat on the stools at the kitchen counter and strategized.

"This is what you have to remember," Xavier had said to me this morning. "The only thing your parents can say is we did this quicker than most. But that's not a sin or a crime." He'd taken my hand. "We'll do this together."

"Are you sure you want to be there?"

He'd leaned away as if he didn't understand my question. "Of course. I'm your husband, and just like I told you, I will always have your back." He paused. "Your parents need to hear this from both of us."

By the time we'd ridden the elevator downstairs, then hugged and kissed at the curb before he hopped into an Uber and I headed toward Ninety-Sixth Street to catch the train, I was convinced my husband was right. My parents would be surprised, shocked even, but like my mother had told me before I left for New Orleans: *If Xavier is the man God has chosen, then your father will be the first to step up and not only accept him but love him. We both would have no choice. Because God has the final say.*

While I might have to remind my mother of her words, I had no doubt what she'd said was her truth. They'd get over any shock; my mother would see the similarities between Xavier and my father, and Papa would see my happiness. They'd come to the same conclusion—that I'd done the right thing.

But as the clock ticked and time passed, my apprehension returned. Because of my father. From my experience, I knew God never told my dad everything . . . just enough for Papa to become suspicious, sit me down for my interrogation, and ask so many leading questions that I always confessed to every accusation. I was confident my father didn't know this end—he just knew something wasn't right.

Turning away from the window, I needed to do something to release the anxiety that was rising in me. I glanced at the time on my phone: 6:53. I hadn't realized so much time had passed. Xavier should've been here by now. Right away, I opened up my messages.

Where are you? I texted.

Just a moment later, Xavier replied:

I was just about to text you. I still have an hour here, baby. Can you postpone?

Seven minutes before my punctual parents were to appear at my door, and now he wanted to postpone?

Not possible. They are probably downstairs at this moment.

I tapped the phone, waiting for his response. It took about a minute for him to say:

I'll get there as soon as I can.

I closed my eyes. What was I supposed to do with this? Should I entertain my parents and wait for Xavier? Before I could answer that question, the doorbell rang.

The concierge was supposed to announce all visitors. But my father was Kareem "KJ" Jeffries. Even though he'd never been here, I was sure he'd been recognized. And his celebrity (both past and present) opened all kinds of doors, including the one that led to my condo.

Right before I opened the door, I glanced at my rings. Truly, I wanted to keep them on, but I needed to prepare my parents before I slapped them with this news. I slipped the rings off, slid them into my blazer pocket, and pulled open the door.

"Mom, Papa," I said.

Even though my mother was in front of my father, she stepped aside so he could embrace me first. He rested his hands on my shoulders, and though he smiled, his eyes peered into mine. "Princess," he said. "I'm so happy to see you."

"You sound as if you haven't seen me in a month," I said as he wrapped his arms around me.

"It feels like a month of Sundays has passed since we last shared the same space." Now he was the one to step aside so my mother could hug me, and then together, they entered.

"It's crazy you had to come here," I said, closing the door. After a quick prayer, I faced them. "I feel like I'm back in college, when you would drive all the way to Hanover, when a phone call would have worked just as well."

He nodded. "Sometimes, I might be a little over-the-top,

but I've told you more times than you've ever wanted to hear—you will always be my responsibility."

My mother chuckled. "Except for when you get married."

"Even then," my father said as he lowered himself on the sofa, "when the young man comes to me to ask for your hand in marriage, I will explain that while you will be his wife, I will always be your father."

My mother chuckled. "Well, you and that young man might find yourself at odds," my mother said, the two of them continuing this conversation without me.

I stood frozen in horror. How had the conversation turned to my marriage?

"I get it, Papa," I said, stopping both of them from going any deeper.

"You'll just have to get used to this until you get married," my mother said. "He was the same way when you were in Atlanta. You have no idea how many times I had to stop him from boarding a plane."

"That's crazy. You can't worry about me whenever I'm out of your sight."

He nodded. "It's difficult for any father to get used to his little girl growing up, but I assure you, I wasn't just being an overbearing father this weekend." He straightened his pant legs, then continued, "From the moment your mother told me you were going away, I couldn't shake the feeling that you were in trouble . . . and you needed me."

I took a deep breath. God had definitely spoken to him. "I was fine, Papa, really."

"I can see that, and I'm grateful," he said. "So your trip . . . it was good?"

I nodded, swallowed, and prepared myself, but before the truth could pass through my lips, my father kept on:

"I can't say I was happy about you going away because you and Xavier haven't known each other very long and—"

Before the lecture could continue, my mother said, "Pastor, it was just a little weekend trip." Then she winked at me, her signal that she was coming to my rescue. She added, "Remember how it was when we were young? They just wanted some time together. My goodness, you're acting like she ran off and got married." Her chuckles took it beyond torture for me. "She's young, she's single, and—"

"Mom, Papa," I interrupted her, "there's something I have to tell you."

Their heads tilted to the right in unison, their synchronization one of the manifestations of their thirty-five years of marriage.

I inhaled the biggest breath, then exhaled the words, "Xavier and I got married." Then to add a bit of levity, I said, "Mom, I guess God was talking more to you than to Papa this time." I laughed, though I sounded deranged.

My parents sat like twins, eyes and mouths as wide as the tea saucers my mom used to serve guests, and as still and stiff as any wooden board. It occurred to me that maybe I should have given my parents more of a preamble. Because with the way they sat in shock, I'd never forgive myself if either of them had a medical emergency behind this news.

They just sat, for seconds that turned into at least a minute. It was the loudest silence I'd ever heard. And then . . . my mother burst out laughing. As I stared at her (and my father stared at me), my mother laughed. She pressed her hand against her chest, threw back her head and let it rip, almost roaring, something my delicate and decorous mother never did.

But while my mother's shoulders shuddered with her chuckles, my father did not move. There was no laughter in his expression, just understanding and the realization of what had been stirring his spirit.

"Oh my goodness, Chastity," my mother said, "you really do tease too much." It was our silence that made my mother pause, her glance volleying between us more than a few times before she said, "Oh my God. Chasity, tell me you were kidding."

Before I could speak, my father said, "She's not."

I held up my hands as if that would stop the impending attack. "Please let me explain."

"Explain?" My mother's tone was filled with incredulity. "What's there to explain? Your father and I know what 'I got married' means."

"I want to explain . . . We didn't plan this, it just happened."

"How could this just happen?" my mother asked.

"Xavier and I got to New Orleans and we were having such a good time being together, it seemed like the right thing to do. Truly, it just happened."

My father shook his head. "These things just don't happen." He finally broke his gaze from me, lowered his head, and pressed his hands together. I'd seen that stance before. He was pray-think-speaking . . . that's what he called it. Talking to God while he was trying to make sense of what I'd said.

"Papa, it did just happen." I sat next to him and faced them both. "The weekend before Xavier and I went to New Orleans, he asked me to marry him, so we'd already made the decision to spend the rest of our lives together. We already knew we were going to be married; we just didn't know we were going to do it this weekend."

"You were . . . engaged . . . and you . . . didn't tell us?"

My mother sounded like she was hyperventilating, and so I spoke fast: "I wanted to, but I knew you'd be upset thinking I hadn't known Xavier long enough to be engaged."

"Oh!" She tossed up her hands. "So it was better for you to come home and tell us you were married instead?"

"No. We just—"

"You didn't 'just' anything, Chastity," my mother interrupted. "You got *married*."

"Sisley," my father said, "let Chasity speak."

I'd just turned the world inside out. Because it was my mother who'd always jumped to my defense. She was the one who chided my father into being silent so I had a chance to make my point.

My mother blew out a long breath, folded her arms, and my father nodded for me to continue.

"Xavier and I have been moving in this direction since the day we met, and by last week, we knew we wanted to spend the rest of our lives together. When we got to New Orleans, we realized there was no need to wait. Yes, it was spontaneous, but it wasn't done totally without thought."

"It wasn't spontaneous." My father shook his head again. "This took some planning."

"Why do you keep saying that? I'm telling you what happened, but you don't believe me?"

"I believe you, and I also believe this was planned."

My eyes narrowed. What was my father saying? Did he think Xavier had manipulated me? Had set this up?

Offended, I folded my arms. "I'm sorry this has come as such a shock. But I'm thirty-four; I'm not twenty, like you were, Mom." It wasn't meant to be a shot, but my mother's head reared back. I was sorry about that, but reminding them of that fact was all I had left. I continued, "I've lived, I've worked, I've taken care of myself. I was ready and wanted to do it."

My father nodded as if he were trying to hear me. "I can

understand all of that. So you're in love . . . but what's the rush? Why did you have to get married *right now*?"

His accusation was inside his tone, and I had a hard time believing what he was saying. First my father insinuated I'd been manipulated, and now . . . Was he really asking this?

"If you're asking if I'm pregnant, I'm not!" I snapped.

My father held up his hand. "Of course you're not pregnant. You haven't known him long enough to be pregnant. And that is my point. You don't even know this man."

"Lots of people have gotten married knowing each other with less time than me and Xavier."

"And none of those people are my concern."

"And I'm not your concern either, Papa. At least not in this way. I'm telling you, I know marrying Xavier is what I was supposed to do. He's my purpose, just like you and Mom are each other's."

My mother moaned. "You're comparing what I have with your father to you and Xavier?" She didn't give me space to answer. "Yes, I was young, but I'd known your father for two years before we married."

I pressed my lips together and swallowed all the words I wanted to say—like how she had married my father even when her parents didn't want her to.

My parents had met on a commercial shoot in Philadelphia; she was a young dancer from South Carolina whose mother had escorted her to her first professional gig, and he was KJ Jeffries, the star, rookie point guard of the New York basketball team. *Smitten* was the word they'd both used the many times they'd told me their story. The seven hundred miles between them did nothing to keep them apart. My father courted the young girl (he was five years older), even taking my mom to her high school prom.

They often talked about the barriers they encountered: the distance, their ages, his celebrity, her conservative parents, who didn't want her anywhere near a professional athlete—but none of that stopped them.

My mother had convinced her parents when she told them about her purpose. So couldn't she see I felt the same way? If she was able to see purpose in her late teens, why couldn't I see mine when I was almost double that age?

"Okay, you knew Papa for two years, but what does time have to do with purpose?" I said, finally responding to my mother.

"So because that was my journey, you feel as if you had to do the same?"

"No, of course not. I just want you to understand that I really believe we do have that in common, Mom. I do believe Xavier is my purpose." When my parents exchanged disgusted glances, I continued, "I know this down to my soul. Papa, you're the one who always says there are no coincidences. So explain to me why Xavier and I have so much in common, why we feel so connected, why everything just fell into place? We are the missing puzzle piece for each other."

Just as I said that, the doorbell rang, and I was filled with relief. I rushed to the door, and the moment I opened it, Xavier pulled me into his arms as if he knew I needed the strength of his embrace.

"My parents are here," I whispered.

He nodded, then entered my condo with the smile that always brightened my world. "Hello, Pastor and Mrs. Jeffries."

One of the things I always said was that I'd been raised right. My social lessons came from watching Pastor and Mrs. Jeffries and then emulating their behavior. But the reception they gave my husband made it seem as if the pastor and his wife didn't have any manners at all.

Their aloofness didn't faze Xavier. "I'm sorry; I really wanted to be here when you arrived, but I was held up with a client."

My parents remained silent.

I said to Xavier, "I told them."

He raised his eyebrows as if that surprised him, and I wondered if he had expected me to wait. There was a question in his eyes when he glanced at me, but only for a moment. He turned his attention back to my parents. "I wanted Chastity and me to tell you the news together," he said. "I didn't want to put this all on my wife."

Both of my parents flinched at how Xavier addressed me.

He continued, "I know this comes as a shock, but what I want you to know is that I love your daughter, and I promise you, Pastor and Mrs. Jeffries, I will take care of her."

For the first time my father spoke. "The question that Chastity can't seem to answer for me is—why the rush?"

Xavier nodded. "I know you think this was fast. And it was. But this was about us wanting to start the rest of our lives together now. I didn't want to wait when I knew she was the one."

"And so you took my daughter to New Orleans and tricked her into marrying you?"

Xavier and I spoke at the same time:

"Is that what she told you?"

"Papa, no!"

I added, "I told you what happened. Why are you doing this?"

"Because I believe this was planned," my father said, his voice calm, but his tone stringent. "This was planned in the dark."

I shook my head. I'd known this was going to be rough, but my parents' reaction was much worse than I'd ever imagined. And then Xavier spoke, taking it over the edge:

"Well, the only thing I can tell you, Pastor Jeffries, is that Chastity wanted to marry me as much as I wanted to marry her." His eyes were still on my father when he said, "And no matter what you think, she is my wife now."

There was a challenge in his tone, and I wanted to shake my husband. Why would Xavier speak to my father this way? He had to give my parents room for their shock. This was tough, but this would pass. Now though, with the way Xavier was speaking . . .

If his objective had been to piss off my father, he'd landed the punch. My father pressed his lips together, and his nostrils flared. He stood, rising to a height that seemed beyond his six-foot-seven stature, and he glared at Xavier with a death stare. "Sisley, it's time for us to go."

He took one step, but before he could take another, my mother jumped up. "No, wait," she shouted. "We're not going to leave like this, Pastor." She turned to me and Xavier. "You both have to understand how this looks to us."

I took Xavier's hand and squeezed it, hoping he would let me lead the conversation from this point.

"Yes," I said to my mother and father, "but what I'm hoping is that your surprise will not be greater than your love for me. And I'm hoping you trust me, knowing I would only be with a man that God had chosen, because that's how you raised me."

My mother nodded. "Your father and I know that, don't we, Kareem?"

Even though my father's eyes were still on Xavier, he nodded at my mother's use of his name.

Continuing, my mother said, "Here's the bottom line. Beyond our shock, we are sad. We weren't part of our only child's wedding. And your father should have been given the opportunity to perform the ceremony. This is something we've looked forward to since you were a little girl."

Her words squeezed my heart.

"And I'm sure one of the other issues, Xavier, is that my husband didn't get the courtesy of a visit from you. So that the two of you could sit down and talk before you moved forward. That's a tradition in some circles—in our circle—you know."

I flinched at my mother's elitist words, and Xavier tightened his grasp. But his voice was even when he said, "You're right, Mrs. Jeffries. I got caught up in how I feel about Chastity. But I love your daughter, so I can't be sorry. I don't regret what we did."

My mother took Xavier's challenging tone better than my father had. "Well, all we can do now is move forward, and I have a suggestion." She looked from me and Xavier to my father, then back to us. "I guess you had a little civil ceremony down in New Orleans."

I wanted to be offended by the use of the word *little*, except that our ceremony was probably smaller than she even imagined. We nodded at her assumption.

"Well, I'd like for us to have a reception for you. This way we can celebrate together. This should be a happy occasion, and I want us to find a way to get to that." She paused. "Does that sound fair?" she asked, sounding more like a hostage negotiator than my mother.

I nodded. Xavier nodded. My father still glared at us.

My mother said, "I'm hoping we can all agree to this," facing my father. "And I'll plan it. We'll have a wonderful time, and it will give us a chance to be part of"—she sighed—"your marriage."

Xavier spoke up first. "I'd really like that, Ms. Jeffries." When my mother gave him a hint of a smile, he turned to my father. "And, Pastor Jeffries, I apologize for not asking for Chastity's hand in marriage, but what I would like, if you're amenable, is on the day of the reception, if Chastity and I could stand before you and you can perform the ceremony." He glanced at me, and I nodded. Xavier continued, "It would mean a lot to us." He held out his hand to my father, but my father ignored his offer of peace.

"I don't do mock ceremonies," he said with such disdain. "If you're married, you're married. There's no need for me to perform a fake service." He turned to my mother. "Sisley, are you ready." It was a question, but his tone carried a period. This discussion was over.

Without saying anything else, he walked to me, huffed out a breath, and then brushed my cheek with what was supposed to be a kiss. With barely a nod to Xavier, he turned his back, making my eyes burn with unshed tears.

My mother followed him, but she did what my father should have done. She hugged me and held me for the time that I'd missed with him. "Your father will come around," she whispered.

I nodded as I rested my chin on her shoulder.

Still holding me, she added, "Remember what I told you— if this is God's choice, your father will have no choice." Then she turned to Xavier. "I hope you can understand."

Xavier said, "I do," even as his tone sounded as if he didn't.

"If you love my daughter, and you treat her with the love and respect she deserves, then I . . . and Pastor . . . will come to love and respect you." She gave him a smile, but no hug, and then followed my father out the door.

Xavier and I stood, shoulders touching, as we watched them walk out. I stood waiting, thinking the bell might ring again— my father returning with an apology.

But there was nothing.

With a sigh, I turned to Xavier and expected him to do what

he always did—pull me close and embrace me in this moment when I felt almost estranged from my parents.

But when I faced him, I was surprised by the glare in his eyes. And then my surprise went straight to shock when he spun around and stomped into my bedroom.

31

Xavier

'd been battling to hold it. From the moment I walked in and her parents met me with their steely stares, I'd been trying. No matter how many times I inhaled, no matter how many times I flexed, that flame flickered inside.

It wasn't cooling as I paced Chastity's bedroom, circling around her canopied bed. My back was to the door when I heard her. I wished to God that she hadn't followed me.

"Xavier? What is wrong with you?"

I clenched my teeth as the minutes replayed in my mind: her father accusing me of tricking her, her father not having the decency to shake my hand, and then the ultimate insult—his refusal to perform our ceremony.

I'd wanted to tell him to keep his ceremony, that we didn't need him. But we did; we needed him to make our marriage legal—and the fact that he wouldn't do it burned me even more.

"Xavier," Chastity called me again.

I faced her, and, by her changing expression, I knew she saw my rage.

"What is wrong?" she asked again. "Why are you upset with

me?" she pressed, not knowing this was not the time. Not knowing that her words were like kindling. "Are you going to say anything?"

I exploded, "What did you say to them?"

My roar sent her two steps back, but it was too late for me to care. Something she'd said had caused her parents' reactions. Made them glare at me as if I were a piece of crap stuck on the soles of their shoes.

"What are you talking about?" Her voice didn't have any volume this time.

But mine did. "You said something that made them treat me that way. What did you say?"

"I told them we got married." She spoke slowly. "I told them it wasn't planned. I told them we did it because we"—for a moment her next words seemed stuck—"love . . . each other."

My eyes narrowed as she stuttered. "Why did your father say I tricked you?"

She raised her hands, cutting through the air with each word she spoke. "I don't know. All I know is that they were upset. The way they talked to you, they talked to me." She shook her head, sounding calmer now. As if she'd forgotten there was a volcano brewing in front of her. "I guess I didn't consider just how angry they'd be."

"Are you saying you're sorry we got married?"

Her head snapped back. "What I'm saying is I didn't expect their reaction to be so severe. But, Xavier, I don't understand your reaction at all. Why are you upset with me?"

"Are you blind? Didn't you see how they treated me?"

"You need to calm down," she said so softly, I had to strain to hear her.

She stood steadfast, though I could see her fear, in her eyes, in the way she trembled. I wanted to pull back, but her father's voice rang in my ears—telling me I wasn't worthy, his sentiments just like Gran's.

"Your parents treated me as if I'd done something wrong."

"Because to them, you did. To them, we did."

Her words made me pace once again.

She said, "Have you forgotten we're on the same side?"

That made me stop, made me turn to her, with the fire so hot, flames shot from my eyes. "If you were on my side, you would have waited for me. Why did you tell them before I got here?" I didn't let her answer. "Because you wanted to control the narrative."

Her eyes widened, then narrowed as if she were studying me. "You're acting crazy right now and—"

Crazy? The rage took control of my legs, my arms, my hands, my mind. I stormed toward her. "Are you calling me crazy?"

She backed up but didn't have anywhere to go.

"I am not crazy!" I thundered and slammed my fist into the wall, inches from where she stood.

Chastity shrieked. The wall cracked.

And I felt . . . relief.

I stood there for a moment, until my heart rate slowed. That was when I saw Chastity crumbled on the floor, whimpering. I glanced at where the wall had received my rage, then I fell next to my wife.

She screamed and scooted on her butt across the carpet, trying to get far from me . . . until she was backed into the corner.

Lord, what had I done?

"Chastity," I whispered her name and crawled to her, then wrapped my arms around her. "Baby, please."

She cried, "Get away," and wrestled to release herself from my grasp.

I closed my arms around her, so all she could do was kick. But still, I held her tightly, knowing if I let go, I'd lose her.

"Get away," she screamed and trembled.

"No, Chasity, please. I'm so sorry," I said. "I'm so sorry."

She fought like she was in a battle for her life. But I held her, rocked her, and repeated, "I'm so sorry," until she stopped squirming, until she stopped sobbing.

Even then, though, I held on until I felt her body relax against mine. And then, with one arm still wrapped around her, I used my hand to lift her chin.

Inside, I groaned. Not because of the tears that streaked through her makeup, and not even because of the tremble of her lips or the tremors that still raked through her. It was because of her reddened eyes, which were still wide with fear as she looked at me.

I had done this to the woman I loved.

"Baby, I am so sorry."

She lowered her eyes as if she had nothing to say.

So I tried to explain, "I was just upset. It seemed as if your parents didn't accept me."

She shook her head. "That's not what happened." Her voice was low, still shaky. "They're upset with both of us, but you went berserk. As if you . . ." She stopped; she wasn't going to repeat *crazy* again.

I said, "It seemed as if they weren't giving me a chance, and it kept getting worse . . . I didn't know what to do."

She nodded, then her gaze wandered to the wall. "So you decided to punch something? Oh my God, Xavier, I thought you were going to hit me."

"No." I wrapped both arms around her again because the sight of that wall would make her run. "Baby, I would never hit you. You know that." Her doubt made her stiffen, and I continued, "Remember, last night you were upset with me. And I gave you grace," I said using the word she'd spoken in her vows not even seventy-two hours ago. "I just need you to extend that grace to me."

My words touched her, made her relax more into me.

I kept going. "I have never done anything like that, but I promise you, this will never happen again."

The way she sighed, then nodded, I knew I could release her. But still I stayed close . . . just in case.

She leaned against the wall, and I did the same. We sat under the mark of my wrath. I knew my thoughts, but I wondered about hers. I had to make her believe this was a one-time thing.

I leaned toward her, and when she didn't flinch, I pushed toward her until my lips were on her forehead. Then my lips were on her eyes, her nose, and her cheeks, until I found her lips. And when she received me, my heart wept.

It was soft, not very long, but it was enough. When I leaned back, I held her against my chest, hoping my heartbeat spoke to her, making her forget what I'd done.

I was so grateful I'd fixed this, but my gratitude was beyond this moment; I was so thankful for my foresight. Chastity believed we were married. That's why she wasn't going to leave. Because Chastity thought she was my wife.

Thank God for that.

32

Chastity

The knock on the door made me swivel my chair. But unlike the many times when I'd been caught slacking because of my love of this city view, I didn't rush to awaken my computer.

"Come in." I watched the door open before the young deliveryman stepped into my office. His eyes were filled with a bit of sheepishness and a lot of awe.

"I'm back," he said.

This time he held a vase with about three dozen rainbow roses. Without saying a word, the young man and I scanned the office in search of a space. But every inch of every surface was covered with roses.

I gestured to him with my chin. "On the floor by the door."

He frowned as if the flowers were too lovely for that, but he followed my request, then brought me the slip to sign. Like the dozen times before, I reached into my purse for another ten-dollar bill. I'd had to go to the ATM after the third delivery this morning.

"It's after five," I said. "Hopefully, this will be the last time today."

He nodded, but his expression said he wouldn't mind returning. With these tips, this was probably his greatest gig this year. When he stepped out of the office, I spun my chair once again.

My second day back to work after a wondrous weekend, and once again, I couldn't focus. Yesterday it was my dad; today it was my husband. Like I'd done a couple thousand times, I shook my head at the memory of last night. Xavier taking a swing at me didn't line up with the man I knew.

Or maybe it did. Because as my parents reminded me, I didn't know Xavier. Closing my eyes, I allowed my mind to wander, to the times I'd fought hard today not to remember.

A flashback: *Xavier slammed his hand on the steering wheel, startling me, making my head rear back. "Why would you do that?" he shouted. No, he screamed, a sound that made the windows rattle.*

Another moment: *With a grunt, he pitched the velvet box across the room, sending it crashing against the window, making the glass (and me) shake.*

Then last night. Xavier's fist. Through the wall, but next to my head.

Was this a pattern, or was I making too much out of this?

One side of my brain answered: pattern or not, Xavier swinging was unacceptable.

My internal debate continued: I'd known Xavier for ten, almost eleven weeks. Just under three months . . . but there'd been only three incidents. Was I going to allow three bad times to negate the hundreds of glorious moments?

Another knock on the door made me sigh. Was Xavier kidding? Drowning me in the fragrance of flowers wasn't going to fix this. But then a quick glance at my desk clock reminded me before I said, "Come in."

This time, my door opened wide and hard, banging against the wall, and Tasha blew in. She sashayed toward me, wearing dark glasses and some kind of purple fur coat, but once she was halfway to my desk, she stopped. She pushed her sunglasses down the bridge of her nose, scanned my office, then turned to me. "I'm assuming nobody died up in here."

Those were not words I expected. "What do you mean?"

"Well"—she continued her stroll toward me—"the last time I saw this many flowers was at Aretha's funeral, God rest her soul. So what's up with this?" She spread her arms wide, then shrugged off her coat, letting it drop to the floor.

I said, "Gifts. From my husband."

Tasha was about to sit, but she paused, her butt in midair. Then, slowly, she stood straight. "I didn't know you were married."

I said, "We kept it a secret . . . for a while," thinking that was easier than explaining.

"Well, congratulations, I guess," she said, not sounding at all like she was giving me well wishes. Before I could thank her (in the same tone), she asked, "So why all the flowers?"

"He was just in the mood." I looked to the files stacked on my desk.

She studied me through narrowed eyes. When she said, "Sure," I heard every bit of her sarcasm. "Chastity, we haven't known each other very long, but if you want to talk—"

"The only thing I'd like to talk about is this." I pointed to her folder, then picked up mine.

"I remember the first time Derrick filled our home with flowers . . ." she said, ignoring my request. "I'm trying to remember how many weeks it was after we were married."

I inhaled and held that air in.

She continued, "He was so sorry, there wasn't a space or a spot I could pass in our home that didn't remind me how sorry he was." She shook her head. "It took me twenty years to admit that, yeah, that man was way too sorry for me."

I didn't want to get into this kind of discussion with a client, but I couldn't resist asking, "You said weeks? He abused you in the first weeks?"

She waved her hand. "Have you not been listening to me all this time that we've been meeting?"

Yes, Tasha had told me how she'd been beaten. But she talked a lot, making me scour through her ramblings to get the information I needed to protect her and her assets as her marriage ended.

But I didn't get a chance to say anything before she said, "Yes, it was in the first few weeks. Right after we had that big ceremony. We were still opening wedding gifts when he tried to knock out all of my teeth."

Tasha stared at me and I stared at the five vases of flowers on my desk until she said, "You've helped me, so let me tell you this: You cannot fix an abuser, you cannot change an abuser, you cannot help an abuser, because what a therapist told me was their rage comes from a place you can't touch. They need professional help."

I leaned back, filled with indignation. "My husband is not abusing me."

She stood and swiveled her hips, exaggerating her glance around the room. "He's doing something, whether you admit it or not. I'm just saying he has to be the one to fix it, not you."

I hoped she didn't hear the way my voice quivered when I said, "You've made a lot of assumptions about some flowers."

"Because this sh—" She stopped herself and held up her hands. "Sorry, I forgot you're Pastor Jeffries's daughter." She backed up and began again, "Because this *ish* ain't normal. When a man—or a woman—has to go to this extreme, something ain't right. This is how people pay for their abuse."

Her words made me think about my mom. Sisley Jeffries

had a plethora of gifts: minks, diamonds, a whole floor in the brownstone designated as her closet filled with designer clothes.

She said, "There needs to be a twelve-step program for survivors, and the first thing you have to admit is there's a problem. That's where I was at fault."

I wanted to move on to business, but I had to say, "How was his abuse your fault?"

She held up her finger. "My fault is that it took me too long to admit there was a problem. The first time he laid his hands on me, I should've had him arrested. Because maybe then, he would've gotten help instead of believing that I was his punching bag." She paused. "If I had admitted Derrick had a problem, that could have saved us. At the very least, it would have saved *him*. Look at him today, he can't find a job, he has difficulty in relationships, he's already on his third attorney with this. If he'd learned how to channel his rage, he'd be a better man today." Her shoulders sagged. "That's why I'm culpable. I should've kicked his ass out the first time, and we would've started healing from there."

Her words made my heart beat harder, so I leaned across the desk and handed her the folder. "These are all the items we'll be presenting in arbitration."

She gave me a long look, then a little shrug, before she turned her attention to her case. She fell right into it, answering my questions, asking her own. For the next forty or so minutes, we weren't sitting in the middle of a flower garden— we were taking care of the business of breaking every part of her marriage.

At the end, when I stood, Tasha hugged me. "Please don't waste all the time that I did," she said, once again taking us back to the conversation I didn't want to have.

I watched her as she did one of those dramatic strolls, her fur dragging behind her. Even when she was gone, her words remained: *Don't waste all the time that I did.*

Just as I returned to my desk, my cell rang, but I didn't check the screen; I knew the ringtone. A few seconds later, I heard the text notification.

Xavier had been calling, texting, all day. I heard his words on my voice mail: "I'm so sorry. You will never know how sorry." I read his texts on my phone:

I will spend the rest of my life making this up to you.

I wondered if that meant an office filled with flowers for the rest of my life. The thought of that made me chuckle, but the laugh didn't last.

My thoughts returned to three months . . . three incidents.

I should've kicked his ass out the first time.

Her words were like a soundtrack as the movie of my life with Xavier played. I sat at my desk, with that video in my mind and her words still in my ears. Outside, darkness began its descent, and still I sat.

I should've kicked his ass out the first time.

When night had completely claimed the city, I opened my phone to my messages, and texted:

Can we talk, please?

The quick response surprised me:

Please!

I'll be there in about thirty minutes.

The return text:

♥

That made me smile. Then I closed my eyes and prayed, "Lord, I'm looking for a sign from you. Please send me a sign. Tell me what to do."

JUMPING OUT OF the taxi, I trotted through the parking lot, then rang the bell at the side door of the church. Within a few seconds, Thelma, my father's assistant, pushed open the door.

"Hey, Chastity," she said. "What's going on?"

"Not much." I stepped past her.

"That's not true. Your mom and dad told me you went away for the weekend." She sounded as if she was about to break out in a cheer.

I held my breath, waiting to hear the spin my parents had put on this, but all Thelma said was, "Did you have a good time?"

"I did," I said, surprised there was nothing more.

Thelma had been with my father for about fifteen years, having replaced Cynthia, my father's assistant who had ensured her departure when she'd given my mother those pictures of her and my father. My mother had interviewed and hired Thelma herself, and over the years, the older woman had become a confidant to both of my parents.

So if they hadn't mentioned my marriage to her, no one in this city knew. Maybe my parents believed if they didn't speak it, it wouldn't be true.

As I moved down the hall, Thelma stopped me. "Your dad is waiting . . . but he's in there," she said, pointing to the left.

My eyebrows rose a little, but I was not surprised. My heels clicked on the parquet floors, but once I crossed the threshold that led to the 2,500-seat sanctuary, my movement was silenced by the carpet.

I took only a few steps in before I stopped, soaking in the grandeur of the church. It was more than its size, more than the architecture of the domed ceiling and the dozen custom-designed stained-glass windows, which glowed especially under the night sky.

It was the aura of this place. When I was little, I'd been sure God lived here. I couldn't see Him, but I felt Him. Especially when the sanctuary was silent, that was when I felt the most peace. That was what I'd come looking for tonight—peace, signs, and my father.

My father sat in the center of the front pew, leaning forward, his elbows on his knees while his fingertips touched. He was doing his pray-think-speak thing again. Praying and thinking before he had to speak to me.

Without raising his head, he said, "Thank you for reaching out to me, princess."

When I sat down next to him, he hugged me before we leaned back and stared at the altar. The peace of Wednesday evening's quiet surrounded us.

Just about an hour before, this sanctuary had been packed, I was sure, for midweek prayer. My father didn't keep the people long. Started at five thirty, and they were done in an hour so they could go home to their families.

After a while, my father said, "Do you remember the first time we sat in here, just so we could talk?"

My glance stayed on the huge golden cross that hung high behind the altar. "The weekend before I left for college."

He nodded. "Do you remember what I told you then?"

"What I remember most—you said I could always come home." Those words had made me feel so safe then. "You said no matter what I was going through, home was always my sanctuary."

"I wanted to make sure you remembered that then."

I sighed. I guessed this was the sign I'd come looking for. God had told my father to remind me that I had a home, that I didn't have to stay with Xavier.

"I'm glad you remember that now."

"Is that why you were glad I reached out to you? To remind me of that?"

"No." He shook his head. "I wanted to see you so I could apologize. I should never have come at you and Xavier the way I did yesterday, and the next time I see him, I will apologize to Xavier, too."

"Apology accepted," I said, though I felt a bit discombobulated. This apology didn't go along with what he'd just said about always having a home. After a beat, I asked, "Does this mean—"

He didn't let me finish. "I'm not pleased you got married so quickly, and there's nothing wrong with me letting you know that. But I should never have walked out of there with you having any doubt that I love you and support you no matter what."

"I never doubted that. I knew you were just angry in the moment."

"I was more shocked and saddened. But that didn't give me a right to react with anger. And then to not reach out to you last night . . ." His head dipped a bit.

Even during the worst of times, my father lived by Ephesians 4:26. He never laid his head down with anger in his heart.

"I wasn't happy, but I support you . . . in your marriage."

"Thank you."

I turned my attention back to the altar, back to the cross, and my father did the same. He was back in his pray-think-speak mode, and as I waited for him to get to the speaking part, I thought *this* was the sign. My father supporting me and Xavier was the sign that I was supposed to be with him.

My father said, "It's not that I don't like Xavier," as if he was beginning in the middle of a thought. "From what I saw in the half hour we spent together"—he paused, letting the absurdity of that fact settle—"he's a young man who's achieved a lot against what sounds like tough odds."

This was where I was supposed to rise up and shout out all that Xavier had conquered. But although the words and the sentiment were inside, what I wanted to say stayed stuck in my throat.

So my father continued, "I'm hoping he's the good man you say he is."

I nodded, unable to speak my affirmation.

"I still believe he may be holding on to some of his grief, although that's more of my feeling than a fact."

Was that what it was? Grief? Was that what happened last night? Was grief at the center of those three incidents?

"But Xavier and I will get to know each other, man-to-man; I want him to know I'll be here for him as well."

"You don't know what this means to me."

"I think I do." He nodded. "I'm going to stand by you as you stand by Xavier. He's my . . . son-in-law now. Your mother and I accept that."

His words were the companion to the peace in this sanctuary. This was my final sign.

He took my hand. "So, princess, we've reached a new phase, haven't we? You're a married woman." There was so much wonder in his tone. "I'm looking forward to moving ahead from here."

I sighed with so much relief. "Thank you, Papa."

"Now, your mother is already way ahead of me. She's ready to make the announcement, plan the reception, but the first thing I must do is get together with Xavier and apologize to him."

I closed my eyes, filled with gratitude for the signs that I'd wanted and my father's support, which I needed.

"There's one last thing. Last night, Xavier suggested something, and I couldn't hear him then, but"—he pointed to the altar—"I would like both of you to stand right there in front of God, me and your mother, and all of our guests . . . I want to perform the ceremony I've dreamed of since you were born."

I wrapped my arms around him and held on tight. "That would be amazing."

"It's going to be pretty amazing for me, too. Me, the father of the bride." He chuckled, leaned back on the pew, and I rested my head on his shoulder. Once again, my eyes turned to the altar, to the cross and the peace.

The altar, the cross, the peace. Three. Just like three months . . . three incidents. Three . . . the number of divine wholeness, the resurrection. Maybe that's what this was all about. With me and Xavier, a family unit, joining with my parents, this would be Xavier's rising. His new life—one of support and love. With my father, he'd be able to come to terms with his past, his grief, if that was what he needed.

Last night had been so scary, but because of this night, I knew where I was supposed to be. Xavier was my purpose, and I was going to help him overcome. Whatever help he needed, he would get from me. And my mom and dad, too.

33

Xavier

hastity's voice mail once again told me to leave a message, and with a roar, I hurled my cell phone across the room. I heard the snap, then the crack, finally, the crash against the wall, but I didn't care. I was frantic.

I sank onto the sofa, feeling the first flicker of the flames, but it was doused by my regret. How could this happen? Marriage was supposed to protect me, to save us. Yet it was clear: a marriage license wasn't enough. It was just a piece of paper, not heavy enough, not opaque enough, not dense enough to cover up what I'd done. Not enough to make the best woman I'd ever known stay.

But just when I wanted to stop breathing . . . I heard the key. I sprang up but paused at the end of the hallway, not wanting to scare her away.

She stepped into the condo, and I whispered her name. "Chastity." When she closed the door behind her, I said, "I was so worried. I've been calling you."

"I turned my phone off and then I went to my place first. I guess I didn't know where we were going to . . ."

She stopped, combed her fingers through her hair, and I almost collapsed from my relief. Where we were going to stay, to sleep . . . that's what she was going to say.

I took one step toward her; she didn't back away, though she stayed by the door with her coat still closed, as if that would be her quick getaway. But still I had more hope. "I'm so happy to see you. Baby, I'm so sorry."

"I know you are." She paused. "There are over one hundred roses in my office that kinda prove that."

I chuckled but stopped when she didn't even smile.

After a couple of beats, she asked, "What happened last night?"

I didn't want to talk about that. Didn't want to remind her of what she'd seen. But she'd gone straight to it, so I responded, "Nothing. Everything. I lost control because what your parents think means the world to me."

She nodded as if she understood, giving me more hope, until she added, "But you got so angry."

"It was just I didn't have a chance to speak up for myself."

Again, she nodded, then surprised me with, "My father thinks . . ." She paused. "Do you think you could still be grieving in some way and that's where your anger comes from?"

It took everything in me not to squeeze my hands together. What had she told her parents? "Your father knows . . . what happened last night?"

"No." She shook her head as if that was a ridiculous question. "That is between you and me. We'll work it out." I breathed until she said, "Do you think that's it?"

"Grieving what, Chastity?" It was a fight to keep my volume down, my tone steady. "The only person I would grieve is my mother, and she died twenty years ago. I'm over that. Last night was just about it being too much at that moment. But it will never be too much again. That will never happen because I don't want to lose you."

Now she took a step toward me. "Xavier, you've got to stop talking about losing me."

I breathed.

"Whatever challenges we have, we'll work through them, but you're not going to lose me. I'm your wife now."

I wanted to make her say a promise and make a pledge.

"But there's something going on with you," she said. "Haven't you noticed how mad you get?"

She was pressing, and I was already on the verge from the hours I'd waited for her. I turned around so she wouldn't see the emotions boiling. "I mean, yeah, I get angry . . ." After a couple of seconds, I faced her again. "But so do you, so does everyone."

"Okay," she said, holding up her hands as if she wanted to stop the conversation. "Let me rephrase. I do get angry. But yours is different. Yours is a rage—it's like there's this wrath burning inside of you."

I was shocked at how close she'd come to describing what I felt. We were connected for sure.

Still, I said, "Really? You're saying this because of what happened last night?"

"It wasn't just last night. I've seen you like this a number of times. Remember when you met my mom . . ."

I had to take a breath before I said, "You set me up," so she wouldn't hear the anger that I felt.

"And then again, on the day we got engaged."

Another breath. "Forgive me if I was upset when I thought you were saying no."

"All of those are good reasons to be upset, but you go beyond that."

"Baby, please." I moved closer, and again, she didn't back away. "I've just been under so much pressure. So many big moves and changes. My biggest case . . ." I paused. "My beautiful wife. It's been a lot." I pulled her into my arms, and when she held me back, I exhaled. "All you need to know is this won't happen again," I whispered. "Please forgive me."

She leaned into my chest, and I knew not only did she forgive me but she believed me. Because she was my wife. And that ring on her finger had worked.

I HID MY yawn behind my fist. This week had been exhausting, working a major case and still worrying about my wife. As if she knew I was thinking about her, Chastity squeezed my hand, and I turned from the car's window and smiled at her. When she laid her head on my shoulder, I sighed and returned my attention to the passing landscape as the Uber sped uptown.

It was difficult to believe we'd only been married a week. I'd put so much into the last four days, paying penance for what I'd done. But I didn't mind. Like I'd told Chastity a thousand times, I would do anything to make our marriage right. That's why after I'd filled her office with flowers on Wednesday, on Thursday, I sent a designer to her firm with a dozen outfits for her to choose her favorites, on Friday, a driver picked her up from work and whisked her off to the Red Door spa, and then last night, for our one-week anniversary, I'd taken her back to the Times Square hotel where we started. This time, I didn't have the suite lit with candles or fragranced with roses. What I had was a diamond-and-pearl silver cable bracelet waiting for her under the pillow.

Now, this morning, I was giving her what she wanted most,

though the invitation had come from her father. On Thursday, he'd called, apologized, and asked me to join them today.

"I want a reset," he'd told me, and I'd been thankful for his invitation.

Today was my shot to make it right with all of them, the Jeffrieses, who were now my family. In front of Greater Grace, we exited the Uber, and we made our way through the masses, heads down, eyes averted, just like when I'd been here before. At the side of the church, this time, we were cognizant of the camera that watched us.

When her mother opened her door, she hugged Chastity before she turned to me. Taking my hands into hers, she said, "I'm so glad you're here with us, Xavier. Welcome," I smiled . . . and then she added, "son," with such sincerity, that single word snatched away every one of my cognitive abilities.

Chastity's mother didn't seem to notice how she'd muted me as she spun and began to stroll down the long hallway.

"Now, Pastor won't be able to meet with you this morning. He's still preparing his sermon."

"Really?" Chastity said. "He's usually finished by Friday."

"I know, but he was in that place where his spirit was stirred. He told me he just might preach backward."

"Oh, no," Chastity said, her tone a mixture of amusement and concern.

"What does that mean?" I asked.

"Well, I've told you about my dad's gift—this connection he has with God. He believes his messages are for everyone, but there are times when he believes God is using him to speak to someone specifically."

"And"—Chastity's mother picked up—"Pastor doesn't like knowing who God is talking to, especially if it's a tough message. So he turns his back."

"Wow," I said, not quite able to imagine a man standing in the pulpit with his back to more than two thousand people.

"Chastity has been calling it preaching backward," her mother explained, "since she was a little girl. So that's what everyone in the church calls it." She paused as she stood in front of a door. "We still have about twenty minutes before the services begin. You can wait in our guest room. There's juice, coffee, tea, and danishes in there, and then someone will come when it's time to go into the sanctuary."

"Thanks, Mom," Chastity said as her mother pushed the door open.

But before I could give my own thanks, someone inside shouted, "Surprise!" startling both of us.

My wife recovered before I did. "Oh my goodness," she exclaimed, pulling the shorter woman into a hug. Behind her, a gentleman who reminded me of Steph Curry in both stature and sway stood from the sofa and joined us.

"What are you doing here?" Chastity asked.

"Excuse me," the woman said. "I'm the one who should be asking questions. Married, girl? Married! How did this happen?"

She was petite, but she filled the room with her joy, and just standing there, all I wanted to do was laugh.

Chastity swung around and pulled me closer. When I stepped to her side, I recognized the woman who'd been speaking.

She held out her hand to me. "You probably don't remember me, but I'm—"

"Melanie," I finished.

Her eyebrows rose. "I made that much of an impression?"

I nodded, and, with my hands around Chastity's waist, I said, "You did. Because if it weren't for you, I wouldn't have met my beautiful wife."

She tilted her head. "Good answer," she said, and I was sure, by her tone, she remembered the way I'd pursued her.

But although she was attractive, I would never have noticed her if I'd met Chastity first.

Melanie continued, "You are a smooth one. Almost as smooth as my man." She reached for the guy behind her.

He chuckled, then hugged Chastity, and introduced himself as Melanie's husband, Kelvin. Before any more words were spoken, Melanie and Chastity slid across the room, shrieking like schoolgirls, leaving me standing with this guy I didn't know.

Except for Bryce, there was no one else I'd ever called a friend. New York had been pretty much like Mississippi. I'd been so used to isolation, it was a safe place for me. So I wasn't even sure what I should say to Kelvin.

He said, "I guess congratulations are in order."

"Thanks."

"Well, let's have a toast with some juice or something." He chuckled, patted me on the back, and right away, I could tell why Melanie and Kelvin had married. His voice was filled with the same cheer as hers. He poured a glass of juice and then handed me the pitcher. "It happened pretty quickly, huh?"

I nodded. "Yeah, it did," I said and waited for signs of his judgment.

He said, "I hear you. I knew right away I wanted to marry Melanie, but I was a poor college student." He shrugged and chuckled again. "Good for you."

I relaxed as I grabbed one of the crystal glasses and filled it, then Kelvin and I sat at the opposite end, far away from our squealing wives.

"Chastity is really happy," Kelvin said as we watched them.

That made me beam.

He continued, "I've known her since college. And she and Melanie have been besties since the womb, to hear them tell it."

This time, I chuckled with him, and we fell into a rhythm. We talked about the New York sports teams first (a short conversation) and then moved to working out.

"Yeah, I haven't been able to hang out there as much as I'd like 'cause I've been so busy at work, but Sweat Box is my go-to."

"What?" Kelvin leaned back and laughed. "Are you trying to die? Those cats up there are serious. They box like they got issues."

I laughed with him. "Yeah, but I love getting that kind of workout in."

He shook his head and glanced at me with new respect. "That's as bad as getting on the courts in the village."

"I used to do that, too," I said. "You know, I still got time to get that NBA contract."

We cracked up so loud and for so long, our wives turned toward us, then strolled to where were sat.

"What's so funny?" Chastity asked as she sat on the arm of the sofa.

"I don't care what y'all are laughing about," Melanie piped in. "It needs to stop now unless you bring us in on the joke."

But before we could fill them in, our wives' attention turned to the opening door. "Aunt Estelle," Chastity and Melanie sang together.

After they hugged the woman with waist-long locs, she embraced Kelvin before she faced me.

The way she grinned, I had to do the same thing. "You must be Xavier." She wrapped her arms around me. "Welcome to the family."

Then, as she led us into the sanctuary, I once again marveled at all I'd received by making Chastity my wife. I'd wanted just one person, just Chastity, so that we could form a family. But my wife came with an extended support system. There were so many who wanted to include me, a feeling I'd never had before.

I was just so grateful, and so church was the perfect place for me to be right now.

34

Xavier

Greater Grace was already rocking, the praise team already rolling when the four of us strolled into the sanctuary. There was so much pomp for this circumstance—having us enter after the service had already started as if we were dignitaries.

A moment later, Mrs. Jeffries came through the same door, and as she passed, she kissed each of us—Kelvin, Melanie, Chastity—and it was only then I realized I was standing where Chastity should have been.

I said to her, "Change places so you can sit next to your mother."

Before she could answer, Mrs. Jeffries said, "No, you stay right here, son," as she grabbed my hand.

For a moment, I felt awkward, but then in seconds, I relaxed into her grasp. When she released me so she could raise her hands in praise, I wanted to grab her back. But while she worshipped and Chastity did the same, I stood with my hands at my sides, even as a part of me wanted to do what my wife and her mother were doing. I wanted to give that kind of thanks.

The praise team sang, the congregation danced—it was a

Sunday-morning celebration. When another door opened and Pastor Jeffries came through, I expected him to enter bobbing his head, the way he had the last time I was here.

But as the people partied around him, Pastor Jeffries eased down into the pastor's chair, pressing his hands together as if he was praying. His eyes were open, though, and at the end of the song, he nodded toward the minister of music. With a final chord on the keyboard, the celebration ended. There were murmurs throughout as the praise team moved to the choir stand, and then the church became quiet. No one moved for so long I wondered if something was wrong. Next to me, Mrs. Jeffries sat with her head bowed as if she was in prayer herself.

By the time Pastor Jeffries stood, the atmosphere had shifted from celebratory to solemn. He lifted his giant Bible and then moved in a manner that matched the mood he'd set.

"My spirit is stirred this morning, church."

There were more murmurs.

"It's been this way for the last few days."

Chastity shifted next to me, and when she reached for my hand, I wondered if she knew what her father was talking about. Was he solemn because of us?

I remembered his call on Thursday. He apologized, then said he wanted to move forward, have a reset. We didn't talk long—I had a meeting—but he'd sounded sincere. Was this another setup?

Pastor Jeffries continued, "I had some very good news this week that I wanted to share." He glanced to where we sat, and his lips twitched into a slight smile. "But I'm afraid that on this morning, I have to get straight to the message. I can't hold back any longer."

Now I was like everyone else, shifting to find a comfortable place.

"We've been talking about the seven deadly sins, and today we need to talk about wrath. I was really surprised when this subject stirred me so. Because, you see, I know folks who are envious and folks who are greedy, and everyone sitting within the sound of my voice knows of my own *past* personal struggle with lust."

"Amen!"

"I am not ashamed of the truth," the pastor said.

"Tell the truth, shame the devil," someone shouted out from the other side.

Pastor Jeffries nodded. "But I can't say I've come across too many people who struggle with the sin of wrath." He paused and glanced out into the sanctuary. "Because *wrath* is not even a word we use very much in today's lexicon, right?"

The congregation agreed with their mutters.

"So, to begin, let's define *wrath*. I'm going to start with words we know, like *anger*. Anger is a strong feeling of displeasure, even hostility, toward someone or something, and when anger is taken up a notch it becomes rage. Rage is anger that is combined with action." He interlocked his fingers. "And the action is usually something that satisfies that strong urge to harm that rage brings. Now, that's bad, because you've moved from an internal feeling to expressing anger with action to harm."

He held up his finger. "But wrath?" He paused. "As the kids would say, that's leveling up. The dictionary says wrath is extreme anger, extreme rage. And it's the adjective of *extreme* that has stirred me so. Because if you already want to harm someone with rage . . . what is the extreme action that goes beyond rage? What kind of harm comes with wrath?"

Now, the people mumbled, but my eyes stayed on Pastor Jeffries. Chastity told me she hadn't discussed my . . . issues . . . with her father—and I believed her. So he couldn't be talking about me . . . and Tuesday night.

He said, "It doesn't take a genius to figure this out, church. Wrath is extreme anger that carries the energy of violence and vengeance." Those words hung in the air before he kept on, "Now, how does one get from anger to wrath? Because, like I said, it does begin with anger. But it's an escalating feeling of anger to the point of uncontrollable action. It's surging anger that takes you to the violence. Wrath does damage; wrath leaves wreckage."

I twisted my neck, loosened my tie, straightened my pant legs.

"Let's look at Proverbs nineteen-nineteen." Next to me, Chastity opened her Bible on her phone, but I didn't have one of those apps. Mrs. Jeffries offered me her Bible, and although I felt so uncomfortable that I wanted to get up, I read with her as Pastor Jeffries did the same: "'A man of great wrath will suffer punishment.'" He paused and everyone in the congregation looked up. "Oh, there's more, but I can stop right there. Because this is the *Lord* talking about punishment. This is not the punishment that comes from man. But let's read on." He continued, "'For if you rescue him, you will have to do it again.'" He slammed his Bible shut, startling everyone. Then he paced across the altar, stopping on the right side. "Here's the thing. Anger is a human emotion. That's why throughout the Bible, God teaches the appropriate way for us to handle our anger. He teaches that it's going to come, but it must be controlled. It's going to happen, but it must not last."

My eyes followed Pastor Jeffries as he took long strides to the other side of the altar:

"But when God talks about wrath, He gives no instructions. He speaks only about the suffering that will come as punishment for the wrathful man."

"Amen," someone shouted out.

Pastor Jeffries kept on, "And because wrath is the *extreme* of anger, the Lord is warning that anyone who goes to that extreme is a person who will do it again and again and again."

"Whew," Melanie shouted out.

"But the warning in the Word is not only for that person filled with wrath. The warning"—he paused—"is for you." His voice began to rise with each word. "Because when I began to study the scripture in all the translations, when the Lord talks about having to rescue that person again and again and again, I came to realize . . ."

Once again, Pastor Jeffries paced, until now he stood in the center of the altar. This time, though, he stepped down and stood right in front of us, though his eyes looked out into the congregation.

"If you find yourself with a wrathful person, this is what that scripture is saying: You cannot save a wrathful man from the consequences of his intemperance. You may do it once, you may do it twice. But if that man is unchanged, all of your efforts will be useless, and the help you have given will only make him believe that he can continue to indulge his wrath with impunity."

Still standing in front of us, Pastor Jeffries pressed his hands together as if he was praying. His eyes closed, and I never knew two thousand people in one place could be so silent.

His eyes were still closed when he said, "This is the part of my study that stirred me so much." His voice was so low, even though he was just standing a few feet away, I had to strain to hear him. "Today, I'm not talking to the wrathful man; it's the brother or the sister in Christ who tries to rescue him whom I want to reach. Because what I know today is that after you rescue and rescue and rescue, there will come a time"—Pastor Jeffries opened his eyes and stared straight at us—"when the wrathful man you're trying to save will turn his wrath on you."

It felt as if the entire congregation inhaled at once. Everyone except for me. I had already been holding my breath. Now it felt like I was melting under the heat of his stare, and I didn't exhale until he turned to return to the altar. With my handkerchief, I wiped my brow.

Mrs. Jeffries patted my arm. "Are you okay? It is a little hot in here."

I nodded. "I'm fine."

"Don't worry," she whispered, "he gets everyone worked up. He's good, huh?"

Her words made me smile for one reason—if her husband hadn't told her the message was for me, then it wasn't.

He was back at the altar when he began again: "According to the Bible, there is only room for His wrath. That is reserved for the Lord because in His infinite wisdom He knows what to do with it. We do not."

From the pulpit, Pastor Jeffries held out his hand. "Someone in this place is suffering from this. Do not be dismayed; do not be embarrassed. There is hope; come, let me pray with you."

I was grateful he didn't gesture toward me. His eyes were on the couple of guys who walked down the aisle toward him.

As they lowered themselves on the kneeling bench, Pastor Jeffries said, "Anyone else? I feel as if there is someone chained to their seat."

I felt a nudge, but not from Chastity. It came from inside, but I didn't move. I just bowed my head, rewinding the pastor's words, matching what he'd said with how I felt at times. I did get angry, but it wasn't to the extreme. I'd never been punished . . . had I?

Still, I wondered if this was about me. That was the question in my mind until I looked up. And Pastor Jeffries was glaring straight at me.

35

Xavier

*B**ut when God talks about wrath, He talks about the suffering that will* *come from the punishment of being a wrathful man.*

Pastor Jeffries's words echoed in my mind. Those words and his stare had me twisted. What did he see when he looked at me? And now what would he say at dinner?

In the background, I heard Chastity and Melanie still chatting. Kelvin had been called to Harlem Hospital, where he worked, so the two of them were in the back of the Uber while I sat in the front passenger seat, my eyes trained on the outside, my mind scrolling through the sermon.

"Babe," I heard Chastity say, "we're here."

I had to blink to bring myself back. Chastity and Melanie had already slid out, and the driver was glancing at me with a frown.

When I finally jumped out, Chastity took my hand. "You okay?"

I nodded. "Yeah, was just thinking about some things."

"Well, I hope you let work go for a few hours. I really want to hang out with Melanie and Kelvin after we leave here."

"Oh, yeah, I'm good," I said, although I wasn't. The truth: I didn't want to face her father.

But I took my wife's hand and we trotted up the brown-stone's steps. Before we reached the top, Mrs. Jeffries opened the door as if she'd been waiting.

"You're missing one," she said as we stepped into the parlor. With a sigh, she added, "Don't tell me, Kelvin was called to work."

"He was, Mama Sisley, but he's going to meet up with us later."

"Well, I'm getting dinner together, so Xavier, come with me," she said, though I didn't understand. What about Chastity and Melanie?

Before I could ask any questions, Chastity kissed my cheek. "I'll be right back, babe." Then she and Melanie shot up the stairs, giggling like they'd been doing since before church began.

I was confused and turned to Mrs. Jeffries.

She gestured for my coat. "Those two, whenever they're here, they spend the first fifteen minutes upstairs in Chastity's bedroom, reminiscing." She beckoned me to follow her, and as I passed through the living room, I realized I'd never seen my wife's old bedroom or any part of her childhood home except for this first floor. There was so much for us to learn about each other.

Those thoughts were wiped away, though, when I stepped into that gourmet kitchen. The aromas of macaroni and cheese, collard greens, fried chicken—and, wait, was that a hint of catfish?—assaulted me. "Wow!"

She laughed. "Don't be impressed. Remember I told you about my friend?" She grabbed an apron from a hook on the wall. "Melba delivers every Sunday morning, so all I have to do is this." She folded back the foil from the macaroni and cheese and reached for a bowl.

"Do you want me to help, Mrs. Jeffries? Though, honestly, I'm not really good in the kitchen."

She chuckled. "No, thanks," she said, as she began opening cabinets. "I just wanted to save you from your wife and her best friend."

My wife.

"Take off your jacket. Get comfortable." She lined bowls and pans on the center island. "This is your home now, son."

That word seemed so natural as she went about the business of putting the dinner together. I hung my jacket over the back of one of the kitchen chairs.

"So," Mrs. Jeffries began as I faced her. "Pastor told me you two talked."

Her words took me back to the sanctuary. "Yes, ma'am. We didn't have much time, but I was grateful he reached out to me."

She held a pan in midair and glared at me, but the ends of her lips twitched into a smile that belied her eyes. "First, you called me 'Mrs. Jeffries,' and now 'ma'am.' That is *not* going to work." She held up her hand before I could explain. "I know it's that good Southern upbringing; that's how I was raised. But now that I'm ma'am age, I prefer young people with a little more of a northern edge."

I laughed. "Yes, ma—" We both laughed as I stopped myself.

"What's so funny?"

I stiffened when Pastor Jeffries entered through a side door that led right to the kitchen. Mrs. Jeffries was still chuckling when Pastor Jeffries kissed his wife, then loosened his tie. "You know I hate it when you don't wait for me at church." Turning to me, he added, "I don't like to do anything without my wife, not even ride home."

She giggled, and though he laughed with her, I knew he meant what he'd said. He reached his hand to me, and I searched his eyes. But there was nothing except warmth as I accepted his handshake. "It's good to see you, son."

If Mrs. Jeffries stopped me from speaking with the use of that word, Pastor Jeffries was about to take me out. Had I just imagined that death stare from the altar?

And then . . . he said, "Come with me up to my office so we can talk before we sit down to dinner."

She gave her husband a long side glance. "Don't be up there too long. All I have to do is heat up these dishes."

He kissed her again, then guided me to another hallway, which led to another set of stairs.

As I followed him, I reminded myself that this was Chastity's father. I couldn't get into another confrontation with him.

When I stepped over the threshold of his office, I knew whoever had decorated his church office had probably been the designer here, as well. From the desk to the bookcases and the rug covering the parquet floor, the black-and-burgundy decor was very masculine, very traditional. I was drawn to the two cherrywood gun cabinets with backlights that showcased about a dozen firearms.

Before I could take a detour to check them out, Pastor Jeffries gestured for me to have a seat in one of the chairs across from the love seat. As he sat, he said, "I've been wanting to talk to you from the moment I walked out of Chastity's apartment Tuesday night." He jerked off his tie. "I'm sorry for the way I reacted. I was shocked, but that's no excuse."

I exhaled with relief. Now I knew for sure, I'd just imagined his stare. "I appreciate you saying that, sir. Your apology means a lot because I really love your daughter."

He nodded. "I can see that."

"And I will take care of her all the time, in every way."

"That's all I can ask," Pastor Jeffries said. "That you will love and honor Chastity." He paused, but I knew more was coming, and I braced myself on the edge of the chair, waiting for the conversation to go left. Squeezing my hands into a fist, I breathed in air and held it.

He began, "You know, from the moment I saw Sisley Darbonne, I knew I loved her."

I squinted at his words; he'd taken a right turn instead.

He continued, "She was young, but she was brilliant and feisty, and I don't have to mention that she was gorgeous. But although I loved her, once we were married, I didn't always honor her. And while I've given up the guilt, I live with the regret.

"I do thank God for my Damascus experience. I knew if I didn't have a complete change in my life, my wife and daughter would be gone." He shook his head. "If it wasn't for the saving grace of God"—he held up his hand—"I have no idea where I'd be, but I know I wouldn't be here."

I nodded, not quite sure of what I should say.

"I'm telling you this because I want you to know the blessings that come from honoring a covenant God has ordained."

"Well, I'm looking forward to those blessings," I said.

When he smiled, I relaxed my fingers, loosened my shoulders. Settled into the chair and the conversation. Until his words sent me to the edge again.

"You asked me something the other day, and I'd like to address that. About the reception and me performing the ceremony." A pause. "I would very much like to do that. Thank you for giving me that opportunity."

I wanted to pump my fist in the air. This was the real relief I needed. Now Chastity and I would be legally married. I'd have to figure out the paperwork, but I wasn't concerned—I'd come this far; I'd come up with something. "Thank you, Pastor Jeffries. You don't know what this means to me."

He chuckled. "That's what Chastity said."

"I keep saying we're connected."

With a nod, he said, "Indeed." But then he peered at me, and his stare and his silence made me stiffen again. The intensity in his eyes was just like what I saw an hour ago. He was studying me, and I tried my best not to writhe beneath the heat of his glare, but it was hard not to prepare for the punch.

"You haven't had many male role models in your life, have you?"

Again, he'd taken a different turn than I expected. "No, sir."

He heard my caution, because he held up his hand. "That's not a judgment, son. You've done well with what you were given. But you need to know you have someone now. While you have a responsibility to my daughter, I have a responsibility to you as your father-in-law, and as your pastor. As your father-in-law, I want to be that man you come to when you need to talk about anything. And as your pastor, I want to be that spiritual leader you come to about everything."

I had to pause, swallow, and blink back all the feelings that welled up in me. "I don't even know what to say," I whispered. "No one . . ." I stopped, but I didn't need to finish, because Pastor Jeffries nodded.

"I know," he said. "Just know that I'm here. Now, our talks won't always be easy, especially the spiritual ones, because my job is to help you get straight with the Lord. But our talks will always be truthful and always done in love."

In love. His words lifted me to a place I'd never been. I'd never felt this—acceptance, complete inclusion. Before I could speak, I was saved by a voice that came through speakers I couldn't even see.

"Pastor, you and Xavier come on down. I'm going to call the girls, too."

He glanced at me with a grin. "We've been summoned."

We chuckled together and I said, "Pastor"—he smiled—"thank you. No one has ever accepted me this way."

I reached for his hand, but this time when he took it, he pulled me into an embrace and patted my back, though it felt like he was punching me. I guessed not everything had changed. He was still letting me know he was Chastity's father and was willing to drag me if it ever came to that.

We moved toward the door together, but before we crossed the threshold, the pastor paused.

"Speaking of saving grace," he began, taking us back to the beginning of the conversation, "one of my saving graces after we were married was that Sisley's father didn't get in his car and bring a couple of his double-barreled shotguns with him to have a little talk with me. He didn't live close enough, since her parents were still in Savannah." He paused. "That was *my* saving grace," he said before he stepped out of the room.

I stood there for a moment, shocked. But then I chuckled as I followed him. The threat had been given, the message received, and I had nothing to worry about. I'd waited so long to be married to a woman like Chastity. There was nothing I would do to mess this up.

36

Chastity

I t felt like old times, but everything was new. It was old the way we sat around the dinner table and ate that good food until we were stuffed. It was old the way we chatted and laughed and solved all the problems of the world.

But it was new because I sat next to my husband. And my parents and Melanie played a silly game where, whenever they clanged their silverware against the glasses, Xavier and I had to kiss—which we didn't mind at all.

The whole day I'd been swaddled in love, which had seemed impossible just days before. But now my parents called Xavier *son*, and when we left, he hugged them like he hoped to one day really love them.

The memories made me sigh when we slid into the back of Kelvin (who'd joined us in time for the sweet potato crumb cake) and Melanie's SUV and I snuggled into my husband's arms. Who would have thought this was where we'd be five days ago? On Tuesday, I'd thought I'd be a seventy-hour bride, but Xavier had not only told me, he'd shown me his apology, and with the grace I'd learned from my mother, I'd forgiven him. After Tuesday, we'd lived five days of euphoria. This wouldn't last—it couldn't—but this was our foundation; we'd build our marriage on this time.

The four of us chatted like longtime friends on the ride to this wine bar Melanie had been raving about. Less than forty minutes after we left Harlem, Kelvin slowed his SUV onto Eighth Street in the Village.

He eased the truck to a stop in front of the valet stand, and after we slid out of the car, Melanie and I held our husbands' hands as we strolled toward the red-framed glass door. Melanie and Kelvin stepped inside first, and just as we were about to follow, a couple pushed their way out.

Xavier and I stepped aside, and I smiled at the guy, who strutted with his arm draped around his girl, but then the two of them paused.

"What's up, X-Man?" The guy reached for Xavier and pulled him into a hug.

By the time the woman squealed and hugged Xavier, too, I kinda had an idea of who these two were—at least the guy.

"Oh my goodness." I pressed my hand against my chest. "Are you Bryce?" Before he even responded, I said, "I'm Chastity."

His smile was broad and bright. "What's up, sis?" He wrapped his arms around me. "It's about time we met."

"I know. It's crazy"—I pulled back from his hug—"that after all this time, I'm just meeting my husband's best friend." When Bryce's eyes widened, I realized Xavier hadn't told him, just like I hadn't told Melanie. I said, "Oh my goodness, you didn't know we got married."

Bryce shook his head, then stood like a zombie. But while he was catatonic, the woman with him clapped.

"This is insane. I'm Samantha, by the way. Congratulations. Can I see your ring?"

With pride, I held up my hand as Samantha oohed and aahed over the diamond, which sparkled even under the night sky.

Finally, Bryce found his voice. "Hey, let me have a look at that." He held my fingertips and peered at the ring as if he were a gemologist. He studied it so hard, it made me wonder if he was considering making that move with Samantha.

"That's really nice." He glanced at Xavier. "Well, all I can say is congratulations."

"Thank you." I hooked my arm through Xavier's.

"So you got married," Bryce repeated, his unbelief in his tone. His expression was just like Melanie's this morning. Then he said, "That was fast."

I chuckled. "Everyone says that, but even my parents have come around. Especially now that they've seen how happy we are."

"Awww," Samantha sang. "I think it's the most romantic thing ever. There're lots of stories of people who get married after knowing each other for just a weekend." Turning to Xavier, she said, "I'm glad for you, Xavier. I was so worried after Rox—"

Xavier spoke over her. "I'll check you later, Bryce," he said before he shoved me inside the bar, without even a chance to say good-bye.

I stumbled across the threshold. "Hold up, Xavier." He held my arm to steady me. "What was that about?"

"What?" he asked as if he always pushed me through doors.

"You just pushed me and walked away when Samantha was in midsentence." I was more confused than anything else.

"Bryce told her about my story," he snapped. "And I didn't want to hear how happy she is because of all I'd been through." He shook his head like he was annoyed, and now I just wanted to bring him back to where he'd been ten seconds before.

"Ah, come on. She's just happy for you, babe." With my kiss, I relaxed him. "Let's enjoy the rest of the night."

His smile told me he agreed, and with a quick scan of the bar, Xavier spotted Kelvin and Melanie. By the time we sat down, both of us were back to that happy place.

I was beginning to understand my man, knowing what I had to do to keep his anger in check. That was a good thing, I knew. It was all part of my purpose.

37

Xavier

I yawned as I pushed through the revolving doors leading into my office building. But instead of walking toward the elevator bank, I detoured to the right and sat on the edge of one of the decorative planters. Pulling out my cell, I pressed my fist against another yawn. This was going to be a long day, after a short night.

We'd gotten back to my condo early enough, and after two glasses of wine, I was in a mellow zone. But once I laid my head on the pillow, my mind never released me to rest. Even as Chastity slept beside me, a cacophony of voices echoed in my head:

But when God talks about wrath, He talks about the suffering that will come from the punishment of being a wrathful man.

Then there was Bryce: *You have some deep issues . . . do something about all of this rage . . . before it's too late.*

What had surprised me most, though, was hearing Roxanne: *What's inside of you, Xavier, that's not anger. It's not even rage . . . it's worse.*

I hadn't thought about her in weeks, certainly not since I'd given my heart to Chastity. But in the middle of last night, Roxanne had stayed, along with the others—their words, their tones, all rebukes.

They were wrong, though. I wasn't an angry black man. I was a black man in an angry world.

Glancing at my cell, I hesitated before I awakened the screen. After I tapped the name and held the phone to my ear, I wasn't surprised when my call was answered on the first ring.

Bryce said, "I was waiting to hear from you, fam."

It wasn't only those voices that had kept me awake. Seeing Bryce and Samantha had rocked me. I hadn't put much thought into what I was going to tell him; I figured I'd wait a few weeks, if not a month, and by then, I'd have time as proof that Chastity and I were good.

But by coincidence, I'd been outed, so now I had to face him. As New Yorkers rushed past to get to their nine-to-five desks, I said, "What's up, black man?" as if this were going to be the most casual conversation we'd ever had.

"Really?" Bryce said, not impressed. "This is how you're going to handle it?"

I sighed. "Okay, I got married."

"Uh, yeah. And I saw you, like, twelve days ago. Were you already married when we met up at Sweat Box?"

"Nah, we got married last week, over the Columbus Day weekend," I said leaving out the New Orleans part.

"And you didn't think you should hit a brother up?"

"Come on, Bryce," I said, then lowered my voice. "Call you and say what? I knew how you'd react."

"You don't know jack!"

"Apparently, I do; just listen to you. Instead of wishing me well, you're in attack mode."

With a sigh, he backed up. "You're right. 'Congratulations again' is where I should have started. Especially since Chastity seems like she's not only great but in the two minutes that I talked to her, she seemed happy."

There was so much surprise in his tone that I said, "She *is* happy, bruh. We both are. We made this decision together."

After a moment of silence he said, "I just wanted this to be different for you than—"

Before he began the litany of names, I jumped in, "Don't go down the path of the past. Chastity is my wife. That already makes this different."

"You're right." He sighed, then started over. "I truly wish you the best. That's all I've ever wanted; the best of everything for you. But, uh . . ."

My fingers curled, preparing for Bryce to do what he often did: take me to that place.

He said, "Couldn't you buy her a new ring?" and laughed.

"Why?" I asked, exhaling at the same time. "You know how much that ring is worth?" I shook my head. "But thanks for not saying anything about that."

"What kind of brother would I be if I blew up your spot like that?"

"Clearly, Samantha doesn't agree with you."

"Yeah, that kind of slipped out. But at least she didn't say anything about the ring."

"Thank God." I paused, wishing I could end the conversation here, but the yawn that was rising up inside of me made me say, "Listen, I want to ask you something."

"Whatever, bruh, I got you."

"Remember the therapist you mentioned when we were at Sweat Box?" I didn't wait for him to respond. "If you still have her number . . ."

Holding my breath, I waited for his judgment. But right away, he said, "You know what? I did keep her information. Hold on."

I explained, "I'm still talking to Chastity's father, and KJ has really been good, but I want to make sure I handle this. Not that there's anything wrong," I rambled, "but I want to be the best I can be for my wife."

I didn't need to be on a video call to know Bryce was smiling; I felt his grin. Without any questions, he said, "Her name is Dr. Daniella Escobar. She comes highly recommended. I'll text it to you."

"I appreciate you."

"It's what we do. Let's get together soon, bruh . . . I mean, married man."

After a laugh, I clicked off the phone, then swiped over to my text messages. The doctor's name and number were there. I stared at the text for a moment, thinking about the sermon, thinking about my past, thinking I'd do anything to make sure Chastity and I would always be solid.

With a nod, I turned toward the elevators.

ALL MORNING I'D been wavering. Did I really need to see this doctor? But I finally called after I had to hide too many yawns in too many meetings. I was on the phone for less than ten seconds before I received the first sign that I'd done the right thing: Dr. Escobar answered her phone. When I told her I was surprised to be speaking with her directly, she explained her assistant was at lunch.

Then the second sign: After introducing myself, I asked for her first available appointment.

"Actually, I just hung up from a cancellation. Are you available this evening for my last appointment at five thirty?"

I was still doubtful, but then, these were signs. At least I could go and ask questions. So I agreed to be at her Turtle Bay–area office at five thirty, and after eight hours that felt like eighteen, I left my office two hours earlier than normal. Hopping out of the cab on First Avenue, I entered a gray brick building that blended with the others on the block. With each step, I asked, *What am I doing here?* and the question remained even as I was buzzed inside Suite 104.

The office was bland and basic, much like the building, with its industrial steel-colored carpet, eggshell-colored walls. Metal had been the designer's decorating choice, with six metal folding chairs lined against one wall and a gray desk along the other. The bright red of the braids of a twentysomething young woman was the only color in the room.

"You must be Mr. King." She greeted me with a smile that matched her singsong voice. "I'm Louise."

Louise handed me a clipboard, then pointed me toward a chair. It just took a few moments to fill out the form, since I included only my name, made up an address, and left off my phone number.

When I handed Louise the half-filled-out form, she frowned. Before she asked, I said, "I'm paying out of pocket." There was no need for me to share my insurance information; there'd never be a paper trail between me and this office, especially since one day I hoped to be in politics.

The office door opened, and Dr. Escobar stepped out. "Mr. King." She held out her hand. "It's nice to meet you." She was polite, curt, all business.

I shook her hand, then followed the dark-haired beauty into her office. I'd seen her picture from the research I'd done, but she was more striking in person. I wasn't sure if it was her jet-black waist-length hair, which swung with her stride, or her blue eyes, which were shocking against her olive skin. It was because of her résumé that I guessed she was around my age; in person, I would have thought she was ten years younger.

Her office had been designed with a lot more care than the reception area. The stark white furniture (desk, chairs, book-shelves) and dozens of plants gave the space an oasis aura, and I got it, because right away, I relaxed.

Dr. Escobar didn't have a sofa for me to stretch out, but she did direct me to one of the cushy chairs, and I sank into the softness. Was this how psychologists manipulated clients into revealing their darkest secrets? Readjusting, I shifted to the edge of the chair.

"So," she began and leaned back in her chair as if we were about to just chat, "I can tell you a little about me if you'd like."

I shook my head. "I did my research and was impressed." I paused long enough for her to thank me, and then I added, "I'm here because I'd like to ask a few questions."

"That's interesting." She smiled, letting me know she wasn't offended. "Usually, I'm the one asking questions."

"Well, I just got married, and I want to be the best husband I can be."

"Congratulations. It isn't often that a man walks in and says that, but this is something I believe. We're all trained profession-ally to become doctors, lawyers, teachers, but we don't receive training for the most important roles in our lives: being a spouse and a parent. So I commend you. Before we start, though, are you aware I do couples' counseling?"

I held up my hands, wanting to stop that thought. "This is all about me."

"All right. What about you?"

Now that I was here, I wasn't sure where to begin. I decided to start with the one who'd been bugging me for the longest. "A good friend of mine thinks I have some anger issues."

She didn't even blink when she asked, "What do *you* think?"

I shrugged. "I don't think I'm any different from other black men. We live in America. We're angry."

"Is your friend a black man? Living in America?"

I shifted, looked away. "Yeah."

"And even with that, he thinks you have anger issues." Her tone, sounding as if she was surprised, was part of her point.

But her tactic didn't deter me. I said, "He's known me for a long time. Since I came to New York from Mississippi."

"How long have you been here?"

"About sixteen years. Came here when I was eighteen."

"Did you come here for school?"

That made me chuckle. "No, I came here to get away, and I was actually homeless for a while." I paused, waiting for her reaction. But there was none, which surprised me. Being homeless wasn't something I often shared because of the reactions. People's opinions always changed (not in a positive way) with that revelation. Keeping on, I said, "I came here knowing no one, and when I got off the bus, I didn't even know where I was. But I was here with a duffel bag filled with clothes, almost a thousand dollars, and enough street smarts to get a job as a dishwasher in a restaurant where I was able to wash up and change clothes. When the restaurant closed at two in the morning, I hung out on the streets, like a whole bunch of other people."

Even with all of that, she had no reaction. Just another question. "What made you want to get away from Mississippi?"

A plethora of Gran's attacks rushed me, and I shook my head to silence her voice. "Sleeping on park benches was a step up from where I'd been. I met Bryce a few weeks after I got here;

his father was one of the restaurant's owners, and Bryce hung out there after school. We became friends, his dad found out I was homeless, and after a few months of wandering the streets at night . . ." I shrugged. "Good things started happening."

"Bryce is the one who said you had anger issues?"

"Yeah, and it doesn't make sense, 'cause he knows what I've been through."

"When he says you have anger issues, what is he speaking about specifically?"

I shrugged. "I don't know." After a pause, I added, "Sometimes, I raise my voice."

For the first time, a reaction: her eyebrow inched up slightly as if she was telling me that was bull. "Anything else?" she asked, giving me another chance for a better answer.

"There may have been times when my anger escalated from there."

"Turned violent?"

Her tone was nonchalant, but my reaction wasn't. "No!" I shook my head. "I'm not a violent man." Her blank expression made me add, "I mean, there have been times when maybe I've gotten a little, you know."

"I don't know."

I inhaled. "I've never been violent with a woman."

"Interesting you said 'a woman.'"

"I've never been violent with anyone. I mean, there've been people around when I've lost control."

Her head bobbed, almost as if she were listening to music. "You've used the words *escalated, lost control* . . . would you say you've gone beyond the boundaries of anger?"

"I don't know." This time, her expression was filled with surprise. As if she couldn't believe I would lie right to her face. "That's why I'm here. I wanted to know what constitutes anger issues, what are the boundaries, and if, by some chance, I have a few issues, how would I fix that?"

She rolled her chair closer to her desk and leaned forward as if she was ready to get to work. "I wish it worked like that. I wish I could define anger for you, then we could determine if you had issues, and finally, I could give you a prescription and send you home. But it's much more complicated.

"You see, anger is one of the core birth emotions." She sounded as if she was about to give me a lecture. "We're all going to get angry; in fact, that's one of the first emotions we display as newborns. However, we learn how to handle that. Most of us learn to get angry and then let it go. Others have learned what is called chronic anger. That's anger that lingers, and, to use one of your words, it's anger that escalates."

Chronic anger—was that me?

"So starting with the basics, what did you learn about anger as a child?"

I chuckled. "I didn't have to learn a thing, because I lived it," I said. "My grandmother was in a perpetual state of anger when it came to me."

When she asked me to elaborate, I told her (almost) everything about life with Gran and how she'd never spoken a kind word to me.

"Not once," I reiterated to Dr. Escobar. "Every word she ever said was filled with something just short of hate. She told me I was unworthy, I'd never amount to anything, no one loved me."

"What did you do with your feelings when your grandmother spoke to you that way?"

"Nothing. I didn't do anything because I was a kid and she was an adult in search of a reason to . . ." I stopped, but I could see in Dr. Escobar's eyes she knew I'd feared a beating.

"So you held it inside," she said.

I shrugged. "What else could I do? I even stopped crying when she beat me. Which only made her beat me harder, but holding my tears was my victory. I became strong because I held it in."

"But the mind isn't designed to hold anything like that inside. We aren't meant to be beaten, especially not as children. So whatever you held within had no choice but to one day come out. And," she continued, "I'd venture to say when all of that anger was finally released, it was an explosion."

She spoke as if she'd been there the night Gran told me Mama had died. The night my anger first found its way through a wall.

She continued through my silence, "And it exploded over and over, year after year, because it'd been repressed for so long."

My fingers flexed at her description.

"That's what you've learned," she said. "To never show your anger. To hold it until it bursts out as rage."

"Or wrath," I added.

She raised her eyebrows. "Yes."

Okay, there was my professional diagnosis. "So what can I do about it, Doctor? I mean, maybe it's true what you're saying . . ."

"Maybe?"

"I just want to know if I do have any . . . anger issues, how can I fix them?"

"There are no quick fixes. If this has been brewing inside of you for as long as you described, it's going to take time to work it through."

That was fine for someone who had time; I didn't. I couldn't afford to have another outburst. Couldn't lose control again in front of Chastity.

"There are several things we're going to go over in the next few weeks," Dr. Escobar said, "and at some point, it would be good to include your wife so she can help with your triggers and learn actions to help you gain control."

I nodded, though there wasn't a single chance of me bringing Chastity anywhere near this place . . . or my issues.

"Between today and our next appointment, it would be great if you kept a journal so we can come to understand your triggers. Most of us have the same things that set us off, but I want you to focus particularly on which situations escalate the anger within you."

"Sure, I can do that," I said, though I didn't have any intention of following through, since I wouldn't be seeing her again.

She added, "Journaling is also a good way to deescalate a situation. Rather than exploding at someone, you can write down what you're feeling. Everything that you want to say to them." She chuckled when she added, "Even the bad words." The expression on my face made her hold up her hand. "But you're never going to give anyone what you've written. The paper is just the place to release the rage without harm being done."

If I had that kind of time in my life, that might be a good thing. But I couldn't stop my workday, couldn't tell a business associate to hold on while I wrote a letter.

She added, "And exercising is another good tool. It doesn't have to be anything planned or strenuous. The point is to remove yourself from a situation, even if you have to do it abruptly. Go for a walk or run . . ."

That worked, I knew for sure.

"Those are good actions that will help between sessions. And then, as we work together, you'll learn more internal things to do. Do you have any more questions?"

"No"—I shook my head—"you've really helped."

"Great. Well, speak with Louise to set up your next appointment." She pushed back her chair, though she didn't stand. "I'd like to see you once a week in the beginning, and then after a few months, we'll ease back."

I nodded, then followed as she stood. I shook her hand, told her I'd see her soon. But by the time I was outside hailing a cab, I'd all but forgotten the doctor's name. She'd given me enough to work with—I'd exercise my anger away. I'd work it out, literally. In fact, I decided to head over to Sweat Box right now.

38

Chastity

I wanted to savor this moment, so I closed my eyes, then after a couple of seconds, pushed the key into the lock, and stepped over the threshold. Standing at the door, I took in the bare space. How long had I lived here? Seventeen, eighteen weeks? So much had changed since the end of July . . . and the remodeling of my life made me smile.

Walking through the condo, I relished this space, though I hadn't spent much time here since I'd met Xavier so soon after returning home. Still, giving up this apartment was like turning in the keys to who I'd been. My life as a single woman had come to an end.

I smiled all the way through . . . until I entered the master bedroom. Standing in the doorjamb, I stared at the reason for this visit. For the last six weeks, I'd been living out of a suitcase, with trips here every other day to grab another suit or pair of shoes. Our schedules were too busy for us to make that final move, but with Thanksgiving next week, I had to just stop . . . and do this. Packing up and moving most of my things to storage was how Xavier and I had spent the free hours of last week, though today, I was here alone, handling this.

Stepping all the way inside, I glanced at the mark of Xavier's aggression. Today was the first appointment I could schedule to have the spot repaired.

I did what I always did when I faced this wall: I closed my eyes, remembering how he'd stormed toward me, eyes bulging, red with rage. Then the sound of his fist and how I'd been so afraid.

But I needed to finally toss that aside, because since then, there had been nothing but beautiful days. We'd made time for each other—a quick lunch here, a dinner rendezvous there. And then inside our bedroom . . . Married, guiltless sex was the best. I needed to keep my thoughts in the present; I needed to forget those three times.

Three times.

I was grateful when I heard the doorbell. The painter would keep me occupied and away from those thoughts until I met Melanie uptown for lunch. But when I swung the front door open, my best friend bounced into the apartment.

"What are you doing here?" I asked Melanie after she hugged me. To my ears, I sounded like a robot. "I thought we were going to meet at—"

"Yeah," she interrupted, "but it didn't make sense that you were here to inspect the place and I wasn't. I mean, I know it's immaculate, but I wanted to see if we needed to paint or anything." She sauntered past me into the living room.

"Uh . . . you didn't have to come," I said, wondering how to keep her from the bedroom.

She waved her hand. "Now I won't have to do it during the week. So"—she glanced around the living room/dining room/kitchen area—"anything I need to repair?"

She spoke so fast, and moved even faster, that she was in the bedroom before I could keep her out. I was behind her when she stopped and stared at the fist-size indentation in the wall. "What happened here?"

"I'm getting that fixed; a painter is on his way."

She spun around, facing me. "Not one of those words answered my question."

One of the things I'd never done with my best friend was lie, but still I said, "Would you believe it if I said that's where I mounted my TV?"

I chuckled, she didn't. "Chas-ti-ty . . ."

My government name . . . her admonishment. I held up my hands. "I really am having that fixed, but Xavier . . . had a little accident."

"What kind of accident?" Her glance shifted from me to the wall.

"Xavier got upset one night and—"

"What!"

Then she paused as if she wanted me to repeat what I'd said. But with the way she'd just rattled the walls with her scream, that wasn't going to happen.

"Chastity Jeffries, you better start talking."

"I'm Chastity Jeffries *King*," I said, trying to bring down the heat.

"Chas-ti-ty!"

"All right." I moved past her and turned my attention to the bedroom's window, hoping Melanie would follow and stop looking at the wall. She stayed where she was. I said, "He was upset the night we told my parents we got married and . . . he punched the wall. You've heard of guys doing that before, right?"

"No. No man I've ever known in my history of knowing men has ever punched a hole in a wall."

"It's not quite a hole."

Her eyes narrowed as she crossed her arms. "Why are you making a joke out of something so serious?"

"Because I don't want you to get bent out of shape for no reason."

"No reason." She studied me, making me shift from one foot to the other. Then the questions came like rapid fire. "Is he violent? Has he hit you? Are you being abused?"

"No." My eyes widened. "All of that because of this?" I pointed to the wall. "You need to step back, because you know Xavier—"

"No, I don't. We've hung out a few times, but I don't know him, and neither do you if he goes around punching holes in walls when he gets mad."

"Please don't make me regret telling you."

She huffed, then leaned against the wall and slid down. When her butt hit the carpet, she gestured for me to do the same, and I sat across from her.

A minute was so much longer when it was filled with silence instead of chatter. These minutes felt eternal as I watched my friend assess all that I'd told her. Finally, she spoke up: "Maybe I am making this a big deal, so break it down for me."

The truth—I did want to speak to someone because . . . of those three times. I said, "He punched the wall. He was that mad, and it was that scary."

"Did he . . ." She stopped as if she couldn't finish.

I shook my head. "He didn't, but I thought he was going to."

Even though her hand was pressed against her mouth, her gasp still slipped out. "You thought it? Because he's done it before?"

"No, he's never hit me."

"But . . ."

That one word was a huge question, and I answered, "He

gets really mad." Her eyes narrowed. "That wasn't the first time he scared me."

"And you still married him?"

"He's never hit me."

She glanced up at the wall. "But you thought he was going to."

"Looking back, it wasn't that bad. I was scared, but only for a couple of seconds. He was sorry the moment he did it."

"Yeah"—she nodded slowly—"they're always sorry."

Now I was the one who squinted. "I don't think it will happen again because I've learned how to calm him."

Her eyes were even bigger than before, and her voice was louder than any sound that should be coming from someone her size. "It happens that often? That you've had to learn to calm him down?"

"It's just that he's really stressed right now. And when I talk to him in the right way, I can get him settled in a good place."

"So you talk to him," she said with all kinds of sarcasm, "in the 'right' way. You consider that effective therapy?"

With the way she was talking to me, I wanted to punch a wall myself. "I consider that being a good wife. Are you trying to antagonize me?"

"I'm trying to help you, maybe even save you."

In the next seconds, we both took a couple of deep breaths, cleared our minds, and started over.

"Mel, I know this may sound crazy, but I think his anger issues may be one of the reasons why God brought us together."

"You're right, it sounds crazy. Have you ever talked to him about his anger issues?"

"A little. But he doesn't see it. He thinks we all get angry."

Then her head tilted as if she had a new thought. "Does your dad know about this?"

"No, I would never tell my parents," I said, thinking now she was the one who was crazy.

"But your dad knows," she stated as a fact.

"What are you talking about?"

She pushed herself up and pointed at me. "Remember when your father preached on anger?"

"He was finishing the seven deadly sins series."

"So you don't think any of that was about Xavier?" She didn't give me a moment to respond. "You know your father and his discernment."

"If he had been talking about Xavier, he would have preached backward, you know that. But he didn't because it was just the next sin he was teaching."

She shook her head, crossed her arms, paced in front of me. "I don't care what you say, that was about your husband, and your father knows."

"And I don't care what *you* say, it wasn't about him, and my father doesn't know, because if he did, Xavier would be something just short of dead right now."

We glared at each other; the doorbell rang as if it were the referee, sending us to our corners. I moved to stand; she held up her hand.

"Stay there. I'll get it. But we have more to talk about," she commanded as if someone somewhere had told this mighty munchkin she was my mother.

But I sat and waited—and fumed, because I shouldn't have said anything. My cell rang, and when I saw Xavier's picture, I considered sending him to voice mail so I wouldn't have to talk in front of Melanie. But I accepted the call because that's what we always did, and as soon as I said, "Hey, babe," I heard his cheer. "What's up?" I asked, pushing myself from the floor.

"Baby, you're not going to believe this, but the cable company settled."

"What? I thought there was still—"

He interrupted me. "I thought so, too, but that's what this morning's emergency meeting was about. Not only are they settling but this will be the biggest settlement in Steyer and Smith's history."

I pressed my hand against my chest, feeling my own excitement. "Oh my God, Xavier. Congratulations. I'm so proud of you."

"Do you know what this means?" That was rhetorical, because he answered before I could speak, "I'm going to be made partner, baby. Can you believe it?"

"Yes, I can. You deserve it."

"Is the painter there? Because I wanna celebrate."

"He just got here, but"—I turned as Melanie strolled back in, followed by a black dude in jeans and a sweatshirt, carrying a huge bag of tools—"I don't have to stay," I said, leaving out the part that Melanie was with me. "I'll come home."

"Thanks, baby. I can't wait to see you."

I clicked off the phone, and as the painter studied the crack, Melanie said, "I thought we were going to lunch."

"I'll need a rain check. My husband just won a big case, and we want to celebrate."

That news took a bit of the bite from her fight; I could tell she didn't want to say it, but she did. "Congratulations. I know he's been working hard."

"He has, and this will take a lot of pressure off." That was my way of saying there was nothing to see here, nothing to worry about.

I hugged her, though her hands stayed by her sides, then I dropped the key into her palm. "I've prepaid, including the tip,"

I whispered as I jutted my chin toward the painter. "Thank you for staying here."

"Mm-hmm," she hummed.

"And I'll make this up to you."

"Mm-hmm."

I rushed away from Melanie, and that hole in the wall, not stopping till I was out the door. At the elevator banks, I pressed my weight against the wall. Melanie and I had shared everything since we were kids, but I was over that. Now that I was married I understood that no one on the outside could ever understand what was going on inside.

"I'll never do that again," I whispered as I stepped into the elevator. And then I asked myself what was I talking about. It wasn't going to happen; Xavier would never get that angry again. I knew that for sure.

It was time to push every bad thought aside. Time to celebrate my husband's impending partnership and his bright future.

39

Xavier

My eyes wouldn't close. So once the clock ticked past five, I gave up the fight and rolled out of bed. Two minutes later, I was dressed in a sweat suit and sneakers. My plan was to go for a run, even in this December weather. But as I stumbled through the condo, I was overcome by the exhaustion that came from weeks of restless nights.

Inside the kitchen, I crossed my arms and tried to lay my head atop the glass table, but like in the bedroom, closed eyes didn't mean I'd rest. My mind was filled with turbulence, thoughts crashing, then settling, leaving me in a state of sorrow.

Exactly three weeks had passed since I'd received the biggest settlement in Steyer and Smith's history. Three weeks filled with celebrations and recognition . . . It was still being praised on the news.

But as the Christmas season rang in, I didn't feel any kind of festive spirit. It was because among all the praise, there was something not being said. Not once in these weeks had anyone uttered a word about me becoming a partner.

Standing, I turned to the espresso machine, hoping a shot of caffeine would awaken me enough to get a run or a workout in.

That was one thing I'd taken from Dr. Escobar. Since that visit, I'd been to the gym daily, releasing the fury that burned within onto punching bags and opponents. Last week, I'd even left a guy knocked out on the mat. I'd raged like a bull at Sweat Box, all so I wouldn't bring any of that home to Chastity. I sipped the espresso and scanned the kitchen, which could be photographed for one of those cable home shows. My home was immaculate, my career disciplined; there was even a method and a mindset to the clothes I wore. All of it was designed to put distance between my present and my past. Living in this place, being married to Chastity, with educational credentials that had me at the top percentile in the nation—all of it was supposed to bury my Mississippi history.

But it seemed my past hadn't been entombed deep enough. Steyer and Smith had done an extensive background check before I'd been hired; Mr. Steyer had discussed it with me at the time. But my transgressions—being fired from two law firms previously—had all been professional, so I'd thought a personal search had not been done.

It was obvious now that I'd been wrong. What they'd found out about me professionally had been enough to hire me with a warning. But what they'd learned about me personally kept me from being a partner. The firm must have discovered everything I'd tried to keep hidden. Maybe they'd even uncovered the truth of my paternity, or that I'd been homeless. This was the only explanation for this slight, because my results were unimpeachable; I should have been made a partner a couple of years ago.

But it seemed that education and results didn't trump my being a poor black kid from the deepest part of the South.

The sun began its slow rise, filling the kitchen with the golden light of dawn; I returned to the table and rolled my conclusions over in my mind. As time passed, I knew I needed to stop focusing on the problem and turn to the solution. Someone at the firm needed to answer to me.

Her touch was light, but it startled me nonetheless.

"Sorry, babe," Chastity said, then kissed my cheek.

This was a sign of how off I was, because in the two months since we'd been married, I'd always felt Chastity, even if I didn't always hear her approaching; we were that connected.

"Babe, what's wrong?" Chastity slid into the chair across from me. "You've been restless for the past couple of days."

We weren't that connected if she thought it had just been days. "Nothing." Even though I'd been used to talking to Chastity about everything, "nothing" was all I had for her right now. How could I share this? She was already a partner; she'd already been found worthy, and I didn't want her pity.

She reached for my hand, but I edged away. Her eyebrows knitted together in confusion, not in anger. "Why won't you talk to me, babe?"

I lowered my eyes to my coffee. "I told you, it's nothing."

"I know what you said," she pressed, "but I'm looking at you, I'm living with you, I love you, and all of that adds up to me knowing something's wrong."

I shook my head; I wasn't going to give her any more.

When she held up her hands in surrender, I breathed. Still, I sat pensive while she popped a K-cup into the Keurig she'd brought from her place.

While she waited for her tea, she returned to the table and stood over me. I cringed at her touch, but said nothing. Just wished her away, because now, her silence was worse than her words.

When the Keurig stopped, she sauntered away, giving me new relief. But she stood at the counter, sipping, staring, filling me with heat.

I never glanced up, never gave her a word—all hints I wanted to be left alone. But then she said, "If you don't have any plans for today, I was thinking we could look at a couple of places."

What? In the middle of my crisis, she wanted to talk about real estate? I kept my eyes on my coffee.

"There're a couple of town houses for sale on Strivers' Row," she said. "But there are also a couple of fabulous lofts in SoHo." She paused long enough to take a sip. "It just depends. So many different lifestyles right here in the city."

It occurred to me in this moment just how different the two of us were. Chastity's greatest concern for her future was real estate. My concern was life-changing.

"I don't think I ever really considered how expensive it is to live in Manhattan," she continued. "But we're blessed."

Her words made me tremble.

"I've looked at preliminary numbers, and we'll be able to get something nice, especially with selling this place."

I tried to inhale, but I couldn't get enough air. At least not enough to stop the heat.

"And if we run into any snags, you know my parents will gladly help." She chuckled. "They would do anything to keep us in the city, even though if we move downtown, we'll no longer be just a mile away from them. But as long as we're close, it'll be good, because now all my mother can talk about is our reception and grandkids, as if one will come right after the other." She shook her head. "I told her to give us longer than two months."

Her chuckles, her words, made my temperature rise. Why had she mentioned her parents? Did she believe they would have to take care of us?

Once again, I closed my eyes and prayed to the God she listened to, asking Him to silence her. To make her put down her cup and walk away. But only part of my prayer was answered; she set her cup atop the counter, and then she returned to me.

She pressed her hands into my shoulders, kneading the muscles. It should have felt good; instead it felt as if she was grinding in the pain. Leaning over, she whispered, "Babe, I'm here"—she pushed—"if you want to talk"—she pushed—"I'll always be . . ."

I sprang up from my chair and faced her all in one motion. She was too stunned to move, too shocked to dodge my reach when I grabbed her throat. Gripping her neck, I pushed her back against the wall. Her eyes bulged with fear, but I couldn't stop. She had pushed; I had snapped.

"I told you I didn't want to talk." The walls vibrated from my volume.

Her lips moved, but she couldn't speak.

"I told you to leave me alone."

It wasn't until tears seeped from her eyes that my senses returned. "Oh my God," I whispered as I released her and watched her collapse like a rag doll. She gasped and coughed as she struggled to crawl away. The corner was as far as she could go and she curled into a fetal position, her coughs now intermingled with her whimpers. I took a step toward her, but I couldn't do it. Because I was still reeling from the heat.

So I rushed into the bedroom and grabbed my wallet, my cell, and then my coat before I stepped into the hallway, my wife's cries still ringing in my ears.

40

Chastity

couldn't move. Even though I knew I had to. There was no way I could sit and wait for Xavier to return. But I needed a moment to figure out how to breathe again. Leaning against the wall, I closed my eyes.

The irony of this moment wasn't lost on me. How many women had walked into my office with stories like this? How many had I helped get restraining orders? How many had I silently questioned, wondering how they'd allowed themselves to be in such a situation? This was my life professionally; it was never supposed to touch me personally.

But now violence had stormed into my life. Xavier had finally put his hands on me.

Finally. That word made me pause . . . Had this been my expectation?

I pushed myself up, stumbled from the kitchen to the front, and secured the locks on the door. But even as I did, I realized the ridiculousness of that action. Unless I changed the locks on *his* condo, there was no way I'd be able to keep *him* out. There had to be a way to protect myself, though. Because if Xavier came back before I could get out, I was going to fight. He was never going to do that to me again.

He had a gun somewhere; he'd told me when I moved in. But it wasn't going to come to that, I prayed. All I needed was something to threaten him. I settled for one of the butcher knives and took it with me into the bathroom. In front of the mirror, I turned my head from the left to the right, searching for the new mark of Xavier's wrath. The mark that was now on me.

I was shocked; I saw nothing. With the way he'd held me, with the way I couldn't breathe, with the way he stared into my eyes even as it felt as if I was beginning to separate from my body . . . I closed my eyes, never wanting to remember that. I was going to have to exorcise that memory from my consciousness.

Feeling as if my strength was back, I rushed into the bedroom's closet. I had yet to unpack half of my clothes, and I wondered what was best for me to take. Enough for a week, at least. By then, I'd muster the courage to tell someone in my life, who'd return with me to get the rest of my things. Someone who wouldn't walk into this condo and kill Xavier.

I tossed my garment bag and then a roller bag onto the bed, ignoring the wheels on the white duvet. I was a meticulous packer, but it was hard to think with all that was in my head. As I tossed clothes into the suitcase, the image of Xavier's face as he choked me had been replaced with the voice of my mother, words that she'd spoken to me over the years:

Never give up on anybody. Miracles happen every day.

"I'm not giving up on Xavier," I said as if my mother were here watching me pack. "He's given up on me. There's no way he can love me with the way he put his hands on me."

No one is perfect; we can only strive to do better today than yesterday.

"That's the problem; Xavier's todays are becoming worse

than his yesterdays. His rage is escalating, so what will his tomorrow look like?"

When you give people room to be human, you have to give them the same space to make human mistakes. That's what grace is all about.

"Choking me was not a mistake, it was an assault."

It felt as if she were standing above me, looking down with admonishment as she quoted part of her favorite scripture: *Mercy triumphs over judgment.*

But the scripture that had given her the strength to stay with my father wasn't enough for me to do the same.

Finally, I tossed my bathrobe into the suitcase before I slid into leggings and a sweatshirt. It wasn't until I zipped the luggage, wrapped myself in my coat, lugged the bags to the front, and opened my Uber app that I realized I didn't have any-place to go.

It was because I had to sit, do a search for hotels, then make reservations that so much time passed. When I heard the key in the door's lock, I jumped up, trembling before I even saw his face.

Where was the knife? I'd left it . . . in the bathroom? The bedroom? I never considered what I'd do in this moment. Now all I had was a garment bag and an overpacked suitcase to defend myself. But I was going to fight. No matter what.

He stepped into the apartment and paused, his eyes on my luggage, while my eyes focused on him. Even the flowers in his hands didn't distract me. I kept my eyes on his hands.

"Chastity."

He said my name the way he always did, like he was singing a love song.

I gripped the suitcase's handle.

"Baby."

He took a few steps toward me, and I took a couple of steps

back, which didn't make sense. I needed to be heading toward my getaway.

"Are you all right?"

His words made me stop, made me tilt my head. "Is that a real question?"

He frowned, not understanding.

"How can I be all right?" Then I broke it down for him. "You just tried to kill me."

His eyes widened as large as the windows. "No, baby. That's not what happened." As he spoke, his hands jabbed through the air with each syllable, and I watched every move.

"What did you think would happen when you wrapped your hand around my throat and squeezed?"

He shook his head. "No." He continued his protest. "That's not what happened. I didn't squeeze."

Now *I* was the one standing there with wide eyes. "Do you hear yourself, Xavier? You just grabbed my throat, pushed me against the wall, but you didn't squeeze?" Lifting the garment bag and then grabbing the handle of the suitcase, I squared off in front of him. "I'm leaving."

"You can't leave me, baby." His desperation was beyond his tone, it was in his countenance and the slump of his head and shoulders. "I love you."

When he took a step closer, I held up my hand. "If you touch me, I will call the police." It was a threat without a follow-through. There was no way I wanted this to escalate; the stakes were too high for Xavier, on the eve of his partnership, and for me—this was not publicity my father needed.

"Chastity, I can't lose you." His voice shook the way my body trembled. "I'm so sorry, but you kept pushing, you kept talking, and I needed time and space and . . ." He collapsed onto the sofa. His shoulders heaved as he covered his face.

Still, I watched his hands.

"There's just so much going on. You don't even know," he kept muttering.

Of course something had been going on with Xavier. He'd hardly been sleeping. Although I'd noticed it a few days ago, I'd waited for this morning, thinking the weekend was a better time to talk. That was all I'd wanted before he tried to choke my life out of me.

"It's been so hard, Chastity."

Mercy triumphs over judgment. I said, "I wanted to talk to you. I wanted to help."

He nodded, glanced up, and took in the sight of me with the garment bag wrapped over my arm, my suitcase by my side. He blinked, like he was fighting every emotion. I saw his thoughts—another person walking away, abandoning him.

Mercy triumphs over judgment. I lowered the garment bag to the sofa, but I stood, my hand gripping my suitcase.

His hands were still clasped in front of his face. "It's been bad, baby."

His expression made my heart beat double-time. What had he done? Pushing the garment bag aside, I eased down onto the sofa.

Xavier's shoulders relaxed a bit when I sat. "I've worked so hard, and now my career . . ."

When he stopped, I asked, "What?"

It took him a moment to say, "No one has mentioned me becoming a partner." Without taking a breath, he went on to tell me how he'd planned, how he'd worked so hard, how he'd just brought in the largest settlement—all facts I knew, but things he needed to share. So I listened.

Even though I heard his torment, I was relieved. This was something we could handle.

"To them, I'm nothing more than a poor kid from Mississippi," he finished.

"It can't be that, Xavier. What would they know about that time in your life, and if they knew something, why would they hold that against you? If anything, you would be their greatest success story."

"What else can it be?"

That was a question I couldn't answer, and truly, I wanted to help Xavier, to talk this through. But all I could do was watch his hands. There was no way I could sit here and have this discussion with his hands being my focus. "I understand how upset you are, and I want to help, but . . ." I paused so the next words would stand alone. "But we have to talk about how you assaulted me."

He dropped his hands and faced me. "That's not what I meant to do."

It took a moment for me to ingest, then digest his words. I nodded. "I believe that. I believe you didn't wake up this morning planning to choke me." When he parted his lips, I held up my hand. "But you did."

"I'm sorry" was all he had.

"And you did it because you were mad. Xavier, we've talked about this. We've talked about your rage, and it's getting worse."

"That's not what it is. It's just this stress," he said. I could tell he was still battling his emotions.

"And living with this stress is called adulting. Things happen in life, and we handle them. But you . . . don't know how."

"It was just this one time."

Was he serious? Did he not remember what he'd done? "It wasn't just this time. It's now been four times with me, and now I wonder, have you been this way with anyone else?"

"No!" He said it so instantly, so emphatically, I believed him.

"Then it's me."

He frowned and his voice was lower when he asked, "What?"

"There's something about me that brings out the worst in you."

He paused as if he was thinking about my words, or maybe he was thinking about his. "That's not true."

"It has to be. You're telling me none of this has ever happened with anyone else." I touched my neck, swallowed, then said, "So something is happening where this isn't working between us."

"No!" He faced me, and when he reached for my hands, I pulled back. Still, he kept on. "Chastity, this is not about you and me. We're perfect."

Now I was the one to shake my head.

He continued, "This is just about what I'm going through."

"That doesn't make me feel good. Because there will be other issues in life. Especially in our careers. And you talk about going into politics? Every day something will happen outside of our house, but you will come home and take it out on me. I'm never going to be a woman who stands for that."

"I wouldn't. I won't." His tone was filled with his sincerity. "I'm telling you, Chastity, from my heart, this won't happen again." When I just sat there, he said, "I'll do anything to prove it to you."

My next words were instant. "Go to counseling. I want us to go to counseling."

He didn't hesitate either. "Okay. Definitely."

I was surprised; I'd expected at least a little protest. "You mean that?"

"Yes!" This time, when he reached for my hands, I didn't jerk away. He said, "I love you and I'll do anything to fix this. I would die if you walked out that door."

"And I don't want to die because I stayed."

"No!" He sounded as if that thought frightened him. "Baby, I would never . . ."

His vibrating cell made us glance at the phone next to the flowers he'd laid on the table. We probably frowned at the same time when JACKSON STEYER flashed across the screen.

"Babe . . ."

I nodded. "Go ahead and take it. If he's calling, it's important."

Xavier stood, and as he paced, I listened to his greetings with the senior partner. By the way Xavier kept saying thank you, Mr. Steyer was once again congratulating him. But then the conversation shifted.

"Ah, yes, sir, it's true," Xavier said and glanced at me. "I got married a few months ago." He paused. "Yes," he said, as if something Mr. Steyer said surprised him. "Yes, you remembered correctly. Chastity." Another pause. "Thank you so much. I'm more than lucky, I'm blessed." Only a couple of seconds had passed when Xavier's face brightened with a smile I hadn't seen in weeks. "That would be wonderful," Xavier said. "I have to check with my wife, but I'm sure we'll be there."

My eyes narrowed.

"Thank you, and yes, we do have much to talk about. Thank you again."

When he hung up, Xavier stood, staring at his phone.

"Is everything okay?"

"Baby, it's better than okay," he whispered. He turned to me with that half smile, and even though just hours before he'd choked me, that smile still warmed me. "Mr. Steyer just invited us for drinks at his home next Saturday before the firm's Christmas party."

"Wow," I said, and then held back, wanting Xavier to tell me what this meant.

"He said every year he invites someone for a preparty cel-ebration, and this year, he wants it to be me and my lovely wife." He paused, inhaled, and then, as he spoke the next words, his voice was filled with excitement. "He said we have lots to talk about."

His relief was so visible, almost palpable, and now I smiled with him.

"Baby," he said as he dropped the phone onto the table, then knelt in front of me. "This is it."

I nodded. "I think it may be."

"No 'maybe' about it. This is happening because of you." He took my hands into his. "I am so sorry. The thought that I hurt you, hurts me, and I can't wait to go to counseling to make sure this never happens again. Just please don't leave me. I love you."

He rested his head in my lap, repeating, "I love you," as if it were a mantra meant to lull me into surrender. I had no doubt Xavier loved me. Love wasn't our problem.

But if he was willing to get help, and if he was on the verge of receiving the career prize that he'd worked so hard for . . .

Mercy triumphs over judgment.

With that thought, I raised my arms and held my husband.

I was going to stay because I wanted to. I had to. But only after taking a few precautions. I loved Xavier, but now I didn't trust him. That made me sad, but it was the truth, and I would do what I had to do to protect myself.

41

Xavier

I ripped the bow tie from my collar, needing to start all over. As I studied my reflection in the mirror, I smiled. Last week, being in a battle with a bow tie would have shot me straight to the top of the Richter scale. But with this invitation from Mr. Steyer, all my stress was gone.

How had I allowed my mind to go to those dark places? I'd wasted a lot of time, had been filled with too much anxiety—for nothing. And where had that pressure taken me? My hand . . . her throat.

I squeezed my eyes shut, not wanting that memory. As I tried to adjust my bow tie, I did the same with my thoughts, keeping my focus on the night ahead. Tonight, I'd receive the invitation to become a partner at one of the nation's most respected law firms. From there, not even the sky would limit me.

"Here," Chasity said, slipping between me and the mirror. With just a couple of nips and tucks, she had my tie right. With a smile, she whispered, "It's perfect now," then she tapped my lips with a kiss before she stepped away.

Chastity held up the hem of her red gown as she sat on the chaise to slip into her shoes, and as I watched, I once again thanked God for this woman. What she'd just said—*It's perfect now*—was about more than my tie. It was about the last week, seven days of bliss, the best time of our young marriage. It had been filled with family (a dinner with her parents where her mother announced our reception would be February 14 to celebrate our love and our birthdays) and fun, where Chastity, after a long day of work, even joined me one evening at Sweat Box. And then when we came together at night . . . this last week of loving my wife had been the best I'd ever had.

But while the memories brought a smile to my lips, the ache in my heart was just as real. My effort came not just because I loved her, but because of what I done. My hand . . . her throat.

Stop! That was behind me. Not only because the pressure was gone but because I was going to learn how to restrain the fury that raged within me. I'd called Dr. Escobar, though this time I hadn't been able to see her immediately. Her first available appointment was two weeks out, but Chastity and I would be there. Because I was more than serious—I was committed.

A tap on my shoulder startled me.

"A million pennies for your thoughts," Chastity said when I turned to her.

Her words warmed me, took me back to our beginning, and I pulled her close. "Do you know how much I love you?"

She nodded. "This I know for sure."

Then in my mind, it flashed again: my hand . . . her throat. I inhaled. "Chastity, I just want you to know I'm so—"

She covered my lips with hers in a gentle kiss, her response to my unspoken apology. She was a woman of grace, just like she'd promised she'd be on our wedding night.

What I needed to do now was become the man who deserved Chastity. And tonight would be that beginning.

I hated to break our embrace, but I said, "We'd better get going."

"Let me touch up my lipstick, and then I'll be ready."

On the nightstand, her cell vibrated, and when she took a quick glance and frowned, I asked, "Is everything okay?"

"Oh, yeah"—she waved her hand—"it's just Melanie."

I watched her tap out a message, then she grinned. "You know what? I'm ready to get this party started. I'll take care of my lips in the car."

"Or I'll take care of your lips for you," I said.

"Promises, promises," she said as she sashayed in front of me. I always loved seeing my wife come toward me, but watching her walk away . . . I needed to loosen my tie because she was doing it again. Oh, how I couldn't wait to get back here. With this woman, with what was about to happen at the Steyer home, tonight was going to be epic.

ALTHOUGH JACKSON HAD taken a liking to me from our first interview, I'd never been invited to his home. I did know, however, that a few years ago, he'd moved to the tallest residential building in the world, right on Park Avenue.

When the Uber rolled to a stop beneath the glass canopy and then the doorman opened the doors leading to the granite floor lobby, I knew Jackson Steyer was on a whole different level of luxury. Once the concierge announced us, the elevator swooped us up to the fiftieth floor. When we stepped off, there were only two apartments, and the door opened before we even had a chance to ring the bell.

"Welcome to my home, Mr. and Mrs. King." Mr. Steyer gestured for us to enter, and once we did, it was a visual extravaganza.

Everything about the expansive open space, which had two seating areas as well as a ten-person dining table, was magnificent. The cream-colored decor on the oak floors made the space luxurious enough, but the ten-foot windows along two walls were all drama.

"Oh my goodness," Chastity said. "Your home is beautiful, Mr. Steyer."

"Thank you," he said, "but two things. First, I cannot take any credit for this place; this all belongs to my beautiful wife." Then he held out his hand and, as if they'd practiced this, Mrs. Steyer entered.

I'd met the quite-a-bit-younger Mrs. Steyer at a couple of office events, and tonight, as she stood next to her husband in a very fitted, shocking-pink gown, she appeared even more youthful than her fiftysomething years.

Mr. Steyer said, "I would never have even considered moving to a place like this if it hadn't been for Kitty."

"It's nice to see you again, Mrs. Steyer."

"Oh, please," she said as she motioned for our coats, "please call me Kitty."

"And I was going to say the same thing. Please call me Jackson."

"All right," Chastity spoke for both of us as we followed the Steyers to a seating area where an unobstructed view of the southern part of the island was sprawled below us. A million city lights glimmered in the darkness of early evening. The Empire State Building glowed in gold, and beyond, One World Trade Center shined bright.

"I would never get anything done." Chastity shook her head as she turned from the windows. "Seriously. I stare out my office window all day, and it's nothing like this."

Kitty laughed. "And we have these views throughout the condo. It's hard to do anything in any room. I'll have to give you a little tour."

"I'd love that," Chastity said.

"Well, first, let's have a drink," Jackson said. "I want to, once again, congratulate Xavier." He paused. "Kitty, did I tell you what a star this young man is?"

"Oh, yes." She laughed. "Many times. According to my husband, you have quite a future with the firm."

"Thank you," I said, my voice steady, concealing my excitement within.

A young woman entered with a tray of champagne, and then we all toasted to Christmas, the coming new year, and all the wonderful things beyond. As Chastity and I sat on one sofa and the Steyers sat across from us, we sipped and snacked on champagne shrimp, honey-garlic meatballs, and stuffed baguettes.

The conversation was easy, about the warm temperatures for the season and the excitement of a new decade approaching, and Jackson even shared some of his exercise routine.

"I'll have to show you the gym we have in this building. State-of-the-art, I tell you."

I nodded and tried to stay in the conversation. But as time passed, I wanted to stand, to shout and make Jackson get to the point of this gathering.

But right before I lost all my sensibilities, Jackson said, "Darling, why don't you give Chastity a tour."

Chastity put down her glass, then squeezed my hand before she stood. Kitty hooked her arm through Chastity's, leading her from the room.

While I understood that Jackson wanted privacy, I wished Chastity could be by my side to hear this. She was so much of the reason why I was here, and this was the beginning of all the things I wanted to share with her.

"So, Xavier," Jackson said, pulling my attention back to him and this moment that would change my life. "I think you can tell I wanted to speak with you alone."

"Yes, sir," I said, trying hard to stay casual and calm when all I wanted to do was jump up and pump my fist in the air.

He nodded. "What I'm about to say is quite unusual, but after talking to several of the partners, we thought this would be the best approach. Of course, we can make the offer ourselves, but because we didn't want to overstep boundaries, and we know the challenges that come with spouses working at the same place, I wanted to speak with you first. So what would you think of Steyer and Smith offering your wife a partnership with our firm?"

I blinked and blinked and blinked.

"Of course, we would have her in a different division," Jackson went on to explain, "but I understand that it may still be a challenge in your eyes. That's why I thought it best that we talked before any offer was made to Chastity."

He was waiting for my response, but I couldn't speak. He interpreted my shock as me needing more information:

"This isn't something that just came to mind. I was impressed with Chastity from the moment I met her, and I've wanted to add an African American woman as a partner. So I did my research, of course, and everything, from her education to the people she's worked with, is impeccable. What I hadn't known was that she's Kareem Jeffries's daughter." He held up his hand as if he thought I was going to speak. "I don't want you to think that's the reason why we want to make this offer. Of course, celebrity never hurts, but she's a great talent and doesn't belong with that tabloid firm." He shook his head as if he found her employment there unbelievable. "All I know is I've built one of the largest firms in the nation, one great attorney at a time. You were one of my great discoveries, and I believe your wife will be the same."

Still, I stayed silent as I processed Jackson's words. This invitation, this night . . . was about Chastity?

When he finally shut up, I spoke up. "Jackson, excuse me, but I thought we were going to have a different discussion tonight."

He cocked his head.

As I shifted to the edge of the sofa, I was surprised by my composure. "I've been with the firm for seven years, and I've had three major cases including this last one, not to even mention all the business I've brought to Steyer and Smith. I believe—no, I know—it's time I'm considered as a partner."

Jackson's face stretched in surprise and he put his glass down. "Really?"

"Yes, and after what I've just laid out, I'm sure you can understand my frustration. Not only with the holdup at the firm but with you talking about my wife instead of speaking about my career."

He nodded slowly. "Xavier, you know the holdup is you."

His words were like a punch, pushing me back on the sofa.

Jackson said, "When I interviewed you, we talked about this. We talked about the issues you had at the other two firms. We talked about the fact I was giving you a chance when no one else at Steyer and Smith wanted to."

"But that was seven years ago, Mr. Steyer. And when I was hired, you never said I wouldn't be made a partner."

"No, but I never said you would be. You came very close to being the cause of a lawsuit against your last firm. No one else would touch a young attorney who brought those kinds of issues with him. But I saw something in you and wanted to give you this chance." He pointed his finger at me. "I warned you then, and I'm pleased to say you haven't let us down. You've done a great job."

"Just not good enough for partner."

"Just not good enough right now. It's only been seven years."

"But I came with experience."

He raised his thick eyebrows when he said, "You came with issues; your anger was a wild card, and I told you then you'd be starting over." He paused, but I said nothing. "You've done well, and your work has not gone unnoticed. Your bonuses in the past have reflected that, and I think you'll be very pleased with your bonus this year." Again, he paused, and again, when I said nothing, he kept on, "But as far as becoming a partner, give that a little more time. Keep doing what you're doing, and I'll always be in your corner."

I wanted to tell this old man that his being in my corner meant nothing when he could very well be dead soon. But again, I stayed silent, though this time, I stood. I had to because of the heat.

"If that's your final word." That statement slipped through my lips, which hardly moved.

Jackson peered over his glasses, his eyes narrowed as if he could see the rage brewing. Was this a test? Had this been set up to see how I would react? But the little bit of hope that thought gave me went away when he said, "I understand how disappointing this must be. But what I can tell you is that you have a future with us."

I had to take my eyes off of him. Focus on the outside lights right above his head.

"Now, I've mentored a few young attorneys over my career, so let me give you some advice. Of course, with this news, you can leave Steyer and Smith. And with all the publicity you've received lately, you'll be given an opportunity at another firm. There will still be a background investigation, however, and while you'll be hired, you'll be starting over. Or you can stay and build on what you've started with us." He paused as if he wasn't sure I was listening. When I turned my glare to him, he said, "Give it a little bit more time, young man."

"How much more?" I asked, hating that my voice wavered.

"That decision is not mine alone. All of us have a firm to protect. But I think you'll be pleased in the end."

"Are you finished?" Kitty's voice floated over my shoulder.

Turning, I saw my wife moving toward me, her eyes full of hopeful excitement. I had to look away.

Kitty said, "It's time for us to head over to the Four Seasons." Then she asked, "Xavier, Chastity, would you two like to ride with us?"

"That's a great idea," Jackson piped in. "I'll let Jimmy know we'll be down in about ten minutes."

"That would be lovely," my wife said.

But I spoke over her: "No, we'll be fine. We'll get there on our own."

While Jackson and Kitty exchanged glances, Chastity frowned. But she recovered, and her smile returned as Kitty handed us our coats.

When Chastity thanked the Steyers for a lovely evening, I opened the door and walked out, saying nothing.

"We'll see you at the party," Chastity said before the door closed behind us.

As we stepped into the elevator, Chastity hooked her arm through mine, but still I didn't speak. She didn't say anything either, until we reached the lobby. "Do you want me to order an Uber or should we just take a cab?"

I answered my wife by motioning to the doorman for a cab, and when we slipped inside, I told him our home address. I gave no explanation to Chastity. I had no words for her.

Turning to the window, I kept my eyes there. My wife had to know by now that becoming a partner wasn't in my future. I just couldn't tell her why—not yet. I couldn't explain to her why I was such a failure—not now. Not when I was boiling over with so much hurt, so much pain, and the heat of a thousand suns.

42

Chastity

We were going home, and I had no idea why. What could have happened in the fifteen minutes Mrs. Steyer and I had been away? Had Xavier committed some kind of offense? Had he been fired?

No . . . Mr. Steyer hadn't worn the countenance or the body language of a man who'd just fired someone. Glancing at my husband with his eyes still on the window, I didn't read him as a man who'd been fired. But he certainly looked defeated.

All I wanted to do was hold Xavier, but he'd locked me out. I was smarter this time, though. I wasn't going to press, wasn't going to say anything until my husband was ready to talk.

My vibrating cell shifted my glance and my attention. Looking down, I saw the notification for an incoming text.

How's the party?

I texted Melanie back:

Change of plans, heading home.

What??? What happened???

I sighed before I texted:

> Don't know yet, I'll keep you posted.

Is Xavier acting crazy?

That text made me pause, made me wonder if I'd done the right thing last Saturday.

> No, he's fine. I'll text when I get home.

Okay, but you know the deal.

Got it, I replied, then returned my focus to Xavier. I knew he felt my gaze, but still, his eyes (really, all of him) stayed away from me.

So I focused on my window, the other side of Sixth Avenue as the cab sped uptown. *Is Xavier acting crazy?* Those four words made part of me sorry that I contacted Melanie last week, although even with this feeling of regret now, I'd done the right thing. After Xavier had pinned me against the wall on Saturday, someone needed to know what was going on in our home.

When I'd sent out an emergency message Sunday after church, Melanie had met me. It had been easy enough to get away; Xavier was playing golf with Bryce. So I slipped away and met up with her.

Over catfish and eggs at Sylvia's, I'd told Melanie the whole story. To my surprise and relief, she'd sat silently, letting me share every detail until I finished. At the end, she'd wiped her lips with her napkin, pulled her cell from her purse, and handed me her phone.

"What are you doing?"

"You're going to call your mother and father and tell them what you just told me."

342

I was shaking my head before she even finished. "No, I can't. Because my father will kill him."

"Well, after what Xavier did, maybe he needs to die."

TO THIS MOMENT, I wasn't sure if Melanie had been serious; I hadn't asked her because I was afraid of her answer. But what I did ask was for her not to make me regret telling her.

"I told you this because I need a backup, so please help me. I don't want to be in a place where I feel as if I can't share anything with you ever again."

I saw, I felt, I heard her reluctance when she said, "Okay. Whatever you want, but I don't understand, Chaz. I don't know why you're staying with him."

"Everyone in his life has abandoned him."

"Maybe there was a reason."

"Never a reason to abandon a child. I'm staying. This is when he needs me the most, and I know we can work through this. We're going to counseling."

SHE'D BACKED DOWN, and the deal was made. My part: Melanie would keep my secret. Her part: Whenever I was with Xavier, I had to check in every half hour or so. In the last week, I'd done that: even as life got better by the day with my husband, I stayed in touch with Melanie. It hadn't felt right, like I was betraying Xavier, sharing what should have been our secret. But if I was going to stay, it was a necessary safety plan for me.

The cab had barely rolled to a stop when Xavier opened the door, jumped out, and walked away, not waiting for me. I paid the driver and then caught up with my husband at the elevator. Now I had to press down my anger. Whatever had gone down with Mr. Steyer, Xavier was going to have to handle it without treating me this way. But for this moment, this hour, maybe even the next day or two, I was going to extend him grace.

Still, he didn't give me a glance nor a word; I was just happy that when we stepped into the apartment, he at least held the door open for me.

"Thank you," I said.

Xavier tore off his overcoat, then hurled it onto the sofa. I moved to the other side of the coffee table, making sure that was between us before I said, "Xavier, I want to be here for you for all things. So please tell me, what happened with Mr. Steyer?"

My cell vibrated, and I knew it was Melanie, but I couldn't pause right then. Not after I'd just asked this question.

For the first time since we left the Steyers', his eyes met mine, but the disdain in his expression was shocking. Although what he said next was worse.

"You want to know what's wrong?" he spat. "You're what's wrong. You're the problem."

Now *I* was the one who didn't want to talk, because this man was acting the way Melanie suspected. But I'd learned from the last time, so I held up my hands. "Okay, if this isn't the right time, just know I'm here whenever you need me."

"Nah, you wanted to talk, so let's do this," he shouted.

I'd opened the door, and now I couldn't close it. I checked the distance between us and took a couple of steps back. "If you want to talk about it, that's fine. Because like I've said, we're in this together, but—"

He laughed over my words. "We're not in this together. This is your world, and I'm just living in it."

I squinted. If I hadn't just spent the last hours with him, I would've been sure my husband had swallowed a whole bottle of something; he was that different. "I'm talking about you and Mr. Steyer. How did this become about me?"

He said, "I don't know. But all Jackson wanted to talk about tonight was whether or not it was fine with me if they offered you a partnership at Steyer and Smith."

I pressed my fingers against my lips. "What?"

My cell vibrated again, but both of us ignored it as Xavier nodded. "I was right; he wanted to talk about someone being a partner with the firm, but it wasn't me."

"I don't even understand. I'm not interested in leaving my firm."

"Well, according to Jackson, you need to bring your talented ass over to us."

Inside, I gasped. Xavier had never talked this way, but I tried to keep the focus on what he'd just told me. "This doesn't make sense," I said. "So what about you?"

His shrug was nonchalant, but his tone was filled with his pain when he said, "Apparently, I'm not partnership material."

"Oh my God, Xavier. I'm so sorry."

His eyes bore into me. "Are you?"

When my cell vibrated again, I knew I needed to respond to Melanie, but I couldn't stop now. "Of course I'm sorry. What Mr. Steyer said was ridiculous. Why did he even invite us to his home if he was going to talk about this foolishness?"

He laughed so loud and for so long, I hoped in that span of time he'd really found some humor. Then he said, "You almost sound as if you care."

"I do care, Xavier. You know that."

He glared at me, and I took deep breaths, reminding myself that becoming a partner had been Xavier's dream. This had to be beyond disappointing; it had to be a bit humiliating. So I inhaled one last time, then exhaled as much grace as I could. "I understand why you're upset, but all I want to do now is help you figure out your next steps."

A few chuckles lingered as he said, "What would you suggest?"

I took this as a chance to encourage him. "There are hundreds of firms out there, so many that would want you and know they'd be blessed to have you." I took a couple of steps closer to him. "Just look at what you've accomplished. Actually, I'm surprised firms haven't been reaching out to you already."

He began to pace—good! Movement would keep him calm. So I took two more steps closer. "Maybe this is God, maybe a sign that you should consider your options." He kept pacing, his eyes down. "Whether it's to go to a new firm, or maybe this is when you should step out into politics."

He stopped, and I prayed my words had given him some hope. But all he said was, "So you have all the answers now?"

"No, but what I have is a never-ending love for you. I want to help because this should never have happened."

"You're damn straight."

I swallowed. "So then let's figure this out. Let's sit down, make a plan, then on Monday, I can help you do some research, maybe even make some calls. Whatever we need to do."

He scowled. "What is this, pity?"

I shook my head, praying my words, my countenance, my demeanor would calm him. "Not at all."

"I'm so pitiful that I need your help?" he said as if he didn't, maybe even couldn't, hear me. "You think the partners were right about their decision?"

That was when I knew there was nothing I could say. Not tonight. I grabbed my coat from the sofa.

"Where are you going?" he growled.

"I think it's best if I give you some time." I took a step toward the door. "So I'm going to go out." Another step. "And I'll be back in a little while."

His eyes were full of fire when he shook his head. "You're not leaving me."

"Xavier," I said, feeling the beginning of tremors in my voice. "I'm not leaving you. I'll be right back."

"You're not leaving!" he screamed.

His chest heaved, and I knew no matter what he said, I had to get out of this condo. But I said, "All right."

He paced in front of me, blocking my path. And then he paused. "Go in the bedroom."

"What?"

He moved toward me, and I rounded the coffee table just as my cell vibrated again. But there was no time to pick it up. I dashed toward the door, but my gown slowed me down. If I could just get the door unlocked, just get into the hallway . . .

The lock clicked, the door opened, but then Xavier grabbed my hair, yanking me back over the threshold, tossing me to the floor.

"Stop," I screamed. "Xavier, stop!"

"You're not leaving me again." He dragged me, and I tried to fight. But he was behind me, so I was kicking and screaming at air.

"You're not leaving me again." He lugged me across the carpet, dumping me in front of the sofa. I could hardly breathe, though I pushed myself up. And looked into the contorted face of a man I'd never seen.

Fear was the reason I ran, but I only got as far as one step when his backhand slap sent me flying across the room. I tasted blood before I landed headfirst in front of the window. All of my energy, all of my fight, had been knocked out of me. But my fear remained, which was why I crawled from where I'd fallen.

"You're not leaving me again."

The tip of his shoe punched my stomach, and I screamed

in agony. "Please, no." Another kick, and my thoughts turned to death. Xavier was going to kill me. But why? How had his love for me twisted to this?

The third kick knocked the fear out of me, and without fear, there was no reason to run. So I just lay there, curled up, wishing I knew the right words to speak to stop Xavier, wondering if this was truly the end.

It was interesting what flashed through my mind as I was beaten by this broken man: the night we met, the night we'd made love, the night we exchanged vows while kneeling bare before each other.

And then my thoughts made a quick turn to my mom and dad, and now I felt the pain of Xavier's assault beyond my flesh. First he would kill me, and then the news of this would do the same to my parents.

I love you, Mom. I love you, Papa, I thought between my cries. That became the mantra that I hoped would lull me into the afterlife.

"Chastity!"

Still I cried, but now I smiled at the sound of my mother's voice. She'd come to me so I could say good-bye.

But then . . . "Get away from her." It was my mother's voice—no, it was my mother screaming.

My mind . . . I was losing it . . . Was my mom here or was I there? I fought to open my eyes, but my lids were sealed. I tried to part my lips, to cry out, to move, to do something. But there was nothing.

And then . . . two pops. Or were they shots? I screamed and struggled to get to my mother. But no matter what, my eyes wouldn't open, my lips wouldn't move, my body wouldn't stir. I was helpless as I spun into the black.

43

Chastity

The black became gray and now I was surrounded by a thousand voices shouting. But still my eyelids wouldn't part. I cried out for my mother, but my voice stayed inside. And then the sounds quieted, and now I heard nothing, saw nothing, felt only serenity as the black returned.

Until . . . the light. Thousands of watts above me, blinding me, even as I struggled to open my eyes.

"Chastity."

The voice was deep, but not the way I imagined God.

"Can you hear me?"

I blinked. This was definitely not God. The light above me dimmed some, and the face came into focus.

"Kelvin?" I croaked.

He nodded.

"Where . . ." That was all that would squeak past what felt like sandpaper in my throat.

"You're at Harlem Hospital, but you're going to be fine."

Then, "Chaz!" Melanie cried out. "Thank God."

"What . . ." I squirmed, trying to push myself up.

"I need you to chill, Chaz," Kelvin said. "We still have to do some tests." Then he turned away from me. "Mel, I'm going to check on the X-rays. Stay with her."

"Of course. I'm not going anywhere." She grabbed my hand, and it felt as if she held me with a vise grip. I yelped. "Sorry," she said before releasing me.

Kelvin said, "She's hurting everywhere, Mel." Then, to me, he repeated, "You're going to be fine, Chastity," as if he thought I needed to hear that again. "I'll be right back."

My eyes followed him until he disappeared, and then I turned to Melanie. "What . . . happened?"

"You don't remember?"

I tried to shake my head, though I didn't really move. Instead, I squeezed my eyes shut and images filled my mind: Xavier raging, grabbing me, tossing me, kicking me. It all made me groan again.

"What's wrong?" Melanie asked. "Do you want me to call another doctor until Kelvin gets back?"

This time I was able to move my head from side to side. Every part of my body ached, but the pictures in my mind were what caused this pain. Then I remembered the sounds, and now I had another question. "Where's . . . my . . . mom?"

"She's fine, Chaz," Melanie said as she sat on the edge of the narrow bed. "She had to go to the police station—"

"What?"

"But your dad is with her."

Those words were like adrenaline, pushing me up. I winced through the pain, but I had to get answers to questions I didn't even know. But my mother was in trouble, and what I knew was that it was because of me.

"Chaz!"

I had to take an extra breath before I swung my legs over the edge. My feet were bare, but I was still in my gown.

"Hey!" Kelvin said as he stepped into the curtained area. "What're you doing?"

"I have to go." I grimaced through my words. "My mom. She's with the police."

Kelvin glanced at Melanie, and she shrugged. "She asked."

"Chastity." His tone was filled with admonishment. "You're not going anywhere." His nudge against my shoulder was gentle yet firm, just like his tone. "Not for a couple of hours."

"I thought you said I was fine," I said as I lay back.

"We need to do some X-rays, and then I'll know for sure."

"I have to get to my mom."

"Your mother is fine," he said, and once again he passed a look to Melanie that let me know he wasn't pleased. "My job is to make sure you are, too." He glanced at his wife before he said to me, "I'll be right back, but can you please just stay put? I don't want to have to admit you," as if that was a threat.

I leaned back, but it wasn't just because I was told to. My legs were so sore; I wasn't even sure I could walk.

Kelvin nodded, then said to Melanie, "I'll only be gone for a few minutes." He lowered his voice, but I still heard him say, "Please don't say anything else to her."

Melanie folded her arms, and then when he left us alone, she returned to the edge of the bed. We sat in silence for a few moments as more images filled my mind: Xavier kicking, my mother screaming . . . and then the sound of pops through the air.

The memory of the sounds made me blink, made me ask, "What happened to my mother?" When she was silent, I added, "Please tell me she's all right."

"She's fine, Chaz. She really is."

I nodded, swallowed, and said, "She shot Xavier?"

"Do you remember?"

I shook my head. "All I know is that Xavier was . . . beating me and then I heard my mother . . . and . . ." I stopped.

"She was trying to save you. I knew you were in trouble when you didn't answer your phone, so Kelvin called the police, and I called your dad." This time she was gentle when she held my hand, and the pain didn't sear all the way through my body. "Your dad didn't answer, but your mom did, and I told her what had been going on. Chaz"—she paused, then swallowed as if she were pushing her emotions down—"I was so scared. And your mom was, too."

I closed my eyes once again. "And she shot Xavier," I repeated. It took a few moments and everything within me to ask, "Is Xavier dead?" although I already knew the answer. I could feel it. The man I knew, the one I loved, was gone.

"No."

My eyes snapped open.

She said, "He's here—he's hurt, but I don't know how badly."

This time, the agony that filled me had nothing to do with the pain that throbbed through my bones. This time, it was because my mother was with the police and my husband . . . I didn't even know. And it was all because of me.

FOR THE LAST hours, my mind had been whirling, swirling with thoughts of my mom . . . and Xavier, though I didn't know why I thought about him. He'd done more than lay hands on me—he'd beaten me as if he'd never loved me.

I hated to admit it, but I still cared. I cared enough not to want him to die.

As a nurse came in and helped me undress and change into a hospital gown, my thoughts still volleyed. Through my examination, I thought about my mom. Through my X-rays, it was all about Xavier. All I could do was wonder and cry and pray for both of them.

By the time I was rolled back into the emergency room, where Melanie still waited for me, the night had bowed to the day. All of those hours had passed, and I still knew nothing.

Kelvin followed right behind before I could question Melanie some more. When he told me, "You don't have any broken bones or any other injuries," it was hard to keep my focus on his words.

He said, "You're fine, but for a few days, you'll feel like you've been in the ring with a professional boxer," and all I could say was:

"I need to speak to my mother."

"Okay, you will. I'm trying to get you out of here," he said before he continued with, "You've been bruised pretty badly."

"Do you know what's going on with Xavier?"

Kelvin sighed. "As soon as I finish with you, I'll check on him."

I nodded, then shifted and squirmed through the rest of his instructions about prescriptions and medications, but my mind was far away from this emergency room.

But then a few of Kelvin's words broke through: "You will heal."

My head jerked back. Heal—I guessed it was a matter of perspective.

"So why did she faint?" Melanie asked her husband as if she were my mother.

There had to be some medical law being broken with Melanie standing in this room while my doctor was speaking to me. But since these were my best friends, I turned to Kelvin to hear his explanation.

"Fainting itself is not usually serious. It depends on the reason, and in this case, your fainting," he said to me as if I'd asked the question, "was a reaction to an emotional trigger. Your body shut down to protect you. But there's nothing to worry about. Now, I do want you to call me—"

Before he could finish, Melanie's cell phone chirped. "Oh!" she exclaimed when she glanced down at the screen. When she answered, "Pastor," I knew she was talking to my father, and my heart skipped. "How's Mom Sisley?"

I reached for the phone, but it took a moment for Melanie to exhale with a smile and then hand her cell to me.

"Papa! How's Mom?"

"Princess, she's fine, but we want to know, how are *you*?"

It was just a question, but I guessed it was one of those emotional triggers that Kelvin just mentioned. This time, I didn't faint, I just cried.

"Princess, what's wrong? I spoke to Kelvin earlier and he said you'd be fine."

I should have known—more medical laws broken, but rules didn't matter among family. "I'm fine, Papa. Kelvin's taking care of me. It's just that I'm so sorry."

"You don't have anything to be sorry about," my father said. "You didn't cause this."

"But I was the one . . . Xavier came into our lives because of me."

"We're not going to talk about any of that right now. I'm just grateful to my God that you are all right. Will you be leaving soon?"

"Yes, Kelvin is getting ready to release me. Can I speak to her?"

"We just got home, and she's resting now, princess. But Melanie is going to bring you here, so we'll be under the same roof."

Melanie nodded when I glanced at her, and I guessed there had been a whole lot of talking going on around me.

"Okay," I said to my father, glad that I didn't have to make any decisions. I said, "I love you," before I handed the phone back to Melanie.

"So," Kelvin said, "do you have any other questions?"

"Can you find out what's going on with Xavier?"

His smile was sorrowful as he nodded. "Okay, I'll be right back. You can get dressed."

When he disappeared behind the curtain, Melanie held up my evening gown, and for a moment, I had to pause. More than time had passed since I'd put that dress on last night. Love had passed away.

We stayed silent as Melanie helped me to step into the dress. My body ached with every movement, but minutes later, I eased back up on the bed, waiting for Kelvin to return. The longer he took, the more my heart pounded. What would the news be about Xavier?

Finally, I broke our silence. "Are you mad that I want to know about Xavier?" I asked Melanie.

She shook her head right away. "Not at all. I understand."

"Do you?" I looked down at my wedding band, topped by the most gorgeous engagement ring. "Because *I* don't understand."

With her fingertips, she lifted my chin. "He's your husband. You loved him. There's nothing wrong with you wanting to know how he is."

When the curtain parted, I held my breath. "Chastity," Kelvin said as he stepped in with a woman following behind him. "This is Donna Scott. She's one of the hospital's finance specialists."

I frowned. "If this is about my insurance, I'll give you my

information, but first"—I turned to Kelvin, a bit annoyed that I had to handle this now—"what about—"

The woman said, "Actually, I had some questions about your husband, Xavier King."

My head snapped back to her. "Is he all right?"

Kelvin said, "He just got out of surgery."

"Surgery?" I gasped. That meant he was alive, but still, that word filled me with fear—for Xavier . . . and for my mother.

"I don't know anything more than that," Kelvin said, "but I can find out for you."

"I want to see him."

Melanie and Kelvin exchanged a glance, but I shook my head. They were not going to shut me down. "I just want to see him, that's all." Then to Ms. Scott, I said, "Can I give you what you need after that?"

"Of course, I'll be in my office, but we'll need the information."

"Thank you." Then, to Kelvin, I said, "Please, take me to my husband."

44

Chastity

The sun's light beamed through the window, heating my face the way it did when I'd slept in this room as a child. The sun had been my alarm clock in those days, but since I hadn't rolled into this bed until after ten this morning, it wasn't an alarm clock that I needed. I needed something to quiet my mind and my memories. My head was filled with thoughts from last night—the hope that had morphed into horror.

And then the horror of this morning and Xavier lying as still as a stone, two monitors on the side of his bed with green flashing numbers and red squiggly lines, the beeps, the sign that Xavier's heart still beat.

But how long would that continue?

I closed my eyes and remembered the doctor's words from early this morning:

"Mrs. King?"

Even though I heard my name called, it still took a tap on my shoulder from Melanie for me to turn away from Xavier.

"I'm Dr. Bell," he introduced himself. With a gesture of his head, he said, "Would you mind joining me?"

I studied his face, looking for signs of what he was about to tell me. Finally, with a nod, I followed him into the hallway, where piped-in Muzak filled the air.

Santa Claus is coming to town . . .

*Melanie reached for my hand and squeezed it as we passed the waiting room; then the doctor stopped. I hesitated to step inside when I saw the placard on the door—*FAMILY ROOM—*but I followed him.*

"I'm your husband's doctor," he began when Melanie closed the door behind us. He turned his glance to Melanie. "Dr. Meadows," he began.

At first, I was surprised that he knew her name, but then I realized he was a doctor who knew another doctor's wife.

"I need to speak to Mrs. King alone. You understand—"

"No." I held up my hand. "You have permission to speak in front of her. I understand the law, but I really need her here with me."

After a nod, he began, "Your husband is in serious condition. He suffered a penetrating wound to his brain."

I swallowed and pressed the tips of my fingers against my lips.

"He was lucky in the sense that the bullet didn't pass through any vital brain tissue or vascular structures. But when we went in to remove the bullet, he suffered some excessive bleeding."

"What does that mean?"

"Well, that complicated the surgery, but we think he'll recover."

I released a long breath. "So what happens next?"

I OPENED MY eyes and remembered how the doctor said it was all a waiting game now. They were still concerned about the bleeding and what that could mean; the next twenty-four hours were the most critical. He asked me if I'd had any other questions, and then Melanie made sure that he, the nurses, and Ms.

Scott in the business office all had my cell number, since she let everyone—including me—know that after I took care of the insurance papers, she was taking me home.

She'd done that, and I'd lain here recalling all of the worst moments of my life. There was one question that haunted me, though—what would this mean for my mother?

As if my thought was a cue, there was a quick knock on my door, and then it opened. That made me smile; little had changed. There was no waiting for *Come in* with my parents.

"I thought you'd be awake, princess." My father balanced a teacup on a serving tray as he stepped inside, then rested the tray on the nightstand.

I pushed myself up, and he hugged me, holding me the way he had this morning, when Melanie had brought me home. I asked him now what I'd asked him then: "How's Mom?"

"Sweetheart."

I glanced up, and the sight of my mother wrapped in her robe, her hair flowing free past her shoulders, brought tears to my eyes. But when she rushed into the room and wrapped me in her arms, I sobbed. "I'm so sorry."

"Sweetheart," she whispered as she held me. When she leaned back, she wiped away my tears. "There's nothing to be sorry about."

She sat, easing onto the bed in front of my father. He held her as she held my hands.

"I'm so glad you're all right. I was so scared," I said.

"I was, too, but we're both fine now." She held my hands as if she never planned to let go.

Looking down, I whispered, "I don't know if we'll ever be fine, because I wasn't honest with you."

There were tears in my mother's eyes when I glanced up. "I can't believe you've been going through this. When Melanie told me what had been going on and then when I rushed there and saw . . ." She sounded like she choked on the rest of her words. Then she finished, "My prayer had been that the police would have gotten to you first, but . . ."

I hugged her again. "I'm fine, Mom," I assured her. "Kelvin said that I'll be sore for a few days, but I'm fine. I'm more worried about you and the police."

When she nodded and said, "I had to answer their questions," my father's arms tightened around her shoulders. "I shot Xavier, so I had to tell them why."

"Because he was beating me."

"Yes, and because he came after me."

"What?" I shrieked.

"The door was open, and when I rushed in, Xavier tried to stop me from getting to you. That's when I shot him, because the look in his eyes . . . I knew what he was going to do."

"Your mother went there to save you, but in the end it was self-defense."

"Oh my God, Mom, if he had hurt you . . ."

She inhaled and held her breath before she relaxed. "We don't have to worry about that. I'm fine and you are, too."

"The only thing," my father said, "is that you'll have to talk to the police."

"Oh, I'll go right now." I swung the covers away, ready to do whatever to save my mother.

"No," my parents said together. My dad said, "I asked them to give you some time; they'll call."

"And then"—my mother paused—"they'll want to talk to Xavier."

My parents didn't know! My father and I hadn't talked about Xavier this morning; I'd only been concerned about my mother, and he only cared about me. Just as I was about to share what I knew, my cell phone vibrated on the nightstand. I didn't recognize the number, though when I saw the words MAYBE: HARLEM HOSPITAL on the screen, I picked up right away.

"Hello, Mrs. King?"

"Yes," I said.

"This is Dr. Bell. I wanted to update you on your husband." He paused. "He had a stroke . . ."

"What?"

"We had to take him back into surgery."

"All right, I'll be right there," I said . . . and then I looked into the faces of my parents.

Slowly, I put down the phone.

My mother said, "It's about Xavier?"

I nodded, but then added quickly, "He's alive, but he just had a stroke."

The shock on their faces matched my own, and now I was more than confused. "I don't know what to do."

"What do you mean?" my mother asked.

"He doesn't have anyone. He doesn't have any relatives and just one friend that I know of, and I just feel like . . ." I paused. "I don't want to be married to him anymore, but I feel like I should be there to make sure he has the best care."

My mother nodded, though it was my father who surprised me when he said, "I understand." He stood. "We'll get dressed; we'll go with you."

"No!" my mother said. But then she held my hands when she added, "You should go. You and your father should go. But I . . ." She shook her head.

"I'm not leaving you," my father said. To me, he added, "I'll call Melanie."

"Thank you," I said as I hugged them both. "Thank you for understanding."

"This is the right thing to do," my mother said.

Her words were so shocking. It was just about twelve hours ago when she'd shot a man who'd beaten me and would have attacked her if given the chance.

But then, when she added, "Be merciful as the Lord says mercy triumphs over judgment," I understood.

Showing mercy wasn't just something my mother believed, it was what she lived. And that made me hug her again.

EVERYTHING ABOUT US had been so fast and so hard. The way we met, the way we married, the way we ended. Standing, I pulled the chair from the wall and scooted right to the edge of Xavier's bed. My heart ached. In the early hours of this morning, he'd looked as if he'd just been asleep. But now his face was contorted, his suffering obvious.

I reached for his hand, but pulled back before we touched. I'd fallen fast; I'd fallen hard: the carriage ride in Central Park, the intimate conversations about his life, the romantic weekend of our wedding—that was what I remembered, but who I was now was the woman who survived last night.

"Here's your coffee." Melanie's voice floated over my shoulder.

My thoughts had been so far away, I didn't even hear her come back. But without taking my eyes away from Xavier, I grabbed the cup.

"Has the doctor been back?"

I shook my head.

She said, "This is so messed up, all the way around."

"I know, but I feel like I have to be here. There's no one else to make decisions for him."

There was a pause before Melanie said, "I told you I understood. The part I left out is that you're a far better woman than I am."

My eyes stayed on Xavier. "Maybe I just have more of my mother inside me than I thought. All those years that I criticized her for staying with my father. And now here I am."

I felt the heat of Melanie's glare from behind me. "Are you saying you're staying with Xavier?"

For the first time, I wondered if Xavier could hear us. "I'm not saying that at all." Then I wondered if Melanie and I should step out of the room, just in case. But I stayed in the chair, and, with my eyes still on my husband, I said, "I'm not staying with Xavier. I'm just doing what I have to do now."

The door to the room swung open, but still I didn't move my eyes from my husband until I heard Melanie say, "Hi, Ms. Scott."

"Hi." And then to me, she said, "May I talk to you for a moment outside?"

I glanced at Melanie and then said, "Sure."

She didn't take me far, the way Dr. Bell had done early this morning. This time, standing right outside Xavier's room, she said, "These are your husband's belongings—what he had on him when he came into the hospital." I nodded my thanks as she handed me a plastic bag with Xavier's cell and his wallet. "And I need to discuss your insurance. I contacted your husband's insurance company, and he hadn't added you to his policy."

I waved my hand. "No worries. I told you, we were just married. We didn't have time to take care of all of that. I can just give you the insurance information from my job."

"That's fine. We can do it that way or you can be added to his, it's up to you. All his company needs is your marriage license, and the rest they will be able to handle at a later time. And the marriage license will be good for our records, too, since he's unable to make his own medical decisions and you'll be doing that." She shook her head. "You know, with all these medical laws."

"Oh, I understand," I told her.

"Again, don't worry. We'll still process everything, but if you can get that license to us sometime this week."

"Definitely."

She nodded her good-bye, and when I returned to Xavier's room, Melanie asked, "Is everything all right?"

"Yeah"—I sighed—"it's just that with everything else on my plate, now I have to hunt for our marriage license." I explained what Ms. Scott had told me.

"You don't know where it is?"

"I don't know where Xavier put it after the magistrate mailed it. Can you believe this?" I slid back into the chair. "I didn't know him long enough or well enough to even know where he kept his important papers. I guess I'll go back to the apartment tonight and search for it."

"Well, you're going to have to go back there at some point because you can't keep wearing your mother's leggings, which look like capris on you, along with your mink coat." It must have been the look on my face that made Melanie add, "But you don't have to do that right now. Just go online and have a copy sent to you."

"That's a perfect idea. I've had to do that a couple of times in the middle of divorces . . . but, oh, wait."

"What?"

"Why don't I just call the magistrate and have him send it? That'll be faster than even doing it online."

"Yeah." Melanie nodded. "He can fax it to my office and I'll pick it up."

"Perfect." I paused. "Except I don't remember his name . . . but his brother was Xavier's friend." I scanned through my memory. "Will, that was his name." Then I had another thought. "But it should be in Xavier's phone." I slipped it out of the bag, then awakened the screen. Only 12 percent of the battery was left, but that was enough to make one call.

When I tapped the screen, Melanie chuckled. "Well, one thing was good. Y'all were close enough to know each other's passwords."

I shrugged. "Not a big deal. It was a joke with us. We used our birthdays, which are the same, so . . ." His home screen appeared. "I'll have to search for 'Will' in his contacts 'cause that's all I got." And a moment later, I said, "And that's all I needed, because here he is. Will Allen." As I tapped on his number, I stood and walked to the window. For a moment, I glanced out onto Lenox Avenue, still in wonder at how much my life had changed.

And then, "Yo, bruh, what's up?"

I recognized his voice from our wedding day.

Will said, "I didn't expect to be hearing from you so soon."

"Will, this is Chastity, Xavier's wife."

"Oh, yeah, what's up? How you doing?"

"Well, there's a lot going on, but I was calling to get your brother's telephone number."

"My brother?" he asked, as if he had no idea what I was talking about.

"Yes, I can't find our marriage license, and I need a copy." When he was silent, I frowned. "It's really important." More silence, and I sighed. "Xavier is in the hospital," I said, wondering why I had to go through all of this. "I need it for the insurance, and I can't find the one you mailed."

"Man, Chastity, this is messed up."

"It is," I said. "But we think he's going to be all right. So if you can put me in touch with your brother or if you can send it yourself, I would appreciate it. I really need it."

"Man, Chastity . . ."

When he repeated that, I frowned.

"I can't do that for you," he said.

"Why not?"

"Because . . . because," he stuttered. "There isn't a license. You and Xavier were never married."

Epilogue

Chastity

Six months later

eased the car's bumper to the double wrought-iron gates, then glanced up, squinting at the day's bright light, which shined through the rental car's sunroof. The cameras above whirred before the gates parted. I rolled over the narrow graveled road, which was lined on both sides by century-old trees with limbs like bulky arms opened wide to welcome me.

It took a couple of minutes to make it up the winding road to the welcome center, and within another minute, I was inside and stepped to the guest check-in desk at Abundant Care.

"How are you, Ms. Jeffries?" The receptionist, who'd greeted me every time I'd been here, smiled.

"I'm great, Andrea. And how's your son?"

Like she'd done over the last two months, since I'd finally found this rehabilitation and care center, she shared another story of her five-year-old. "Well, I'll let you go." She chuckled. "They're out back today."

The hallway was as winding as the road that led here. At the double glass doors, I paused, then stepped outside into air that felt ten degrees cooler than the ninety degrees I'd left behind in the city.

Today, Bryce sat at one of the picnic tables by the pond, and as I approached, he glanced up and welcomed me with his smile.

"Hey, you," I said before I gave him a hug.

When he stepped back from our embrace, he said, "You're looking good."

"You say that every time."

He laughed. "And I always mean it."

I dumped my bag onto the table and then rounded it so that I could get in front of the wheelchair. Xavier glanced up and smiled. And just like all the other times, I was reminded of that half smile that had captured me that first night. He still half smiled, only now it was because the entire right side of his body was paralyzed.

"Hey." I leaned over and hugged him.

When I stepped back, his lips moved. He grunted his greeting; that was all he could do.

"How are you?"

This time, he gave me several grunts and kicked his left leg forward.

"He's happy to see you." Bryce chuckled. "As always."

With Bryce's words, Xavier kicked again, and now I smiled.

"See?" Bryce said. "He's trying to tell you that I'm right."

"Hi, Ms. Jeffries." Bryce and I turned to the woman, dressed in sweats. "I hope you didn't just get here. It's time for Mr. King's physical therapy."

Which was exactly why I'd come at this time. I said, "Don't worry, I'm good."

The physical therapist kicked off the wheelchair brakes, and as she began rolling Xavier away, he grunted loudly, as if there was more he had to say. Bryce and I stood until they were out of sight, and then we sat at the picnic table.

"So, how is he?" I asked.

"No change physically, but they still work with him every day. The physical therapist, the speech therapist. The doctors say it's good that his brain is functioning. He's aware, knows everything that's going on around him. He responds to them the way he responded to you." Bryce sighed. "I guess we can all be hopeful."

With a nod, I pulled a large envelope from my bag, then slid it across to Bryce. He stared at it before he glanced up at me.

"You're still going to do this?"

"I told you, this is how it should be." Now I paused so that he would really hear what I said next. "You're his family."

"So are you." When I pressed my lips together, he continued, "I know. I still can't believe he did that, but he only faked that wedding because he didn't want to lose you, because he loved you."

"His reasons don't change the fact that he and I are not family."

"It takes more than a piece of paper to make a family, Chaz." He lightened it up with "Look at us. After all we've been through together these last six months, you're my sis."

I grinned. I did feel that way about Bryce. He'd been by my side from the moment I contacted him, the day I'd found out that Xavier and I had never been married.

"I'm so grateful for you," I said. "But it's time for me to move on. It's time for you to officially become Xavier's guardian."

He glanced at the folder, which he still hadn't touched. And then he surprised me with "I was so happy to hear about your mom. The case is closed."

His words lit up the space. "Thank you and thank God. We didn't think there was going to be too much of an issue, especially once I gave the police my statement, but you never know. I just didn't want her to be punished because . . ." I left it there.

Bryce shook his head. "The man who did that to you that night is not the man I knew. I mean, yeah, for years I'd been worried about his anger, but I never thought . . ."

"Neither did I. But it has ended, and all is well. Bryce, I've done my part. I went to court to legally get him to this point. And he's settled now, here in Bear Mountain, a place that means something to him and where he's getting the best of care." I paused. "But I'm not his wife."

"Can you be his friend?" When I stayed silent, he added, "Chaz, I'm afraid of what this would do to him. Yeah, he has me and a few other people, but you're the only one who really gets a reaction from him, because he loves you, and if you just disappeared—"

"Please, Bryce. Don't make me feel guilty."

He held up his hands. "That's not what I'm doing. I just know that you still love him, too, or you wouldn't have done all of this."

After a long pause, I nodded. "You're right. But now I need to love him from afar. So"—I tapped the envelope—"all I need is your signature."

He nodded. "I want you to do me a favor." He slid the package back to me. "Can you give this more thought?"

"No."

"Just one week. It's that important. Just one week. And if after a week, you still want to do this, I'll take you to lunch, sign the papers, and never say another word." When I said nothing, he added, "One week."

"Okay. But you keep the papers and I'll meet up with you."

"No, because if I have these papers, it'll be too easy for you to walk away. Just one week."

After a long moment, I returned the folder to my bag with a sigh. "One week," I said in a tone that I hoped felt like a warning to Bryce.

He grinned as if he had a victory, and I wondered if he did. Why had I agreed to this when I'd already had too many weeks?

When I stood, Bryce stood with me. "You're not going to wait for X to come back?"

I shook my head. "I'm going home to begin my one week."

With a chuckle, he hugged me, and then I made my way back to the front. I arrived at the guest check-in, just as another woman approached and I motioned for her to speak to Andrea first.

"Hello, my name is Roxanne Butler. I'm here to see one of your residents, Xavier King."

"Oh." Andrea glanced at me. I smiled and gave her a small shake of my head before she turned her attention back to the woman. "Well, just sign in here," she said, glancing at me again.

I had no idea who the woman was, but it didn't matter since I was leaving.

Then Andrea said, "Oh, here's Xavier now."

Roxanne and I turned as the physical therapist rolled Xavier toward us. His eyes widened, and the grunts began.

"Oh my goodness. Baby," Roxanne said as she leaned over and hugged him.

He grunted and kicked that leg up a couple of times, his eyes only on me.

"I guess he's glad to see me," Roxanne said. "I haven't seen him in almost a year." She pressed her hand against her chest. "Since last August, I think it was."

Last August. When I met Xavier.

His grunts were so loud now, they echoed through the hall. The physical therapist and Andrea frowned.

"He's never been this way," the therapist said. Leaning over, she asked Xavier, "Mr. King, are you all right?"

He grunted and kicked. Then kicked and grunted.

"I know, baby," Roxanne said. "If I'd known about this sooner, I would have been here." And then she explained some more. "There's nothing wrong with him. He's just glad to see me because we were engaged."

Engaged?

To the physical therapist, she asked, "Are you taking him to his room?"

The therapist glanced at me. "Uh, no, he's going back outside."

"Would you mind if I rolled him out?" She didn't wait for the therapist's response as she adjusted her purse on her shoulder and gripped the wheelchair's handles. "Which way?"

The therapist pointed straight ahead, and then the three walked away, with Xavier still grunting, still kicking. When I turned back to the desk, Andrea said, "She's his fiancée?"

"I guess," I said with a shrug.

"I thought you . . ."

"Oh, no." I shook my head. "Xavier and I are just friends."

She frowned, but before she could ask another question, I said, "Listen, I don't want to disturb Bryce, since he's out there with Xavier and . . ." I couldn't even say her name. I took out the envelope and a pen, and as I wrote Bryce's name across it, my hand shook.

My name is Roxanne Butler. He's just glad to see me because we were engaged.

And now I had another memory:

You must be Roxanne. Nice to meet you.

That was what Will had said on the day of our wedding. I chuckled at that memory, but I felt no joy. What I felt, though, was relief. This was right. I handed the envelope to Andrea.

"Okay, I'll give it to him when he leaves."

"Thanks," I said.

"See you next week," Andrea shouted as I walked away.

All I gave her was a wave as I walked out of the welcome building. And I never looked back again.

About the Author

Victoria Christopher Murray is the author of more than twenty novels, including: *Greed; Envy; Lust; The Ex Files; Lady Jasmine; The Deal, the Dance, and the Devil;* and *Stand Your Ground,* which was named a *Library Journal* Best Book of the Year. Winner of fourteen African American Literary Awards for Fiction and Author of the Year (Female), Murray is also a five-time NAACP Image Award Nominee for Outstanding Fiction. She splits her time between Los Angeles and Washington, DC. Visit her website at VictoriaChristopherMurray.com.